INDISCRETION

CHARLES DUBOW

blue door

Blue Door
An imprint of HarperCollins*Publishers*
77–85 Fulham Palace Road,
Hammersmith, London W6 8JB

First published in the United States by William Morrow 2013

Published in Great Britain by Blue Door 2013

A catalogue record for this book is
available from the British Library

HB ISBN: 978-0-00-750130-4
TPB ISBN: 978-0-00-750131-1

Printed and bound in Great Britain by Clays Ltd, St Ives plc

MIX
Paper from
responsible sources

FSC
www.fsc.org
FSC™ C007454

To Melinda

E cosi desio me mena
(And so desire carries me away)
PETRARCH

Great lovers lie in Hell . . .
JOHN CROWE RANSOM

INDISCRETION

PROLOGUE

THE POET A. E. HOUSMAN WROTE OF THE "LAND OF LOST content," and how he can never return to the place where he had once been so happy.

When I was younger, I greatly admired the poem's sentiment because I was not old enough to realize how banal it was. The young invariably cherish their youth, incapable of imagining life past thirty. The notion that the past is more idyllic is absurd, however. What we remember is our innocence, strong limbs, physical desire. Many people are shackled by their past and are unable to look ahead with any degree of confidence because they not only don't believe in the future, they don't really believe in themselves.

But that doesn't prevent us from casting a roseate glow over our memories. Some memories burn brighter, whether because they meant more or because they have assumed greater importance in our minds. Holidays blur together, snowstorms, swimming in the ocean, acts of love, holding our parents' hands when we are very small, great sadnesses. But there is much we forget too. I have forgotten so much—names, faces, brilliant conversations, days and weeks and months, things I vowed never to forget, and to fill in the gaps, I conflate the past or make it up entirely. Did that happen to me or to someone else? Was that me who broke his leg skiing in Lech? Did I run from the carabinieri after a drunken night in Venice? Places and actions that seem so real can be entirely false, based purely on impressions of a story told at the time and then somehow subconsciously woven into the fabric of our lives.

After a while it becomes real.

SUMMER

1

Eleven in the morning. The backyards of houses rumble by. Here and there an aboveground pool, discarded patio furniture, rusting bicycles. Barking dogs tied with ropes. Dry lawns. The sky is a pale blue, the heat of early summer just beginning to unfurl itself. Every fifteen minutes or so the train stops. More people get on than off.

Day-trippers look for empty seats on the crowded, noisy, brightly lit train. They carry bags filled with sunblock, bottles of water, sandwiches, and magazines. The women wear bathing suits under their clothes, bursts of neon color knotted around their necks. The men, young, tattooed, muscular, the buds of iPods wired to their ears, wear backward baseball caps, shorts, and flip-flops, towels draped around their necks, ready for a Saturday at the beach.

Claire is joining them. But she is not with them. I am not

there either. We haven't met yet, but I can imagine her. If I close my eyes I can still remember the sound of her voice, the way she walks. She is young, alluring, hurtling to a destination that will change her life, and mine, forever.

She huddles against the window, trying to concentrate on her book, but puts it down every few moments to look out at the passing landscape. The jolting of the train makes her sleepy. The trip feels like it is taking longer than it is, and she wishes she were there already. Silently, she urges the train to go faster. Her backpack, the one she carried around Europe, is on the seat beside her, and she hopes no one asks her to move it. She knows it is too big, and it looks as though she is coming to stay for a week or a month and not just a night. Her roommate had taken the other bag, the one on wheels which they shared, on a business trip. She opens her book and tries again to focus on the words, but it's no use. It's not that it's a bad book. She has been meaning to read it since it first came out. The author is one of her favorites. Maybe she will read it on the beach later if there is time.

The conductor collects the ticket stubs. He has a thick, reddish mustache and is wearing a worn, light blue short-sleeved shirt and a round, dark blue cap. He has done this trip hundreds of times. "Speonk," he intones nasally, drawing out the last syllable. "Next station Spe-onnnk."

She consults the schedule in her hand. Only a few stations to go.

At Westhampton, the day-trippers begin to get off the train in small groups. Some are meeting friends with cars. High fives and laughter. Others stand around and gather their bearings in the sunlit parking lot, clutching their cell phones to their ears. Their adventures are already beginning. She returns the schedule to her pocket. She has to wait another thirty-eight minutes before she reaches her destination.

At the station Clive is waiting. Go left when you come out, he had told her. I'll be there.

He is tall, blond, English. The tails of his expensive shirt untucked. She has never seen him in shorts before. He is very tan. It has only been a week since she last saw him, but he looks as though he has lived here his whole life. That the handmade suits he normally wears seem to belong to some other man.

He leans over to kiss her on the cheek and picks up her bag. "How long are you planning on staying exactly?" he asks with a smile.

"I knew you were going to say that," she says, wrinkling her nose at him. "No need to panic. Dana took the good bag."

He laughs easily and starts to walk, saying, "I'm just parked over here. Thought I'd run you back to the house, and then we could all grab a spot of lunch."

She hears the mention of others and is surprised but tries not to show it. "Come out for the weekend," he had said, nuzzling her shoulder. "I want you to. It will be very quiet. Just us. You'll love it."

He opens the door of his two-seater and throws her bag behind them. She doesn't know anything about cars, but she can tell it is a nice one. The top is down and the rich-smelling leather is pleasantly hot against the bare backs of her legs.

Although he is older than she, he has the youthfulness that comes to men who have never married. Even if they travel with a woman, there is something unencumbered about them, never having been weighted down by anything more than their own desires.

When she met him, at the party in a loft in Tribeca, then afterward at the restaurant and then bed, he had reminded her of a boy home from school for Christmas trying to squeeze in as much pleasure as possible before it is all over.

"So who else do you have out?" She doesn't mean to make it sound like an accusation.

"Oh, just the rest of my harem," he says with a wink. Reaching out, he puts his hand on her thigh. "Don't worry. Clients. They invited themselves at the last minute, and I couldn't really say no. Bad form."

They drive past high green hedgerows, behind which there are occasional glimpses of large houses. Workmen, Mexican or Guatemalan maybe, dart in and out, pushing lawn mowers, clipping branches, cleaning pools, raking gravel, their battered pickup trucks parked inoffensively on the side of the road. Other people are on the roads too. Men and women jogging, some on bikes, one or two nannies pushing strollers. Sunlight twinkles between the leaves. The whole world seems manicured, verdant, private.

They turn down a gravel drive lined with newly planted saplings.

"Can't tell you how long it's taken to get this bloody place ready," says Clive. "Nearly strangled my contractor when he told me it wouldn't be done by Memorial Day. They only just finished the pool last week. Can you imagine? Bought it over a year ago. Bloody nerve of some people."

They pull up to the house. It is modern, white. Several cars are parked in front. A Range Rover and two Mercedeses. She has never seen grass so green in her life.

Carrying her bag, Clive ushers her through the door into a large, dark, soaring room. A fireplace dominates one wall, a modern painting the other. She recognizes the artist. She had been to one of his shows that spring.

"Do you like it?" he asks. "Not really my thing. I know bugger-all about art. But my decorator said I needed a whacking great painting there so I bought it."

The ceiling must be thirty feet high. There is almost no furniture, only a long white leather couch and a number of cardboard boxes stacked in the corner.

"The rest should be here next week," he says. "We're just camping out now. Come on, let me give you the grand tour."

He sets down her bag and leads her through the house, showing her the dining room, the kitchen, a media room, and a game room complete with pool table, Foosball, Ping-Pong, and a pinball machine. In every room, a wide, flat television.

"Typical male," she says, knowing what he wants to hear. "You can't be bothered to furnish your new house, but you've already got all the toys set up." He grins, flattered.

"Let me show you where you'll be staying." They go back the way they came and he carries her bag into a large master bedroom, where the bed sits unmade, shoes kicked across the floor, clothes draped over a chair, and a laptop on the desk open to Bloomberg. Magazines and cell phones are scattered on the bedside table. On the dresser is a photo of Clive posing with skis and another with a young woman on what appears to be a sailboat. Without looking closely Claire can tell she is topless.

"Sorry, it's a bit of a mess. Didn't get a chance to tidy. Hope you don't mind." As if he hadn't expected her to answer, he turns and kisses her. "I really am glad you could come."

"Me too," she says, returning the kiss. She needs to pee. The trip out was long, and she is hot and uncomfortable. He places his hand on her breast, and she lets him. She likes the way he touches her and the way he smells. Leather and sand. That he is English. It is like being ravished by a Regency duke. His hand is now under her shirt and her nipples are hardening. She doesn't want to break away and decides she can wait. It is over quickly. He didn't even bother removing her top or his. Her panties are around one ankle, and she is sitting on the bed while he washes up in the bathroom.

"We've just inaugurated the bedroom," he calls to her.

Unfulfilled, she stares down at her naked legs and black pubic hairs, feeling vaguely foolish.

He comes back out. "Right, let's go meet the others, shall we?"

"One moment." She goes into the bathroom now, carrying her underwear and shorts. There didn't seem any point in putting them on first. The bathroom is large and covered in marble. The towels decadently soft. There are two sinks, a bidet, and a shower with multiple heads in gleaming steel that probably cost her entire salary. There is another television screen, this one concealed behind the mirror. She splashes water on her face and wishes she had thought to bring in her toiletries. She has no hairbrush, no lipstick.

"Come on then," calls Clive. "I'm famished."

She walks out. "You look gorgeous, darling," he says, swiveling his hips. "Fancy another go?" He winks and gives her a peck on the cheek. "Here, thought you might like this." He hands her a glass of champagne like a reward. He is carrying another. "Don't want to get too far behind everyone else. They've got a head start."

By the pool are two other couples, the women reclining on

chaises and the men at a table with a champagne bucket on it. It is very hot now, and she blinks in the sunlight. She is introduced to Derek and a blond woman who makes no attempt to rise. Her name is possibly Irina, but Claire doesn't quite catch it. She looks for a ring and sees there isn't one. The woman has an accent Claire can't place, and looks quite tall. She is in good shape. Derek is stubby and also English and wears a red Manchester United shirt. On his wrist is a fat, diamond-encrusted watch. He was in the middle of telling a funny story and clearly didn't like being interrupted.

The other couple is married. "Larry," says a portly, balding man with glasses, "and this is my wife, Jodie." Jodie smiles at Claire, turning her head just enough to inspect her. She, too, is wearing an expensive watch. And several glittering rings. They are all wearing expensive watches. Claire doesn't wear a watch.

Jodie is around forty and has a taut, trimmed stomach that flattens into an orange bikini. Her breasts look too good to be natural. "So where did you two meet?" she asks, taking a sip of champagne. Claire notices that Jodie's fingernails and toenails are painted burnt gold. The veins on her feet and forearms stand out.

"At a party in New York a few weeks ago," says Claire. "It was . . ."

"It was love at first sight, wasn't it, darling?" says Clive with a laugh, sliding his arm around her waist.

"Speak for yourself," responds Claire playfully. "Handsome English hedge fund managers are a dime a dozen these days."

Jodie smiles. She has been here before. Has met his other women. Clive preens.

"Right, chaps," he announces. "I don't have a bite of food

in the house, and even if I did I'm a rotten cook, so I've booked lunch. Let's drink up and go."

Lunch takes most of the afternoon. There is caviar followed by grilled lobster and more wine. It is Clive's treat. "My shout," he said when they sat down. "Order whatever costs the most."

Even though it is hot, they sit outside under large green umbrellas looking over a harbor full of sailboats. Clive points out to Long Island Sound and, in the distance, Connecticut. It was an old whaling port, he says, once one of the biggest on the East Coast. "Settled by an Englishman, of course," he says. "A bit of a soldier of fortune named Lion Gardiner. The family still owns an entire island in the Sound that was given them by Charles the First. Must be why I feel so drawn to the place. I think old Lion and I would have been great mates."

Seagulls wheel overhead. Occasionally a particularly brave one lands and is then shooed away by a waiter. Claire is seated between Clive and Larry, but the men just talk across at each other, and there doesn't seem to be much point in trying to join in because most of the conversation is about either the derivatives market or English football, of which both Clive and Derek are big fans.

As a result Claire drinks more wine than she should and begins to wonder when she could get the earliest train back to New York. Would Clive drive her to the station or would she have to call a taxi? He would be annoyed. She is silently relieved when he proposes a trip to the beach. The other two women make vague noises about not liking the sand and can't they all just go back to the pool, but they are shouted down by Clive and the other men.

After a quick stop by the house to change, Clive piles everyone into his Range Rover—"I'm the only one with a beach sticker and the bloody cops like nothing better than handing out parking tickets on weekends in June"—and Claire sits in the back between Jodie and Larry. Derek sits in front with tall Irina perched comically on his broad lap. When they arrive at the crowded beach, Clive, carrying a cooler, marches down close to the water and stops on a tiny patch of unoccupied sand between two other groups. "You can still get a decent cell phone signal here," he says, opening a complicated nylon folding chair. Claire is holding the towels, a nanny visiting the beach with her employers. The others are straggling behind. Jodie is complaining. "My hat's going to blow away, dammit," she says. "Christ, why'd we have to come here?"

Claire looks out at the sparkling blue water and the small foam-tipped waves gently crashing against the sand. Children are playing, laughing and diving through the surf while parents and babysitters stand in the shallows and watch. It is still early in the season, and the water is too cold for most swimmers. The cloudless sky stretches endlessly back beyond the curve of the world. She wishes she were here alone.

"More wine?" asks Clive. He is filling glasses.

She shakes her head. "No thanks. It's beautiful, isn't it?"

"There's a reason why these houses cost so much, love. See that one over there? It sold last summer for forty million. There's one down there that sold for twenty million the other year. The new owner tore it down and put up an even bigger one."

"You couldn't give me one of those houses," says Larry. "You know what the upkeep is on one of those things? Salt damage, dune erosion, hurricanes, taxes? Only an asshole with more money than brains would buy one."

"That's why I bought one well inland, old boy. I'm an ass-hole with money and brains," Clive adds with a wink.

Jodie walks up. "Do we have to stay? My hair is getting ruined."

Clive has taken off his shirt. His torso is as tanned as his face, the muscles lean. He is a fitness enthusiast, one who practices yoga every day, goes to the gym regularly, pops vitamins. Claire can see the other women admiring him, envying her. She knows that body, has felt it, tasted it. But she has never seen it outside the bedroom. In the sunlight. She looks away, conscious of her desire. Her own arms are pale. She has never been able to get tan the way Clive can. She freckles instead.

"Oh, don't worry about your hair, darling," Clive says. "The windswept look is very fashionable out here."

"You're a riot, Clive. I just had it done and it wasn't cheap." A light wind gusts and blows off her hat. "Shit! Larry!"

She glares at her husband, who goes scurrying after the hat.

"What did I tell you?" she says when he returns. It is all his fault. He is the man. He should have been protecting her. Larry grimaces and says, "Clive, can you drive us back to the house? Jodie really doesn't want to stay." Jodie stands a few feet behind him, victorious, her arms crossed against her torso.

Irina, who has been lying on a towel, says, "I want to go too. I am getting all sand everywhere."

"All right," says Clive, throwing up his hands in mock defeat. "Sorry, love. Day at the beach cut short."

Claire hesitates. "Can I stay?"

"Sorry?"

"I'd like to stay. It's just so beautiful, and I haven't seen the beach in so long. Do you mind? I could take a taxi back if it's too much trouble. I just really want to go for a walk and a swim."

"Water's bloody cold for swimming," says Clive, looking at his watch and then toward the parking lot, where his other guests are now waiting. "Look, I didn't plan on spending the day playing chauffeur, but I could come back for you in half an hour or so, after I've dropped off this lot. That do?"

"Yes, thank you."

He is surprised, she can tell. It has probably been a long time since a woman failed to go along with his plans. In his world that sort of thing isn't supposed to happen. It's a black mark against her. She can tell he is already thinking who he should invite out next weekend. The others are almost back to the parking lot. He turns and follows them, lugging the cooler and the chairs. She feels lighter now.

With a sigh, she looks down the beach and removes her shirt and shorts until she is standing only in her bikini. The sun and wind feel good on her exposed skin. Although it is crowded here, she can see that farther down it thins out. That is where she wants to be, and she starts walking. The sand crunches pleasantly between her toes. The afternoon sun warm against her face. A wave bigger than the others crashes to her left, sending foaming surf rolling up over her feet. Involuntarily she lets out a little shriek and leaps aside. She had forgotten how cold the water could be, but after a few moments she becomes used to it.

When she was a child, her family would go to the beach every summer. The water was always cold there too. Maybe even colder. They would rent an old, thin-walled house on the Cape, near Wellfleet, for a week. There would be lobsters and sailing and sand in the sheets, her father playing tennis with his old wooden racket and a smell of mildew that saturated the whole house that always made her think of summer. That had been a long time ago, before her parents' divorce.

She passes several surfers bobbing like seals in the small waves and watches them for a while. One of them starts paddling and gets up unsteadily as the wave begins to crest. He manages to stay upright for a few seconds before falling. A pretty girl with long sun-bleached hair claps her hands and whistles. Claire thinks it would be wonderful to know how to surf. If only there was time. She thinks she'd be good at it. She is a good skier and used to dance in high school, so she knows her balance is good and her legs are strong.

Crossing over a seaweed-covered stone jetty that juts out into the ocean, she comes to a stretch of beach that is almost completely deserted. Up ahead in the distance is another jetty, and beyond that what looks like a large lagoon. There are signs posted on hurricane fencing that warn against disturbing a breed of bird called piping plover. Imposing mansions occupy the dunes behind her, but for the moment she feels as though she has the beach all to herself.

The sun is strong and she decides to cool off by going swimming. It is too cold to wade in. She waits for a moment at the water's edge, timing the waves, gathering her courage. Seeing her chance, she runs in, lifting her legs awkwardly out of the foaming water, and dives into a breaker. The cold shocks her, but she kicks hard and comes out beyond the swells. As she treads water, tasting the salt on her lips, her body feels strong and clean. She starts swimming a breaststroke, but the current is stronger and pushes her back, and she realizes she isn't making much headway. For a moment, she is anxious, concerned that she might not be able to get back to shore. Knowing that to fight the current would be to risk exhaustion, she swims parallel to the shore until she has escaped it. When she no longer feels its pull, she bodysurfs back to the beach, stumbling wearily out of the water.

"You should be careful out there."

She turns to see a man of about forty standing beside her. He is good-looking and well-built, with sandy hair slowly turning gray. There is something recognizable about him. It is a face she has seen before.

"There's a powerful riptide there," he says. "I was watching you when you went in, in case you got into trouble. But you looked like you could take care of yourself."

"Thank you. I wasn't so sure for a moment." She takes a deep breath and realizes her fear has passed. She smiles at him. He is an attractive man. "I didn't realize this was a full-service beach. Are you lifeguards salaried or do you work on commission?"

He laughs. "We work strictly for tips."

"Well, that's too bad. As you can see I'm not carrying any money."

"You'd be amazed how many times we lifeguards hear that. Maybe I should go into a more lucrative line of work."

"Well, you could start a line of bikinis that come with pockets."

"That's a great idea. I'll bring it up at the next lifeguard convention."

"You should. I hate to think of all those starving lifeguards, saving all those people for nothing. It just doesn't seem fair."

"Well, we don't do it for the money but for the glory—and for the gratitude, of course."

"In that case, thanks again for almost saving me."

He makes a little bow. "It was almost my pleasure. Well, so long. Stay out of riptides."

He walks down the beach in the direction of the lagoon. She watches him get smaller and sees him join a group of people by some canoes. A chill runs through her. She shivers, wishing she had brought a towel. She has to head back anyway. It is getting late. Clive will be waiting.

THAT NIGHT THEY ARE IN THE KITCHEN, READY TO GO OUT. "Where are we going?" Claire asks. She is wearing a simple white dress, low cut over her small breasts. Jodie appears serene. She has forgiven Clive.

"There's a party. Writer chap I know. Gorgeous wife."

"I want to go to nightclub," pouts Irina, applying lipstick while staring at the mirror in her compact. "My friend say they are very good here. You take me, baby?" This to Derek, whom she towers over, caressing his thinning hair. He grunts in assent. "'Ere, what about a nightclub then?"

"Things don't really get going at the clubs until midnight," answers Clive. "We'll have plenty of time."

"What's he written?" Claire asks.

"Who?"

"Your writer friend. What's he written? Would I have heard of it?"

"You may have done. He wrote something that came out the other year. Won a big prize too, I think. I never got around to reading it."

"What's his name?"

"Winslow. Harry Winslow. Have you heard of him?"

"Yes. He wrote *The Death of a Privileged Ape*. It won a National Book Award. I loved it."

"I didn't like it." It was Jodie. "You remember?" she says, turning to Larry. "I tried reading it in Anguilla? Bored the crap out of me."

"Yes, well, my taste in literature runs toward Dick Francis and Jackie Collins, I must say." Lowbrow Clive to the rescue, but Claire doesn't give up so easily.

"How do you know him?"

"Harry? He's a lovely chap. Terribly funny. Wife's smashing. Not sure how I know them. Just do. Met them at parties, I suppose. They have a house out here. Been in her family for years apparently, though I think that sort of thing means rather less here than in England."

"And after we go to nightclub, yes?" puts in Irina.

"Absolutely. After we'll go to a nightclub, and you and Derek can boogie until dawn."

THE HOUSE IS CHARMING. LIVED IN, LOVED. IT'S SMALL, TWO stories, the shingles brown with age, the trim white. Cars line the drive, some parked on the grass. A little boy, the son of the family, armed with a flashlight, helps direct them. Through the tall trees, an open field is barely visible in the twilight. The air smells of salt water, the sound of the ocean just audible. Claire wishes she could come back in the daylight. She can tell it would be marvelous.

Inside is the detritus of generations. Family treasures cover the wainscoted walls. It is as though the contents of several larger houses were spilled into one. Old portraits and photographs of men with mustaches and high collars, women with straw boaters and chignons, captains of industry, forgotten cousins; paintings of prized, long-dead horses; posters; books everywhere, on shelves and stacked in piles on the floor; and model airplanes and Chinese porcelain foo dogs and old magazines and fishing rods and tennis racquets and beach umbrellas jammed in the corners. Overhead a dusty, oversize hurricane lamp bathes everything in a soft glow. Children's toys, scratched tables and scuffed chairs and piles of canvas sneakers, moccasins, and rain boots. The whole place smells of years of mildew, the sea, and woodsmoke.

Claire is the last one in. The noise of the party pours out from other rooms. Clive puts his hand behind her back and brings her up to introduce her to a man with sandy hair. He is shaking hands with the rest of their group.

"It's my lifeguard!" He is taller than she remembers. He wears an old blazer with a button missing and frayed cuffs. "Saved anyone tonight?"

"Just a few. They were dying of thirst."

Claire giggles. "Clive, I met this man on the beach this afternoon. Apparently, I went swimming somewhere I shouldn't have and could have drowned."

"You didn't tell me."

"It was my good deed for the day, Clive," the man says. "Good thing she's a strong swimmer. I was afraid I was going to have to go in after her. Last year a teenage boy drowned there."

"So you're Harry Winslow?" Now she knows why he looked so familiar.

"I am. Who are you?" He smiles broadly. There is an old

scar on his chin. His eyes are gray. A faint trace of wrinkles. He holds out his hand, the nails clean, the fingers tapered. Golden hairs curl around his thick brown wrist.

His hand envelops hers as she introduces herself, a little less confident now. She is surprised that it would be so callused. He is no longer the same man she met on the beach. He has taken on substance in her eyes.

"Well, Claire, welcome. What can I get you to drink?"

"Excuse me," says Clive. "I see a chap over there. I'll catch up later, hmm?" Without waiting for Claire to answer, he is gone, smelling money.

"How about that drink, then?"

Claire follows Harry inside a small living room with an old brick fireplace, painted white. She notices large, worn sofas and comfortable reading chairs. He walks to a table piled high with bottles, glasses, and an ice bucket. On the floor, a faded Oriental carpet. The rest of the party is on the porch and the grass out back. She accepts a glass of white wine. He is drinking whisky on the rocks from a chunky glass.

"I read your book."

"Did you?" he responds. "I hope you liked it."

He is being modest. It is an act, she can tell. One he has repeated with varying degrees of sincerity. He has had this conversation before. Many people have read his book. It has won prizes. Thousands, maybe millions of people have liked it, even loved it. The success for him is a shield, a gift. It lends him an enviable objectivity.

"I did, very much."

"Thank you."

He smiles truthfully. It is like a parent hearing about the

achievements of an accomplished child. It is no longer within his control. It has taken on a life of its own.

He looks around. He is the host. There are others to attend to, other drinks to fetch, introductions to be made, stories to be shared. But she wants him to stay. She tries to will him to stay. Wants to ask him questions, know more about him. What is it like to have your talents recognized, to have your photograph on the back of a book? To be lionized by friends and strangers, to have your face, your hands, your body, your life? But she cannot find the words and would be embarrassed if she did.

"Where are you from?" He sips his drink. He asks the way an uncle asks where a young niece is at school.

"Just outside of Boston."

"No, I meant where do you live now?"

"Oh." She blushes. "In New York. I'm sharing an apartment with a friend from college."

"Known Clive long?"

"Not long. We met at a party in May."

"Ah," he says. "He's supposed to be very good at what he does. I must admit I don't know the first thing about business. I'm hopeless with money. Always have been."

Other guests come up. A handsome man and a beautiful woman with exotic looks and dark hair pulled tightly back. "Excuse us," says the man. They know him. "Darling," she says, leaning in to offer him her cheek. "Great party. I wish we could stay. Sitter," he explains. "You know what it's like."

They laugh with the intimacy of a private joke, the way rich people complain about how hard it is to find decent help or the expense of flying in a private plane.

The couple leaves. "Excuse me," Harry says to her. "I need to fetch more ice. Enjoy the party."

"I always do what the lifeguard tells me," she says, making a mock salute but looking him in the eyes and holding his gaze.

He turns but then, as though realizing he is leaving her all alone, says, "Wait. You haven't met Maddy. Let me introduce you. Come with me."

Reprieved, she follows him happily through the crowd to the kitchen. Unlike the living room, it is bright. Copper pots hang from the walls. Children's drawings decorate an aging refrigerator. A checked linoleum floor. There is a small, industrious crowd here, some sitting at a long, heavy table, others chopping, washing dishes. On a scarred butcher block table sits a large ham. It is an old kitchen. Worn and welcoming. She could imagine Thanksgivings here.

"Sweetheart," he says. A woman stands up from the oven, taking out something that smells delicious.

She is wearing an apron and wipes her hands on it. She is taller than Claire and strikingly beautiful. Long red-gold ringlets still wet from the shower and pale blue eyes. No makeup. A patrician face.

"Maddy, this is a new friend of Clive's." He has forgotten her name.

"Claire," she says, stepping forward. "Thank you for having me."

Maddy takes her hand. A firm grip. Her nails are cut short and unpainted. Claire notices she is barefoot.

"Hello, Claire. I'm Madeleine. Glad you could come."

She is dazzling. Claire is reminded of Botticelli's Venus.

"She liked my book," he says. "Must be nice to the paying customers."

"Of course, darling," she says. And then to Claire, "Would you like to help? As usual one of my husband's cozy little

23

get-togethers has turned into an orgy. We need to feed these people, or they could start breaking things." She shakes her head theatrically and smiles at him.

"The world's greatest wife," he says with an ecstatic sigh.

"I'd be happy to," says Claire.

"Great. We need someone to plate the deviled eggs. They're in the fridge and the platters are in the pantry. And don't worry if you drop anything, nothing's that good."

"You're a wonderful field marshal," says Harry, giving his wife a kiss on the cheek. "I need to get ice."

"Check the wine too," she calls out as he leaves. "We've already gone through two cases of white. And where's that other case of vodka? I thought it was under the stairs." She begins to plate the canapés from the oven onto a platter.

"Is there anything else I can do?" Claire brings out the deviled eggs.

"Yes. Phil," she says to the man with the dish towel, "let Claire do that for a while. Take these out and put them on the sideboard." She turns to Claire. "Is this your first time out here?"

Claire nods. "It's very beautiful."

"It's much grander now than when I was a kid," she says, slicing a brown loaf of bread, using the back of her wrist to push her hair away from her face. "Back then most of the land around here was farms. The place across the road was a dairy farm. We used to go help with the milking. Now it's a subdivision for millionaires. Hand me that plate, would you?"

"You've always lived here?"

She nods. "We came in the summers. This was the staff cottage. My family owned the big house up the drive."

"What happened?"

"What always happens. We—my brother, Johnny, and me—had to sell it to pay estate taxes, but we kept this place. I couldn't bear to part with it entirely. Isn't that right, Walter?"

This is where I come in. Every story has a narrator. Someone who writes it down after it's all over. Why am I the narrator of this story? I am because it is the story of my life—and of the people I love most. I have tried to be as scrupulous as possible in my telling of it. I wasn't a participant in everything that happened, but after I knew the ending, I had to fill in the missing pieces through glimpses that meant nothing to me at the time, memories that flash back with new significance, old legal pads, sentences jotted down in notebooks and on the backs of aging photographs. Even Harry himself, though he didn't know it. I had no choice other than to try to make sense of it. But making sense of anything is never easy, particularly this story.

I walk over, plucking up one of the canapés and popping it into my mouth. Bacon and something. It is delicious. "Absolutely, darling. Whatever you say."

"Oh, shut up. Don't be an ass." Then to Claire, "Walter is my lawyer. He knows all about it. Sorry, Walter Gervais, this is Claire. Claire, Walter. Walter is also my oldest friend."

It's true. We have known each other since we were children. I live next door.

"Hello, Claire," I say. "I see Maddy's already dragooned you into service here at the Winslow bar and grill. I refuse to lift a finger unless it's to join the other four wrapped around a glass tinkling with ice."

I fancy myself to be both witty and slightly indolent. I am

not really either, though. It's a persona, one I use to protect myself. In fact, I am quite boring and lonely.

"I don't mind. I don't really know too many people here, so it's nice for me to help," Claire says.

"You're lucky," I say. "I know far too many of the people here. That probably explains why I'm hiding out in the kitchen."

"Walter's a big snob. I don't think he's made a new friend since he was in prep school," Maddy says.

"You know, I think you're right. I already knew all the people worth knowing by then anyway."

"Claire came with Clive."

"Right, see? There you go. Just met him. Don't like him."

"You don't know me," says Claire.

"You're right. I don't. Should I?"

Here's the thing about Claire: she is actually quite beautiful, but there is something else about her that makes her stand out. In this world, beauty is as common as a credit card. I will try to put my finger on it.

"That's up to you. But we didn't go to prep school together so it looks like I don't have much of a shot." She smiles.

I smile back. I like her. I can't help myself. I tell Maddy to stop working. Maddy is always working. She is a fiend for activity.

"All right." She puts down the knife. "That's all the food we have in the house anyway. Just about the only thing left is the bluefish in the freezer."

"And those are only any good if you pickle them in gin. Just like me."

Why do I always play the bloody fool around her? It can't

be that I am showing off. No, it is Claire I am showing off for now.

"Walter, stop standing around sounding like a moron and go get Claire and me something to drink." Maddy turns to Claire while I'm still in earshot. "You wouldn't know it, but he's actually a hell of a good lawyer."

I could have left this out but I didn't. It appeases my ego. My education was very expensive, and I am a good lawyer. I make a lot of money at it too. I don't really like it, though. Other people's problems at least keep me from thinking too much about my own.

I come back carrying a wine bottle. "Let's go outside and get away from this crowd," I say to Claire. "You come too, Maddy."

The three of us go out the kitchen door. We stand on the damp grass. Claire has removed her shoes now too. Madeleine lights a cigarette. She is trying to quit. The party is roaring on the other side of the house. It is darker here. A large tree with a swing looms in shadow in front of us. The moon and millions of stars fill the night sky. In the distance we can see the lights of a much bigger house.

"Your parents' house?" asks Claire.

Madeleine nods. "And to the left is Walter's. We grew up next door to each other. But he still owns his." It's too dark to see my house through the thin brake of trees.

"The law may not be as glamorous as writing books, but it is more consistently remunerative," I say.

"Don't believe it," says Madeleine. "Walter's rich as sin. Even if he wasn't a lawyer."

My great-grandfather was a founder of Texaco. Unlike

many other families, though, we were able to hold on to our money.

"Don't give away all my secrets, Maddy. I want Claire to fall in love with me and not my money."

"Too bad your money's the most lovable thing about you."

Claire says nothing. She is enjoying herself, I can tell. It is like standing next to a fire; she feels warmed by our friendship and grateful we are sharing it with her. She feels she could stay here all night listening to our intimate banter, not wanting to let it go and return to the world that exists outside this house.

But what is she really thinking? It is always so easy to know what's on Maddy's mind. There isn't a deceptive bone in her body. This one, though, is more difficult. She is more concealed.

MIDNIGHT. THE CROWD HAS THINNED OUT. A SMALL GROUP has gathered on a cluster of old wicker furniture in the corner of the porch. Harry is in the center. Also, a couple named Ned and Cissy Truscott. Ned was Harry's roommate at Yale. A big man, a football player. Now a banker. I have expensively represented his firm on several occasions. In spite of that, we get on quite well. I am fond of them both. Claire is with them, listening like an acolyte. Laughing loudly, showing pretty teeth. She has a lovely laugh. It reminds me of silver bells. Harry is talking. He is a very good storyteller, unsurprisingly.

Clive approaches. He hovers before them, maybe a bit unsteadily, waiting for an opportunity. By this time everyone's had plenty to drink.

"Hello, Clive!" Harry roars. "Come sit down." Harry is

drunk now too, but he handles it well. Always has. Tomorrow he'll be up at six, whistling in the kitchen.

"No thanks," says Clive. "Thanks for the party. Claire, we have to go. I promised this lot we'd go dancing, remember?"

"Oh, can't we stay? A few more minutes. I'm having such fun."

"C'mon, stay for one drink," calls Harry. "What do you want to go dancing for? You can dance here."

"Thanks," says Clive with a forced smile. "Houseguests. They want to see all the hot spots. Do the Hamptons properly."

"Suit yourself."

"Come along, Claire."

Reluctantly, she rises. "Thank you very much, Harry. Please tell Maddy how much I enjoyed meeting her."

Harry stands up too. "Of course. Glad you could come. Watch out for riptides."

They depart, and Harry begins to tell another funny story.

2

SEVERAL WEEKS PASS. IT IS SATURDAY MORNING. CLAIRE HAS rented a car. She is driving out to Clive's house. She hasn't seen him since that weekend. He's been away, in the Far East, he told her. Or was it Eastern Europe? To her surprise, he has invited her out again. She almost declines, but then he tells her that they've been invited for dinner at the Winslows'. How do I know this? I was also invited. What's interesting is I think that it was my idea.

"You don't need to rent a car," Clive had protested. It was a lot of money for her, but she had insisted. She didn't tell him why. She told me later that she hated feeling dependent on him, had wanted to be able to go where she wanted, when she wanted.

As she got closer to Southampton and Route 27 became increasingly congested, she began to regret her decision to drive out. The sun is high over the barren scrub pines that line the highway, and it reflects off the roofs of a thick stream of expensive cars heading east, blocking her way. They inch forward past gas stations and motels, car dealerships and farm stands. None of the glamour is visible from this road. Cars speed past in the opposite direction on the other side of the median. Claire is hot and irritable. Even the radio is annoying her.

When Clive's call came, she had almost stopped thinking about him and was ready to move on. Her roommate, Dana, said she was crazy to dump a rich, handsome Englishman with a house in the Hamptons during the summer. She should at least wait until the fall.

She asks herself, not for the first time, why she is doing this. She knows she will have sex with Clive. He is an exciting if selfish lover, but she is no longer interested. It will mean nothing, a small price to be paid for admittance. She will spread her legs for him, and then, when he is finished, she will close them up again and go to sleep, both having gotten what they wanted. I can imagine her. She will make the noises required, rake her nails across his back, gasp appropriately, sigh appreciatively. She is not what she seems.

Who is she exactly? She is half French, she will later tell me. Proud of the fact. It makes her more exotic. Her father was an American officer with an Irish name, a graduate of an undistinguished college, dashing in his uniform and generous with his small paycheck. Her parents had met while he was on furlough in Paris from his base in Germany. Her mother was younger, barely out of convent school. An only child, the daughter of older parents. The father a professor at the École Normale Supérieure. They lived in an old house in Asnièressur-Seine, a suburb that is perhaps best known for being the home of the Louis Vuitton family. I have been there. It is surprisingly bourgeois.

Her mother married her father shortly before his discharge. It was a small ceremony held in the local Catholic church. Another soldier was best man. It had been a hasty affair, the small bump that was to become Claire barely noticeable under her mother's dress. Afterward they came to live in his hometown in Massachusetts, near Worcester. Before long there was another baby, Claire's younger brother. But her mother could never adapt to the harsh winters or reserved inhabitants of New England. The language had been difficult for her. Her accent too strong, too foreign. Claire remembers her mother withdrawing to her room for hours, days, when the long, dark months enfolded their town. She began to smile again only with the return of spring. Meanwhile, Claire's father strove. He worked as a salesman, then a stockbroker. They bought a new house, a large Victorian in a dreary neighborhood. He had prospered but never became rich. There had been good years and bad. A green Jaguar that once adorned the driveway was replaced by a Buick. Claire had her own room, as did her brother. She went to school, earned high marks, learned how to ice skate and kiss boys. Their mother taught them French and on Sundays took them to Mass.

Every year Claire's mother returned to Paris to visit her parents, bringing Claire and her brother. Claire hated these trips. She found her grandparents old and distant, relics of another century, another life. What she liked best were the walks through the streets and parks of Paris. It was a world unimaginable to her classmates, who had barely been beyond the aging factories that surrounded their town, and who considered Boston as distant as the moon. She would see French boys her age and pretend that she was meeting them, that they were waiting for her. They would let her smoke their cigarettes and ride behind them on their motor scooters, her hands clasped tightly around their thin, hard bellies. Instead she and her mother and brother dutifully toured the Louvre and visited cafés where they would invariably order the prix fixe. Once, for a special treat, their father joined them, and they traveled down to Nice for a week by the beach. By then her grandfather was dead, and her grandmother had become even more remote, sitting in an old chair by the window in that familiar, oppressive room amid stale biscuits and the smell of decay. That had been the last trip. Shortly after, her parents divorced.

Her father remarried. He moved to Belmont, and before long his wife gave birth to a daughter. He was starting over. Claire was sixteen. She lived with her mother in their old house and communicated with her father on holidays and birthdays. By the time she went off to college, two years later, she had learned that love did not give itself freely. That if she wanted it, it had to be taken. The protective shell that had been slowly growing around her finally hardened into place. She did not resent her father. She only knew that neither of them had much to say to each other. A few weeks after she had moved to New York he had sent her a small check. In a brief note he had written *I hope this will help you get started*, but she had left the check uncashed for many months, despite her low salary, and finally tore it up. He never mentioned it to her.

When Claire was in college her mother moved back to take care of her own mother. After the old lady died, her mother inherited a little money and the apartment, which she sold. She did not remarry. Claire had visited once. Her mother was living outside of Paris in the former royal city of Senlis, in a little apartment near the cathedral. She looked older but more serene. Around her neck she wore a small gold cross. They were more like two old friends chatting than mother and daughter. When Claire left, her mother embraced her but said nothing.

All that was years before. Now Claire was a member of that tribe of independent females, working without guarantees or guidance in the city, hoping to find love and, if not love, success or something like it. She was not promiscuous but she was available, which explains Clive and the men who had come before him and would no doubt follow.

The traffic had been worse than Claire expected. When she arrives at Clive's house they are already late for dinner. "You took your bloody time getting here," he says, offering her a perfunctory kiss. He is already dressed, a glass of champagne in his hand. He does not offer her one. "Sorry, traffic," she says, hurrying into the bedroom to shower quickly and change.

Five minutes later she is rushing down the front steps, carrying her shoes while Clive waits in his car, the motor already running. "All right?" he says, barely waiting for her to close her door before accelerating down the drive, spitting gravel over the grass. She will swipe lipstick across her mouth and brush her hair in the car. "I told you it was silly to drive out," he says. "I would have been happy to collect you at the station." She ignores Clive's rudeness. It is not him she has come to see.

When they arrive at the Winslows', it is still light. In the west the sky is turning a startling mix of orange and purple. Harry greets them at the door. He is unconcerned about the time. "Come on in," he says, his hair still wet from the shower. His light blue shirt clinging damply. His nose is sunburned. "Look at that sunset," he says, presenting it like a gift.

Claire offers him her cheek and feels his lips lightly brush her skin. "Thank you so much for having us," she says. "I was so happy when Clive told me."

"Our pleasure," responds Harry. "You made a big impression on Maddy. Let me get you guys something to drink."

The house is more magical to her than before. There is no crush of party guests talking, laughing, flirting. Tonight it has reverted to its own quiet, private self, a house where a family lives, where secrets are shared and kept. On the wall she sees a small painting she hadn't noticed before. A seascape. On a faded, elaborately carved frame a tiny brass nameplate with the name of the artist. Winslow Homer. She is surprised and impressed. Claire wishes she could inspect everything, study the photographs, learn the language.

Harry is at the bar. We have a running joke. Whenever one of us or, as it happened once, all of us find ourselves in Venice, we go to the famed Harry's Bar right off St. Mark's and swipe an ashtray or coaster to bring back to the bar here. On the wall is a photograph of Harry standing proprietarily in front of the frosted double doors, grinning madly. Maddy took the picture on their honeymoon.

"Wonderful day today," he says. "Ned rented a boat in Montauk and we each caught a shark. Jesus, it was incredible."

He uncorks a bottle of wine, wincing. "Cut the hell out of my hand, though." Harry holds up his palm. Claire and Clive can see it is red and blistered. Calmly, gently, Claire reaches out and takes his hand and holds it in her own, running her fingers over the ravaged skin.

"It must hurt very much," she says.

"Oh, it looks worse than it is." His hand escapes to the glass. "Most of the red is iodine."

"What did you do with the shark?" asks Clive.

"Going to have it mounted. Hang it on the wall over there. It'll be quite the conversation piece. You know what people are like out here. It'll drive 'em nuts," he adds, laughing.

They walk outside to the porch. On the lawn Ned is throwing gentle spirals to a little blond boy. Claire recognizes him as the boy with the flashlight from the night of the party. They stop when they see them, and the boy waves.

"That's Johnny," says Harry. "Johnny, come here and say hello to our guests."

The boy runs to them, his tanned legs long and skinny like a colt's. Claire sees he has his mother's blue eyes above a sun-freckled nose.

"How do you do?" he says in a soft voice, putting out his hand the way he has been taught. But he is a shy boy. He does not look them in the eye.

"How do you do, mate?" says Clive.

"Hello, Johnny," says Claire, squatting so she is at eye level with the boy. "I'm Claire. How old are you?"

I am studying her. She is good with children. It is obvious. I imagine she must have worked as an au pair during college. She would have been their best friend.

"Eight." His voice is nearly inaudible, but at least he is looking directly into Claire's eyes. "But I'm almost nine."

"Almost nine? That makes you very grown-up. I'm twenty-six. What do you like to do? I like to sail and read books."

"My daddy writes books."

"I know. I read his book. It was wonderful."

Johnny smiles. Harry puts his hand on his son's shoulder. "All right, buddy. It's time for your supper. What do you say?"

"Good night. It was nice to meet you."

He goes into the house. Claire watches him go, already in love. He is my godson.

Ned comes up. Despite his size, he is surprisingly quick. I have seen him play tennis. He can still beat men years younger and many pounds lighter. "Hey there." To Harry he says, "He's getting a good arm. He'll make the team yet."

Harry smiles abstractedly. Claire senses he is thinking about something else. "Hockey players can do everything football players do, but we do it on ice and backwards," he says. Then to Claire and Clive, "You should see Johnny's slap shot."

"Only girls slap." Ned grins.

They speak in the shorthand of their youth. The two ex-jocks. Members of DKE. Harry was on the hockey team. In his senior year, he was captain.

I remember long, cold nights in Ingalls Rink, huddling under a blanket with Maddy, sharing my flask of bourbon, watching Harry skate. He was good, very good. She couldn't take her eyes off him. His hair was longer then, blonder. He would look up at her every time he scored a goal, seeking her approval, knowing in his heart that he already had it. Already they were inseparable.

Madeleine Wakefield was the most beautiful woman at school. She was the most beautiful woman anywhere she went.

Men hovered around her but she had become inured to such attentions. Magazine editors and photographers had asked her to model, but she always said no. To her, beauty was nothing earned. It was a fact, like being left-handed, and it was nothing she ever thought about. While the other girls would dress up for parties, borrowing clothes from roommates, pulling earrings that their mothers had given them for a special night from the backs of their drawers, Maddy never tried. Her normal costume was an old shirt of her father's, a baggy sweater, blue jeans. Still, wherever she went, the men would forget their dates and stare at her, although few of them were bold enough to approach her, sensing there was something different about her, incapable of knowing the true self beneath that beauty.

I knew, of course. We had always talked about going to Yale together, but after her girls' school in Maryland and my prep school in Massachusetts, the reality was almost better than the dream. She had a car back then. A vintage red MG convertible that had been a present from her grandmother, with the plates MWSMG. Freshman year had been a blur of weekends in Manhattan, nightclubs, and bleary last-minute dashes up I-95 to make it, hungover and hilarious, to classes on Monday morning.

And then, in our sophomore year, she fell in love with Harry. We were in different residential colleges. He in Davenport, Maddy and I in Jonathan Edwards. We had seen him, of course. In Mory's, where he was usually surrounded by his friends, drinking beer or celebrating his latest victory. He was popular and, honestly, it is impossible to imagine him otherwise. Maddy instantly disliked him, which I should have known as a sign. "He's very full of himself," she had said, on those nights when it was just us, which it was most nights. She wanted to make fun of him and to despise him for what she saw in herself. But, in hindsight, it was like watching two lions circling each other. It would have been either death or a lifetime together.

Maddy and I remained friends—how could we not? She had been my late-night companion since she first climbed out of her second-story window so we could go catch fireflies together. As children, we would walk our bikes silently down the gravel drive and meet for midnight escapes on the beach, where we made fires out of driftwood and listened to the waves lap the sand while we shared our most intimate thoughts and dreams.

We had to be careful, though. My parents were often away, and I would be left alone in the care of Genevieve and Robert, the childless Swiss couple who took care of the place. Genevieve was short and stocky and cooked. Robert drove and looked after the garden. Both of them were in bed by ten and assumed I was too. I was an only child, pudgy and bookish, so they hardly would have imagined I had this secret, nocturnal existence. Madeleine's father was more of a problem. He would have beaten her if they had caught her sneaking out. Not that it would have stopped her.

One time we were playing tennis and I saw the welts at the tops of her thighs when she bent over to pick up a ball. He had used a belt. I wanted to do something but she swore it was nothing and let's play another set. God, she was brave. She still is.

The dinner is marvelous. Fresh swordfish, tomatoes and

corn, hot bread, and ice cream, washed down with cold, steely white wine. Maddy has a special way of grilling the fish using pine branches that gives it a wonderfully rich taste. We sit under round paper lanterns, outside on a small, screened-in porch off the kitchen. There are more men than women so I sit between Clive and Cissy. Cissy is very funny. Small, blond, she can talk for hours. She is from outside Philadelphia, the Main Line. She and Ned have been trying unsuccessfully for years to have a baby. I admire her toughness, her lack of self-pity.

Clive keeps trying to quiz me about my clients, but I put him off. When I grow tired of his insistence, I ignore him completely and listen to Harry tell one of his stories, which, if I recall, was about the time when he was seventeen and drove his car into a tree on purpose to collect the insurance money. He had even borrowed a pair of hockey goalie pads for protection. The car was an old heap, and he had hoped to make about five hundred dollars. He thought thirty miles an hour would be a good speed, not too fast or too slow, but the impact was so great, it knocked him out.

"The next thing I know," Harry says, "there's a cop knocking on my window with his nightstick wondering just what the hell is going on and why am I wearing hockey pads in the middle of July?"

We hoot with laughter. Claire, on Harry's right, is in paroxysms of delight. She had been helping Maddy in the kitchen and is the first to jump to her feet to help clear. She is showing off a little, letting us know she is more than just Clive's latest mistress. We are all of us in our forties, and we can't help but be a little enchanted by her potent combination of youth, beauty, passion, and brains. It turns out she does the *New York Times* crossword puzzle, which is one of Harry's favorite distractions too. They groan complicitly about the creeping influence of pop culture in the clues. They argue over a book review they both recently read, and share a passion for Mark Twain. Is this the best night of her life? I think so.

Clive is not part of this. He dislikes not being the star. This crowd is not impressed by his Aston Martin or his fancy watch or the last time he was in St. Bart's. He doesn't really belong here. Claire doesn't belong with him either. I am willing him to leave.

After dinner we play charades, something else at which Harry excels. By midnight everyone is drunk and Harry stands up and says, "It's time." I know what he means, of course. As do Ned and Cissy. Maddy just rolls her eyes.

"Time for what?" asks Claire, but already the others are in motion.

"Time to go to the beach," Cissy says over her shoulder. "We do it after every dinner party."

"You all go on without me," declares Maddy, remaining in her chair. "Someone has to stay here with Johnny." I could have offered to stay. I normally do. But not tonight.

"Come on," says Claire, pulling a bewildered Clive to his feet and dashing out the door to the Winslows' old red Jeep. In the front seat, next to Harry, Ned is carrying a bottle of wine. He is slurring his words a little. Cissy is sitting on his lap. Claire and Clive pile in beside me in the backseat. The house is a short drive to the beach, under five minutes. This time of night the beach is deserted. The moon lights a path across the water for us. The sand is cool beneath our feet.

Harry runs down to the water's edge, pulling off his shirt and then dropping his trousers until, naked, he rushes whooping into the dark water. Ned and Cissy follow close behind,

Cissy shrieking as she dives in. I am slower, but suddenly beside me, Claire is undressed as well. I can't help but notice her body in the moon glow, her young breasts, the roundness of her hips. I catch a glimpse of a triangle of dark pubic hair. It happens in an instant, of course. One second she is standing beside me, the next she is in the water. A surge of desire seizes me as I watch her run. It is just Clive and I now. I pull off my trousers. "Bloody hell," he mutters and strips too. We dive in together.

At night the ocean always seems so much calmer. It is like a big lake, the waves barely more than ripples. The water is waist-high. Most women would be crouching in the water, concealing themselves. But not Claire. It is becoming apparent to me that she is not most women. Harry and Ned are having a splash fight, like a couple of boys. She joins in, laughing, splashing hard. It is impossible not to watch her. Clive stands off to the side, as though he were an interloper and not Claire's lover. Then Cissy climbs on Ned's shoulders and gracefully dives off. "I want to try that," says Claire. But instead of climbing on Ned, or even Clive, she glides behind Harry and grabs his hands. He squats obediently under the water while she places her feet on each shoulder. He lifts her easily, and she balances for a moment, drops his hands, and throws her arms out and her head back before smoothly diving off. When she comes up, she wipes the wet hair from her face and yells, "I want to do that again!"

Once again Harry squats, his back to her, and she confidently mounts. And again, she drops his hands and balances, but this time she wavers and falls with a splash into the water. Harry helps her up. "Careful," he says with a laugh.

"My favorite lifeguard," she pronounces with a laugh and gives him a wet kiss on the cheek and a quick hug, her nipples grazing his chest. "Once again you've saved me from drowning." She stands back in front of him, as if to say, Look at me. This could be yours. I can't remember if anyone else noticed the moment. I tried to catch Ned's or Cissy's eye, but they were in the middle of doing another dive.

Harry says nothing and looks away as Clive comes up.

"Let me show you how it's done, mate," he says.

Claire pulls away from him, but he squats down, saying, "Come on."

She climbs up without looking at him and just dives off, straight and clean. When she comes up, she says, "Can we go? I'm getting cold."

The moment has passed. Claire wades back out of the water, shoulders hunched forward, an arm covering her breasts, a hand in front of her loins. She looks at nobody. No one looks at anyone as we hurriedly pull our clothes over our wet bodies. Our mood is postlapsarian.

We drive back to the house in silence. Even Cissy is quiet. When we get out, Claire and Clive hang back. It is obvious they are going to have a fight. The rest of us go inside.

That's not entirely true. I linger just out of sight and over-hear snatches of what they say. "Don't touch me" and "Stupid cunt" and "Why don't you just fuck him then?"

She comes in, crying, running past me to the kitchen. To Maddy.

"Is everything all right?" asks Harry. I say nothing, and Clive is standing in the hallway, looking angry. He wants to follow her but knows he can't, an unbeliever in the temple.

Madeleine comes out. "Clive, Claire seems very upset. I know it's late, and we've all had a lot to drink. But she asked if she could stay here tonight, and I told her she could."

Clive stares at her, unsure of what to say, of how to react.

43

The words he wants to say fail in his throat. His will is not as strong as Maddy's.

She senses his frustration and puts a hand on his arm. "She'll call you in the morning."

When he gets outside the house, he will find his words again, he will rage, he will think black thoughts, call them all names. But not now. Standing before him is Madeleine, looking like a Madonna. Behind her, Harry, Ned, me. He has no chance. Now all he says is "Tell that cunt I don't want to see her again," and he leaves, his car spitting gravel as it drives off.

Inside, Maddy has her arm around Claire, who is apologizing over and over. Her face is wet with tears. Maddy consoles her. We all do. Or at least try to.

"See, I told you I didn't like him," I say, but all the thanks I get is a dirty look from Madeleine.

"Don't you worry about it," Harry tells Claire. "You're welcome to stay here as long as you like. If you need us to get your things from Clive's, I'll run over tomorrow. For tonight, we can loan you anything you need."

"Thank you," she sniffs.

"We are going to have to put you on the couch in the living room, if that's all right. Ned and Cissy already have the guest room. We'll get you pillows and sheets. You'll be snug as a bug."

I am about to suggest that she would be welcome to stay at my house, as there are plenty of empty bedrooms, but then think better of it.

"Please don't go to any bother. I don't mind at all. You're being so kind. I just feel like such a fool."

"Not at all," says Harry. "I'll be right back." He goes upstairs and returns several minutes later with pillow, sheets, blankets, a towel, and a large gray T-shirt with the words YALE HOCKEY on it. "I figured you could use something to sleep in."

Cissy and Madeleine begin to make up the couch. Harry wanders into the kitchen and starts rinsing glasses. I debate having a last drink but then decide against it. It's already past one in the morning. Instead I say my good-byes, kiss Maddy good night, tell Claire to sleep well and that everything will look better in the morning, and head out to the familiar path that leads through the narrow strip of trees that separates our two houses.

I can imagine Claire, having calmed down, thanks to a few gulps of brandy, getting under the covers on the couch. Madeleine would be there, making sure her newest charge is comfortable and well looked after. Ned, Cissy, and Harry would have already gone up. Then Maddy would have left too, turning off lights, leaving Claire alone in her temporary bed, staring up at the ceiling, happy as a child.

3

SEVERAL WEEKS PASS. SUMMER RAGES ON. THE STREETS OF Manhattan bake in the fierce sunlight. To Claire, the breezes and salt water of Long Island are just a memory. She has been banished to the ordinary world, one inhabited by coworkers, college friends, deliverymen, strangers on the subway. Like Eurydice, she will never again walk in fields of flowers.

Claire has not seen the Winslows. There is no reason why she should. She returned to the city the day after her fight with Clive. Harry and Ned had gone to Clive's to get her bag and retrieve her rental car, but when they pulled up, no one was home and her possessions had been thrown into the front seat.

Even though Harry and Madeleine had asked her to stay and been so kind, she felt like an intruder, a stranger taken in under false pretenses. She would forget about them. Their lives, which had temporarily intersected with hers, would now continue along a different path.

I thought about her on a few occasions during the days that followed. Hers was an unfinished story, and I wanted to know more of it. What would she do? What turns would her life take? And then it seemed she had disappeared for good.

Until one night Harry announces to Maddy and me over dinner in the kitchen, "I meant to tell you. Guess who I saw today?" He had been in New York, lunch with his agent, a few errands. "Claire."

"How is she?" asks Maddy.

"She looked well. I was walking out of the restaurant and talking with Reuben, and all of a sudden, I almost knocked her down. What are the odds of that?"

"I liked her," I say. "Poor thing was wasted on Clive. What a horse's ass."

"Maddy liked her too, didn't you, sweetheart? At least I thought you did. We were standing there chatting about this and that, and she asked warmly after you both, and Johnny, and Ned and Cissy, and she looked a little blue, so I thought, what the hell, and invited her out for the weekend. At first, she said she couldn't, but I insisted. Hope you don't mind. She needs being taken in hand. Maddy, you're just the person to do it, too."

Maddy does love a project. Even as a child she was always taking in strays. I remember sitting up nights with her, helping her watch over a dying rabbit or chipmunk which the local cat (my cat, incidentally, but she never blamed me for it) had eviscerated. She would keep them warm, use an eyedropper to give them water, and inevitably bury them in the woods in one of my mother's shoe boxes.

"I'm glad you invited her, darling," she says. "But we can't have her sleep on the couch again. Where will she sleep? Aren't Ned and Cissy coming?"

"Don't worry about that," I offer. "They can stay with me. I have lots of room."

"Great," says Harry. "Thanks, Walter. And Ned and Cissy can give her a ride out."

ON FRIDAY THEY ARRIVE, LATE. THE TRAFFIC IS PARTICU- larly hellish on Fridays, especially during the summer. What had been a ninety-or-so-minute drive in my childhood can now stretch out to three hours or more, even for people like me who know the back roads. The farms that used to line the roads are almost all gone. The old potato barns are nightclubs. The quaint little stores where I had once bought comic books and penny candy and donuts are high-end boutiques selling cashmere sweaters and virgin olive oil. Last year an Hermès opened in the old liquor store. The beach and the sunsets are just about the only things that haven't changed.

Claire is greeted with hugs and kisses. Her face is bright with welcome. She looks lovely. "I brought this for you," she says as she presents Madeleine with a large, brightly wrapped box.

"It's heavy," Madeleine says. "What is it?"

She opens the box and pulls out a gleaming copper sauce- pan. "Oh, you shouldn't have. These are very expensive." It must have been a small fortune to someone like Claire. She works for a magazine, an assistant editor or something, the lowest on the pole. The generosity of the gift, as well as its appropriateness, overwhelms Madeleine, who is a sucker for cookware. She gives Claire another, longer hug. "I love it. Thank you!"

"And this is for you," Claire says to Harry. She hands him a paper bag. From inside he withdraws a red T-shirt and opens it up to display lettering on the front: LIFEGUARD and a white cross. He puts it on over his shirt. Everyone laughs and claps.

"Another childhood dream fulfilled," he laughs. "All I need now is a whistle and a clipboard."

Wine is brought, glasses filled. Harry carves the chicken. It is from a local farm. There is also fresh sweet corn and long green beans crunchy with sea salt. Everyone is happy to be here. Plans are discussed for Saturday. A beach excursion and a picnic seem to be in order. Then Harry announces that tomorrow night they are getting a sitter and giving Madeleine a night off from cooking—"About time!" she cries and we all laugh—and that we will all be going out to eat.

It's one of our favorite restaurants, a place with red-checked tablecloths and inch-thick steaks dripping with butter. The owners are a diminutive Greek woman and her brother, who spends most evenings drinking by himself in the corner. Some nights I sit with him and listen to his schemes for investing in real estate. Once when I was there, a family of local Indians from the Shinnecock tribe came in. There were six of them, two parents and four children. They ordered a single steak and split it amongst them. It made me feel absurd and fat to be eating the same thing only for myself.

"It's also got the worst wine list in the world, but that's part of its charm," says Harry.

Tonight, though, we are all tired. There will be no midnight swim. Madeleine says she will clean, and Claire offers to help her. Harry excuses himself and goes upstairs to work. I lead Ned and Cissy back through the bushes to my house.

It is late when the two women go to bed. I can imagine them in the living room talking, their feet tucked up behind them on the couch, finishing the wine. They are very different, but there is a growing bond between them. It is hard to resist being idolized.

So much has been made about Harry, yet Madeleine has never protested or voiced any resentment. She has given of herself utterly. Since their marriage I had never thought of Madeleine needing or wanting anything other than Harry because she had so much already. He was the missing piece that made her complete. But she is human, too, something that many of us forget at times because she seems immune to pettiness, possessing a serenity that actually grows more pronounced the greater her troubles. She knew she had Harry and Johnny—and me, of course—but can she be blamed for wanting more? What is important is she thought she was the one making the choice.

As I often do, I sit in my room looking across to her house. In the distance I hear the whistle of the night train heading back to New York. Maddy's light goes out well past midnight, and I crawl into my childhood bed.

4

THE NEXT MORNING CLAIRE COMES DOWN LATER THAN THE
rest of us. It is nearly eleven. We are outside in the sunlight.
Harry has been up for hours. He says it's the time when he
works best. We have all settled into our normal weekend routines. Newspapers. The smells of coffee and bacon. The hum
of crickets, the call of birds. Harry and Johnny are practicing their fly casting on the lawn. They flick and roll the long
line out gracefully, allowing the bare tip to hover for a second
before floating down to the grass. They have been doing this
for nearly forty-five minutes. It is mesmerizing, like watching
water eddy and pool in a stream. It is a skill I have never been
able to master. Johnny already casts like an old pro. Last year
Harry took him to Wyoming for a week along the Bighorn.
Harry once told me that if he hadn't become a writer, he would
have been a fishing guide.

Claire emerges from the house, carrying a mug. Her eyes are slightly puffy. She is wearing Harry's Yale hockey T-shirt. It reaches down to just below the tops of her thighs. Her feet are bare.

"So that's where it is," he says. "Been looking for that."

"Sorry. I took it by mistake. I brought it out last night to give back. Hope you don't mind. It's just so comfortable."

"Not at all. Consider it a gift. I can always get another. After all, you did give me a new T-shirt last night."

"Thank you."

I can't help but stare at her. I can see the curve of her breasts under the shirt, their youthful lift, the barely visible outlines of her nipples. Maybe she senses my eyes on her and excuses herself to go back inside. I have already seen her naked in the dark, but somehow in the morning it's different. Of course, she has seen me naked too, but it's not quite the same thing. I no longer possess the allure of youth, if I ever did.

On a summer day, for us there is only one way to go for a day at the beach—by canoe. My house and Madeleine's former house sit side by side overlooking a brackish lagoon that drains into the ocean. As children we disdained the notion of being driven to the beach, or even biking. We would pack up a battered Old Town canoe with towels, coolers, beach chairs, and whatever else we needed and set off like Lewis and Clark. It is nearly half a mile to paddle, and the winds could be stiff, sometimes forcing us to hug the shore, but the extra effort was always worth it. Unlike those people who came by car and sat crowded in clumps by the parking lot, we had a whole stretch of beach almost entirely to ourselves.

There are two canoes now, and we keep them on racks at my house, the paddles and mildewed life jackets, which only Johnny ever wears, hanging from the thwarts. Harry and I hoist one canoe and walk it past the bulrushes onto the old dock and into the water, our feet sinking in the mire. Ned easily picks up the other one by himself. The wicker on the seats has long since given out and been replaced with crude and less comfortable wooden boards. Spiders dash out from the gunnels, and we scoop them out with our hands. Standing calf-deep in the water, we load up the canoes and take our seats. From long custom, I sit in the stern and Maddy in the bow of one, Harry and Ned in the other. Johnny sits in front of his father while Cissy reclines in the middle on a folding beach chair like Cleopatra touring the Nile. Claire hops into ours and sits on a cooler.

"I feel like a freeloader," she says. "Would it be all right if I got out and pushed?"

"Nonsense," I say. "Enjoy the ride."

"Only if one of you lets me paddle back," she says.

The other canoe is far in front of us. The trip to the beach is always a race. Johnny's and Cissy's extra weight, along with most of the gear, usually evens things out, but now with Claire we are losing ground. Madeleine is intensely focused, reaching her paddle far out to draw as much water as possible, sending miniature whirlpools by me. She is very strong. I paddle hard too, focusing more on speed than on steering. "Oh, it's all my fault," says Claire, seeing how badly we are trailing. She has grasped the urgency of the moment yet can do nothing. "That's it," she says, and takes off her shirt. Gracefully, she dives into the water and we shoot forward. "I wasn't kidding about pushing," she says, and we feel her kicking behind the canoe.

53

Madeleine yells, "We're gaining."

It's true. We are. My arms are tiring, but I keep up the same pace as before. I won't let her down. Madeleine is the most competitive person I know.

"Get a horse," I yell to the other canoe as we pull within several lengths.

"Hey, that's cheating," cries Harry. "No motors allowed."

"Faster, Daddy, faster!"

I feel Claire stop pushing and see the other canoe now veering off to the right. Claire has reappeared by the other canoe. She has grabbed the stern and is forcing it off course.

"No fair," Harry shouts, as he begins to stand up.

Cissy shrieks, "Don't even think about it, Harry!"

Laughing, he tries to grab for Claire, but she ducks under the water. Seconds later her head pops up on the other side, like a seal's. The canoe rocks dangerously but doesn't tip over. Ned is sitting in the bow with his paddle poised in the air, looking bemused.

"I want a do-over," he says.

Madeleine keeps paddling hard as we pass them. My arms feel like they are going to fall off, and my back is on fire, but we keep going until we hit the shallows. There is no way we can lose now. I lean back, exhausted, as we glide to a stop, the nose of the canoe crunching into the sand. Maddy gets out and dances triumphantly in the water. Claire splashes up, and the two hug like tournament champions.

"In your face, Winslow!" crows Maddy.

I am too tired to move.

"Flagrant violation. We are lodging an official protest to the stewards of the yacht club," jokes Harry, as they glide lazily to the beach. "We'll see you barred from these waters for good, Mrs. Winslow."

"You're just a sore loser."

"Me? We had you beat fair and square until you torpedoed us."

"All's fair in love and canoeing, darling." She kisses him.

"You're coming with us on the way back," he says loudly to Claire, and everyone laughs.

I know most people find the beach restful and restorative, but some beaches have special healing powers. For me, this is that beach. It is a place I have explored since childhood, and I feel as comfortable here as I would in my own house. I tolerate the occasional intruder the way any host would but am always secretly glad to have the place to myself again. Put me down on a stretch of sand in the Caribbean or Maine, and I will certainly appreciate it, but it's not quite the same thing. In some places the water's too cold, or too warm, or too green. The shells are alien to me, the smells unfamiliar. But here it is perfect, and I will come here as happily in January as in August. There are few days I look forward to more than that first warm day when I feel brave and resolved enough to withstand the still-frigid temperatures and the only other creatures in the water are neoprene-clad surfers and the fish, and I dive into numbing, cleansing cold.

My father did this every year too. He and I would drive to the beach in the old station wagon and plunge in. No one else was on the beach at that time of year, and he would say, "It's polar bear time, Walt." Now, I partly do it for him, and if I had a son, I would do it with him too.

By midsummer the water warms up, and the bathing becomes easier, although it rarely gets above seventy degrees. I am by no means a sun worshiper, though, one of those people who lie immobile for hours courting melanoma. For me the beach is about movement, about swimming or walking or playing, some food, and then a chance to doze in the sun and recharge before beginning the paddle back.

Maddy spreads out the blankets on the sand while Harry and I plant the umbrellas. We are fanatical about making sure the pole is deep enough. A sudden gust could pick up a poorly entrenched umbrella and send it skittering across the beach like a headless chicken. The sure sign of a beach rookie. We dig deep, packing the base with wet sand, tamping it down. Then there is football. Johnny, Claire, and Harry on one team. Ned, Cissy, and me the other. Claire is surprisingly good. She catches several of Harry's passes and runs by me twice, making me feel old and fat. When her team wins, Claire jumps up and down, grinning with delight. This is her day; she is making an impact on all our lives.

We are all hot and sweaty. Harry proposes a swim. "Let's make it a race." We are used to his races.

Cissy groans and tells Harry he's too energetic.

"I'll race," says Claire.

"Fantastic." Harry beams. "What about you, darling?"

We all know the answer. Maddy says nothing but smiles and removes her old green cotton pareo, the one she bought years ago in Spain. She might be over forty, but she still has the same figure she did when she was in her twenties. A long, lithe torso, surprisingly large breasts, strong shoulders, a flat stomach, small backside, and slender, slightly bowed legs. It is a body that an adolescent boy would have dreamt up.

"You have an amazing figure," comments Claire as she watches Maddy stretch. "What's your secret?"

"Are you kidding? I'm fat." She has always said that. She hates compliments about her looks. She is not fat.

"See that white buoy?" says Harry to Claire. "Out around it and back, okay?"

The three swimmers dive into the water and strike out through the surf. Claire is swimming hard, but Harry and Madeleine swiftly outdistance her. Madeleine knifes through the water with long, powerful strokes. Her speed is incredible. She is well around the buoy by the time Harry reaches it. Claire is far behind them both. Maddy strides easily out of the water first, barely winded. She turns and waits for Harry. He follows closely, panting hard. Ned, Cissy, Johnny, and I all whistle and clap.

"You're too good," he says. "One day I'll beat you."

"Maybe for your birthday, darling," she answers with a smile. It is part of their old routine. It is like the Greek myth where the outcome is always the same. I think if by some fluke Harry were to almost win he would hold back. A world in which Maddy doesn't always win their swim races is a world neither of them wants to live in. I am not sure I would either.

Claire staggers out of the surf. She looks exhausted and surprised that she lost.

"Cheer up, Claire," Harry says with a laugh, clapping her on the back. "I guess I should have mentioned that Maddy was an Olympic-level swimmer in school. She won the Maryland regionals in high school and was an alternate for the U.S. team. I've never even come close to beating her."

It's true. Maddy is an extraordinary athlete. You should see her swing a golf club.

Hands on hips, bending slightly at her slender waist, Claire is still breathing hard. She takes in this information without saying anything, but I watch her watching Maddy. She is still a little incredulous. With the arrogance of youth, it is hard for her to believe someone a decade or so older could beat her so easily, especially when she had thought she was going to win. She is seeing in Madeleine something she hadn't seen before. I know the feeling.

She walks up to Maddy, who is drying her hair, saying, "That was incredible. I had no idea you were such a great swimmer. Why'd you give it up?"

Maddy turns, the sun illuminating her. She is like a being from a more advanced species. "I didn't give it up. I just found other things that were more important."

I can tell Claire is puzzled by this response. I watch her face. Talent for her is not something to be taken for granted. "If I was as good as you are, I would have kept at it."

Maddy smiles. "Come on and give me a hand with lunch," she says.

They kneel down at the coolers. There are bottles of beer wet with ice, cold chicken legs from last night, egg salad sandwiches, homemade potato chips. Peanut butter and jelly for Johnny. We huddle on the blankets, munching happily. Sitting on a low, old-fashioned beach chair, I am wearing my beat-up straw hat with the slightly ripped brim to keep the sun off my increasing baldness.

Claire leans in to me and whispers, "What happened to Johnny?"

Johnny has his shirt off. There is a long white scar down the center of his tanned chest.

"Heart," I whisper back. "He had several operations when he was very young."

"Is he all right now?"

I nod yes. It is something I prefer not to think about too much.

She goes over and sits with him. They begin playing in the sand. Building a castle. The adults are discussing politics. Harry and Ned are, as usual, on opposite ends of the spectrum. Maddy is reading, ignoring them, also as usual. Cissy is lying on her front, the straps of her bikini top unclasped. I think about reading too but feel my eyelids beginning to lower. In the distance, I see Johnny and Claire strolling alone together down the beach collecting shells before I nod off.

5

THE RESTAURANT IS IN AN OLD FARMHOUSE SET BACK FROM the highway. Local legend has it that in a former incarnation it had been a speakeasy. Across the road sits one of the area's last remaining farms, the fields of young corn hushed in the twilight. The hostess, Anna, is barely five-foot, with close-cut red hair and a beaklike nose. She has never married. Her mother, who died a few years ago, was very fat, and she would sit each night on a chair in the sweltering kitchen waiting for the last customer to leave. When Anna sees us, she gives Maddy, Harry, and me a hug, a sign of favor that we know has as much to do with Harry being a respected author as it does with us having been loyal patrons for years. One wall behind the bar is covered with faded framed and autographed book jackets from regular patrons. Vonnegut, Plimpton, Jones, Winslow.

"You're late," she reproves us. We had waited at home to

watch the sunset and are already a little drunk. Harry had mixed martinis. "I almost gave up your table. We are very busy tonight."

Waiting customers crowd into the small bar, where Kosta pours drinks. We wave to him and follow Anna to our table. The decor hasn't changed since I first started eating here in the 1970s with my parents and probably not since it opened in the 1950s. The walls are brown with age. "You wanted to sit inside, right?"

There is an outside dining porch during the summer, but it is too brightly lit for our tastes. It's where the millionaires sit. The interior room is cozier, the tables and chairs wooden and solid, not the cheap plastic found outside, the red-and-white checkered tablecloths patched and worn. An enormous old cast-iron stove sits unused in the corner. We order more martinis from one of the Vietnamese girls who work there. There is a family of them. They all live in a trailer behind the restaurant.

"Wait till you try this meat," Harry tells Claire, leaning across the table. "It's the best steak in the world."

She looks at the prices and whispers to me, "Walter, it's very expensive."

It is expensive. This is not the kind of place where she would normally come if a man wasn't paying. I can see her doing the math in her head. I remember what it is like to go out with a large group with expensive tastes when you only have a few dollars in the bank.

Once in college I joined some classmates at a restaurant on the Upper East Side, students down for the weekend on a spree. My first credit card sat chastely in my wallet. When my father had given it to me, he said, "Now, Walt, this is for use only in emergencies." I had about fifty dollars in cash too, a fortune back then. One of our group, the son of a wine importer who had been raised glamorously in both Connecticut and England, casually informed us that he was having the caviar. Several others, equally privileged, did as well. I gulped when I saw the prices. He then ordered wine, champagnes and Bordeaux.

This was not the way I normally lived. Part of me was greedy for the experience, the other part appalled by the extravagance. And, mind you, we weren't poor. But a closely controlled lifetime of allowances, boarding schools, country clubs, and college had kept me sheltered from this kind of decadence. Scrupulously, I ordered the cheapest thing on the menu. Chicken of some kind. It didn't matter, of course. When the bill came we all divided it up equally. I was horrified to see that my share was nearly one hundred dollars. I had never spent anywhere close to that on a meal in my life. If my companions were equally aghast, they hid it. As I found out, that was the code. Gentlemen don't quibble about the check. As I reluctantly handed over the card, I felt a tremendous fool, especially at the thought of those who had gorged themselves at my expense.

When I told my father what had happened, he assured me he would pay the bill. This time. "I hope you learned a lesson," he said. "Next time I won't bail you out."

I turn to Claire and whisper, "Don't worry. This is our treat. You're our guest."

She doesn't say anything, thanking me instead with her eyes. They are truly lovely.

We order. Our drinks come. Then hot plates of saganaki,

which is basically melted Greek cheese. Incredibly delicious. Taramasalata, bread, and olives. Wine. We are all laughing a lot, and Harry is standing up and telling a funny story in some kind of accent and doing a little dance, which has us all roaring.

Finally the steaks arrive. Large hunks of seared beef, thick, charred crusts of salt, pepper, and sparkling fat dripping down the sides. We fall on them like sled dogs.

"Oh my god, this is the most delicious thing I've ever eaten," gasps Claire.

The rest of us grunt appreciatively, too happy to stop chewing.

In midbite, I sense Claire tense. I look at her, thinking she might be about to choke. But it is not that. She sees something. I look around, following her gaze.

"What's the idea, Winslow?"

It's Clive. He's standing over the table. Staring hard. He looks flushed.

"Clive," says Claire. "What are you . . . ?"

"Quiet. I'm not talking to you."

Harry puts down his knife and fork. The rest of us sit expectantly. Ned pushes his chair back. The muscles bunch in his neck. Harry says, "Clive, I'll ask you not to speak to Claire like that."

"I'll speak to her any bloody way I like. So," he says, now turning to Claire, "have you fucked him yet?" Turning to Harry, he continues, "She's a pretty good fuck, isn't she, 'Arry?"

I notice him dropping his *h*'s, revealing his true origins. Yes, I know, I am a snob. But is that worse than pretending you are something you are not?

"Get out of here, Clive. You're drunk."

"So what if I am?" To Maddy he sneers, "You better watch her, or she'll be shagging 'Arry the moment your back's turned."

"All right. That does it." Harry is on his feet, moving toward Clive.

For a minute I think he is going to hit him. Clive seems to think so too because he involuntarily flinches, awaiting a blow that never comes. And Harry is a powerful man, maybe not as strong as Ned but big enough. You don't play hockey the way Harry did and not be good with your fists. Instead he grabs Clive fiercely by the lapels.

"Clive, I don't know what you're talking about, but obviously you've had too much to drink," he says. "I want you to apologize to my wife, Claire, and Cissy. Then I want you to pay your check and get out of here."

Clive looks nervous but responds, "What if I don't?"

"Then I'll take you outside and beat the hell out of you."

By this time Anna is at our table, and diners sitting around us are staring. "What's going on? Mister Harry, what are you doing?"

Harry releases Clive. "Nothing, Anna. One of your guests was just leaving."

"Fuck off, 'Arry," says Clive, regaining his composure as he retreats from the room. To Claire: "And fuck you too, you slag."

Ned is about to go after him, but Harry puts his hand on his shoulder. "Let him go. It's not worth it." To Anna, he says, "My apologies, Anna. Hope that didn't spoil any of your other guests' appetites."

"I don't like that kind of thing here, Mister Harry," she

says. "I don't want him coming back here. You can always come back. You're almost like family, you, Mrs. Winslow, and Mister Walter."

"Thank you, Anna." Then he turns to Claire and puts his hands on her shoulders and asks, "Are you all right?"

She nods, her eyes red. "I'm sorry," she chokes. "I'm sorry."

"Some men just don't like being dumped, eh?" someone jokes to break the tension. I think it is me.

"Harry," says Maddy, rising regally to her feet. "I'm going to take Claire into the ladies' room. Come on, Claire. Cissy, you come too."

After they return, Claire is quiet. She doesn't look at anyone. Maddy leans into Harry. "We should go."

"Of course. I'll go see Anna about the bill."

The ride home is suffused with awkward silence. Ned and Cissy are in their own car, the rest of us in the old Jeep. Harry tries to make light of what happened. For once his natural charm is ineffectual. It is impossible to tell what Maddy is thinking. She is keeping her thoughts to herself. What will the two of them talk about later in bed, in the privacy of their own room? Will Maddy be angry? Will she be frightened? And what will Harry do or say? Would they say anything? I have no idea. This is unexplored territory. They have been married for nearly twenty years, and are so inseparable she even went with him on his book tours.

It is Madeleine who saves the moment. She turns in her seat, looks at Claire, who is sitting in the back next to me, and says, "I hope you know I think what Clive said is complete shit."

Claire sniffs gratefully. "Thank you, Maddy."

"No. You don't have to thank me. It just sickens me that someone like him feels he can go about poisoning people's minds just because he isn't happy. He's a stupid man, and he was trying to hurt you and us. We offended his vanity, and he had to lash out."

I have almost never been more proud of her. She has always had the ability to cut through the extraneous and focus on the essential.

Harry is driving, concentrating on the road. Briefly, he looks at Maddy and smiles, and she smiles back. Unpleasantness has been forgotten; order, trust have been restored. Harry asks, "Did you see his face when he thought I was going to hit him?"

Maddy laughs. "I know! I thought he was going to start crying. Why didn't you hit him, anyway? God knows he deserved it."

"It's not the way it used to be, darling. For all I know, he could have come to dinner with a table of lawyers hoping I'd do just that. You can't hit anyone anymore without getting sued. Happened to a friend of mine a few years back. Got taken to the cleaners. Lawyers take the fun out of everything. Sorry, Walter, no offense meant."

"None taken," I answer.

Maddy turns back to Claire. "Would he have done that? Is he like that? God, how awful."

Claire, shocked into response, answers, "I really don't know. At first he was so nice. It was only once we came out here that I saw a different side of him. In New York, he was charming and handsome and successful . . ."

"Quite a catch," comments Maddy.

"Yes. No. I suppose. But out here he seemed so different, so, I don't know, he just wasn't . . ."

"Wasn't what?" asks Harry.

"He wasn't . . ." She starts but catches herself, and she says instead, "He wasn't genuine. Yes, that's it. He just seemed like a phony. Do you know what I mean? All of a sudden, here, in this beautiful place, next to all of you, he just seemed so fake. The way a paste diamond looks when it's held to a real one in the right light."

We pull into their drive. A few lights are on. The sitter's awake. Ned and Cissy have evidently driven straight to my house. I say my good-nights and follow them over, picking my way like a blind monk through a familiar maze.

6

LABOR DAY. THE SUMMER'S LAST HURRAH. ALREADY NIGHT is falling earlier. Autumn is waiting on the doorstep. People bring sweaters when they go out in the evening.

Claire is driving with me. She has been out every weekend. She is now one of the gang, part of a nucleus that never changes even when minor characters drift in and out at restaurants, cocktail parties, lazy afternoons at the Winslows' or at the beach, nights playing charades, sailing in my little sailboat, Johnny's ninth birthday, skinny-dipping in the ocean, or sitting under the stars listening to Verdi. We are all tan.

I insisted on leaving Thursday night, telling her to call in sick to work. No one will be around anyway, I said. Everyone goes away. We leave in the early evening. We will have dinner and a chat. This is my chance to get to know her better. She will be staying at my house this weekend. As will Ned and

Cissy. They arrive tomorrow. The Winslows have other house-guests this weekend.

I order martinis for both of us. She has adopted them now too. Never more than two, I told her once. I repeat an old joke about why martinis are like women's breasts; one is not enough and three are too many. Words to live by.

We are in an Italian restaurant in town. It has been here since 1947. The booths are covered in red Naugahyde, the menu features a drawing of the Leaning Tower of Pisa. It is the last remaining business on Newtown Lane from my child-hood. Even the hardware store has been replaced. There are two things I appreciate about it. One is that it is devoutly dem-ocratic. I have seen movie stars eating at tables beside weather-necked fishermen and their families. The other is that they make delicious thin-crust pizza.

I am deposing her. Where she was born, where she lived, where she went to college, what she studied, why she does what she does, who she is. My right hand itches for a yellow legal pad to scratch it all down, but I will remember it well enough.

She is a willing witness, her tongue loosened by gin. And I am on my best behavior, not aggressive, but solicitous, empa-thetic. She tells me about her father, her French mother, her younger brother, who lives in California, where he works for a software company. But I also know witnesses have their own motivations. They will lie, or twist facts, if they have to. They can be resentful or closed, releasing only the most meager in-formation. Others want me to like them, thinking that will color my interpretation of the law.

And it is clear that Claire wants me to like her. Not roman-tically, alas. No, she is too easy around me for that. Instead, she treats me the way one would treat a prospective employer. She wants me to see her in the best light, to gain my approval. And she is hard to resist. She laughs at my jokes, she asks me questions, gets me to tell stories. There is nothing a man likes half as much as the sound of his own voice and an appreciative, preferably female, audience.

The conversation steers to Harry and Madeleine. "Tell me more about them," she says. "I know you've known Maddy your whole life. I have never met anyone like them. Are they really as happy as they seem?"

We have almost finished the wine now. Crusts and a few lonely olive slices are all that remain on the platter.

I shrug. "Who's to say? I mean, happiness is a chimera. The real question is, does the happiness outweigh the bad, because every relationship has both. I guess it's a question of having more of one than the other. And in the case of Maddy and Harry, I would have to say that, yes, there is more happiness. I know them pretty well, and I have to admit I have never known a couple so well-suited for each other. They know how to work together and have fun together."

I don't blame her for being curious. Some couples have that effect. They have a golden aura about them, something almost palpable that makes them shine more than the rest of us. It is as if they walk through their lives with a spotlight trained on them. When they enter a room, you can't help noticing them.

She gets me talking. In a way, it is a relief to share little secrets. I have seen so much and know so much about them. This must be how a servant feels, whispering over the kitchen table, intimate but still apart.

"Does he love her very much?"

It is a question I have never asked, had never thought to ask.

The answer, to me, is blindingly obvious. Who would not love Madeleine?

"Of course," I answer. "Theirs is one of the great love stories of our age."

It sounds flip, but I mean it. Not in a tragic, fatal way, where love is denied or thwarted, as one might read in a romance novel. They are not Tristan and Isolde, or Abelard and Héloïse. I can think of no heroes of literature who would fit their paradigm. Their story lacks the obstacles to passion. They met and fell in love. It is one of the simplest and, at the same time, most difficult things to do. The drama of their lives is that they know how to keep love alive. And they are not selfish about their love. They share it with so many people. It is what draws the rest of us to them. It's not that he is a respected author or she a great beauty, or even that they occupy a charming cottage near the beach, or any of their many other attributes. It is the strength of their bond that draws us and inspires us. We look at them and want to be them. I say as much to Claire. I am probably a little drunk and slightly embarrassed by my loquacity.

Later, on the ride back to my house, I make a pass at her.

"Walter, please don't," she says. "Let's not complicate things."

I apologize. The idea of forcing oneself on a woman is repellent. Maybe if I felt otherwise, I would have been kissed more.

After a few moments, she says, "I hope you don't mind."

"Not at all," I answer gamely. "I felt it was the polite thing, to have at least tried. Didn't want you to feel insecure."

She laughs, briefly placing her hand on my knee. "Thank you, Walter. You made me feel much better."

We are friends again.

At home, the house is silent. She has never been here, I realize. The center of the action was always at Maddy and Harry's. "Would you like a tour? I promise I won't pounce."

"I'd love it."

The house was built by my great-grandfather. He called it Dunemere. All houses then had names, but it has been a long time since anyone called it that. Back then people rarely built on the beach. Instead, they preferred to be closer to town and arable land, and away from the storms that periodically devastated the shoreline. It was at the end of the nineteenth century that wealthy New Yorkers began to buy beachfront property, where they built enormous summer homes, only to desert them each year shortly after Labor Day.

In the 1960s, my father had the place winterized, primarily so we could spend Christmas here. He insulated the walls, which had been filled with nothing but old newspaper and beer bottles left by the original builders; he also installed a furnace in the basement and radiators in the bedrooms, but it wasn't until after my parents died and the house fell to me that it really came to be used all year round, though I do shut it up in January and February and drain the pipes so they don't freeze.

Unlike many of the modern houses in the area, the interior is dark, its dimensions modest for a house of this size. There is no media room. No family-style kitchen. Real estate agents out here would call it a teardown because the new crop of home buyers would find it too old-fashioned. The design is Italianate; cream-colored plaster on the outside, something that would not have looked out of place in Lake Como or Antibes. In old black-and-white photographs, there are striped awnings over the windows. Inside you walk into a high-ceilinged center hallway covered in the dark stucco that was once so fashionable. The stucco keeps it cool. The walls have family portraits and a large, faded Gobelins tapestry my grandfather brought back from the First World War. Straight ahead and out a large door is a wide brick patio, where my parents held their wedding reception. It runs the entire length of the house and overlooks a lawn that slopes down to the large brackish pond that leads to the ocean. Flanking the door are matching life-size portraits of my great-grandparents. My grandfather, a little boy in a sailor suit, stands next to his father, bespectacled and stern. Opposite, my great-aunt, dressed in crinolines, her hair long, leans on her mother's lap.

A long table takes up most of the left side of the hallway, and on it sits an old leather-bound visiting book. The book is almost full. The first entry is nearly as old as I am. The older books are in the library, full of spidery script and long-dead names.

"Please sign your name if you want to," I say.

She does. I have never seen her handwriting before and am not surprised that it's clear and elegant. My handwriting, like most lawyers', is appalling. She writes her name and date, and then "You have a lovely home."

To the right of the table is the door to a large formal dining room, the site of many endless dinners I was forced to endure as a child when my parents were present, spooning soup and eating heavy meals prepared by Genevieve and served by Robert. The walls are covered in Zuber wallpaper depicting El Dorado. I love that paper. It is a gateway to a different dimension, and on the rare occasions when I throw a formal dinner party I am still capable of losing myself in its magical jungles, canoeing down the Amazon or fighting off Indians with my trusty revolver.

There are eight bedrooms on the second floor. The largest was my great-grandparents'. It is known as the Victorian Room. I think I will have Claire sleep here. The canopied bed is too short for me, but it is where I always put first-time guests. The ones whom I like, at any rate. I still sleep in the same room I occupied as a child, over the kitchen in what had been the nursery wing.

Finally, there is the playroom on the third floor. The biggest in the house, it contains an old pool table, bookshelves crammed with popular novels of my parents' youth—Kipling and Buchan, Ouida, Tom Swift and Robert Louis Stevenson—and chests of drawers filled with exotic costumes brought back over the years by relatives and friends that we used to wear for fancy-dress parties. Along the wall is my great-uncle's oar from Henley and window seats where I would curl up with a book on rainy days.

"We should do a costume ball," says Claire. She is rummaging through the drawers. She pulls out a Pierrot costume I had worn as a child. It would just fit her. Then a burnoose my father used to wear that made him look like Rudolph Valentino. I had always admired it most because it had a real dagger. "That would be such fun." It has been a long time since our last costume party.

For a second I almost make another pass at her but think better of it. Maybe she would have said yes this time. Expensive real estate can be a powerful aphrodisiac.

We go back downstairs, and I lead her to her room. It is large, with windows facing over the pond. I imagine it is probably bigger than her entire apartment. The bed is just to the right as you enter, the French linen part of my great-grandmother's trousseau. Matching bureaus, a dressing table with my great-grandmother's silver-backed Tiffany hairbrushes still on it, a fireplace, an escritoire, a pair of Louis XV armchairs. Silvered family photographs. My grandfather in his uniform. My grandmother's three brothers. Heavy, pale damask curtains. A wide stretch of carpet, a chaise longue, and a table with an old-fashioned upright telephone and an equally ancient radio, neither of which has worked in years but which remain in place because that's where they've always been.

"What a wonderful room."

"It was my great-grandmother's. It's something, isn't it? You know, back then husbands and wives rarely shared a room. My great-grandfather slept next door." The room as spare as a Trappist's cell.

"And where do you sleep?"

"On the other side of the house. In the nursery. Now don't look at me like that. It's not like it has Donald Duck posters on the wall. I've updated it somewhat over the years. It's just where I feel most comfortable."

"But you could sleep in any room in the house."

"Exactly. And I could eat in the dining room every night and throw costume parties. But I don't. I come here to relax and sleep and work."

"Don't you get lonely?"

"Never. And besides, Madeleine and Harry are right next door."

We say our good-nights, and I pad off down the familiar carpet past my parents' former bedroom and the "good" guest room to my old lair. As I lie in bed that night, I fantasize that Claire comes into my room. Once or twice I even venture to the hallway, thinking I may have heard the sound of her feet, but when I finally fall asleep around dawn, I am still alone.

7

After graduation Harry was commissioned in the Marine Corps. As a college graduate he was automatically entitled to become an officer, and he entered flight training school. Madeleine followed him. They had been married the day after graduation. It was a small ceremony held in Battell Chapel, followed by lunch at the Yale Club. Ned was best man. Madeleine's father and brother, Johnny, came, as well as her stepmother at that time. Mister and Mrs. Winslow. I had never met them before. His father was a prep school English teacher. Tweedy, articulate, wry, the same broad shoulders. Harry had grown up a faculty brat in Connecticut, living on borrowed privilege. A pet of the upperclassmen as a child, and a guest on classmates' ski trips and holidays while a student. Unlike most of them, he worked during the summer, one year as a roustabout on the Oklahoma oil fields, another on an Alaskan fishing boat.

Why the Marines? It struck me as an odd decision at the time. No one we knew was joining the military. Our fathers had been raised when there was a still a draft, but most of them were of an age that fell between the Korean and Vietnam wars. Maddy's father had actually left Princeton to enlist to fight in Korea, an act that had always been difficult for me to square with the debauchee I knew in later life. Or maybe it partly explained it. I wouldn't know, having never been a soldier or even heard a shot fired in anger.

We never heard Harry discuss going into the military in those waning school days. Most of us had been obsessed with softening the impact of graduation by lining up jobs at investment banks, newspapers, or earnest nonprofit institutions, or obtaining postgraduate degrees. I had known for months that I would be entering law school in the fall, so I simply let the days of May spool out without any particular anxiety.

I had been aware that Harry echoed my outward calm, but he rarely spoke about the future. When he had revealed his intentions over one of those endless farewell dinners to a table consisting of Maddy, myself, Ned, and few other confidants, I could tell I was not the only one surprised. Even Ned, who had landed a job in Merrill Lynch's training program and was Harry's best friend, goggled.

"You're joking, right?" he had asked.

"Not at all," Harry had responded. "I wouldn't joke about something like that. I've always wanted to learn how to fly. Anyway, I'm not good enough to become a pro hockey player, and I have zero interest in working on Wall Street. I really have no idea what I want to do, so I figured while I am making up my mind the least I can do is serve my country."

Maddy, of course, knew. What's more, she obviously approved. If he had told her he was going to become a lion tamer or a salvage diver, she would have followed along just as happily.

As a married couple, they lived off base at the Naval Air Station in Pensacola for the first year. Harry flew fighters. They had a dog then, a brown mutt named Dexter. Maddy drove the same red MG she had at Yale. They cut a glamorous path wherever they went. Senior officers would be found at their frequent cocktail parties. Their new friends had been football legends at Ole Miss and Georgia Tech, now married to former cheerleaders.

This is when Maddy discovered her talent for cooking. Inspired by the local cuisine and with plenty of time on her hands, she tackled shrimp étouffée, rémoulade, fried chicken, pecan pie. Then she began working her way through Julia Child, Paul Bocuse, James Beard. Soon she was making béchamel sauces, coq au vin, salmon terrines, beef bourguignon, cheese soufflés. Invitations to her dinner parties were as sought after as presidential citations.

During the day, Harry flew endless training missions and sorties, and attended ground school. But luckily there was no war. On weekends, they traveled, driving all night to visit friends on Jupiter Island or to go bonefishing in the Keys. I visited a few times from my first year at Yale Law. They also got moved around by the Corps. Bogue Field, North Carolina. Twentynine Palms in California. A year in Japan. Maddy says this is when Harry began to write. His first efforts went unread by anyone other than her, but she encouraged him. There were numerous short stories and even a novel. All now destroyed.

Once she told me, "When I fell in love with Harry, I never thought of him as being a writer. He was simply the most confident person I had ever met. He's always determined to be the best. He was the best hockey player, then he was the best pilot, and I guess it just makes sense that he would be the best writer. If he wanted to be the best jewel thief, he could probably do that too."

He kept at it. At some point he began submitting short stories to magazines and literary journals, most of them obscure. Finally he had one published, then another. When his six years were up, he resigned his commission to write full-time. A few years later his first book, a roman à clef about an Air Force officer, met with modest praise and milder sales. Critics recognized him, though, as someone who needed more time in the bottle.

He and Maddy moved to New York, then outside of Bozeman for a year, and after that Paris, where they lived above a Senegalese restaurant in the distinctly unchic 18th Arrondissement. Maddy's trust fund subsidized them, allowing them to get by but not live extravagantly. Johnny was born, and then Harry's second book, which took seven years to write, won the National Book Award. There is even talk of a movie.

But he still loved flying. When his second book was published, he fulfilled a promise to himself and bought a used plane that he fixed up and now kept at the airport near their cottage. On fine-weather days, he would take the plane up. Sometimes he'd invite others to come with him. They'd fly over to Nantucket, circle Sankaty Head and return. Or up to Westerly. Sometimes he'd touch down for lunch, but he preferred to remain aloft. I flew with him many times. It is very peaceful. Madeleine rarely went. Small planes make her nervous.

⁓

FRIDAY MORNING. THE AIRFIELD SITS BEFORE THEM, TANKER trucks idle in the background, the planes of the local elite parked, waiting like ball boys to spring into action. It is just Harry and Claire. She and I had gone over early to the Winslows'.

"I'm going flying," he announced as we walked in. "Anyone want to come?"

I declined. "I'd love to," said Claire. "Do you have your own plane?"

"Yep. A single-engine Cessna 182. She's a little beauty. She's been in for repairs. This is the first time I've been able to fly her all summer."

"Do I need to change?"

"Nope, you're good to go."

At the airport he files his flight plan and does the preflight inspection. Today they will fly over Block Island. The plane is old, but he loves it anyway. The sky is a cloudless blue. It's already warm, a late-summer heat. The little cockpit is stuffy. Harry opens the windows. "It'll cool off when we get higher," he says. He is wearing an old khaki shirt and a faded Yale cap. Around his neck hangs a gold chain. He tells her it is a Saint Christopher he wears for luck. Maddy bought it for him when he was in the Marines. They taxi to the runway. Only one other plane is ahead of them.

Claire is excited. She feels like a child, practically pressing her nose against the plastic of the window. The engine starts to rev, and they begin to taxi down the runway for takeoff. Harry pushes the throttle and they race forward. One second their landing gear is on the ground, and the next they are in the air, climbing, climbing. The earth falls away beneath them, and when they bank, Claire can see they are already hundreds of feet in the air, the people on the ground, houses, trees rapidly diminishing below her.

At cruising altitude, Harry says, "Some view, eh?" He has to yell now above the engine.

She nods her head, leaning forward in her seat. She can see the curve of the earth and beyond, stretching to the end of the horizon, the blue of the Atlantic. She is amazed by how fast they are moving. What would have taken an hour in a car now takes seconds.

"I've never done this before," she says. "I mean, fly in a small plane. It's incredible."

He points to his right ear. "You'll have to speak up," he yells.

"Okay," she yells back, smiling.

He smiles and gives her a thumbs-up, his eyes hidden by his sunglasses. As they fly he points out landmarks. They have now left the mainland behind, soaring godlike over the ocean. A fishing boat, white against the dark blue water, bobs like a toy. Block Island looms in the distance, and then suddenly they are almost over it. She sees the waves crash on the rocks.

"That's Bluffs Beach," he shouts. "Over there is Mohegan Bluffs and Southeast Lighthouse. In between is Black Rock Beach. It's a nude beach, but I don't think you can see much from up here." He smiles.

She looks at him. He is wearing shorts and moccasins, his legs strong and tanned, covered with golden hairs. She wants to touch them. This is the first time they have been alone together. It is hard to speak. She had no idea it would be so loud.

Words formulate in her mouth, but nothing comes out.

There is so much she wants to say, but this is the wrong time. In addition to the noise of the engine, he is wearing a headset, further blocking his ears.

"Did you say something?" he asks, lifting the right earpiece to hear her better.

She shakes her head no. Relieved, she feels like someone who has stumbled on a precipice but miraculously regains her balance. Her heart is racing, her palms are sweaty. Nothing has changed.

"Do you want to try it?" he yells, indicating the controls in front of her.

"What? You mean fly the plane?"

"Sure, it's easy," he shouts. "Put your hands on the controls. It's not like a car. The tiller controls the altitude, which means it lets you go up, down, left, and right. If you pull on it, the plane will go up. Push and it goes down, get it? The throttle controls acceleration. See that? That's the altimeter. It tells you how high you are. Keep at one thousand feet. That's your airspeed indicator. You're going about a hundred and fifty-five miles an hour now. And see that little instrument that looks like a plane? That's your attitude indicator. Keep it level unless you turn. Okay?"

"What should I do?"

"Don't worry. I'll have my hands on my controls the whole time. Just go ahead and take your controls. They won't bite."

She puts her hands tightly, too tightly, on the tiller. The vibrations from the engine course through her. The plane bucks slightly, and she jumps. "Not so tight," he says. "Relax."

"I'll try." She inhales and exhales quickly several times and then resumes her grip, this time lighter, on the tiller.

"Good. Now just keep her level."

He lets go of the tiller. "See? You're flying the plane now."

"Oh my god. That's amazing." She is giddy. She can't believe how easy it is.

"Want to try a turn?"

She has to strain to hear him. She yells back, "Yes. What do I do?"

"Turn the tiller slightly to the right and then straighten out."

She does, and the plane turns but begins to drop.

"Pull up a bit—but not too much."

She does and the plane levels out again.

"Very nice. Now just keep heading on this course. See over there? That's our airfield." When they get closer, he yells, "You better let me take over now."

He contacts the tower, tells them they are approaching, and receives permission to land.

He reaches out his right hand and points. "We're going to pass over our house. We're right on the flight path. Look down."

She cranes her neck. Below is the house, like a diorama in a museum, a microcosm. She is a giant. He begins the landing, flaps down, reducing airspeed. The treetops rise up to meet them. Objects become larger again. They touch down with a slight shudder and a bounce as the air pressure resists the wings. He taxis to his parking spot and kills the engine.

"Not bad," he says, looking at his watch. "And it's not even noon yet."

"Thank you so much. That was one of the most amazing things I've ever done," she says.

Her eyes sparkle. Descending from the cockpit, the rest of the world feels flat and ordinary. She wishes she could return to the clouds.

On the drive back Claire, emboldened, now a risk taker, a conqueror, asks, "What happened to Johnny? I mean, his scar. Walter said he had an operation when he was younger."

"That's right. He was born with a congenital heart defect. A hole in his heart."

"Oh my god. What did you do?"

"There was a series of operations. We took him to the Children's Hospital in Boston. The first time we were up there for months. He could have died."

"How old was he?"

"The first was right after he was born. The last when he was four."

I remember sleepless nights in the hospital, the monotonous beeping of the monitors, concerned surgeons in blue scrubs, the small, deflated, unconscious form beneath a transparent shield. It was hell.

"Is he all right now?"

Harry rubs his forehead. "I don't know. I think so. The doctors are optimistic he'll be okay. It's been a long time since we had a scare, thank God."

"He doesn't seem sick. He seems like an ordinary healthy boy."

"It's been hard. He tires easily. And Maddy watches him like a hawk. She's always on the lookout that something might be wrong. We've had some false alarms, but we can't be too careful. Even if he looks like an ordinary healthy boy, he's not."

"I'm sorry."

"No reason for you to be sorry. We give him love and confidence and try to make his life as normal as possible. He could live another six years or sixty. It's impossible to know. It's hard for him at school, though. He can't play sports. Children can be cruel."

"It must be very hard on you. I mean on you both."

"At times it is, but he's a great kid. He knows what we're up to, and he tries to make us feel better. He'll say things to Maddy like, 'It's okay, Mommy. I don't feel sick. Don't worry about me.' But you just can't help feeling so goddamn helpless sometimes, you know?"

"I'm sorry. He's a lovely boy. He's such a wonderful combination of Maddy and you."

They pull up to the house. The boy comes running out. "Daddy, Daddy," he shouts as the tires crunch to a halt on the gravel. I am sitting by the window, reading the newspaper.

"Hey, sport."

"Daddy, there was a telephone call for you. From Rome. Mommy took the message."

"Thanks, pal. Tell Mommy I'm back, okay?" The boy trots back inside.

To Claire, "Got to make a call. Glad you could come along." He gets out of the car.

"No. Thank you for taking me. When can we do it again?"

"Maybe not for a while."

"What do you mean?"

He looks at her, a bit puzzled. "I thought you knew. That's what that call is about. Maddy, Johnny, and I are leaving for Rome in a week. I have a grant to write there. I'll be working on my new book."

"No. No, I hadn't heard." She feels like she is going to be sick. "How long will you be gone?"

"Almost a year. We'll be back next June. For the summer."

"Oh, I see." And then, "You must be very excited."

"We are. An old friend of mine found us a place to stay near the Pantheon."

"What about Johnny? Where will he go to school?"

"There's an American school. And we have the names of good doctors there."

"Oh good. I'm so happy for you all." She tries to make it sound like she means it.

"Thanks. It'll be a lot of fun. I've always wanted to live in Rome. So has Maddy. As you can imagine, she's very excited about the food. She's already enrolled in both a cooking and an Italian class."

"I'm going to miss you." She throws her arms around his neck and pulls him to her, his cheek next to hers.

He pats her on the back and uncoils himself, smiling at her. "Hey, we're going to miss you too."

"Thanks again," she calls after him as he heads into the house. "I had a wonderful time."

"I'm glad you enjoyed it. You were very brave. Not everyone likes to fly in small planes."

"I loved it."

He smiles and walks inside the house. She does not notice me and I watch her standing there for a long time after he is gone. Finally, she turns and leaves. I am sorry to see how sad she looks.

I FIND HER SEVERAL HOURS LATER. SHE IS SITTING AT THE end of my dock, staring out over the pond, her feet dangling in the water. A family of swans swims by. A pair of Beetle Cats, the small, gaff-rigged sailboats popular with residents who live on the pond, tacks in the distance. It is very peaceful.

"Where have you been?" I ask. "We've been looking everywhere for you. We're going to play tennis."

Yes, I have a tennis court too. It's an old-fashioned clay court. I know a lot of people prefer acrylic these days, but I actually still enjoy rolling the court. The preparation as important as the play.

She looks up. Surprised at first and then disappointed, as though she were hoping for someone else. I am in my ratty old tennis whites.

"I'm sorry, Walter. I needed to be alone for a while."

"Everything all right?"

"Did you know that Harry and Maddy are going to Rome?"

"Of course."

"I didn't."

"Is that so terrible?"

"Yes. I mean, no. I don't know."

"You have something against Romans? Did a principe ever break your heart, or did you trip and fall on the Spanish Steps?"

I am trying to be light, but I can tell, too late, she is not in the mood.

She shakes her head silently.

"Anything I can do?"

She shakes her head again.

"Right. Well, I'll just leave you to it then, shall I?"

"Thank you, Walter. I just feel like being alone. Maybe I'll wander up later and see how the tennis is going."

"I hope so. You owe me a rematch." She manages a smile at that. The week before she leveled me, 6–4, 6–4.

We don't see her again until evening. After tennis, I tiptoe up to her room and see that her door is closed. At seven she comes down. I am in the kitchen, putting hamburger patties into a cooler. We are going to a cookout on the beach. It's a Labor Day weekend tradition. There will be about fifty people there. Ned, Harry, and I had gone to the beach earlier to build a bonfire, digging a pit in the sand, filling it with driftwood.

"Sorry I didn't make it to tennis," she says as she enters. "I wouldn't have been any fun."

"Feeling better?"

"Yes, thanks." She looks beautiful. A low-cut pink dress. She is not wearing a bra. The sides of her breasts peeking out from behind the fabric. I try not to stare.

"You look lovely, but you might want to bring a sweater or something," I suggest. "It can get pretty cold on the beach at night this time of year."

"I could really use a martini, Walter. Do you think you could make one for me?"

"With pleasure," I say, washing my hands and going to the bar. It is a form of communion. I drop the ice cubes into an old Cartier silver shaker that belonged to my grandfather. Add Beefeater gin and a dash of dry vermouth. I stir it, twenty times exactly, and pour it into a chilled martini glass, also silver, which I garnish with a lemon peel.

"Hope you don't mind drinking alone. I want to pace myself."

"Oh, you're such a fuddy-duddy, Walter." She takes a sip. "Perfect."

Ned and Cissy come in. "Priming the pump, eh?" says Ned.

"Want one?" I ask.

"No thanks. Plenty to drink at the beach."

"Sorry not to see you at tennis today," Cissy says to Claire. "Everything all right?"

She nods her head. "Yes, thanks. Just a bit tired, that's all. You know how it is."

"Just as well, I suppose. You missed seeing my man get his big butt kicked by Harry."

"Harry had a hell of a serve today," I put in. "He could do no wrong. Don't feel too bad, Ned. Pete Sampras couldn't have beaten him today."

"Yeah, well. I'll get him the next time."

"You'll have to wait until next summer then, won't you?" pipes up Claire. "Unless you're going to go all the way to Rome to play a few sets."

We all stare at Claire, surprised by her tone. Then Cissy says, "Look at it this way, Neddy. At least you'll have a whole year to practice."

Everyone laughs at that. "C'mon, Claire, drink up," says Ned.

We take my car, Ned in the front with me, the women in back.

"Aren't we going with Harry and Maddy?" asks Claire.

"They're going to meet us there," says Ned. "They are bringing their houseguests."

A Dutch couple. Wouter and Magda. He is in publishing. They have just dropped off their daughter at boarding school and are passing through on the way back to Amsterdam. Their English is flawless.

The sun is setting low over the ocean when we drive up. A finger of brilliant orange extends from one end of the horizon to the other, as far up and down the beach as we can see. There's already a good crowd. I recognize many of the faces, some from the club, others from Manhattan, the rest a scattering of literary types, friends of Harry and Maddy's. The fire is roaring. Tables have been set up. There are hurricane lamps and coolers full of wine and beer. Liquor bottles, ice cubes, and mixers. Plastic cups. Several large trash bins. There are a few children. Labradors. By the lip of the parking lot, piles of shoes.

"Can you make me another martini, Walter?" Claire asks. I notice she didn't bring a sweater after all.

"Of course. But remember the old rule about women's breasts."

"You have such a dirty mind." She winks at me. "Don't worry, Walter. This is the last big party of the summer, right? Loosen up. Let's have some fun."

There's no shaker, but I still make her a drink. "Not my best effort, I'm afraid," I say.

"You're very sweet, Walter. Thank you." She gives me a little peck on the cheek.

"After this, though, you'd better stick to wine."

"When will Harry and Maddy be here?"

"Haven't a clue. Soon enough, I should think."

I excuse myself to drop off the hamburger patties. When I look around, I notice that Claire has moved. She is talking to three young men. They are about her age, tanned, slim-hipped as soccer players. The sons of rich men. I should know. I was one of them once, lifetimes ago. She is laughing. I can tell she is mesmerizing them.

Harry, Maddy, and Johnny arrive with Wouter and Magda. "Sorry we're late," Harry says when I see him. "We're still packing up. A year's a long time to be gone."

I am already planning on spending Christmas with them in Rome.

By nine o'clock the first stage of the party is winding down. It gets dark quickly this time of year. Parents carry sleepy children to their cars. Tables are folded. Empty wine bottles clink in recycling bins. The fire remains high, still being stoked by those who aren't ready to go yet. For the young the night is just getting started. Flames shoot up into the night. Faces flicker in the firelight. The sand begins to feel cool underfoot. I am about to put on my sweater, but I look around for Claire, worrying that she might be cold.

She is still talking with one of the young men, holding a drink in one hand, rubbing a bare arm with her hand. I go up to her. "Sorry for interrupting. Claire, are you cold? Would you like my sweater?"

Claire looks at me, her face luminous, eyes glazed. She is drunk.

"Walt," she says. "That's so sweet. I'd like you to meet Andrew. His parents have a house out here. He's going to business school."

We shake hands. Andrew is wondering about me and where I fit in. I am possibly too old to be a boyfriend but too young to be a father.

"I'm staying with Walt. His parents have a house out here too, but they're both dead and now Walt lives there all alone."

Ignoring her, I repeat, "Are you cold?"

"No, I'm fine. Feel great."

"So you don't need my sweater?"

"I have a sweater if she gets cold," Andrew says pointedly.

She ignores him and asks me, "Have Harry and Maddy arrived?"

"Yes. They've been here awhile."

She looks around and sees them. She frowns. "Oh yes, there they are." She turns to Andrew. "I have to go say hi to some people. I'll be right back."

She walks over and gives Maddy a hug. "I didn't know you were going away. Harry told me this morning. I know I should be happy for you both, but it makes me sad."

"Don't worry. We'll be back before you know it. The summer's over anyway."

"Well, that's just it. I don't want the summer to end. Just knowing that you won't be here makes it so much more final."

Maddy squeezes her hand. "I know. I never want summer to end either."

"It was just such a surprise."

"I am sorry we didn't tell you. It had all been settled last winter, and it just never occurred to us that you didn't know too."

"You don't need to apologize. You have both been amazing to me. I love you both so much." She gives Maddy another hug.

"We'll miss you too."

Claire turns away and walks back to Andrew, who gets her another glass of wine. I am not sure this is such a good idea, but it's not my place to say anything.

"Everything okay?" Harry asks, munching a hamburger. He and I had stood aside while the two women talked, and now we rejoin Maddy. "You worried about something?"

"I'm not sure," I say. "Claire seems to be drinking rather a lot."

Harry laughs softly. "Yeah, well, she won't be the only one at this party."

Maddy looks at him. "I think she's taking the news of our trip hard. Why else would she be getting drunk? We've spent plenty of nights with her, and she's never been like this. What was she like when you told her this morning?"

"Well, I could tell it was a surprise. I felt like an ass because obviously she had no idea what I was talking about."

"I saw her down by the pond before tennis," I add. "She looked pretty glum."

"Well, I can understand that," says Maddy. "We sort of adopted her and now we're dropping her."

"Oh, she'd have gotten tired of us before too long anyway," says Harry. "I mean, she needs to spend more time with people her own age. We're just a gang of middle-aged old farts with receding hairlines and expanding waistlines."

"Speak for yourself, fatso," says Maddy, punching him playfully in the arm. Actually, both of them look great for their age. I, on the other hand, look every one of my forty-two years.

We see Claire on the other side of the bonfire and watch as she stumbles and nearly falls. Andrew helps her, and she hangs on his arm, laughing. Have I said she has beautiful teeth?

"She does look pretty sozzled," says Harry. "Do you think we should do something?"

"I'll go over and talk to her," says Maddy. "You two stay here."

Across the fire I can see Maddy speaking with her. The boy stands sheepishly off to the side. Maddy has a hand on Claire's shoulder. Claire is shaking her head, attempting to back away. But it is very hard to say no to Maddy.

They come back. "Harry, do you mind driving Claire back to Walter's?"

"Please," protests Claire. "I'm fine. Please. I don't want Harry to drive me back."

"Hey, what's going on?" It's Andrew.

I step in and tell him in my most lawyerly voice that he should probably get the hell out of there.

"Don't make me," Claire shouts. "Maddy, can you drive me instead?"

"It's okay," says Maddy. "We need to help clean up." Maddy hates driving at night. Her eyes aren't as good as they used to be, and she dislikes wearing glasses.

"Come on, Claire," says Harry gently. He puts his hand on her arm.

She pulls it away. "Leave me alone."

She starts walking unsteadily to the parking lot, Harry following. "I'll be right back," he says.

By the car she is sick.

"Oh god," she says. "I'm sorry. I'm such an idiot."

He tells her not to worry. We've all been there. He offers her his handkerchief, and then insists she wear his sweater when he sees she is shivering. "Are you all right, or do you think you'll be sick again?"

She shakes her head. "No, I'll be fine," she answers, her voice faint.

On the way back, she is weeping softly, embarrassed and anxious. Harry asks if she's all right. Why is she so upset? Claire says she doesn't want to talk about it. He says that it's all right, they're friends. If it's something he can help with, he'd be happy to.

"I'm in love with you," she blurts. "There, I've said it. I'm sorry."

He laughs and tells her that it's only the liquor talking.

"Don't laugh at me," she says.

He tries to reassure her. That he is not laughing at her.

"Stop the car," she says calmly. "I think I have to throw up again."

He pulls over, headlights illuminating the road ahead. The houses slumbering. She jumps out and instead of being sick starts running across a field in the dark. Harry curses under his breath, gets out and runs after her, yelling at her to stop. She is barefoot, and he catches her easily. Panicked like an animal, she tries to escape, twisting her body and swinging at him with her little fists. He grabs her wrists. She is gasping for breath and sobbing about how stupid she is, that he should go away. He tries to soothe her, telling her to calm down, saying what a wonderful, beautiful girl she is. She embraces him fiercely, still sobbing. He strokes her hair. She looks up at him, and he looks down at her.

Her face rises to his, her lips on his, her tongue in his mouth. "Make love to me," she pleads, placing his hand on her breast. Immediately she can feel him hardening. "I love you. I need you. Now. Here."

But he does not. "I can't," he says. "I'm married. I love my wife. Don't do this."

"But what about me?" she asks. "Do you love me?"

"You're a beautiful girl," he says. "You shouldn't be doing this. I'm married."

"I can't help myself," she says. "I need you. Please."

"Claire, for God's sake. Don't make this more difficult than it already is. We should go. Come with me. Please." He holds out his hand, but she refuses it, walking past him to the car.

They drive in silence. There is nothing to say. He gets out of the car to open her door but she is already out and heading toward my house, the key under the mat. She says nothing.

"Will you be all right?" he calls to her. At the door she pauses and looks at him before disappearing inside.

The wax seal of a secret letter has been broken. Nothing can make it whole again.

When he returns to the beach, everyone asks after Claire. He laughs and says he's glad he won't have her hangover in the morning.

THE NEXT DAY THEY ARE LEAVING. IT'S A TIME FOR LAST swims and the final packing of bags. In the morning, I find a note from Claire in my kitchen. She has caught an early train back, thanking us for our kindnesses. Harry's sweater has been left folded neatly on the counter.

Our lives will never be the same.

FALL

1

THE POET LAMARTINE WROTE THAT A WOMAN IS AT THE BE-
ginning of all great things. It's indisputable. After all, women
give birth to us, so they are always at the beginning. But,
whether they mean to be or not, they are also present at the
beginning of terrible things too.

The Winslows move to Rome. The latest in a long line
of expatriate writers. Keats, of course, who died there. In
no particular order, Byron, Goethe, the Brownings, James,
Pound.

Harry and Maddy live off the ecclesiastical version of
Jermyn Street. In Rome, even the priests are fashion-conscious.
During the daytime the street is full of archbishops and cardi-
nals of every size, shape, and color, from Soweto and Ottawa,
Kuala Lumpur and Caracas, shopping for cassocks, chasubles,
zucchettos, and surplices. Garments of red, gold, white, and

purple fill the shop windows. Painted wooden statues of saints and the Virgin. Gammarelli's, it's said, is the best.

They live in a fine apartment. The *piano nobile*. The owners are on sabbatical. The ceilings are high, the furniture elegant, portraits of noblemen with perukes, cuirasses, and long noses hang on the walls. Every channel on the television seems to show women with bare breasts, and they decide to hide the set in a closet because of Johnny. There is an old woman, Angela, who comes with the apartment and speaks no English. Maddy tries to talk to her in rudimentary Italian, adding in school-girl French when she doesn't know the word. It doesn't matter. They like each other.

Johnny can do no wrong in the old woman's eyes. *"Ma che bello,"* she exclaims, pinching his cheek. She cooks and cleans. To his delight, Harry finds she even irons his boxer shorts.

Rome in early autumn. The Tiber sparkles. People still eat outside. There is a café near the Piazza della Rotonda where Harry, Maddy, and Johnny go in the morning for caffe latte and sweet rolls. Johnny drinks fresh carrot juice. They read the *International Herald Tribune* and struggle through the *Corriere della Sera,* a dictionary at their elbows.

Maddy sends me e-mails describing it all. As ever, I envy them their life. They spend the first weeks walking and eating, wandering through museums and churches, marveling at St. Peter's Basilica. Every street is a history lesson. They follow in the footsteps of saints and vandals, poets and tourists. There are names of contacts, friends of friends. Bettina and Michaeli, Romans who live in a floor of a palazzo on the Piazza dei Santi Apostoli. One of her ancestors was a pope, which is a source of both great family pride and amusement. They have a large portrait in the dining room of the pontiff in question. Michaeli works at Cinecittà. Other friends. Mitzi Colloredo. The Ruspolis. The Robilants. English bankers. A Hapsburg and his wife.

It doesn't take them long before they are going to parties and making even more friends. "You only need to know one person in Rome," Bettina says. "Then you know everybody." Harry's book has been translated into Italian and has already had three printings. One evening he does a signing at a bookstore near the Piazza di Spagna, and the store is packed.

There are weekends along the coast at Ansedonia, with the Barkers. A Yale classmate who married an Italian woman, a contessa. Maddy tells me it is the Hamptons of Rome. Harry buys a Vespa.

They discover trattorias. Nino, Della Pace, Dal Bolognese in the Piazza del Popolo for the people watching but not the food, the Byron in Parioli, but their favorite is in the Piazza S. Ignazio, located on a hidden square not too far from their apartment. I went there with them when I visited early on. It is one of those fine old Roman restaurants where, at the end of the meal, they place on the table bottles of *digestivos,* Sambuca, Cynar, amaro, homemade grappa steeped with figs or fruit. On the wall, photographs of unfamiliar Italian celebrities.

What is most remarkable about the restaurant is the staff, who, appropriately enough, are out of a Fellini movie. Every one of the waiters has something wrong with him. One has a pronounced limp. Another a speech impediment. The third a tumor like a truncated horn projecting from the top of his forehead. They are all very nice and adore the Winslows, who dine there at least once a week.

"We don't even bother looking at the menu anymore," Harry says. "They just bring us whatever they have special, and it's always good."

At some point in everyone's life, whether in a restaurant, watching one's child play soccer, or walking through the streets alone, the question is asked, what else do you need? It is a question that once asked is almost impossible to answer. You may require nothing more at that exact moment to eat or drink, or you may be content with the bed in which you sleep, a favorite chair, the immediate wants and possessions of life. Then there are the intangible things, love, friendship, passion, faith, fulfillment. But you think about the question over and over again, because few of us have what we need—or few of us think we do, which is almost the same thing. It can become a drumbeat. What else is there? Have I done enough? Do I need more? Am I satisfied?

There is an innate greediness that is part of the human condition. It drove Eve to eat the apple; it impelled Bonaparte to invade Russia and caused Scott to die in the frozen wastes of the Antarctic. We have different names for it. What is curiosity other than greed for experience, for recognition, for glory? For activity to distract ourselves from ourselves? We hate the idea that we have come as far as we are going to go. And we are not content with what we have or how far we have come. We want more, whether it is food, knowledge, respect, power, or love. And that lack of contentment pushes us to try new things, to brave the unknown, to alter our lives and risk losing everything we already had.

HARRY OFTEN MADE UP STORIES FOR JOHNNY AT BEDTIME. ONE OF my favorites was about the Penguin King. Johnny was mad about penguins. He knew all about the different types. The emperor, the Adélie, the rockhopper. Where they lived, what they ate. Many nights at Johnny's bedtime, I would stand by the foot of the bed with Maddy while Harry told the story. Each time it was slightly different, but it always started out the same way.

"There was once a Penguin King who lived at the South Pole with his family, Queen Penguina and all their princes and princesses. The princes and princesses were very cute. The Penguin King was the biggest and strongest penguin, and even the sea lions were afraid of him. But the Penguin King was sad."

"Why was he sad, Daddy?"

"He was sad because he was tired of snow and ice and sea lions. He was tired of swimming. He was even tired of Queen Penguina and the princes and princesses."

"Oh, no. That's terrible. So what did he do?"

"One day he told Queen Penguina and the princes and princesses and all the other penguins at the South Pole that he wanted to see the rest of the world. He wanted to see New York City and France and Beijing and deserts and skyscrapers and trees. All the penguins started to cry and said, 'Don't leave, don't leave. You're our king.' The princes asked, 'Who will protect us from sea lions? Who will feed us krill?' The princesses asked, 'Who will keep our feet warm?'

" 'I've made up my mind,' he told them. 'I need to see the world.'

"They all cried as they watched him waddle off. He waddled farther than he had ever waddled before. He waddled for two whole days. He came to the ocean and saw a big ship. 'Perfect,' he said. 'That's just what I need to take me to see the rest of the world.' "

"No, don't go on the ship," Johnny would interject.

"Well, too bad you weren't there to warn him because that's exactly what he did. The Penguin King waddled down to the ship and commanded the men there to take him aboard. They were very tall but did what he told them. They took him on the ship and gave him lots of fish to eat.

"Some time later, he couldn't tell how long for sure, the ship stopped. To his surprise, he was put in a box and taken off the ship. When the box was opened again, he was surrounded by other penguins. There was a funny smell. Like rotting fish. 'Where am I?' he asked. 'You're in the zoo,' the other penguins told him.

" 'What's a zoo?' he asked.

" 'It's a prison,' they told him. 'No one ever gets out of here.'

" 'But I am the Penguin King,' he said.

" 'Not here you're not. Here you're just another penguin.'

" 'What have I done?' asked the Penguin King. 'I should never have left my family and my kingdom. How could I be so stupid?'

"He sat down and cried and cried. He missed Queen Penguina, and all the penguin princes and princesses. He would never see any of them ever again. He would never again protect them from sea lions or go swimming in the deep ocean or warm the feet of his children. 'If only I could go back home, I'd never leave again,' he said."

"So what happens next, Daddy?"

"What do you think should happen?"

"I think Queen Penguina and all the penguin princes and princesses become ninjas and find a boat and rescue him!"

Harry laughs. "Great idea. Okay, so one night when he was

dreaming of snow, there was a tapping on his cage. He looked up. It was Queen Penguina and the princes and princesses. All his children were there, even the youngest, who had grown now and had lost their childish gray feathers. They were all wearing black. Outside the guards had all been tied up.

" 'What are you doing here?' asked the Penguin King. 'Run away or else they'll put you in the zoo too.' He couldn't bear the thought of them suffering as he had.

" 'No, they won't,' said Queen Penguina. She had never looked so beautiful. 'We have traveled for months to find you, and no one knows we are here. Come with us quickly, and we can all get away.'

"So the Penguin King followed his beautiful wife and their children to the river, and they all jumped in. He was so happy to be swimming again, and he gave his wife and children the biggest hugs in the whole world. 'I am so lucky to have such a wonderful family. I can't believe I didn't appreciate you all more. I promise I'll never leave again.' And then they all swam home, and they all lived happily ever after. The end."

Johnny almost always wanted a happy ending, and Harry was always willing to oblige. But one night after Johnny had gone to bed, Harry confessed that he really thought it should have a different ending.

"How do you see it ending, sweetheart?" asked Maddy.

"The Penguin King is left to rot in the zoo. Serves him right too, if you ask me."

2

IN EARLY NOVEMBER A CALL COMES FROM HARRY'S EDITOR in New York. He wants to discuss the new book. Can Harry fly over for a day or so? The publisher will be there. Other executives. They'll book the ticket. Business class, of course. This is a lavish gesture, one that reflects their high expectations. The Winslows' New York apartment, the bottom two floors of a brownstone east of Lexington, has been sublet. It won't be a problem to put him at a hotel. When can he come?

He doesn't want to make this trip but says he will. Maddy has to stay in Rome, though, because Johnny is in school. In New York, they had sitters who could look after him, but not there. It's not the same thing. "What if something happens? I need to be here," she says. He will only be gone for two nights. Three at the most. It will be the first time they have slept apart since he left the Marines.

A week later he lands at Kennedy. A driver is standing out-side customs, waiting with his name on a sign. After the old stones of Rome, New York seems ridiculously modern. It is jar-ring yet reassuring to be surrounded by the sound of English being spoken, the advertisements for familiar products, Yan-kees caps, the large cars.

The day is spent in meetings. The weather is colder here than in Rome. He is wearing a new blue cashmere coat Maddy bought him at Brioni. He shakes hands with the senior people, many of whom shepherded his last book through. He is hailed like a returning hero. A young woman brings him espressos. "Would you like anything else, Harry?" asks Norm, the pub-lisher. A lunch is brought in. Sandwiches, pasta salad. There is a PowerPoint. Charts, graphs, sales projections. Hollywood is interested. Later in the hotel he takes a nap. Reuben, his agent, is taking him out for dinner. Afterward there are several par-ties they could stop by.

They eat in a restaurant popular with publishing execu-tives. The maître d' shakes Harry's hand warmly, and says how good it is to have him back and how everyone can't wait to read the new book. When is it coming out? Many people stop by their table. Some sit down for a drink or to swap industry gossip. Harry is tired. He is drinking to keep himself awake. He tries to beg off, but Reuben insists they go to at least one of the parties. It's in Chelsea, near the river. Another of Reuben's clients. He promises it will be fun. The younger generation. Not like us. You'll learn something. Come on up for just one drink, says Reuben. Harry agrees but finds himself yawning and glancing at his watch in the car downtown. It is too late to call Maddy.

How do I know all this? Harry wrote it all down, and I read about it later. Every moment of the trip and much more besides. Isn't that what writers do? It isn't real until it's on the page. Although I didn't know a lot of the details until years after.

The party is in a cavernous loft. Reuben introduces Harry to his other client. He is much younger than Harry was when his first book was published. Harry is fairly sure he and Reuben are two of the oldest people at the party. The young author is friendly and tells Harry how much he admired his book. He is skinny, with dark curly hair, intense brown eyes. He looks about twelve. The face of a trickster. Harry cannot even remember his name. He knows he has never heard of the young man's book, let alone read it. I've been living in Rome, he says by way of excuse. Reuben tells me it's terrific.

There is a meritocracy among writers. Even if Harry is older and has won a prize, he knows he is not much further ahead of this young man. He does not have a corpus of published novels to fall back on. His career can still go either way. It is the next book that will prove whether his is a real talent or just a fluke.

And then it happens—inescapably, inevitably, like turtle bones being thrown, like the tide going out.

A woman's voice behind him. "Harry. What are you doing here?"

He turns around. Claire.

"Great to see you," he says easily, giving her a kiss on each cheek. Her skin is warm, soft. "That's how they do it in Italy," he laughs. "It's a great custom."

The days slip away between them. For a moment, she is flustered.

"I thought you were in Rome. Are you back already?"

"No. My publisher needed me to fly over for a few days. I arrived this morning."

"How's Maddy? And Johnny? Are they here?"

"Both are very well. They stayed in Rome. How are you?"

"Fine," she says. "Really good. Look, I'm sorry about what happened. Between us, I mean. I hope you forgive me."

"Nothing to forgive," he says. "If anything I should be flattered. Water under the bridge, right?"

They get a drink. His tiredness has left him. They talk about Rome. She has never been there. It's magical, he tells her. Everyone should live there at least once in their life.

"You look well," he says. There is something different about her. She has a new job. An editorial position at a magazine. Better money, more respect. She is coming up in the world. There is something else. She has cut her hair. During the summer her hair was long. Now it is shorter, more stylish. It makes her look older, sophisticated.

I have also seen her. We had a drink shortly after the Winslows left for Rome. I had never seen her in high heels before.

"Well, you know," she says. "What are you doing here?"

"Reuben brought me. He's my agent. Remember, you met him on the street that time? He felt I should become acquainted with the younger generation."

"Does he represent Josh?"

"Is that his name?"

"Yes. It's a party for him."

"Friend of yours?"

"We dated for a while."

"You don't know how happy I am to see you. I don't know a soul at this party except Reuben."

"Let me introduce you to some people," she says.

Soon a small crowd has gathered around them, wanting to meet the famous Harry Winslow. The men thin and studiously scruffy, dressed in black. The women waiflike, many of them drinking beer from bottles. He is seated on a sofa. The center of attention. A peddler of stories opening his sack. He takes out one first, then another. Claire brings him a whisky on the rocks. He has lost count of how many he has already had. But he knows precisely when she leaves and when she returns. He is performing for her.

The room is a blur, but he is enjoying himself. Young men and women want to know about his new book, his views on modern literature, terrorism, the Middle East. Is it true he was really a fighter pilot? One young man asks if he had ever shot down an enemy plane.

"No," he answers, "I was a peacetime soldier." He tells a story about the time he was forced to ditch a plane in North Africa during a training flight and had to spend the night in a Moroccan whorehouse. Everyone laughs.

Claire is perched behind him on the arm of the sofa. They are like magnets drawn to each other. He is a hit, as she knew he would be. His success is hers. I didn't know you knew Harry Winslow, she is told. Oh yes. We're old friends.

It is past midnight. The waiters are packing up. The party is winding down.

"We're going to a bar," she says. "Want to come?"

Harry looks around. No sign of Reuben. "Sure, why not?" he answers. It's already morning in Rome.

Outside they hail a cab. Claire gives an address. He is carrying her laptop and gym bag.

"Where are we going?" he asks.

"We have to stop at my place first. I want to drop off my bags. We won't be a minute. The bar's practically right around the corner. Do you mind?"

"No, it's fine."

She lives in the East Village. It is a new apartment for her, rented in early September. The building is modest, an old tenement. No doorman. Rusty fire escapes hang over the sidewalk. A key to get in, an intercom with the embossed names of tenants, many covered over by newer arrivals, some handwritten. Then a heavier second door with security glass. "I'm on the third floor," she says. "There's no elevator, we'll have to walk." He carries her bags.

The marble stairs are rounded with age. This has been the first stop for generations of New Yorkers. The difference is that now the neighborhood is fashionable, the rents expensive. Worn tiled floors. Cast-iron banisters. Water-stained walls. Chinese menus slid halfway under doors.

"Here we are," she says. More keys to get in. A dead bolt. "It's not really that unsafe," she says. "These locks are left over from the eighties."

The apartment is small, unfinished. She could have been here a week or a year. A bookshelf along one wall. A small kitchenette on the other. A couch, a small dining table covered with scattered papers, a pair of shoes, an empty wineglass with crusted sediment in the bottom. Dishes in the sink. Boxes stacked in the corner. The untidiness of single life. A bedroom off to the left. He can tell the refrigerator is the sort that would be empty except for maybe old milk, a brown lemon, wine, decomposing Chinese food, jars of mustard.

"It's not much, but I don't have to share it," she says. "Would you like a drink? I won't be a moment."

She finds a nearly empty bottle of whisky and pours the remnants into a coffee mug. "Sorry," she says. "I don't entertain very often."

"No, no. It's great. This you?"

There are photographs arrayed along the top of the bookshelf. A little girl on a street in Paris. A smaller boy, obviously her brother, stands next to her. The colors have faded. It is the face of a disappointed child.

"Yes. I was about eight when that was taken."

"And this one?"

"My mother."

It is a small family history. These are photographs set out to remember what one leaves behind. There is one of her with friends at what looks like a college football game. Another with a friend, a garden party. Each is wearing a white dress. On the shelves there are the usual books. *The Bell Jar. Les Fleurs du Mal.* T. S. Eliot. Vonnegut. Tolstoy. Gibran. Some newer titles too. Both of his books. The first one only recently back in print. He grins self-consciously and runs his index finger down their spines.

"If you don't mind, I suppose the least I could do is sign them for you," he says, taking out his pen.

"No, I'd love it."

With a flourish he writes *To Claire, who has excellent taste in literature. Harry Winslow.*

He hands them to her. She reads the inscriptions. "Thank you," she says, leaning in to give him a quick kiss on the cheek.

"One day they'll be worth just about what you paid for them," he says with a smile.

She smiles back. "I'll be right out," she says.

Harry collapses in the chair. He is tired. There has been too much to drink. It is time to leave.

There is noise from the other room. The sound of glass shattering. "Oh fuck that hurts."

"Are you all right?"

The room beyond is dark.

"Claire?"

"I'm in here," she says. "I cut my foot."

He walks through the small, dark bedroom to the bathroom. The light is on. On the wall is a poster for a French film festival. She is sitting on the toilet. There is blood on the sole of her foot. Shards of glass on the floor.

"Sorry," she says. "I dropped it. I am such a spaz."

He examines the cut on her foot. "I could bandage it. It doesn't look too bad."

He goes to the medicine cabinet and rummages around for an antiseptic. "Do you have anything like hydrogen peroxide?"

"I don't think so."

"Let me do this first." He takes out his handkerchief, wets it with soap and water, and cleans the wound. Then he applies a Band-Aid. The sole of her foot is pink, the nails painted red. She has beautiful feet, delicate ankles. He has to crouch awkwardly in the tiny bathroom. He has the patience of a parent. "No need to amputate," he says with a smile. "Do you think you can walk?"

"I can try."

He puts his arms around her and lifts her up, surprised by how light she is. He has to turn sideways to walk through the door.

"On the bed," she says.

He places her on the bed, and suddenly her arms are around him, pulling him down. Her lips pressed to his. Her hands on his body, his arms. This time he doesn't resist, he can't. Then she is on top, straddling him. She pulls her dress over her head, flinging it carelessly in the corner. The dark points of her breasts stand out against her pale body in the blue glow of the room. Her arms enveloping him, her smell, the softness of her skin, her warmth. Her tongue searches his mouth, warm and alive. Her hand on his hand, guiding him first to her hard breast, then next between her legs, rubbing his fingers over the thin silk, feeling the wetness, before bringing it back up. Then he is on top, her legs around him, drawing him in. Hands now undoing his belt, searching the tops of his flanks, her fingernails beneath his boxer shorts. Still entwined she unbuttons his shirt, lowers his trousers, running her hands through the hairs on his chest. She reaches down and holds him in her hand, feeling the hardness, the blood pumping, heart racing. Embracing him, she whispers in his ear, "I love you. I am yours."

She kneels before him on the bed. Her tongue now darting in his ear, caressing a nipple, his navel, slowly lowering herself until she takes him in her mouth, first slowly, then longer, deeper, until he cannot stand it anymore.

"I can't do this," he says. "I can't. I'm sorry. I have to go."

But he is powerless. His muscles, his strength fails him. The curtain has been torn, the border crossed; now there is only the other side. He is falling into it. It is something he has secretly yearned for. She pulls him back to the bed, caressing him, wrapping her legs around him, her body burning him, feet in the air, rhythmically back and forth, gasping for breath, pushing and pulling, slick with sweat, her mouth searching for his, his mouth on her breast, her clavicle, her neck, fingers scoring his back, panting, moaning, her screaming, his roaring, until they collapse together.

"Stay inside me," she whispers. Her arms wrapped tightly around him.

Lying there, breathing. His head on her pillow, staring into each other's eyes, hands clasped, their breath mingling, their bodies melded. He cannot remember when he has felt such peace.

"I think I love you too," he says. Or does he? Maybe he only thinks it and is confused by the thought. Maybe the words mean different things to him than they do to other people.

She sighs and kisses him, already asleep, exhausted by jet lag, whisky, and sex.

3

IN THE MORNING HE IS AWOKEN BY HER AS SHE RETURNS TO bed, limping slightly from the cut on her foot. Early sunlight filters dully through the curtains. "I thought you might like this," she says, kissing him on the mouth. Her breath is musty. She places two mugs of tea on the bedside table. He sits up, leaning back against the pillows. She is naked. Her skin white, supple, firm. A mole on the back of her thigh. The hair between her legs dense and black. She moves like someone who could spend her whole life naked. He would like to see that.

"Good morning," he says. "Come here."

On her hands and knees, she advances to him, like an animal, her eyes locked on his. She kisses him hungrily. He moves her onto her back, his face between her legs. She is already wet. She moans, grabbing the back of his head as his tongue flickers in and out. "Oh god, yes. Don't stop." The intimacy of making love in daylight. There is nowhere to hide. Everyone else is going to work. He enters her. They stare silently into each other's eyes, hers brown, his gray, an unspoken communion. And then her lids lower, and she tilts her head back, her mouth open, pelvis bucking, long, short, long, short like a lover's Morse code until the pace increases as her eyes open again, and they go faster and faster and faster, eyes locked on each other, she shouting, "Yes Yes Yes."

"I HAVE WANTED TO WAKE UP NEXT TO YOU EVER SINCE WE first met on the beach," she says after. They lie splayed on the bed, exhausted like athletes. "But I never thought it would happen."

"Well, now it has. Is it everything you hoped it would be?"

"Better," she says, kissing him.

"What time is it?"

"Almost eight. I don't want to, but I have to get going. What are you doing today?"

"More meetings. A lunch. Drinks. A dinner."

"I want to see you. Can you get out of the dinner?"

"I was planning on it. I would much rather see you."

She smiles radiantly. "What time can we meet? I can try to get out of the office early."

"Is seven-thirty okay?"

"Perfect."

In the shower, he soaps her hair and her breasts, the cleft of her buttocks against him, making him hard. Slowly, wordlessly, she widens her stance, lowering herself, her back to him, arms bracing against the tiles. His legs bent to compensate for the difference in height. He watches himself penetrate her. This time it is quick. The water sluicing off their bodies, splattering on the floor. She has a beautiful back.

"I don't ever want to stop fucking you," she says.

"You might have to," he says with a smile. "I don't know if I can keep up this pace. I'm not seventeen anymore."

"Then we'll just have to feed you lots of oysters."

Out on the street, they part with a kiss. She gives him her number. "I'll call you later," he says. He watches her walk away through the cold, gray morning, memories of her warmth still on him.

After a cab ride uptown, he enters his hotel. It is his favorite in the city. Quiet, secluded, a block from the park. Black and white marble floors. The bar makes the best bullshot in Manhattan. "Good morning, Mister Winslow," says the doorman. Maddy's father lived here for the last two years of his life, ravaged by alcohol.

In his room, there is a blinking red light on the phone. It is a message from Maddy. "Hi, it's me. Guess you had an early meeting. Call us later. Johnny sends his love. We miss you!"

There is also a message from Reuben, one from Norm, another from me. We are meant to have drinks tonight. He calls down to room service and asks them to send up a pot of coffee and scrambled eggs and bacon. Then he removes his clothes and goes into the bathroom, where he stands under a scalding shower for several minutes before shaving. Breakfast arrives. He signs for it and leaves the tip in cash.

He will call Maddy later.

At three he telephones Claire. "I've been waiting to hear from you all day," she says. "I can't stop thinking about you."

"Sorry, this is the first chance I've had. Are we still on for tonight?"

"If you still want to."

"Of course I do. I'm having a drink with Walter at his club at six. I can meet you after."

She laughs. "Oh god. You are?"

"Yes. I can't get out of it. And besides, I like Walter."

"I like Walter too, but it just seems so coincidental. Do you think he'll suspect anything?"

"Why should he? He doesn't know I saw you."

"So where shall we meet?"

"I don't care—as long as they have plenty of oysters."

She laughs. "I know a place on Spring Street. It serves wonderful oysters," she says, giving him the name and address of the restaurant. After he hangs up, he is surprised by how excited he feels.

Harry and I meet at six. As usual he forgets to wear a necktie, but my club keeps spares on hand precisely for people like him.

He looks well, if a bit tired, which is to be expected given the time difference for him. We sit in the bar. Several other members are playing backgammon.

"How did the meetings go?"

"Fine." He shrugs. "The whole industry is so nervous these days, and they want to check on the progress of my book. After all, they did make rather a large investment in me. I can't imagine Hemingway doing it like this, though. He'd probably have told them to go fornicate themselves."

We talk about Rome, about plans for Christmas, about Maddy, Johnny's health. The new book.

"How's it coming?"

He takes a drink. "Slowly."

"Why?"

"I don't know. I thought moving to Rome would be an inspiration, but it's been almost too stimulating. I sit down but I can't concentrate. Instead I find myself walking for hours."

"Does that help?"

"Not really. The book just hasn't kicked in yet. Maddy loves being there, though. She's got her cooking classes and her Italian lessons. And Johnny's having a ball. One of his best friends is the Australian ambassador's son. He's teaching Johnny how to play cricket."

He is his normal charming self. There is a funny story about getting lost when they drove out to the Villa d'Este. But there is something different too. A lack of ease. Later it occurs to me that this was one of the only times I had ever seen him without Maddy. At ten of seven, he excuses himself, saying, "Sorry, Walt. I need to go." We shake hands, and he dashes out. I don't mind. There had never been talk of anything more than a drink. I order myself one more and wait to see who else will be coming in. If I am lucky another member will also be stag, and we can dine together. Later, on my way out of the club, I am told that Harry forgot to return the necktie.

4

SHE IS THERE WHEN HE WALKS IN THE RESTAURANT. OUTSIDE it is already dark. She rises, beautiful, expectant, from the table, whispering in his ear, "The oysters can wait, but I can't. Come with me."

He follows her down a flight of stairs. The bathrooms are large. There is a lock on the door. She embraces him as though making up for lost time, one hand pulling him to her, the other reaching for his zipper.

"I'm not wearing any underwear," she whispers as she hikes up her dress. She is already wet. He lifts her, pinioning her against the wall, her hands grasping his shoulders, his hands under her thrusting, her breath coming in short, sharp gasps, eyes closed, covering her mouth to keep from crying out.

They return to their seats, cheeks flushed, sharing secrets within a secret. The waiter comes to take their drink orders.

She leans forward and asks conspiratorially, "Do you think he knows?"

Harry leans back in his chair and slowly, melodramatically begins to survey the room, one eyebrow raised higher than the other. She giggles.

"Yes, definitely," he answers. "Everyone does. You can see it in their faces. They're trying to be discreet, of course."

"Of course."

"That's why no one is looking at us, and the waiter is treating us like any other customers, but you can tell."

She nods, suppressing a laugh. "You're right. I can tell."

"We may as well have neon signs over our table reading 'Just Bonked in the Bathroom.'"

"Very embarrassing. How will we live it down?"

"By showing them we're better than that. Rising above it."

"Or maybe we could just do it again?" She leers at him.

The waiter returns with their drinks. They are both having martinis.

"Christ, you're insatiable. Can I at least have a drink first?"

"You've earned it." Her hand is under the table on his thigh.

They consult the menu. "What are you having?" she asks.

"I know I'm having the oysters to start."

"You'd better be."

"How many do you think I should order?"

"Is there some kind of mathematical formula to it? I mean, do so many oysters get burned up per so many orgasms? Is it a dozen oysters for every orgasm? If you had five dozen oysters, does that mean you could have five orgasms?"

"You know, I have no idea. I don't know if I could eat five dozen oysters though."

"It does seem like a lot. Do you have to eat them all at once or can you space it out over the course of a night? You know, eat a dozen, fuck. Eat a dozen more, fuck again."

"That's an excellent question."

"Well, it certainly seems more practical than gorging on fifty or so oysters in one sitting. What if you just had one enormous orgasm and that was it? Fifty oysters, boom, gone at once."

"What if it was the greatest orgasm in the history of the world? Fifty oysters could really pack a punch. Wouldn't you rather have one unbelievable, mind-changing, earthshaking orgasm than a bunch of little ones?"

"Let me think about that. You know, I think I'd prefer a series of little ones. Because even after I just had the most incredible orgasm of my life, it would only be a few minutes before I'd want to do it again, but I'd be too shattered. Or at least you'd be."

"Good point. Women don't need oysters."

"Maybe we should consult a doctor to find out the proper proportion?"

"Or an oysterman?"

"Better yet, an oysterman's wife."

It is raining lightly when they leave the restaurant. The autumn is more advanced here than in Rome. Most of the leaves have already fallen. She wraps her arm tightly around him. He lessens his stride to accommodate her shorter legs. It is a new city to them both. The lights are shining only for them.

They stop for a drink in a bar near her apartment, but after they place their order she says, "I don't really want it. I thought I did because you did. But what I really want is you. Do you mind if we just go?"

"Let's get out of here then," he says, placing some bills on the bar beside the untouched drinks.

Upstairs in her dimly lit bedroom, he stands behind her.

"I want you to undress me," she says.

Slowly he unzips the back of her dress and slides it off one shoulder at a time until it falls to the floor. She is wearing a pale pink brassiere, which he unhooks gently. Then slowly, like a supplicant, he moves around her and kneels before her, nuzzling her belly. He turns her to sit on the bed and removes her shoes. Naked, she stands up, facing him now.

"Touch me everywhere," she whispers.

He does, caressing her breasts, her back, her arms, between her legs.

"Kiss me," she says.

"Now you undress me," he says.

She removes his borrowed tie, sliding it off around his neck, and, taking it in both hands, she skims it up and down her body. Then she wraps it behind him and uses it to pull him closer to her. Standing on her toes, she kisses him softly on the mouth before tossing aside the tie with a giggle. She unbuttons his shirt, working her hand down through his chest hair, kissing and licking him until she stops at his navel. She walks around, removing first one arm of the shirt, then the other until she is standing behind him, her hands reaching around his front to unbuckle his belt.

"Don't move," she whispers. "Let me do it."

She pulls down his trousers, kissing and licking the backs of his legs, and then slips her hand beneath his boxer shorts to feel him already straining at the cloth. She slowly rubs her hand back and forth and then lowers his shorts.

"Oh god," he says.

Still behind him, she removes one shoe, then the other, allowing her to pull off his trousers. She turns him to face her and then takes him in her mouth, slowly, slowly, along the shaft and back again, teasing, looking up at him.

As if on cue, he steps back and turns her around so that she is facing the bed. She inches forward and leans her weight on her forearms and calves. He enters her from behind, and when he is all the way in, she shudders and cries out. He watches himself go in and out of her, fascinated by this most primal of motions. He looks down the plain of her back, his hands on her haunches. She moans, clenching herself like a fist. He wants to be in every part of her at once, to feel what she feels, to know what she knows. This is as close as we can come to truly being with another person, and yet even this is not enough. He slides her down so that she is on her side, her right leg in the air, his right hand behind her head, his left hand on her breast. They are side by side. Equals now. Without meaning to he slips out of her, and, with a warm laugh, she puts him back.

"I love you inside of me," she says.

She rolls over on her stomach, and he drives deeply into her, arching his back, going deeper, deeper, deeper, deeper. Her eyes open wide as she clutches at the bed covering, repeating My god, My god, My god, My god until her voice dissolves into uh uh uh uh uh uh, as he goes faster and faster, and she gasps for air, her face driven against the bed until they both cry out as though in pain not pleasure.

Afterward, she uses the bathroom. When she comes back, she asks, "Do you really have to leave tomorrow?"

"Yes. The ticket's already been bought."

"I don't want you to leave," she says, reaching for his hand. "Now that I've found you, I don't want you to go. Is there any way you could stay just a few more days?"

"I don't know. It's not that easy. Maddy . . ." It is the first time he has mentioned her name. "She's expecting me."

She sighs. "I know."

Neither of them says anything.

"When can you come back?"

"I don't know."

"What if you said you had to check on something out at the house?"

"We have a caretaker. He'd call if there was a problem."

She turns away from him. "So, you're leaving. And I can't do anything to get you to stay?"

"It's not that I don't want to." He puts his hand on her back.

"What are we going to do?" Her voice wavers. "Is this it? I get you for a few days, and then everything goes back to the way it had been?"

"I don't know."

She turns back to him. "I know you don't know," she says. "Neither of us does. But things are different now. You know it, and I know it. I am not trying to ruin your marriage. I want you to understand that. I love Maddy. But I love you more. And I can't bear the thought of not seeing you, of not holding you."

"What reason would I give? I need a reason."

"You need more of a reason than a girl who wants to fuck your brains out?" she says, laughing.

"That's a pretty good reason." He smiles, kissing her gently on the shoulder.

"Will you do it?"

"I'll see. I'll check with the travel people."

"I'll tell my office I'm sick."

"What shall we do?"

"I'd like to go to the beach. I've never been out there this time of year."

"It's beautiful. Much quieter. No one's around. Especially during the week."

"We can have a picnic."

"We can't stay at the house, though. The water's off. It's all shut up."

"We don't have to. We can stay at an inn. Or just drive back to the city. It would be an adventure."

The next morning he calls Maddy from his hotel room. "Something's come up," he says. "I need to stay another day. Is that okay?"

She sounds disappointed. "No, of course. Johnny was so looking forward to you coming back. He made a sign for you at school. It's in Italian."

"He can still give it to me. I'll be back Saturday. It's not such a long time."

After he hangs up, he sits by the phone, staring at it. For a moment he thinks about calling back to say he will be coming after all. That he won't be staying. That he misses them and can't wait to see them. That it's all a big mistake. A big joke. But then the phone rings instead, and, startled, he answers it.

"Mister Winslow," the voice says, "it's the front desk. Your assistant asked me to tell you she is out front. She's waiting in the car."

"Oh, yes," he says. "Thank you. I'll be right down." He closes the door behind him. If there was ever a chance to turn back, it is past.

THERE IS NO TRAFFIC. THE EXITS ZIP BY. CLAIRE IS WEARING an oatmeal-colored sweater with a high, ribbed neck that she keeps playing with. She sits forward in the passenger seat of the rental car, alert, not wanting to miss a thing, a child on a school outing. As he drives he tells funny stories, and she laughs the laugh that was one of the first things I noticed about her. Silver bells. A laugh you never want to end.

It is well before lunchtime when they drive through town, shorn now of its summer plumage. It is like visiting a dress rehearsal, with the cast in their street clothes and the seats in the theater empty. Once again the town is home to locals. Pickup trucks idle on Main Street. Signs advertise a spaghetti dinner at the firehouse. The high school football team practices under a sky the color of clay.

"This is my favorite time of year out here," he says. "It's so peaceful. It's easy to see why so many artists and writers have been attracted to it. But a lot of the old places have closed down. Rents get more expensive, locals can't afford it. Most artists can't afford it anymore either. See that place?" He points to a storefront that sells expensive bath fixtures. "That used to be a bar. Big Al's. Jackson Pollock drank there."

A few doors down he turns and parks across from the train station. "I hope this place never goes out of business," he says. "Food's too good."

They walk in. On the right is a refrigerated display case containing links of sausage, cheeses, hot peppers, hams, olives. The opposite wall rows of pasta, homemade sauces, soups, drinks, and gelati. The smell of olive oil and fresh bread. In the middle is a queue of men, most of them general contractors, manual laborers, some white, others Hispanic, ordering sandwiches. On the walls are photographs, postcards sent by loyal customers.

"This place is almost as good as Rome," he whispers in Claire's ear.

"Hey, Harry!" says one of the men behind the counter. "How you doing? Where you been? Haven't seen you for a while."

They shake hands. "Hey, Rudy. Been away. Working on a new book."

"How's it going?"

"Good. Good."

"How's Mrs. Winslow?" He is looking at Claire.

"She's fine, Rudy. Thanks for asking. This is Claire. She's a friend. I told her that you sell the best prosciutto this side of Parma."

Rudy holds up his hands deferentially, accepting the compliment. "So what can I get you?" he asks.

They order. Bread, cheese, meat. The food of workmen, of Italian peasants. Food to be eaten with the hands.

"I don't think Rudy approves," says Claire when they are outside. She is trying to make light of it.

He deposits the bag in the backseat. "It was a little awkward," he admits.

"Maybe we shouldn't have come out."

"Nonsense," he says with a smile. "Now get in. We still have to buy wine."

The beach is deserted. The gray waves crash roughly on the sand. It is too cold to go barefoot. He carries a blanket and the food.

"The water looks so different this time of year," she says. "Almost like it's angry."

He kneels in the sand, spreading the blanket. From his pocket he takes out a corkscrew.

"You're such a Boy Scout," she says, grinning.

"Always be prepared, that's my motto. Hope you don't mind drinking from the bottle."

"Just try to stop me."

After lunch they lie on the blanket, her head on his stomach, staring up at the sky. It is less cold closer to the ground. A lone seagull stands nearby, waiting for an opportunity. "Beat it," says Harry, throwing a piece of driftwood at the bird, which flaps its wings and lifts itself off to a short distance away.

"Poor thing's hungry," she says.

"Sure, he's hungry. But if we feed him, all his friends will want to join the party—and so much for our peaceful picnic."

They walk down the beach, past the stone jetties and the empty houses of millionaires. "I had an ulterior motive in coming here." She smiles. "This is where we first met."

She turns and faces him, burrowing into his coat, his arms around her, her hair ruffled by the wind. He is still not used to how short she is.

"How can I forget?"

"You're my lifeguard," she says in a soft voice, raising her mouth to his. "I could have drowned, and you would have saved me."

"But you didn't need saving."

"I did. I still do."

He doesn't say anything.

"I want to start the clock again. Go everywhere we went this summer, but this time, it will be us. I want to go to the same restaurants, the same stores, fly again in your plane."

"All right."

"And I want to go to the house."

"But it's shut up. There's nothing there."

"I don't care. I want to see it. Please?"

He assents. I have often wondered why he did. I know why Claire wanted to go there. But why would he take her? This was his home with Maddy, with Johnny. A special place for them. For us all. Why would he defile it? But I suppose a man in his position is already spending money he doesn't have. What's a little more?

They drive down the familiar driveway and park. It is not as big as Claire remembers. From the outside the house looks inanimate, an empty shell. The leaves have fallen from the trees. Their feet crunch on the gravel. Harry removes the key from under the flowerpot. Inside it is gray, the air still. It is like entering a tomb. Claire is surprised by how neat it is. The shoes have been put away, the tennis racquets stacked out of sight. The doors and windows closed.

"Brrrr, it's cold," he says.

She stands in the middle of the living room. It is at once familiar and strange. The ghosts of summer fill the room. Half-remembered conversations, the *thwock* of croquet balls on the lawn, the hum of insects through the screen doors, the smell of steaks sizzling on the grill, laughter. "I wonder if it's glad we're here," she says. "The house, I mean."

"Let me start a fire," he says, moving past her.

He opens the flue. The wood is dry, the newspapers from late August. In a few moments flames are crackling in the fireplace.

"As long as we're here, let's look around," he says. "A few years ago a raccoon chewed its way through the roof, and we found a whole family living in Johnny's closet. You can't imagine the mess."

They start in the attic, he scampering ahead boyishly. It's stuffy, smelling of mothballs, crammed with dusty trunks, abandoned suitcases, garment bags, cast-off toys, broken fans and chairs, bedsteads, old magazines, boxes of old Christmas decorations, cracked riding boots that will never again be in a stirrup.

"Looks critter-free to me," he says.

"There's so much stuff. I could explore up here for days."

"Yeah, our stuff but also stuff from Maddy's family. There's a whole rack of her great-grandmother's tea gowns somewhere around here. I have no idea why we keep them. Believe me, they'll never come back into style."

"What's this?"

"My old footlocker."

"What's inside?"

"Oh, a bunch of stuff from the Marines."

"Can I see?"

He opens it. On the top his dress tunic. "Let's see if it still fits." He takes off his coat and slips it on. "A bit snug." He grins.

"Very handsome."

On the second floor, they inspect the bedrooms. Johnny's room first, then the guest room. Finally his and Maddy's. It is her first time in it. She wouldn't have dared before. It is a simple room, comfortable. The walls and wooden floor are painted white. Through the window, she looks out at their private view, past the bare tree limbs to the fields beyond. On the bed a patchwork quilt. Slippers underneath. Books on the nightstand. On the bureau photographs, hairbrushes, perfumes, cuff links, loose change in a bowl. The secret life of families.

Claire shivers. "I don't feel right being here," she says. "We should go downstairs."

He finds her on the couch before the fire, chin in her hands. "I don't know if it was such a good idea for us to come here," she says, staring at the burning logs.

"Why do you say that?"

"Because this is your place. Yours and Maddy's. I thought I could make it mine, but I was wrong. I had thought we would make love on your bed. I know that sounds awful. I'm sorry. I wanted to prove something, but when I was actually in your room, I couldn't go through with it. It's the first time I really feel that we've been doing something wrong. Before, I felt like it was just us, you know? That the two of us being together would change everything, and that it would all be all right. But now I'm not so sure."

He reaches out and holds her hand. "Do you want to drive back to New York?"

She nods her head. "Yes," she says. "I'm sorry."

For most of the drive back, they are silent. The radio substitutes for conversation. When they pass the old World's Fair grounds, he says, "Do you want me to stay with you tonight?"

"Yes. I mean, do you want to?"

"Yes."

It is late afternoon when they park near her apartment. The rest of the world is still at work. They go upstairs, stopping to collect her mail.

"About before," she says. They are sitting on her couch. "It was too much, you know?"

"I know. I've never done this either."

"Never?"

"No."

"You've never had an affair?"

"No."

"Have you ever wanted to?"

"Not until I met you."

Wordlessly, she stands up and takes him by the hand into the bedroom.

AFTERWARD, THEY LIE IN BED, THEIR BODIES EMPTY, THE sheets knotted at their feet. "How many lovers have you had?" she asks.

"Not many. There were a few girls in high school. One

or two in college, freshman year. But since Maddy, there has been no one else."

"Then why me? I can't believe there weren't other women who wanted you."

"There were a few."

"And?"

"And I did nothing."

"Why?"

"They weren't important."

"So why am I important?"

"Because you're you. Because it's us."

"You mean there's an us?"

"There is now."

"Are you happy about that?"

"I don't know if I am happy about it, but I know I would be unhappy if there wasn't."

"Why?"

He takes his time to answer.

"That's a good question," he says. "I don't know. It may be because I can't stop thinking about you. Even when you first came into our lives, there was something special about you. When I met you on the beach, I thought you were beautiful, but I wasn't thinking about that. It was only when you came to our house that night, to our party, that I found myself angry that you were dating that jerk Clive. I knew you deserved better. I wanted you to have better."

"And are you better?" she asks with a laugh.

"I don't know. I just know that you mattered to me. I knew it almost immediately."

"I had no idea."

"No, nor did I want you to. You were our guest. Our stray. Maddy's summer project."

"That's what you thought of me?"

"Yes. No. I mean, that's what I wanted to think. I couldn't have lived with myself if I'd allowed myself to think otherwise."

"And when Clive said those things at the restaurant?"

"Exactly. I guess I was so angry because somewhere I knew that part of what he said was true. But even I didn't know it yet. At that time you were under our protection, if you know what I mean. The thought never entered my mind that this would happen."

She moves closer to him. "I'm sorry."

"No. Don't be."

"Have we made a terrible mistake?"

"I don't think so. I hope not."

"But you're married. You have a life with Maddy. And Johnny."

"I know."

"I don't want to hurt her. I wish there was a way we could just create a little parallel universe where you and I could be together, and where you could still be with her, and no one would get hurt."

He kisses the top of her head—the same way he would a child who wished a river could be made of chocolate or every day was Christmas. Yet part of him wants to believe it too.

"All I know," he says, "is that I spent a lot of time wandering through the streets of Rome thinking about you. Wondering what you were doing. What your day was like. Who your friends are. If there was anyone holding you."

"Really?"

"Yes. But I had no idea I would ever see you again. It was a fantasy. I guess I'm at the age. Some men buy sports cars. I dreamt of a beautiful girl thousands of miles away."

"And now it's real," she murmurs, playing with the hairs on his chest.

"Yes, now it's real."

"So what are we going to do?"

"I don't know. I do know that I am flying back to Rome tomorrow. I do know I have to work on my book."

"Your book. You haven't talked about it, and I haven't wanted to ask. How is it going?"

"Ah." He sighs. "Not as well as I would like."

"Why?"

"I was telling Walter the other night that it was because I was distracted by the sights and sounds of Rome. That's true up to a point, I guess. It's easy to be distracted in Rome. But it's easy to be distracted in New York too, and that hadn't stopped me before."

"So what's the matter?"

"I had a friend in the Corps who was a great pilot. He was from Texas, a real good ol' boy. Square-jawed, brave, great reflexes. One day he was in a crash. It wasn't his fault. There was a technical malfunction. But it was the end of his flying career. He was given a chance to fly again, but he just couldn't. Couldn't bring himself to get back into the cockpit. So he just quit. I never saw him again."

"And?"

"And now I know how he felt."

"But you didn't crash a plane. Your book was a success. Thousands of people around the world have read it. You won a National Book Award, for God's sake."

"What I mean is that I feel fear. I'm scared to get back into the cockpit because I'm not sure I can do it again. What if my next book is a dud?"

"You can't let yourself think like that."

"I know. But every time I sit down to write I feel an uncertainty I never felt before. I try to write, but before long I need to get out, and I start walking."

"How much have you written?"

"Well, that's just it. I've written hundreds of pages, but I've thrown most of them away."

"Why?"

"The direction keeps changing. What I am working on now is almost completely different from what I started out to do. I wrestle with voices, characters. I'll sit down and write something that I like, but when I go back and read it a few days later I hate it."

"Can I do anything to help? I mean, I know it sounds stupid, but if you need to discuss it with anyone, to bounce ideas off of, you can always talk to me."

"Thanks, but what I need is to get back to Rome and hole up for a few weeks and concentrate on nothing but the book. Hopefully by then, I'll have figured out some things."

"All right. But I mean it." She gets up and goes to the living room to change the music. Her bottom is white, round, her legs a bit too short for her body. He likes watching her walk.

"Do you want to get some dinner?" he asks. "It's still early."

They dress and go out. Their hours are different from the rest of the world. There is a little French restaurant near her apartment. They walk there, her hand in his. "I'm famished," he says.

"Me too."

"I'm going to splurge and order a really good bottle of wine," he says.

It costs several hundred dollars. It will be, he thinks, the most expensive wine she has ever drunk. It is a gift he wants to give her, one of many. Money is of no importance. All he wants is her happiness.

The waiter decants it. When it is ready, he pours the wine. "That's amazing," she says, taking a sip.

"It's always been one of my favorites. It's a Pauillac. A fifth growth. Not as expensive as a premier cru, but in my opinion every bit as good. The '82 was a particularly good vintage."

"You sound like Walter," she says, giggling.

He laughs. "I suppose I do. It's probably because he's taught me a lot of what I know. Yale and the Marine Corps are great for learning about a lot of things. French wine isn't one of them though."

Over dinner they talk about her, her family, her job. They are still getting to know each other. Filling in the blanks. He learns that pears are her favorite fruit, that she doesn't like Renoir but adores Degas, that she knows how to tap-dance, and that she wore eyeglasses in high school until she switched to contacts. His life is known, he has lived in public. Hers is still to be discovered. But like in the child's game of connecting dots, the more connections he makes, the more she becomes the person that in his heart he already knew her to be.

"What would you do if we saw someone you knew?" she asks. "I mean if they saw us, here, together?"

"I don't know. I've thought about it, sure. I suppose it depends on who it was—and what we were doing. I mean, there is nothing especially suspicious about us having dinner, is there? We are friends. You did spend a lot of time with us over the summer. What's the harm in that?"

"Some people might misinterpret it, but they wouldn't know for sure."

"But they'd be right. It's hard to hide body language, especially when you're sleeping together. There's a kind of heat that two lovers give off, even if they're on opposite sides of the room. It practically burns off your clothes."

He reaches out and takes her hand, threading her fingers through his. "I would love to travel with you," he says.

"Where would we go?"

"France. I would like to visit Paris with you, and the South of France. Afterwards, Morocco, Tangier, Zanzibar."

"I'll get my toothbrush."

"I'm not kidding. We could find somewhere cheap and live for a year on the beach. You'll go topless and your breasts will become the color of caramel. But first I want to take you to bed in the Ritz. Order room service. I know you've been to Paris with your parents when you were a kid. When was the last time you were there?"

"During college. I backpacked around after my junior year."

"But you never stayed at the Ritz."

"It was a little out of our budget."

"Where else did you visit?"

"Well, besides Paris there was Madrid and Barcelona. Then Florence and Venice. Finally, two weeks in Greece. On Santorini. I got very sunburned."

"Were you there by yourself?"

"I was with my boyfriend. His name was Greg. We broke up soon after. Isn't that always the way? You travel around with someone and it's easy to get fed up with them. Their habits begin to get on your nerves."

"You know what they say about Venice?"

"What?"

"That if you go there with someone you aren't married to, you will never marry them."

"That's okay. You're already married."

He lets that slide by, but for a moment she wonders how he will react. It had come out of nowhere.

"So you don't mind traveling with me? What if I got on your nerves too?" he asks with a smile.

"The opposite is true too. If you can travel with someone and still like them, then you know you're with the right person."

"Well then, I guess we'll just have to find out, won't we?"

The wine drunk, the food eaten, he pays and they leave. It is his last night in New York. Tomorrow evening, he will fly back to Rome. They spend the next day in bed. Sleeping, making love. The last time for almost an hour, slowly, care-fully, like pearl divers filling their lungs with oxygen. Uptown, his bags are still at his hotel, a room he has barely seen. At four in the afternoon, he has to leave.

"I wish I didn't have to go," he says.

She is sitting on the bed, a black robe wrapped loosely around her, her arms folded protectively. The room is lit only by the fading sun, an in-between hour. She is distancing her-self, waiting for the blow.

He wants to say something, to reassure her. But he cannot find the words.

"Is this it?" she asks, not looking at him, her voice rising up from miles inside her.

He wants to say no, but he doesn't want to lie. He doesn't even know what the truth is anymore.

His coat is on. He is ready to return to his other life.

"I know I can't ask you to stay," she says. "I know you have to go back to Maddy and Johnny."

"I do."

"And I am not going to ask for any promises."

"I know you won't. And I'm sorry I can't give any."

"But I did promise myself I wouldn't be a bitch or make you feel guilty, so I won't." The rims around her eyes are moist. There is a catch in her voice.

He walks over and takes her hand, her clean white fingers soft and limp. They are beautiful hands, with no adornment, no rings, no polish. They are the hands of an aristocrat, a geisha.

"I don't want to lose you," he says. "I'll be back. I don't know how, but I'll figure something out."

"I'll be waiting."

"Maybe you could come to Europe. I have a tour next month. We could meet somewhere."

"What about Maddy? Won't she be coming?"

"No. She won't want to. She'll want to stay with Johnny. And it wouldn't be that long. Only a couple of days."

"I'll take it," she says with a smile.

"Good. I only wish it could be more."

"Me too."

She stands up and walks over to him, her robe falling open, placing her naked body against him. "Now you better get out of here," she says, her lips brushing his, "or I'm going to start seducing you."

He throws his head back and laughs. "I am going to miss you," he says. He can't remember when he wanted her more.

"I love you, Harry," she says.

"And I love you." This time he said it. There is no doubt.

A last embrace, then the door, the lonely hallway, the old stairs down to the street. His footsteps echoing dully as he descends. From the other floors the smell of cooking, the chatter of television. Normal lives. He does not stop until the lobby, and he knows she would not be watching. On the street, he does turn and look up, counting the floors to find her apartment. She does not appear, and, after a moment, he hurries down the street looking for a taxi. The smell of her on his fingers.

6

WEEKS PASS. THE RIPPLE FROM THE CAST STONE HAS NOT been felt. Life continues as it had before. Mundane chores, taking Johnny to school, paying bills, walking to the *salumeria*. There are still parties, drives in the country, visits to churches to admire the frescoes. There are still kindnesses, shared jokes, acts of love. One night Harry comes home from one of his rambles with an enormous bouquet of flowers. Outwardly nothing has changed.

But he is not sleeping, and he has always slept well. He has the soldier's ability to sleep anywhere.

In their borrowed bed, he lies staring up at the ceiling. He is waiting. "What's wrong?" whispers Maddy, surprising him. He thought she was already asleep. It is the middle of the night.

"Nothing. Can't sleep. That's all."

"That's been happening a lot lately."

He thought she hadn't noticed. He had tried to be so quiet.

"Is it your book?"

"What? Yes."

"Can I help?"

"No, no. Thank you. I just need to work some things out in my head. I think I'm going to go work for a while. I'm sorry I woke you. Now go back to sleep."

"Good luck, darling," she says, nestling back into her pillow, sleep already returning, confident in her love. He kisses her gently on the forehead and closes the door quietly behind him as he goes out.

At his computer, he begins his nightly betrayal. There are messages from Claire, full of passion, declarations of love, vivid descriptions of what she would like to do with him. His daytime mask falls off, and, aroused, he responds in kind, communing with her through the ether.

I cannot wait for Paris, he types. *There is an old Spanish song where the woman says make love to me so that the bells on my ankles jingle in my ears. I will make your bells jingle. I will even bring the bells.*

Outside the wind beats the branches against the window. His is the only light. Even the city's cats are asleep.

He is surprised by how easy it all seems. How naturally he can deceive. And yet it is not all lies. He loves his wife, his son. They are everything to him. But he has discovered that there is something more, something he had never known about before, an extra dimension where time and space exist on a different plane. Like an explorer who has discovered an earthly paradise, he has lost his taste for the world beyond and all he can think of is crossing the snow bridge back to Shangri-la.

Thanksgiving arrives. Maddy cooks a feast. She has located

a butcher in Trastevere where she has special-ordered two whole turkeys, a bird that rarely features in the local cuisine. Other dishes are easier to obtain. Potatoes, of course. Stuffing. Creamed onions. I mail her several cans of impossible to find Ocean Spray, which we have both always preferred to the gourmet stuff. She is making apple pies, even pumpkin. A large group of Americans arrive, friends of friends, children. They are local diplomats, artists, a journalist or two, people who can't or won't be able to return home for so brief a holiday. There are more than twenty of them. The guests bring wine, champagne. They sit on every available chair in the house. The invitation said drinks at two, dinner at three. They sing "We Gather Together," and Harry says grace. The only thing missing is football on the television. Johnny sits between his parents. The wife of an architect sits on Harry's left. He discusses his favorite Roman buildings, but soon he realizes she doesn't share her husband's enthusiasms. It is like talking to a shortstop's wife about baseball, only to find she has no interest in the sport.

After the main course but before dessert, everyone goes for a walk while the pies cool. They head en masse to the Piazza Navona, where they admire Bernini's fountain. For the Romans, it is just another Thursday. It seems decadent to be eating and drinking in the middle of the day when everyone else is working. It is like playing hooky.

They continue to the Tiber and then back again. By now it is getting dark. Office workers are on their way home. A few people have begun filling the cafés, teenage boys navigate the streets looking for girls. Shops are closing down.

"I love Thanksgiving," says Maddy when everyone has

gone. They are in the kitchen. She is washing glasses, he drying. *La forza del destino* is playing in the background.

"I have to go to Paris," he announces. "I just found out. I didn't want to say anything before and spoil the day. I'm sorry."

She looks over at him. "You have to go away again? Ugh. Why can't they just leave you alone and let you write?"

He shrugs. "I've been invited to meet with the French publishers. And they want me to give a talk. Apparently, I'm quite popular in France."

"The French also think Jerry Lewis is a comic genius," she says with a smile. "So, when do you have to go?"

"Next week. Monday. I'll be gone about three days."

She wipes hair out of her eyes with the back of her hand, careful not to get dish soap on it. "I won't be able to come, you know. Johnny has school."

"I know." He is busy inspecting the glass in his hand. "I'll miss you."

"I wish I could go. It's been a long time since we were in Paris."

"Maybe the next time. It'd be boring for you anyway. I'll be busy all day with meetings, and then there will be business dinners at night. Everyone wanting a piece of me. You hate that sort of thing."

"God, yes."

"And maybe I'll bring you back something, a little frock," he says lightly. "Maybe a new bag? The latest fashions?"

She gives him a wry look. "Ha. You know perfectly well the last thing I want is some silly dress I'll never wear anyway."

"Beautiful, great cook, wonderful mother, and hates to

shop. You really are the world's most perfect wife." He gives her an affectionate kiss on the cheek. Inside he is elated. A sailor given a three-day leave.

That night he tells Johnny once again the story of the Penguin King. Then he and Maddy make love. At first she resists, claiming she is too tired and full. Over the years, they had made love with less and less frequency. I find this out from Maddy later. Theirs had become a working relationship, and had long ceased being a passionate one. They were a team, she explained to me. After twenty years, some things change.

It would be overly simplistic to say this was the reason Harry did what he did, but it may have had something to do with it. My sex life has never been what one could call satisfactory, but I think that, like a muscle or a foreign language, it can be diminished if not practiced regularly. I had fewer expectations from sex, so I set my bar lower and found other pleasures of the flesh, namely food and drink. And, as with food, a person is less likely to patronize another restaurant if the cooking at the one he visits all the time continues to stimulate his appetite.

I have often thought about Maddy at this time of her life. How trusting she was. How ignorant. She made a vow and kept it. There had never been any question she wouldn't. But despite her beauty, she was not a very sexual person. Not that she was indifferent to sex, but she regarded it the way someone else might consider chocolate or physical exercise. It had its benefits, even its pleasures, but it paled in comparison with what was truly important to her, which was love and family.

Like those born without money, those born without love want it all the more. It becomes the great solution, the answer to all problems. When Madeleine was just six months old, her mother left. Before her marriage her mother had been very beautiful, a highly paid fashion model from a humble background, but she didn't leave to run off with another man. She was forced out by her mother-in-law, a wealthy and powerful woman who disapproved of her son's choice in a wife. And he did not put up much of a fight. For him, it came down to a choice of love or money, a decision made easier for him because I honestly question whether he ever loved anyone. He never told Maddy the truth either, saying instead that her mother was crazy, a drug fiend.

It was easily handled. People were able to do things like that back then. There was one rule for the rich and another for everyone else. A telephone call to a lawyer was all it took. Threats were made, papers signed. Maddy lived with her grandmother for the next several years, until her father remarried, this time to someone deemed more suitable. Her older brother, Johnny, had stayed with their father, and together they left the country for a few years, living in St. Croix. But her mother, beaten by a system she never really understood, vanished from their lives. There had been one or two attempts at phone calls, usually on Maddy's birthday or Christmas, but the calls had always been intercepted by her father, who simply hung up.

One time, when Maddy was seven or eight, still wearing her party dress, she came into the room just as her father was replacing the receiver. Who was that, Daddy? she had asked. Wrong number, he told her. She hadn't learned yet not to trust him.

It wasn't until Maddy was a freshman in college that she saw her mother again. She was living outside of Boston, near where she had grown up. For days Maddy debated contacting her, wondering if there was any point, if any good could come of it, but knowing in her heart that she had never been told the full story. Finally Maddy called her mother on the phone, arranging a meeting, unsure of what to expect. What kind of woman doesn't fight for her own child? Maddy was then at an age where she still expected answers.

Her mother lived in a poor neighborhood of an old industrial town. Multifamily houses with plastic siding, children playing in the street, shuttered stores, cracked sidewalks, pit bulls barking behind chain-link fences. I still don't know how Maddy located her. She doesn't lie, but she can be selective in what she chooses to reveal.

When she arrived, her mother greeted her. The apartment was sparsely furnished. The paint on the walls was chipped, and it smelled of cat. I am sure Maddy had never been in a house like this before. She moves in a different world completely. A man sat in one of the only chairs watching television. He didn't even look up. In the background, a pretty little girl with long blond hair peered out shyly, half-hidden by the kitchen door.

In the same way that we form an image of a character in a book, Madeleine had always had a picture in her mind of what her mother looked like. She had been too young to remember her mother, and her father had destroyed all photographs of her. Was her imagined mother drawn from a vague half memory, the dim recollection of a face above her, lifting her from a crib, holding her to her breast? Would seeing her mother be like looking in a mirror, and seeing an older version of herself?

This woman standing in the doorway was certainly not the

mental image Madeleine had held for so long, and there was little of the beauty she had supposedly once possessed. It was a face worn down by poverty. Her teeth were bad. Her hair hung limply. For a moment, Maddy wondered if she was even in the right house.

"I'm Madeleine," she said. She didn't kiss her mother. She didn't even know what to call her. "Mother" seemed wrong. It had been too long. They were total strangers.

"Hello, dear," answered her mother, her accent pure Boston. "Come in."

There are two sides to every story. The two women sat in the kitchen, sipping the coffee Maddy had brought from paper cups. There were no accusations, no remonstrations, no tears. On either side. How do you get back almost two decades? You cannot. But it was obvious to Maddy that her mother had suffered during that time. Awkwardly they chatted about what Maddy was studying; her brother, Johnny; even, delicately, her father. "He was such a good-looking man," said her mother. "No one could resist him." Why had she left? It wasn't my fault, her mother answered. They held all the cards. What could I do? The old woman smiled humorlessly. The smile of a prisoner serving a life sentence. It was a long time ago, she said.

It was too much. After an hour Maddy found an excuse to go. When they parted, the two women embraced. There was no talk of a future meeting.

When Maddy returned to her room that night, I asked her what she had expected to find. Did she think it would be a tearful reunion? Did she expect them to fall into each other's arms after being separated for nineteen years?

"It was awful," she said. "You have no idea."

"I'm sorry."

"It wasn't just that she was so poor. It was that all my life I had felt so sorry for myself. That she must have been some kind of monster for not wanting me. But that wasn't the case at all."

"What do you mean?"

"She didn't come out and say it, but I could tell she was the real victim here, not me. It made me realize how horrible I have been to think these things about her all these years. I had always hated her for abandoning me, for making me the girl who didn't have a mother. But they made *her* leave. They threatened her. What choice did she have? They had the money, the lawyers, the police if necessary. She had nothing. We destroyed her life."

"We? You had nothing to do with it."

She thought for a moment. "I didn't, but I still did. It was about me. My grandmother didn't want me raised by her. She was from the wrong side of the tracks. They told me she was crazy. That she had to be committed. That's why she had gone. But that wasn't true. They told her she would be arrested if she ever tried to find me. They would ruin her brothers. They lied to her. They lied to me."

She was in tears now. I had seldom seen her cry. It was unnerving. I remembered the grandmother. A formidable dowager who had terrified me as a child but who had never been anything but loving to Maddy. The father, charming and monstrous, a wonderful athlete who had smashed nearly every club record, was still alive at that point, having divorced his third wife. He was the only parent she ever had. She would hear nothing bad said against him, even when he had been at his worst, wanting to believe in him, feeling that a false god was better than none at all.

Soon after that, she met Harry and never looked back. He was her family now. It would all be better. They waited to have Johnny. She wasn't ready to share Harry with anyone. Then, she was. I was there the day Johnny was born. Everything was a movement away from what she had known to something better, something positive. I was, I am, so proud of her.

Why am I recounting all of this? Isn't it obvious? For years people have thought I was sexless, or gay. Neither was true. I have never married because I was already in love, of course. Maddy was the first and the only woman I ever loved. I have tried others, but no one had her goodness, her sense of honor, her strength. I was ruined from an early age. But you have to understand that it wasn't a selfish love. When she first met Harry, I understood. They were perfect together. I was old enough then and aware enough of my shortcomings to know that she needed someone like him. Someone strong. Someone true. Someone who could lift her in his arms and protect her. I was a confidant, a companion, and I resigned myself to that role because it was best for her.

There was one time when I tried. We were teenagers, maybe fifteen, and one night on one of our nocturnal outings, I tried to kiss her. But she laughed. "What are you doing?" she asked.

"I love you," I said, the epitome of adolescent angst. We were on the beach. We had snuck out on one of our moonlight sprees. I had brought marshmallows and a bottle of wine I had stolen from my parents' cellar. I had been working up my courage all week. No, my whole life.

She was silent. It seemed to last for centuries. Then she

spoke and told me I was her best friend, in many ways her only friend. She didn't want a boyfriend. She wanted a friend. By then her breasts had grown in. They were—how can I put this delicately?—deliciously large. Surprisingly so. I ached to touch them. But she detested them. "I feel like a freak," she said. She was already astonishingly beautiful, and I wasn't the only one who thought so.

Even if I was the one with whom she chose to spend time, other men became part of her life. It was impossible to stop them. They surrounded her, but she wanted little to do with them. There was one Spanish boy she had met in Switzerland, but I think it was more of an experiment. To see what it was like. It didn't last long. We never spoke in detail about it. I am grateful for that. I hated him, though I never met him. Gonzalo or Felipe. I can't even remember his name, but he became my enemy when she told me about him and I couldn't see what she would see in him.

But I understood Harry. He was the sort of man with whom she should have fallen in love, and she did. He was handsome, confident, talented, kind, and loving. He was what she needed, and I, the eternal eunuch, the faithful friend, at least knew she was happy. And while it was cold comfort, it was enough.

7

I SEE THEM IN THEIR HOTEL ROOM. HARRY AND CLAIRE. I AM not there but I can imagine. The heavy curtains have been drawn. The room is purple in darkness but objects are discernible. Above, an ornate ceiling maybe twenty feet high. Queens and movie stars have slept here. Outside, it is midafternoon, the weather dreary. Cars circle the *place*. Motorcycle messengers race by. Taxis idle, waiting for fares. Diamond necklaces glitter behind bulletproof glass in vitrines lining the hallway, and well-fed bankers return from lunch.

They are on the bed, fucking. Urgently, desperately, like starving men at a banquet. She is still wearing her shoes, her blouse. Their bags where the chasseur left them. The bottle of house champagne is untouched in its sweating ice bucket. The only sounds primal. The slap of flesh on flesh, the grunt of effort, the moan of pleasure. Two halves of a whole joined.

An amulet, the key to a kingdom. There is nothing else in the world.

Afterward she tells him it was the best ever. She holds him, her hands cool around the tender flesh.

"Yes," he smiles, exhausted. "God, yes."

He lets her sleep, tired from her long flight and the time change. For him, the time is the same. He dresses and slips out, quietly closing the door behind him. Instead of taking the elevator, he walks down the carpeted stairwell. He nods to the clerks at the front desk and the concierge, who smile urbanely back at him. He is unknown to them. He hasn't been here in years. He has yet to make an impression. They take in his coat, his shoes. Is he a good tipper? They will know him by name, grant him the benefit of their knowledge, their network of contacts, doors will unlock. If he tips poorly, monsieur will find that tables cannot be procured, tickets are regrettably unavailable. It is a simple relationship, the simplest.

For Harry the anonymity is a thrill that he wears like a protective veil. On the street he turns down Rue de Castiglione to Rivoli, heading under the colonnade, past the cafés and shops catering to tourists. On the far side, the trees of the Tuileries are barren, the grass brown, the benches empty. He carefully crosses the Place de la Concorde, heading toward the Seine. This is not the real Paris, the Paris of students, Algerians thin as blades, old women who feed stray cats. Of cheap shops, trade unions, and streets whose names celebrate long-forgotten victories. The France of working people, of eating lunch at home, of market day and bad shoes. This is the Paris of visitors, of the rich, of diplomats, and of those who cater to them. It is a façade, but a pleasing one nevertheless.

Years ago he knew a homosexual *comte* who lived in an apartment nearby. It was a fabulous apartment, on the *grand etage*, decorated like an Egyptian nightclub. Harry and Maddy had been drinking with him all night and had gone everywhere. Ledoyen, Castel's, Le Baron, and finally, as the birds began to sing, they went back to the *comte*'s for a last drink. It was dawn by that point. The *comte*, who was middle-aged and chubby, told Maddy that Harry was lucky his wife was along. Harry, who was younger and stronger than the *comte*, smiled, unthreatened, amused by the Proustian decadence of it all.

Tonight, it is raining lightly, droplets dampening his hair. He has no hat or umbrella, but he doesn't mind. He is a walker. New York, London, Rome, Paris. It doesn't matter. That is why he dislikes Los Angeles and most American cities. There are not enough sidewalks.

He walks down the river and then up to the Place des Vosges, the oldest in Paris, before turning back. He finds himself on Saint-Honoré. He walks past the famous shops, Hermès, Longchamp, Gucci. Their elegant wares redolent of beautiful lives, ski trips, Mediterranean islands, wealthy tanned men, aristocratic women. He stops in front of one of the greatest and on impulse walks in, uncertain of what he is looking for. The tall, elegant *vendeuses* watch him. He is unused to being in stores like this. Unlike many husbands, he has not been dragged along on shopping trips, waiting idly outside a fitting room, watching the elaborate dance between customer and clerk.

Self-consciously he browses through the racks, inspecting the price tags, trying not to be astonished. There is a black cocktail dress that catches his eye. It is thousands of dollars. Maddy had never bought anything this expensive in her life.

But the cost isn't important. He needs, he wants to buy Claire something. He has the generosity of early love.

He calls to one of the saleswomen who, less disinterested now that she sees what he is looking at, comes over. He struggles to remember his French and not to confuse it with his even more rudimentary Italian. Unlike Maddy, languages never came easily to him.

"*Je veux acheter cette robe.*"

"*Mais oui, monsieur. Savez-vous la taille?*" With her hands, she carves a woman's body in the air.

He looks at her blankly. He realizes he has no idea what size Claire is.

"I don't know," he says, feeling stupid.

The saleswoman holds her hands to her hips. "Like me?" she asks in English. "*Comme ça?*"

He has forgotten the word. "No, smaller. *Petite?*"

"*Ah, pas de problème,*" she says. She locates the same dress in the next size down.

"If it doesn't fit, I can bring it back?"

"*Oui, monsieur.* Of course."

It is almost dark now. He walks back to the hotel swinging the bag, the dress cocooned in its box, protected by layers of tissue paper. This is not him. It is someone else. Someone who stays in expensive hotels, patronizes stylish shops, is meeting a woman not his wife. It is a role he is inhabiting, a dream. Nothing is real. If someone pinched him he'd wake up. But he doesn't want to wake up.

He goes up to the room. It is as dark as he left it. Naked under the covers, she is just stirring. Her body warm, hair ruffled, breath sour.

She smiles, eyes half-closed. "Did you have a nice walk?" she asks drowsily, stifling a yawn.

"I did. I love walking in Paris. It was certainly the most expensive walk I've ever taken in Paris, though." He shows her the shopping bag, with a smile. "I bought you a present."

She brightens and sits up in bed. "You didn't! Oh my god, I love that store."

She takes the bag from him and opens the box. The cover has fallen now, revealing her breasts. The nipples soft and pink. He thinks about what is underneath the covers.

Holding up the dress, she cries, "It's beautiful. I can't believe you did this." She jumps out of bed and embraces him. "It's the nicest present I've ever had," she says, kissing him. "Thank you so much."

"Try it on. See if it fits. I had no idea what size you were. The salesgirl told me I could return it if we wanted."

"I'll be right back." She runs to the bathroom. The light comes on. The heavy door clicks behind her. He sits on the bed, waiting for her answer.

"It's perfect!" she cries from within.

"Let me see."

"No. I want it to be a surprise."

She comes out of the bathroom, provocatively naked. She walks to him and, bending over, dangles her breasts in his face like two ripe pears, lightly brushing her lips against his cheek. "Let me show you how much I like my present."

That evening she wears the dress to dinner. Black hair, black dress, pale skin. She is all youth, all vitality, all sexuality. She is the most beautiful woman in the room. Other diners look up from their meals and watch her as she enters. It is as if she is not wearing any clothes at all. It is vertiginous following her. The maître d' proudly leads them in.

Harry marvels at the transformation in her. From the artless young woman of the summer to this figure dressed in the latest style. What would her life have been like if she had never met him on the beach? If she had never come to that fateful party?

"I can't believe we're in Paris," she says excitedly. Tonight they are dining in the hotel. It is a two-star restaurant. A Belle Epoque temple to Escoffier. Tomorrow they will go out.

They discuss plans. This is a city she knows from her childhood, parts of it forever associated with dreary Sundays and airless rooms. He wants to show her the other side.

The waiter hands them the menus. They order cocktails. Her French is impeccable. The waiter tries not to look surprised. He had taken her for an American.

"I had no idea you spoke so well," Harry says. "My French is pretty much limited to what I can order from a menu or a wine list."

"It's been a long time," she says. "I've been practicing for the trip but I'm still a little rusty. I've forgotten so much though. My mother always said I had a good accent. They say you never lose that." She pauses. "I had a French passport for years. I was a dual national before they made you choose. I still have it. In a drawer at home. The photograph is from when I was twelve or thirteen. I keep it because it does remind me that, after all, I am half French."

"Have you ever wanted to spend more time here? I mean, to live?"

"Not when I was a child. It was awful coming here. I suppose I was lucky. While most kids my age were going to Disneyland, I was going to Paris. But it was a Paris without joy, without fun or beauty or art or any of the things people come here for. My grandparents didn't even have a TV. My brother and I would spend endless hours sitting on a hard settee in their living room while my mother chatted with them, drinking tea and nibbling on biscuits. It was agony. I could see the sky outside, imagining that the other children, the real French children, were playing in the park or going to the zoo. When my grandparents died, I was relieved. I know that sounds horrible, but it's true."

"At least you saw the real France. I've been to France, oh, I don't know, maybe two dozen or so times, sometimes longer, sometimes shorter, sometimes coming through Paris, sometimes not, but I've never seen what you saw. I've only seen the Hollywood version, the version that France wants us to see. You lived behind the curtain."

"I suppose, but I like this better. The food isn't as good behind the curtain." She laughs. Her face lights up. Her teeth are white. He can see the pink of her gums.

She orders lobster bisque laced with pistachio followed by truffled sole. He orders the same.

Harry calls over the sommelier. They decide on a Montrachet.

"I'm starving," she says.

"And no need to worry about eating too much. They have a beautiful spa with a pool. Pamela Harriman died while swimming laps in the pool."

"Who?"

"A famous courtesan," he explains. Then he adds, "Actually, she was the American ambassador to France. She married a lot of rich men and had affairs with even more."

After dinner they stroll down a long corridor to the back of the hotel. It is midweek and a reception is winding down. Businessmen are exchanging cards. They head to the little bar, down a few steps. The smell of expensive cigars perfumes the air.

"This is my favorite bar in the world," he tells her. He would come here even when he couldn't afford to stay in the hotel.

They walk in. Claire is surprised by how small it is. It is already crowded. Smoke plumes in the air. All the tables are occupied, but there are two seats at the narrow bar. George, the bartender, is mixing drinks.

"Mister Winslow," says George in an English accent. "Lovely to have you back with us, sir." He is slightly taller than average, balding, white-jacketed, precise in his movements. Harry has already sent him a note saying he would not be coming in with Maddy.

The two men shake hands. "Good to see you again, George. This is Claire."

"Welcome," George says. "You've just dined, I believe. Might I suggest a digestif?"

Harry looks to Claire. "Whatever he offers, agree to it. He is to the cocktail shaker what Picasso was to the brush."

"All right, George. In that case I would very much like a digestif."

"Lovely. Now, may I inquire whether you are fond of Armagnac?"

She nods. Behind the bar he wields the tools of his craft. His hands deftly lifting, chopping, swirling, pouring. Finally, a flower petal as a garnish.

"Voilà."

She takes a sip. "Delicious," she says.

Pleased, George permits himself a smile. "I thought you would like that."

"What is it?" asks Harry.

"It's called a Hôtel de France. Two parts Armagnac. One part crème de cassis. Seven parts chilled champagne. A shot of pear liqueur. I make the liqueur myself. And for you, Mister Winslow?"

"Surprise me."

Once again the hands fly over the bar. It is like trying to watch a man cheat at cards.

"And voilà again."

"Excellent," says Harry. "What is it?"

"It's a variation on the classic French 75. Before dinner I use London gin. After dinner, cognac is best. Then, of course, sugar, lemon, and champagne."

"Superb."

"It was my pleasure. Excuse me."

Another customer is beckoning. George begins speaking in Spanish to him. Others come up, he responds in French. He is like a brilliant financier or someone who has the hot tips at the racetrack; everyone wants him.

"What a fascinating man," Claire says. "I have never met a bartender who revered his work so much."

"You're right. To him, this is the sacred mountain. There has to be a best in everything. The best lawyer, the best shoemaker, the best baker. He is the best bartender. He has devoted his life to it. Do you know that he wakes up every morning and reads newspapers in five languages just so he will be able to converse with his clients on any topic that might interest them?"

"Does he know Chinese?"

"Not yet."

"He should."

"Maybe, but the Chinese don't come here yet. At least not many."

She sips her drink. "Just wait."

As happens most nights, George facilitates introductions. They meet a Spanish couple from Madrid. Then some Germans. Finally, two American girls traveling on their parents' money. Claire chats with them. Harry is smoking a cigar. A fat corona from Cuba.

"Are you having fun?" he asks when she turns back to him.

She squeezes his hand. "I am," she answers. "Are you? Are you glad you're here? With me?"

"There is nowhere else in the world I would rather be. And with no one else. Have I told you how beautiful you look?"

"Not nearly enough."

"You look beautiful."

"Thank you. For this, for all this."

Later, in the room, he stands behind her, watching her brush her teeth. The water pouring from a faucet resembling a golden swan. She is very thorough. As he brushes his teeth, she uses the toilet, leaving the door open. He can see the white of her knees. Hears the roll of the paper as she unwinds it off the spool. He is overcome by intimacy, intruding upon her, her underwear around her ankles, knees together, her breasts bare. He stands in the doorway watching her. Her hand between her legs. Surprised, she looks up at him.

"Sorry," he says. "I wanted to watch you."

"It's all right."

"I've never done that before."

She flushes and stands up, leaving her underwear on the floor. "I understand," she says, kissing him. "This is all about new things."

She is in bed waiting when he comes in. He can see that the message light is flashing red on the phone. He ignores it as he lowers himself into her arms.

8

THEY SPEND THE DAY AS LOVERS DO. IN THE MORNING BREAK-
fast is wheeled into their room. Claire hides, giggling under the
covers, while Harry, wearing only a terry-cloth robe, signs the
bill. The waiter maintains an attitude of Gallic indifference.
He has seen it all before.

There is hot coffee, croissants, buttery eggs, crisp bacon.
The linen is starched and white as paper.

"Try this coffee," he says, handing her a cup and saucer.
"It's the best in the world."

"You say that about everything at this hotel. Oh my god,
you're right. That's really good."

"It ought to be. At the prices they charge."

"And these eggs. They're incredible. I can't imagine I'd be
hungry again after last night's dinner, but I'm starving."

After breakfast they go out. The sky mirrors the gray of the stones on the *place*. Drivers in sunglasses and dark suits stand in front of Mercedes parked beside the entrance talking on cell phones and waiting for passengers.

They turn up the Rue de la Paix, heading toward the Opéra.

"Where shall we go?" she asks, her arm tucked under his. She is wearing woolen mittens and a scarf. I never wear hats, she has told him.

"Wherever you like."

"I don't feel like going to a museum. I know I should. But it's like waking up on Sunday and going to church. It feels like duty, not fun."

"So that rules out churches too, I take it?" he asks with a smile.

"Oh. Well, yes, I suppose it does. I mean, I've been to Notre Dame. It's beautiful and awe-inspiring but we only have a short time. I'd rather not spend it in a musty church."

"Where would you like to go?"

"Besides back to bed at the hotel, you mean?" she says, grinning at him. "I'm happy just to walk until we're both hungry and then stop at some random place for lunch. How does that sound?"

"It sounds perfect."

They head north. In his mind they are heading vaguely toward Montmartre, but he is willing to choose another direction if one suggests itself.

They walk in contented silence, occasionally pointing out something amusing or odd. It feels so natural, her hand in his.

"The cars are all so small," she comments. "It's like a race of midgets drives them."

At the bottom of Montmartre, they take the funicular to the top of the hill. Once there, they walk to see the Basilica of Sacré-Coeur, the highest point in Paris.

"I've never been here," she says. They stand there looking out over the city, the Seine writhing like a lazy silver snake in the sunlight.

"Some people think the Eiffel Tower is the best place to see Paris, but I still think this is," he says. "Did you know that the tower is older than the basilica?"

"Really?"

"It's true. The basilica was only completed after World War One. The Eiffel Tower was dedicated in 1889. But people had been coming here for centuries. They say druids used to perform rituals on this site."

"Stand there," she says. From her purse she takes a camera. Behind him Paris falls away to the horizon. "Smile," she says. He does. "Now you take a picture of me."

They get a fellow tourist to take one of them together. I have seen it. They look like so many other tourists in Paris. I wonder if that's how they felt.

They stop for lunch in a small restaurant full of Dutch tourists. After, they wander through Montmartre to Pigalle, past the Moulin Rouge, the Bateau-Lavoir, its great days, when Lautrec, Picasso, and Utrillo lived in the neighborhood, behind it. They turn down the Boulevard de Clichy and see a sign for the Musée de l'érotisme.

"This looks promising," she says.

"I thought you didn't want to go to a museum."

"This is different. Come on."

"Are you sure?"

"You never know. We might learn something new."

Harry pays and they enter. The museum is clearly popular with tourists. On the walls are pornographic images from around the world. Carved images from India, contemporary photographs of naked women in leather, cartoons, phalluses of exaggerated length, an entire floor devoted to Parisian brothels, the *maisons closes* of the nineteenth century. They almost burst out laughing at several of the images.

On the way out, there is a gift shop selling books, posters, and erotic postcards.

"Wait here," she says.

A few minutes later, she returns carrying a brown paper bag. "I found it."

"What?"

"Look."

She hands him the bag. In it is a French copy of the Kama Sutra.

"They say there are sixty-four different positions," she says. "I can't wait to start."

BACK IN THE HOTEL THEY ARE SITTING OPPOSITE EACH OTHER on the bed. She translates, " 'the kinds of sexual union according to dimensions, force of desire or passion, time.'

"It says that man is divided into three classes, the hare man, the bull man, and the horse man."

"How flattering."

"Shhh, be quiet. It depends on the size of his lingam."

"You mean the . . ."

"Exactly. And that women are divided into three classes

169

based on the size of their yoni: a female deer, a mare, or a female elephant."

"A female elephant? Good lord."

"Stop it."

"Why is there no male elephant? It hardly seems fair."

"To whom?"

"To everybody. Poor female elephant, for one. No male elephant to satisfy her. And to me. I mean, who's to say I'm not a male elephant? I've always thought of myself as being rather elephantine."

"You are, darling. Now be quiet. It says here about three equal unions, based on corresponding dimensions. Look, there's a diagram. It says that a male hare and a female elephant are an unequal union."

"That makes perfect sense. It's like the old joke about the elephant and the flea."

"Do you want me to keep on reading or not?"

"Of course," he says, stroking her white thigh. "Go on."

"It says that when the man exceeds the woman in point of size, that is the highest union."

"So what are we?"

"I am the deer, and you are the horse."

"I would rather be the elephant."

"Shut up."

Her hair keeps falling in front of her face, and she keeps pushing it back with one hand. It is not quite long enough to stay behind her ear.

Suddenly, like an alarm bell, the phone on the night table rings, low and long, shattering the silence. "Shit," says Harry, rolling over on his side with the speed of a guilty conscience.

"Darling," he exclaims too loudly. "I'm so sorry I haven't called. It's been crazy."

He sits on the edge of the bed, his naked back to Claire. A narrow expanse of white sheet separating them, an impassable boundary.

"No, no," he says. "I was just taking a little nap. How are you? How's Johnny? Tell me all the news."

Claire sits there frozen, initially too terrified to move. She can barely breathe. It is almost as though Maddy is on the other side of the door. But he doesn't even turn around once to put a finger to his lips or otherwise ask for silence. Or even to acknowledge her. It is as though she doesn't exist. They are no longer in the same room, on the same bed, in the same world. No longer lovers on the verge of intercourse. Or maybe, like Lot's wife, he doesn't want to look back and be turned into a pillar of salt.

She keeps staring at his back, unsure of what to do. For a moment she considers making a noise to elicit a reaction from him, even if it is one of horror. It would be so easy. A word. A sound. A slammed door. It would all unravel. It would be that easy. But she does not.

Instead she lies there listening to his domestic intimacies, her back against the pillow, deciding whether she should pull the sheet up to cover herself or not. She stares at her toes, at the clock and the now-forgotten book that had promised so much just a short time before.

"I'll be home on Friday," he says. "Yes, yes. I love you too. And I miss you too. Give a big kiss from me to Johnny. *Ciao bellissima.*" His little joke.

He replaces the phone in the cradle but continues sitting there motionless, his face to the wall.

She can wait no longer. A line has been breached, a moment shattered. She says nothing and instead quickly gets out of bed and goes to the bathroom, closing the door behind her. A few moments later she emerges, clothed, her hair hastily brushed. She stops, pauses as though about to say something but doesn't. Her heart is racing.

Finally he turns. "What are you doing?" he asks.

"I need some air. I'll be back later," she says. She takes her coat and rushes out of the room. The big, heavy doors are too well-balanced to slam.

"Wait! Come back," he cries, but it's too late. She doesn't hear the rest, if there is anything. Would he follow? She can picture him struggling with his pants, searching for his socks. She walks faster.

She passes through the hotel lobby and finds herself on the street, slipping into the culture. There is something familiar, comfortable even, about the signs in the store windows, the words on the newspapers, the overheard snatches of conversation of the pedestrians. It is not foreign to her. Like a mermaid, she is able to live in both sea and air.

A light rain falls. Already it is growing dark. The rain mingles with her tears. She is furious at Harry. Furious that he would answer the phone when they were about to make love, furious that he would ignore her so completely, furious that he could sound so easy and natural with Maddy, furious with herself for her betrayal of Maddy, and furious at the position in which she now finds herself.

She walks through traffic to the Tuileries. The benches are empty. The gravel crunches underfoot. The world is going home. In the twilit distance, the elegant ponderousness of the

Louvre, lights burning from its myriad windows. I am a fool, she thinks. This is a car that is heading for the cliff. Do I jump out now or do I stay in?

After an hour she returns, her hair soaked. The doorman smiles in greeting.

"*Mademoiselle,*" says the front desk clerk.

"*Oui?*"

"Monsieur Winslow left you a message in case you came back before he did."

He hands her an envelope of heavy paper with the hotel's crest printed on the back, and she opens it. The note reads: *Went to find you. If you get back before I do, wait in room. Sorry. X Harry.*

She returns to their room. Like a murder scene, it is exactly as she left it, the sheets rumpled, the pillows dented. The Kama Sutra lying where it fell.

A quarter of an hour later, Harry returns. "Thank God," he says, striding up to her and embracing her. His arms and face are still wet with rain. "I was worried. What the hell did you do that for?"

"I'm sorry. Maddy's call freaked me out."

"Well, it freaked me out too," he replies with a laugh, taking off his coat.

She lets out a little half smile. "I hadn't thought about that. Of course it would bother you. It was just that we were having this special moment, and all of a sudden, you switch off, and you were talking with Maddy, and it was like you had forgotten me completely. I'd never felt so alone in my life."

"I understand. But Maddy's my wife. I do love her."

She looks down. "I know."

"And it would be damn odd for me to go away on a trip and not speak to her. We don't want her getting suspicious. That would ruin everything."

She nods her head. "I know."

He kisses her, and she lets him. Her anger has passed but not the fear. "Your hands are freezing," he says. "Do you want me to order some tea from room service?"

She smiles up at him. She has never wanted, needed him more. "No, I have a better idea," she says, pulling him toward the bed. "And this time don't answer the phone."

THAT NIGHT, AROUND EIGHT, THEY ARE IN A TAXI HEADING TO THE Marais, leaving the glittering lights and privileged streets of the Premier Arrondissement. It is an unfashionable neighborhood, the streets narrow. This is the Paris of cheap hotels and peeling posters. The taxi stops in front of a nondescript restaurant. Its simple façade paneled in dark wood, the interior concealed by red-and-white-checked curtains. On the window the words RESTAURANT A LA CARTE FOIE GRAS A LA MODE DES LANDES.

"Don't be put off by the way the place looks," he says, as he holds the door for her.

They enter. The room is well-lit but dingy. There are only twenty or so tables, but every one is occupied. In the corner Claire thinks she recognizes a famous film star. She looks again and realizes she was right.

They sit. The waiter presents the menus. "It's practically impossible to get a reservation here," Harry says. He orders champagne.

"What is this place?" she whispers.

"The best restaurant in Paris. Maybe the world."

"You're kidding."

"Nope."

"Why is everything about the best with you?"

He takes a sip of champagne. "As Oscar Wilde said, I have the simplest tastes. I am always satisfied with the best. Well, actually, I think it's the best, and so do a lot of other people. It also horrifies just as many others. You won't find it in the Michelin guide, that's for sure. As you can tell, they don't spend a lot on their decor. But the food is amazing."

"So what makes it so good?"

"The secret is fat, if you want the truth. And ingredients."

"What do you mean?"

"Most restaurants in Paris these days are mindful of the fact that their clientele cares about their weight. Not this place. This place is a heart attack waiting to happen."

"That's good?"

"It is when you taste the food. There are many different kinds of cuisines in France. Some are about oil, some are about butter, this place is about fat. They make the best roast chicken in the world here, which we are going to order by the way. The skin is covered in crackling hot fat. The chicken is a Coucou de Rennes, which are the best in the world. They also have the best foie gras I've ever tasted. It comes direct from Aquitaine. I don't know if you noticed but on the window outside it says 'foie gras des Landes.'"

"I guess."

"Well, anyway, 'des Landes' means it comes from Landes in Aquitaine. Again, the best. You can't find any other foie gras in Paris to compare. So, you see, ingredients."

"So we're ordering the foie gras?"

"You bet."

The waiter returns. They order the foie gras and chicken, as well as a galette of potatoes. From the wine list Harry selects a Gevrey-Chambertin.

"Get ready to feast," he says. "The potatoes are purely superfluous, but they're so damn good I can't help myself."

They drink the champagne. The foie gras arrives. Three pink slabs streaked with yellow fat. Slices of toasted baguette. A block of unsalted butter.

"You're going to turn me into a fat pig." She slathers the foie gras and butter on the warm toast, melting, merging them together. She sighs. "This might just be the best thing I've ever tasted."

"Isn't it?" he says, grinning at their mutual pleasure. "Americans never get really good foie gras. The stuff they ship over is full of preservatives. This is the real thing."

They finish the foie gras. Greedily, she uses the last piece of bread to wipe the remainder from the plate.

"Save some room," he says.

"I'm sorry. I can't help it."

The chicken comes out. Brown and glistening, fat dripping off the skin. Beside it, the potatoes, sliced and layered, steamed and fried before being baked in duck fat and garnished with garlic.

"This is insanely good," she says, taking a bite.

"I know. You couldn't eat here every night though."

"It makes me understand why people get fat. They need to. A small person couldn't possibly consume all this food even though I want to. If I was fat I'd have more room."

"I forgot how big the chickens are here."

"I know. It's enough to feed a family of four."

"I don't think I can finish."

"No way. I can't either. If I have another bite, I'll explode."

"We'll get it to go. I know it's considered bad form, but I can't leave this behind. It's too good."

They leave the restaurant hand in hand. The street is cold, the wind whirling pieces of paper through the air. Storefronts are shuttered. They pass a nearly empty café. A few cars drive by, a motorcycle. There are no taxis. They walk west, in the direction of their hotel. The noise from televisions blares from behind curtained windows.

"It's too far to walk," he says. "Don't worry. We'll come across a taxi soon."

"Oh, I don't mind. I need to walk off some of that meal. Thank you, by the way."

"For what?"

"For this, for everything. For the best days of my life and the best meal. God, now you have me using that word."

Other couples pass them on the sidewalk. A taxi drives past. Harry almost doesn't see it. He whistles and shouts, and it comes to an abrupt halt. They pile in and give the address of their hotel. The lights of Paris are shining only for them. There is no other reality. They are here, now. Lovers in Paris. They are like gods living in secret among mortals. They are all who matter. The outside world does not exist. The world for them is this France, this Paris, this room, this bed.

9

THEIR LAST DAY. THE BOULEVARDS ARE SLICK WITH RAIN. Wearing only panties, she is sitting on the bed reading the newspaper and eating an orange. Stacking the rind neatly in a pile. He is at the desk, typing.

The room is peaceful. A simulacrum of domesticity. On the table a tray with empty coffee cups. The remains of breakfast. Her plane leaves this afternoon. His is not until evening.

She sighs.

"Are you all right?"

"I just don't want it to end, you know? To go back to reality. I don't mean staying in the Ritz. I mean being together. I don't know when I'll see you again."

"I know." He walks over to the bed and sits next to her. She takes a wedge of orange and feeds it to him. "It doesn't have to end," he says, placing his hand on her thigh.

"Can you make that promise?" Her eyes are wide, searching his. "I want to believe you."

"Yes, I can."

She nods. "It's too much to ask."

"Can't we just try this for a bit more? What if you get tired of me? What if you meet someone younger? It's not like I'm in a position to complain."

"I don't want anyone else."

"You say that now. Once my hair and teeth fall out you may think twice," he says with a laugh. "I'm a lot older than you. You don't want to be changing my colostomy bag at dinner parties."

"Nonsense. You'll be one of those devastating older men."

"You're right. I could become incontinent. That's pretty devastating."

"Stop," she says, hitting him with a pillow. "You're making me laugh again, and I don't feel much like laughing."

"That's ridiculous. How can you not feel like laughing? Remember, laughter's the best medicine. Have you ever been to a funeral? Nothing people like better than an old friend of the deceased telling wildly inappropriate stories."

They are like children on a cruise ship. Somewhere over the horizon is the port where they have to get off. For now they are only pretending.

I have often wondered what was going through Harry's mind during these days. Was there ever guilt or remorse? It is as though he didn't have a wife or a child. Had he forgotten their years together, the shared laughter, the shared pain, the people whose lives they had touched, whose lives he and Claire could ruin? What direction was he taking? Did he think that he could maintain this affair without Maddy knowing? Did he even want to?

WHAT I FIND SO PUZZLING ABOUT HARRY'S BEHAVIOR IS HOW natural he was about it. It was as though he was a born adulterer. It is possible that sort of thing comes more easily to some men, especially writers, actors, or spies, those who become so used to inhabiting other personas, other lives, that they lose touch with the one life that really matters.

Some men, I imagine, would have felt pangs of guilt, or at least some anxiety. They would have been scared of being caught. Their deception exposed, their home life broken upon the rack.

But it was easy for Harry. Maybe he didn't think life possessed real pain or real tests. Things just came to him. I suppose he was struggling with his new book, but, after all, wasn't that part of the creative process? Weren't artists supposed to suffer? In some ways it seemed unfair. He who already had so much and wasn't satisfied with that. For so much of his life, he had only to put out his hand and whatever he wanted was there. True, he had never had much money, but that never seemed to matter. He had something more important, namely the ability to inspire love. Was it such a surprise, then, that he had inspired Claire? After all, who hadn't loved him? Dogs, fellow students, friends, readers, strangers in bars. He had collected love the way a car accumulates miles. What was a surprise was that, having inspired love, he wanted it back.

Even in college he had been the hero, the beloved, and yet it was Madeleine he had cleaved to. She was the one who needed him most, and he had pledged himself to a sacred trust. Perhaps he sensed something broken in Maddy, something only he could fix, and, knowing that, he permitted himself to give himself to her utterly. I am not saying he didn't love her. I believe he did. I know he did. But she needed him, or someone like him. And I don't think he truly needed anyone, at least not in the same way. He was always a self-contained unit, someone so supremely confident in his own abilities that he never once questioned them. He had never needed to. I know he worked hard, but it was the work that a gifted athlete puts into his training regimen. It helps to elevate his game, a game that most of us could never hope to play and never pretend we could.

Had he sensed something in Claire he could fix, something that only he could provide? Or was it something more selfish? Was she someone who was only for him? After years of being someone everyone else thought he was, or should be, was he now allowing himself to take what he wanted, even if it meant destroying everything else?

Of course, it's never anything so abstract. His betrayal was as natural as a disease, as a cancer that builds up quietly inside the body and then erupts unbidden when there is nothing else to keep it in check. And when it happened, it consumed him.

And Claire? I have never held her to blame, even if some think I should. She was a young woman, beautiful, sensitive, and impressionable. Alive. Tapping life to the roots. In need of love, or attention, or direction. Or all three. I am not sure which.

How could she not be dazzled by Harry? He was handsome, successful, charming. She might as well have been asked not to feel the grass under her feet or taste the salt of the sea. It would have been like telling a moth to resist a candle, or telling a flower not to bloom. No, the one I blame is Harry. He, the schoolboy hero, the ex-Marine, he is the one who lacked courage and dedication. It is easy to tempt, but only the truly strong can resist. He should have been able to but he, paragon that he was, was weak.

I could describe even more how they fucked, how she sucked his cock, how many orgasms she had, how they walked through streets hand in hand like true lovers. How they kindled passion in each other, passion for life, passion for love, passion that burned only for passion's sake. After all, that is selfishness and greed. Wanting more than is good for one. And they devoured it, exulted in it. Who can blame them? There are few things more powerful, more intoxicating than knowing there is someone who desires you utterly. And if it is illicit, secret, forbidden, that makes it all the more exciting. Who cares at that point about other people? Others don't matter when it is just the two of you in your own little lifeboat. Desire is all. Shame does not figure into it.

She wanted him, and he wanted her. Beauty enraptures you, sex defines you, the simplest things become objects of envy to others. When one is on fire, one burns. It is impossible not to. It is elementary physics. Even a child could understand that. It is so simple.

But fire has no qualms. It burns everything, regardless of what is in its path.

WINTER

1

VICTOR HUGO WROTE THAT THE SUPREME HAPPINESS OF LIFE is the conviction that we are loved, but that conviction is based on an assumption of such love. If we are proven to be wrong, the void left behind is often filled by resentment and rage. Hugo could also have written that the supreme unhappiness of life is discovering we are not loved. It is one thing if we already suspect the absence of love in our life, but what truly crushes us is finding out that the love we cherished was a lie.

I arrive in Rome a week before Christmas. Coming from New York, I am surprised by how mild the weather is. Even though the Romans are bundled up in coats and scarves—no one knows how to wear a scarf like an Italian—they still sit outside in the cafés except on the coldest days. I travel light, knowing that everything I need, I can buy there.

My first night we all go to see the nativity scene outside of

St. Peter's. The huge square is jammed with people, Romans and tourists alike, nuns from Africa, businessmen, families, shopgirls on their way home from work, coming to admire this grandest of crèches. Harry is carrying Johnny on his shoulders. The floodlit façade and street hawkers selling pictures of the Pope lend the whole scene a carnival air. After, we go for dinner at the restaurant on S. Ignazio. Despite the brightly lit streets and the jostling, happy crowds chattering back and forth in Italian, our little group is subdued. Maddy is remote, Harry preoccupied. Neither of them seems to have much appetite. After we finish talking about mutual friends back in New York, the conversation falters. Johnny is already asleep, his head resting on his mother's lap.

Back in the apartment, I ask Maddy, "What's the matter?"

Johnny has been put to bed, and Harry, too, has said good night. It is just us. There is a fire going. My jet lag has left me. A bottle of red wine has appeared. Two glasses.

"What do you mean?"

"Is everything all right?"

"Of course. Why do you ask?"

"Well, I ask because things seemed strained. I don't know what's happening, but I've never seen Harry or you so distracted."

"We're fine. It's hard adjusting to a new city sometimes. You know how it is. The language. The customs. Plus, Harry can get moody when he's writing. It's a lot of work, and he's been having trouble sleeping. And he's been traveling too much, which hasn't helped."

"And that's it?"

"That's it."

But that is not it. I know Maddy well enough to know when she is avoiding something.

"Okay." I smile. "If you don't want to talk about it, that's fine. I'll be here for a week. We have lots of time."

"Oh shut up, Walter," she says, playfully. "If I had anything to talk about, I'd tell you. You know that."

"When I saw Harry in New York the other month, he said he was having a hard time with the book."

"Yes, it's true, I suppose." And then, "Maybe it wasn't such a good idea to come to Rome."

"Can't you leave if you want?"

"We could, but we made a commitment. There are the people who awarded Harry the money, the people who own this apartment, the people who rented our place in New York, Johnny's school. And then there's Harry. I know he'd never want to say that being in Rome caused him problems. He'd hate the idea of giving in like that."

"Naturally."

YOU HAVE TO REMEMBER I HAD NO IDEA WHAT WAS REALLY going on. Neither, of course, did Maddy. If anyone had asked if we thought Harry was capable of having an affair, we would have laughed in their face. You may as well have asked if he was building a thermonuclear reactor in the basement. The notion was inconceivable.

But all too often we find out that the people in whom we had the most faith are capable of deceiving us. The newspapers are filled with stories of bankers, politicians, priests, and athletes who cheat their clients, have affairs, abuse altar boys, or use steroids. The regularity of these exposures may have caused them to lose the power to shock. We live in an age when we are no longer surprised that people let us down. The only surprise is that we are so constantly willing to allow ourselves to be deceived.

Sometimes we are betrayed by friends. One of my grandfathers had been in the CIA. He served in the OSS during World War II and later in Washington. He befriended an Englishman, a fellow spy. The Englishman was a regular at my grandparents' house in Georgetown. They'd go on fishing trips, swap trade secrets over glasses of bourbon, secure in the knowledge they were both on the same side, fighting a common enemy. Until, of course, it was discovered that the Englishman was a Soviet mole, recruited at Cambridge before the war, and that he had been feeding back Western secrets, some of which doubtless came from my grandfather, for decades. It's a famous story. The revelation not only ended my grandfather's career but, more important, destroyed his faith in others. It turned him despondent, paranoid, miserable; the pain of the treachery was too great for him to stand. Because he was a spy himself, deception was a way of life, but it stung all the more when he was the deceived. It was a blessing when he died a few years later. The Englishman lived until a ripe old age in an apartment in Moscow, a decorated full colonel in the KGB. It was in all the newspapers.

Then there are the betrayals we choose to ignore. Toward the end of his life Maddy's father had a girlfriend, Diana, whom he had been dating for a decade or so. She was beautiful, a widow who worked at Sotheby's. They never married, but traveled constantly, dining out in the best restaurants. But he was living a double life; there were other women, just how many I never found out. There was a pattern. Every few years he would disappear for days or weeks at a time on a bender, washing up at the Waldorf or the Plaza Athénée until Maddy could track him down and take him to the emergency room. There he would hover between life and death for a week or two before invariably, impossibly pulling through yet again. His once-powerful body ravaged by years of self-abuse, his feet with their unclipped toenails protruding from under the sheets, and still, in his lucid moments, able to use his matchless charm on the nurses. Diana would disappear at these moments. Some might say she had every right to do so, that she didn't want to enable him, that he deserved to be punished. But I think her refusal to visit him in the hospital was more about self-preservation than self-righteousness. Seeing him in the hospital would have forced her to confront the reality of the situation, and she could never bring herself to do that, knowing full well that, once his strength had returned, he would only go out and do it again.

Another betrayal is the kind we perpetrate ourselves. It is one thing to be lied to, but it is something else again to be the liar. But even then, most of us don't look at it like that. We make up our own excuses, justifying the betrayal, clothing it in nobler raiment. It is easy to pretend that maintaining a lie is in the best interest of those we might hurt, supreme in the confidence that we will never get caught. Of all deceptions, that is the most common and the most foolish—and the one for which people have the least sympathy.

During the winter after my Christmas visit, Maddy sent me e-mails and told me Harry was often away for several days at a time. He was meeting with a publisher, giving a talk in Barcelona, back to Paris for a literary conference. I found this surprising because, before they went to Rome, it had been unthinkable for them to spend a night apart. But he was a success now, and I supposed such things came with the territory. Maddy wasn't worried. At least not about their relationship. There was no hint of concern, except she and Johnny missed him, and when he returned from his trips, he was often irritable, locking himself away in his study for hours or disappearing on long rambles through the city and never asking her to join him.

In February, I called Claire again, missing Maddy, and looking for someone who shared my affection for her. I hadn't seen or spoken to Claire in months, but thought if she were available, she would be willing to put up with me for a night as long as I could promise her a decent meal and agreeable conversation. It was good to hear her voice after so long, and we made a plan. But the next day, she called me back to change it.

"Walter," she said. "I'm so sorry to do this to you, but I have to take a rain check on dinner tomorrow."

"That's quite all right," I said. "Is everything okay?"

"Yes, yes. Everything's fine. I just found that I have to fly to Paris tomorrow for work. I hope you don't mind."

"Not at all," I said. "I understand completely."

Only later did I register that Maddy had said Harry was making a quick trip to Paris as well. His second since December. In New York we think that flying to Paris is such an undertaking, but really, when one is living in Rome, it's no more than a trip to Long Island. A direct flight is only two hours, after all. And the price these days is nothing. I remember marveling at my English friends who would jet off to Verbier or Gstaad for a weekend of skiing. For them it was practically next door.

I nearly called Claire back to tell her Harry would also be in Paris and she should look him up. But then I thought better of it. I was sure they both already had plans and the last thing they would want to do would be to race around Paris trying to have a quick drink together. There's nothing more boring than an obligation drink, something quick, early in the evening, when the other person keeps looking at their watch because they have to dash off to something else.

WHEN HARRY RETURNS FROM THAT PARIS TRIP IT IS LATE. He enters the apartment expecting, hoping that everyone will be asleep. A single light burns in the living room and he goes to turn it off. But the room is not empty. Maddy is sitting there, staring out into the black Roman night, the ghost of her face reflected in the window. A glass of red wine sits in front of her.

"I thought you'd be in bed," he says.

"How was Paris?" She does not look at him. Her face is still turned toward the window, her voice neutral, contained.

"Fine. You know how it is. It's less fun being there when it's all about work. I never thought I'd get bored of Paris, you know?"

She doesn't respond. He is standing in the middle of the room, not advancing toward her as he normally would, sensing danger like an animal.

Finally she looks at him. "Harry, what's going on?"

"What do you mean?" He begins to walk boldly to her, the best offense, smiling, his hands outstretched.

She recoils from him, and his hand stops just short of her shoulder. "Don't."

"What's the matter?"

Still seated, she whips her head around to look at him. He has never seen her so angry. Not a screaming, violent anger. Something worse. Something cold and hard and withering. Her eyes are two pieces of cobalt.

"Are you having an affair?"

"What? Of course not." He tries to sound surprised, as though the very idea were ridiculous. "Why . . ."

"Don't lie to me," she shouts, standing suddenly, cutting him off. A single index finger, thrust out like a knife. "I am warning you. Never, ever lie to me."

"Can you please explain to me just what the hell is going on?"

She glares at him. "Nina Murray e-mailed me. She said she saw you in Paris last night having dinner with a young girl."

It had been in a little bistro near the hotel. The concierge had recommended it. Harry thought he had recognized a familiar face in a group of Americans on the far side of the restaurant but only now was he sure. Nina Murray and her husband, Burt. She was a plain woman. Their daughter had been in Johnny's class. He barely knew them. She and Maddy had been better friends.

"That's right," he lies. "I had dinner with Michelle, the head of marketing at my French publisher."

She looks at him evenly. "Just dinner? You aren't sleeping with her?"

"No, I am not sleeping with her." And then he sits opposite her. "I love you."

"Do you?" she asks, softening, wanting to believe him. "I used to think so. But lately I haven't been so sure."

He takes her hands in his. "I'm sorry. I have been very self-ish. Traveling so much. Working on my book. I didn't think how hard it might be for you and Johnny."

She sits back and sighs, withdrawing her hands. "I don't know what to think."

"It's okay. Maybe it wasn't such a good idea coming to Rome. When we talked about it last year it did, you know? But the book isn't coming along well. And now all this traveling is taking me away from you so much."

"Maybe. It's just that ever since Nina e-mailed me, I have been sitting here thinking about you having an affair and thinking how it all made so much sense. You've been gone so much, and when you're home, you've been irritable. Isn't that what men do at your age? Hit middle age, buy sports cars, screw twenty-year-old girls, leave their wives."

"Not all of us."

She looks as though she is about to cry. "Maybe you're right. Maybe Rome wasn't a good idea. I don't know. Can we do anything about it? Can we go back to New York?"

"I'll look into it in the morning. Come on. It's late. Time for bed."

He holds out his hand, and she accepts it, lifting herself to her feet. She is precious to him at this moment.

In bed, they make love. Silently, sweetly. Her kisses pas-sionate. They know each other's bodies well. When it is over, he washes in the sink. For the first night in months, they lie in each other's arms, her head on his bare chest. He is asleep. She closes her eyes, but stays awake for a long time.

2

LIFE IS A SERIES OF REMEMBERED IMPRESSIONS. A SMELL, A touch, a sunset, carved angels in a cathedral, the death of a parent. We cannot take in everything we see, so we make sense of what we can, using these fragments to make up a whole. Patterns emerge, sometimes randomly; sometimes they mislead. Sometimes they reveal the truth.

Around this time Maddy e-mailed me a video she had taken of Johnny and Harry skating in Rome. During the winter, an outdoor rink is set up in the shadow of Castel Sant'Angelo, burial place of emperors. Harry and Johnny are skating easily clockwise around the rink, free as birds. Every time they pass, they stop and wave, smiling at the camera. The sky is white behind them. Other faces occasionally fill the screen: children holding on to the edge, young girls, pure faces surmounted by woolen caps, snatches of Italian from their mouths as they pass by. In the center of the ice, a young man is showing off, spinning and twirling. A light snow is falling. Everyone looks so happy.

It took several weeks for Harry and Maddy to extricate themselves from Rome. Arrangements had to be made, but it was easier than they had thought. They agreed to pay their landlords the remainder of the rent. The prize committee was understanding and regretted that the Winslows had to leave but did not penalize them. They had had other families leave early. Artists—they shrugged—need to be where they can work best. The tenants in New York were unhappy, but a clause in the contract gave the Winslows the option to revoke the lease early with thirty days' notice. Even Johnny's old school was cooperative, permitting him to return so late in the year. If he needed extra help to catch up with the rest of the class, the Winslows would have to hire a tutor. Harry stopped traveling.

I had been surprised to hear they would be returning within the month. It seemed out of character, but I also knew how important home was to both of them. Maddy e-mailed to tell me they would be back sometime in March. I was, of course, overjoyed. I even offered to let them stay with me in my small apartment (I never needed anything more). That's when she told me their tenants were leaving. She made no mention of what Nina Murray had told her.

Carelessness is the handmaiden to tragedy. Cataclysmic events often have their origins in the mundane. We turn left when we had meant to go right, and the world changes forever.

It happens in late February. It is only a matter of days before they were to leave Rome. Maddy has rushed out to the *macelleria* near their apartment to purchase chops for dinner. It is almost five, and the shop is about to close. Harry is out for one of his walks. He will not be back for hours. In her hurry, she has taken his credit card, which he had left on the front hall table. When she tries to pay with it, the cashier tells her it has been declined. He is apologetic. He tries again, but the response is the same. Embarrassed, she leaves the shop empty-handed even though the butcher insists she could come back and pay tomorrow. She has been a good customer, after all. These things happen.

But not to her. Every quarter, the trustees at her bank deposit money into her account. And she is good with money, never spending too much, keeping track of her withdrawals, always knowing to the penny what is available. For years she and Harry had lived off her income, with his officer's salary supplementing where it could. When his book became a success, he was able to pay for more things on his own, but they had always maintained separate accounts. He had been very proud of finally being financially independent. But she knows money flows through his fingers like water. He is generous, yet irresponsible to a fault. That is one of the reasons they kept their accounts separate.

She returns home, an agonizing suspicion gripping her. In a drawer in his office, jammed in the back, she finds unopened bills from his credit card company. She opens the most recent one and is shocked to see the balance. There are hotels in Paris, restaurants, and airfare. She had assumed the publisher had paid for all his trips. Then she spots the name of a famous shop on the Faubourg Saint-Honoré. The date is from his first trip to Paris. It is for several thousand dollars. She knows that whatever was purchased had not been for her. Then she opens another envelope from the credit card company. It contains a notice requesting immediate payment; failure to comply will result in suspension or termination of privileges.

Maddy closes her eyes. She can't think, can barely breathe. She places her hand on the table to keep herself upright. The truth rushes in on her. With a scream she rips the envelopes in half and then heaves Harry's desk over with a loud crash. Papers flying everywhere. The laptop smashing on the floor.

"Bastard!" she yells. "Bastard!"

The noise brings Johnny and the maid running. "Mommy, are you okay?" asks Johnny. The child peers nervously from behind the door.

"Signora, stai bene?"

"Sì, bene, bene," Maddy answers, struggling to regain her composure.

"Johnny, darling, Mommy's fine."

"What happened to Daddy's desk?"

She kneels down and hugs her son, to reassure herself as much as him. "It's nothing, darling. You know how you feel when you get angry, and sometimes you just want to hit something? Sometimes mommies get angry like that too."

"You're crying."

"I know. I know. It's okay, sweetheart."

She knows what she has to do. To the maid she says: *"Angela, per favore, impacchettare vai valigia di Johnny. Siamo in partenza stasera."* We are leaving tonight. *"E la sua medicina."* And his medicine.

"Per quanto tempo?"

"Non lo so." I don't know.

The maid says nothing. She can read the signs. She has

been married, has brothers, uncles. Roman men don't even try to be discreet. Taking Johnny with her, she goes to pack.

Maddy hurries to her room and pulls a suitcase from under the bed. She throws in a few important things—jewelry, underwear, warm sweaters—and removes their passports from her bureau. Her cell phone. American dollars. She can't stop to think. If she did, she might not have the courage.

"Where are we going, Mommy?" asks Johnny.

"We're going home, darling. To New York," she answers. She hadn't known the answer herself until just that moment, but it seems the only possible response.

"What about Daddy? Isn't he coming too?"

"He'll come later. We need to go now."

The old woman says nothing but picks up Maddy's bag and carries it down the stairs to the street. *"Stronzo,"* she mutters under her breath. Asshole.

Maddy takes Johnny's bag and her purse, giving the apartment a last look before closing the door. There is nothing she wants to remember. She does not leave a note. Maybe she will send one later. Harry should be able to figure out for himself what happened. Or not. Right now she doesn't really care.

On the street she runs to a cash machine and withdraws the daily limit. She hands five hundred euros to Angela. "I will send more later. *Io manderò più tardi.*" Then she gives her a hug. *"Mi dispiace molto.* Thank you for everything. *Mille grazie."*

Angela has hailed a taxi, and the driver has already put their bags in the trunk. She kisses Johnny, her eyes ringed with tears, pressing his small form to her. *"Addio bel ragazzo."*

It is time to leave. Maddy doesn't want to start crying again. "Leonardo da Vinci airport, *per favore,*" she says. They will buy tickets there. Johnny huddles close to her in the car. "When will Daddy join us?"

"Shhh," she says. "Soon, sweetheart. Don't worry."

The industrial suburbs flash by as in a dream. She inspects small things. The back of the driver's seat. The veins on her hand. The strands of hair on her son's head. The thin fibers mesmerize her. It is the same as when her father used to beat her; she would stare at his shoes, fascinated by the pattern of the seams, the grains, the texture of the leather, pushing out the pain. Johnny sings softly to himself an Italian nursery rhyme he had learned in school: *"Farfallina, bella e bianca, vola vola, mai si stanca, gira qua, e gira la poi si resta sopra un fiore, e poi si resta spora un fiore."* He flutters his hands together like the wings of a butterfly.

At the airport she pays the driver, and they enter the vast departures hall, a testament to postmodernist architecture. She sees the logos of many airlines. Royal Air Maroc. Air China. Air Malta. TAP. The endless possibilities. The chance to start over completely, randomly. Pick a place on the map blindfolded and go there. But that is too much. She knows what she wants, where she needs to go. She sees the same American carrier that brought them over. Walking to the ticket counter, she asks the agent for the next flight to New York.

"I am sorry, *signora*," he says in excellent English. "There are no more flights this evening. The next is tomorrow morning at six. But nothing until then." Maddy has forgotten that there are no flights to the United States this time of day. It wouldn't have made a difference.

"Grazie, signore," says Maddy. She shoulders Johnny's bag and grabs the handle of her roller bag. "Come on, sweetheart. We need to go try a different airline."

The news is the same at the British Airways counter. There are no more direct flights this time of night. They would be happy of course to book the *signora* tickets for tomorrow morning. What time would she like to leave?

"How about London?" she asks. "Are there any flights left to London tonight?"

"*Sì, signora.* There is a flight at 20:25. It gets in at 22:25."

"I'll take it," she says, handing over her American Express card and their passports. "And can you book me on a connecting flight from Heathrow to JFK tomorrow? Both one-way."

"Of course. What class would you prefer?"

"Business, please."

"*Bene.* You are booked on the 20:25 to London Heathrow. Your flight tomorrow leaves at 15:05 from Heathrow, arriving in New York at 18:10, eastern standard time. Would you like to check your bags?"

"*Sì.* Thank you." She places first her bag and then Johnny's on the scale. Her hand trembles as she writes their names and New York address on the luggage tags. They have never flown without Harry.

"*Prego.* Here are your tickets. Present them at the British Airways Executive Club on the second floor of Terminal C. The agents there can help facilitate your passage through security."

In the lounge Maddy finds a quiet area for Johnny to sit among the well-dressed executives chatting urgently in many languages or staring intently into the brightness of laptops. She hands Johnny his Game Boy and says she'll be right back. "I have to go talk to the concierge, sweetheart."

She asks the concierge to book a hotel room for them tonight in London. Does the *signora* have a preference? It has been a long time since Maddy stayed in a hotel in London. They usually stay with friends, but she doesn't feel up to that right now. She remembers a hotel where she once stayed with her grandmother. It was charming, discreet, on a cul-de-sac off St. James's. She doesn't know if it is still there. The concierge affirms that not only is it still in business but it has availability for tonight. A deluxe king room. The price more than seven hundred dollars.

"Fine," sighs Maddy. "We'll take it."

Returning to where Johnny is sitting, she looks at her phone. She had purposely put it on silent mode. She sees several missed calls from Harry. She doesn't want to talk to him. Not now. Maybe not ever. She checks her e-mail. There are also several e-mails from him. She doesn't open them. *Where are you?* reads one of the subject lines. *Call me* reads another. She cannot. She ignores them and puts the phone back in her pocket. But it doesn't stay there. She has to think, to plan ahead. So what does she do?

She e-mails me, of course.

I am sitting in my office when her message arrives in my inbox. The subject line is *Maddy,* and it reads, *Johnny and I flying back to NYC. Arrive from London. Stay with you for few days? Thank you. Love, M.*

I immediately e-mail her back. *Mi casa su casa. U ok????*
Fill u in tom. Thx. U R an angel.

My fingers tap out *Can I do anything? Pick you up at airport?*
Not ncssry, comes the reply. *Arrive @ 6. Take taxi.*

3

And what of the third person in this drama? Naturally I don't include myself. I am merely the amanuensis. What of Claire?

I am filling in details I learned only later. When she is not with Harry, she lives her normal life. He had told her he would not be able to see her for a few weeks, and that he and Maddy would be returning to New York sooner than originally planned. She was excited but also nervous. How would this proximity change their relationship? Would she be able to see him more? Or less? It was a question she ignored, like a crack in the ceiling, knowing that at some point, it would have to be addressed. So she waited.

Waking early while it is still dark. Showering, selecting clothes, underwear. Riding the subway to work. Alone in her thoughts, in her bed. Spending the day on the computer, attending meetings, making phone calls, lunching at her desk or maybe with a colleague, writing e-mails and articles. At night there are yoga classes or dinners with friends. She is popular, as she would be. Pretty girls and ironic young men in narrow suits. Restaurants in Tribeca, Williamsburg. Parties and openings.

The days pass waiting for Harry to call and tell her about their next adventure. She keeps a bag packed by the door. She is content, wrapping herself in a secret, her unguessed-at other life. Hoping for something none of them really wants. Terrified of the consequences but doing nothing to forestall them.

To everyone else she is a single woman. At a dinner party one night, she is seated next to an architect. The hostess, an old friend of hers from college now married, had told her about him. He is about her age, handsome. White teeth. He has sensitive fingers and an easy laugh. He has just come back from Shanghai. It is his third trip there. The city is growing like an anthill, he says. His firm is very busy. The incredible wealth, the drive to create a new future. He is studying Mandarin. Halfway through dinner, it is understood that he will take her home. On the stoop he kisses her. There is a light rain. Can I come up? he asks. She bites her lip, avoiding his eyes. Her hand rests warmly on his chest.

"I'd like to but I can't," she says.

"Is there someone else?"

She nods her head. "I'm sorry."

"I understand," he says. "I had fun anyway."

She watches him walk off into the night, turning around and waving at her from the corner. In the taxi, she had decided she would sleep with him but had then changed her mind. For a moment, she almost calls after him.

Why doesn't she? Why shouldn't she take her pleasure

where she finds it? Why does she deny herself? Does she think that being loyal will swing the balance in her favor or even exonerate her? A sacrifice to appease the gods? That somehow, miraculously, a small act on her part, like pulling petals off a daisy or avoiding cracks on the sidewalk, will make things turn out all right? No, she knows by now that it cannot. It is too late. Whatever happens will be terrible for at least one of them, maybe for everyone. Like a sailor in a storm, she prays for dry land.

She is at work when his e-mail comes. The subject line reads *Maddy knows*. A momentary horror grips her. Her hand cups her mouth as she screams silently. She stares dumbly at the screen. Disbelieving the words, reading them several times. She opens the e-mail, fearful of what she will see, but there is nothing more. The lack of information makes it even worse.

What does Maddy "know"? How much does she know? She e-mails him back. *Are you sure? What happened? Where are you?* Her words disappearing into the void, uncertain of a response. There is none. She waits. Five minutes. Ten. It is torture. She sends another e-mail with simply the subject line *Hello?* but, like pulling up a lifeline that has been severed, there is nothing at the other end.

She cannot stay at her desk. She needs to get outside, walk, escape. "I have to go," she tells her editor. "I'll be back later." On her way out, she stops in the ladies' room and throws up.

It is late when she returns home. She stares at her reflection in the mirror. Her eyes look haunted. Her face pale. She has been checking her phone all afternoon, waiting for the familiar beep of an incoming message. The fear she felt earlier has now been replaced by anger. She feels cut off, adrift, abandoned. Why won't he write or call? It would be so easy. Just a word or two to offer comfort, information, guidance, absolution. The screen looks back blankly at her. The usual e-mails come in from colleagues, friends, but she ignores them. They are unimportant, a dinner reservation during an earthquake. Pouring a glass of wine, she puts on music and sits on the couch. She stares at the photograph of them taken on Montmartre. There is nothing else to do.

When the call comes, it is after nine, past three in the morning in Rome.

"It's me," he says.

"Why haven't you called? I've been going out of my mind."

"Me too."

"Where are you? What happened?"

"I'm in Rome." His voice is thick. She can tell he has been drinking. "Maddy's gone," he says. "She took Johnny."

"Oh my god."

He tells her about coming home. About finding his desk overturned, and Angela yelling at him, abusing him in a language he does not speak. She had been waiting to tell him what she thought of him. It wasn't hard for him to understand the gist of what she was saying. *"Sono partiti stronzo stupido. Non si poteva tenere il cazzo nei pantaloni."* They are gone, you stupid asshole. You couldn't keep your prick in your pants. She spat on the floor and slammed the door on her way out.

He called Maddy's cell, but she did not answer. He had no idea what had happened. He looked around the apartment for clues. Open drawers, empty hangers. He righted his desk and had started collecting the papers when he noticed the crumpled-up credit card bill. He closed his eyes, the enormity of his stupidity piercing him.

"I've been calling hotels, friends," he tells her. "I can't find them."

"Did you try Walter?"

"Not yet. He's my last resort."

"Could they have left Rome? Would they come back to New York?"

"I don't know. It's too late to fly to New York. They'd have to wait until morning."

"What will you say when you find them? What will you tell Maddy?"

"I don't know."

"Does she know about me?"

"I honestly don't know what she knows."

She does not respond, and for a moment there is silence on the line. "What about us?" she asks finally. It is the only question she cares about.

He sighs. "I don't know. I need to talk to Maddy first."

"Of course. I understand," she responds. A light scrim has fallen between them. It was not the answer she had hoped to hear.

"I'm sorry," he says. "This is a big mess. I need to sort it out. It's very late here. Right now, I'm tired, anxious, scared, and a little drunk. I'll call or e-mail you when I know more, okay?"

She puts down the phone. "Fuck you, Harry," she says and starts to cry.

4

I COULD BARELY SLEEP THE NIGHT MADDY TOLD ME SHE WAS coming. Partly I was excited about her staying with me. I even took the rest of the day off and rushed home shortly after her final e-mail and began tidying up, making beds, going to the market, looking for food that a nine-year-old boy might like. I bought cookies, cereal, fruit juice, popcorn. What else? We could always order in pizza if he wanted, but he'd just been living in Rome so he might not find Italian food as appealing as he otherwise might.

But I was also worried. In my e-mail in-box the next morning there were several frantic messages from Harry sent very late. Had I heard from Maddy? Did I know where she was? Where Johnny was? I stared at the screen, my insides hollow. Clearly something terrible had happened. But I didn't know what. I wavered, wondering whether to answer or not, worrying if by doing so I was somehow betraying Maddy. Finally I wrote: *Maddy and Johnny are flying to New York. She e-mailed me last night. What the hell is going on?*

There was no response though. At least nothing immediate. I could only imagine the worst.

Needless to say, I ignored Maddy's request and hired a limousine to take me to the airport so I could meet her there. I was early, of course, not wanting to risk missing them. I saw them before they saw me. Maddy looked drawn, but still beautiful, her mane of strawberry blond hair haloing her face. Johnny straggling after her like a nine-year-old refugee.

"You're too much," she says, hugging me. "I thought I told you not to bother."

"I know you did. Since when have I ever listened to you?" Then to Johnny, "Hey, tiger, how you doing?"

"I'm okay, Uncle Walt. Have you talked to Daddy?"

Maddy shoots me a look. "Why, no," I answer. I ruffle his hair and say, "Great to see you, pal. I bet you must be tired."

He nods his head and says nothing.

"You must both be tired. Let me help you with that," I say, taking the bags. Maddy is too drained to argue, which she normally would. "I have a car waiting just outside."

"Cool," says Johnny when he sees the limo. I hired a stretch. I normally find them vulgar but had hoped it would elicit that kind of response. Johnny clambers in, sits on the seat that runs along the side of the car, and begins fiddling with the glasses and decanters and different knobs and switches.

"Have you ever been in one of these before?" I ask.

"No," he says.

"God, after Europe I forgot that there even were cars this size," Maddy says with a laugh. "It's so big."

"I know. Completely ridiculous, isn't it?"

"I feel like a rock star or a prom queen," she says. Serious, she turns to me. "Thank you, Walter." She puts her hand on my knee.

"Cone of silence?" I ask.

She nods. "For now, if that's okay. Let's talk about other things. How are you? Any news?"

Taking the cue, I fill her in on the little gossip of the town, studiously avoiding any allusion to marital strife. Who's broke, who's drunk, who's come out of the closet, whose children got into Yale, whose didn't. I conducted alumni interviews with several of them. I don't know what surprised me more, how young they seemed or how hard they all worked. And not just schoolwork but community service, drama, violin lessons, summer jobs, sports. I know I never had that intensity or diligence at their age.

One of the boys I met with didn't get in, I tell Maddy. He had gone to a good school, had good grades, and seemed a personable youth. I had given him a positive review, but for some reason the powers that be in the admissions office found a reason to reject him. I tell Maddy about the angry phone call I received from the boy's father, a classmate of ours, demanding to know what happened and what was I going to do about it. I opine to Maddy that the admissions office would have probably been happy to take the boy if the father hadn't been part of the package.

"He always was a pompous ass," she says and laughs, shaking her head. I am glad to make her smile. She had looked so sepulchral getting off the plane.

We arrive at my building. I am just off Park in the 70s, not far from my parents' vast old apartment. I still get my hair cut at the same barbershop I went to as a boy. Attend the same church in which I was baptized and confirmed, patronize the same restaurants. My life is defined by the geography of my childhood. On the streets are boys from my old school wearing neckties and blazers looking eerily like me and my friends several decades earlier. Is it any wonder that I don't feel that I have really grown up yet?

One of the doormen helps us with our bags. I introduce Maddy and Johnny to him, saying, "Hector, this is Mrs. Winslow and her son. They will be staying with me for a few days." He welcomes them and tells me he will put them in the book. He cannot do enough for me. It pays to tip well at Christmas.

We go upstairs. I help carry Maddy and Johnny's luggage to their room, which is actually where I read or watch television most nights. The couch unfolds to make a double bed. It is also my library. I love this room. Books, mostly histories and biographies, line the Chinese red walls. Military prints. On the shelves are miniature painted model soldiers. Mamelukes, hussars. One of my hobbies. I am especially fond of Napoleon's Grande Armée. A sword that had reputedly belonged to Murat, and for which I happily paid a small fortune, hangs over the mantel. There's a small bathroom and a closet where I store odds and ends, ancient skis, winter coats, suitcases. I had cleared out a lot of my old junk to make room for Maddy's things.

"I hope you'll be all right in here," I say.

"It's perfect, Walter. Thank you."

"I'll leave you to unpack. There are fresh towels in the bath. Let me know if you need anything else."

That night we order in. "I'd kill for a hamburger," Maddy

confesses. After dinner, she puts Johnny to bed and joins me in the living room, where I have made a small fire and opened a bottle of good claret.

I know better than to launch questions at her. She will tell me. Or not.

"You know, actually I wasn't entirely truthful at the airport," I confess, handing her a glass. "I have heard from Harry. He sent me several e-mails asking if I knew where you were. I wasn't sure what to do. So I wrote him that, yes, I had heard from you and that you and Johnny would be staying with me. But that I didn't know what was going on. I hope that was all right."

She nods her head. "Yes, I suppose that was the best thing. I did leave in a hurry."

"That was the impression I had. Sort of a spur-of-the-moment decision on your part, was it?"

"You might say that."

"Care to elaborate?"

"I knew I couldn't stay."

"You weren't in physical danger? Or Johnny?"

"No. Nothing like that."

"Then what happened?"

She put her glass on the table. "He's cheating on me, Walter. I had some suspicions about a month ago, and I asked him point-blank about it. He swore he wasn't. Then I found out yesterday that he was. That it's been going on for months. You know, it's not even that I really care that he was having an affair. What I can't forgive is the lying. I just had to go. I don't know what I would have done if I hadn't."

We sit there in silence, staring at the fire. I am letting all of this sink in. It is obviously still a shock to her too. I am amazed by her once again. If I had discovered my spouse of twenty years cheating on me, I'd probably collapse in a self-pitying pile on the floor.

"Do you know who he is having the affair with?"

"No. He's been traveling a lot, though. Mostly Paris, but also London. Barcelona. He told me it was for business. Meeting publishers, giving readings, interviews. Then a few weeks ago this woman I knew from New York e-mailed me that she had seen him in a restaurant in Paris with a young woman with dark hair. When I asked him about it, he said it was someone from his French publisher. I didn't doubt him. We've never lied to each other. At least, I didn't think we did."

"Then how do you know he was having an affair? Do you have any proof?"

She tells me about the credit card bills, where he had been, what he had bought. The banality of the discovery, the carelessness. Her eyes are rimmed with tears. "I couldn't believe it, but I just know it. I know it in my heart."

"I'm sorry. But, I mean, it's Harry we're talking about. Your Harry. Our Harry, for Christ's sake. It just doesn't seem possible. I would never have imagined such a thing in a million years."

"That's what I thought too. Shows how wrong we both can be."

"Do you want to find out who it is? I mean, who the woman is?"

"Actually, I couldn't care less. It's all beside the point. Maybe I will in a week or so. I'm not jealous. I'm angry, hurt, disappointed, shocked, and, frankly, very tired."

"So what are you going to do?"

She sighs. "I don't know. Right now, I'm just going to take it one day at a time. Get Johnny settled. Move back into the apartment. Baby steps. Is it all right if we stay here until then? It's just to the end of the month."

"Of course. You don't have to ask, you know that."

"I know. But you're such an old bachelor. You aren't used to having people underfoot. Especially nine-year-old boys and mopey middle-aged women."

I smile. "Not at all. In fact, I'll rather enjoy it. It'll be nice to have the company. But then what? What about Harry?"

"I don't know yet. That's still a big question mark."

"Are you going to talk to him?"

"I honestly don't know what there is to say."

She is not the sort of person to do things by half measures. "Are you thinking of divorce?"

Stiffening, she says, "Don't push me. I really haven't thought that far ahead. All I know right now is that I don't want to think about it or him."

"Sure. You'll let me know, okay? In case you need a good lawyer."

She rolls her eyes. "Knock it off, Walter."

"I'm serious. If it comes to that and you need someone, I hope you'll let me help—or at least find you someone good."

"Okay. I promise."

5

I more or less take the next few days off. I head into the office late in the morning and then come straight home around one so I can spend the time with Maddy and Johnny. We go for walks in Central Park, where there are still patches of snow and most of the grass has been fenced off. The winding lanes. The bare trees. The ground underfoot is beginning to thaw. Johnny climbs on the rocks. We eat hot dogs and ride on the carousel. The same deranged-looking bas-relief clowns that used to terrify me when I was a child still line the walls. One night we go to a Broadway show. Something puerile and entertaining. Johnny loves it. I must admit I sort of do too. Another night we have a mini-feast in Chinatown. Maddy tells me the Chinese food is terrible in Rome.

We are on holiday. The real world is waiting for us to rejoin it. I am in my office when my secretary informs me that Harry is on the line. It is not the first time he has called, she reminds me. I can't put him off forever.

"Walt, thank God."

I am not sure how to proceed, my emotions conflicted. We have not communicated since Maddy arrived. I am angry with him, angry for Maddy and angry for our friendship. He has let us all down. I am not especially happy to hear from him, and I let my tone show it.

"Harry."

"How are they? How's Maddy? How's Johnny? I am going out of my mind."

"They're as well as can be expected, under the circumstances," I answer coolly. There had never been any question of whose side I would take.

He doesn't respond to my gibe. "Walt, you need to get Maddy to answer my calls. I need to talk to her. I must have called a hundred times."

"I can't make her do anything. She'll talk to you if she wants to."

"I'm coming to New York."

"When?"

"Tomorrow. Please tell her that I want to see her. And that I love her."

"I'll tell her, but I'm not sure what good it will do."

I can hear him sigh on the other end. "Thanks, Walt."

"Not at all." I hang up. If I wasn't so angry with him, I'd feel like an utter bastard.

HAVING MADDY LIVING IN MY APARTMENT ALLOWS ME TO indulge in more than a few domestic fantasies. What if this was all mine? What if she was my wife? What if Johnny was my son? What a different arc my life would have taken. When we go out on the street, each of us holding Johnny's hand, we look like a family. I even wake up early every morning to make waffles for Johnny. They are one of his favorites.

Tomorrow Harry will be coming to my office. He had begged me. I haven't even heard her so much as breathe his name.

"Do you want to talk about it?" I ask Maddy after dinner. Our new ritual is to eat, read Johnny a story before bed, and then have a glass of wine in my living room. It is my least favorite room in the house. I rarely sit here, preferring my library. It has the same salmon pink silk sofas and chairs, antique end tables, English landscapes, carpets, and lamps that were once in my parents' apartment. Of course this room is considerably smaller than their living room, so I had to wedge in what I could and put the rest in storage.

Maddy has started smoking again. I can't blame her. I even join her in the occasional cigarette.

"Not really," she replies. "Thank you for seeing him, I suppose. I am sure it's a comfort to him, but I am not ready to see or talk to him."

"I understand. What do you want me to tell him?"

"Tell him just that. I am still in shock and can't really get my head around what I need to do. I need to first figure out what is best for Johnny and me."

"Very well." I pause. "Do you mind if I ask him one thing?"

"What one thing?"

"Well, it's the lawyer in me, but in this country we presume that people are innocent until proven guilty."

She looks me, her eyes narrowing. "What do you mean? I saw the credit card bill. What more proof do you want?"

I hold up my hands. "I agree it's damning, but it's not conclusive. What I propose to do is to ask him directly whether or not he had an affair."

"Why? I already know."

"You think you do, but what if you're wrong? What if there's some perfectly simple explanation and this whole thing is one huge misunderstanding?"

"That's impossible."

"No, it's not. Until you are one hundred percent certain, nothing is impossible."

She sits quietly, taking in what I have just said. "I have asked myself that same question thousands of times. What if it's just one terrible overreaction on my part? But each time the answer is the same. I can't tell you how I know it. I just do. And I wish to God I was wrong."

"As do I."

"And what's to prevent him from lying to you? He lied to me."

"I don't know. Maybe nothing. But remember, I don't know he did lie to you. I need a confession. Or some other way to prove his guilt or innocence."

She nods her head.

"So it's all right with you? If for no other reason, it would assuage my lawyerly soul."

"Fine. Suit yourself," she says, extinguishing her cigarette in the full ashtray. "I'm going to bed."

She stands and leans over me, her breath strong with tobacco, to place a sisterly kiss on my cheek. "I know you mean well, Walter. Ask him anything you want. If he says anything that you think I should hear, I know you'll tell me. Thank you again for seeing him. I honestly don't think I could."

⊱─

IF IT HAD BEEN UP TO ME, HE WOULD HAVE BEEN FORCED TO travel to New York on bleeding knees like a Mexican pilgrim, praying for forgiveness the whole way. Even that would not have been enough, but it would have been a start. I know that sounds harsh, but it's not entirely wide of the mark. It was his job to protect her, and he let her down. Now it's my job. At least I am taking it on. Part of me just wants to punch him in the nose.

Needless to say, this time I don't go out to the airport. He wanted to go to my apartment, but I told him it would be best if he came to my office instead. From both his charm and potentially his fists, I wanted the protection offered by the dignity of my position and the accoutrements of the law, the impressive desk, the shelves groaning with legal books, the ridiculous modern art decorating the hallway walls, the sweeping aerial view of midtown, the helmet-haired receptionists. My secretary, Marybeth, a formidable creature whose personal life I do as little to learn about as possible, I keep starved of affection so that, like a lion deprived of meat, she is particularly fierce with clients.

She calls me when Harry arrives. He is on time, but I tell her to keep him waiting. I have nothing especially pressing to do, but I want him to sweat a little more under Marybeth's feline gaze. A quarter of an hour later, I ask her to send him through. It is a shock to see him. He looks haggard, as though he hasn't slept or bathed in days. His clothes rumpled. His natural jauntiness has been replaced by a heaviness I have never seen in him.

"Thanks for meeting me, Walt. I came right from the airport."

I say nothing, but swivel slightly, impatiently in my chair, steepling my fingers. I do not rise to shake his proffered hand.

He retracts it and looks at me warily, aware of my hostility but knowing I am his only interlocutor; he needs to subordinate himself to me. I indicate for him to take a seat and he obeys. "How is she, Walt? How's Johnny?"

I have no interest in the niceties. I raise my eyebrows and, in a measured voice, attack. "Did you do what Maddy thinks you did? Did you have an affair?"

He doesn't look at me. With an effort, he admits, "Yes."

He hangs his massive head. I seize the advantage. I know it is almost cowardly of me, but I cannot help myself.

"And have you said as much to Maddy?"

"No."

"I see."

"I haven't had a chance to. She won't talk to me."

"She doesn't want to talk to you."

"But I need to."

"Why exactly? To what possible end? I'm sorry, Harry, but I'm not really sure what earthly good it could do. You've just admitted to me that you did have an affair. Maddy told me she asked you directly a month ago if you were having one, and you denied it. You lied to her. To her face. You know her. She's very intelligent and very perceptive. She probably would have forgiven you if you had told the truth—then. You know how important honesty is to her. And how much she despises dishonesty. You of all people should know that by now."

I watch my words stabbing him. I am embarrassed to admit I hoped they would.

"Yes, yes, I know all that. But for God's sake, she's my wife. Johnny's my son. I love her. I love him. I love them."

"Well, you should have thought of that before you had an affair," I say, allowing myself some emotional latitude. "And whom, may I ask, did you have the affair with?" I consciously employ the dangling preposition.

He says nothing and looks away. I do not press. Some Frenchwoman, no doubt. If Maddy wants to know, I will find out later. We have people who do that sort of thing. It is not important now.

He looks at me, his eyes burning fiercely. His voice low. "I need to speak to Maddy, Walter. If you don't cut out all this bullshit, I will go directly to your apartment and find her."

I sigh patiently. "Look, Harry, I know you know where I live. But why do you think you're meeting me first instead of her? If she had any desire to see you, she'd be the person you're talking to, not me. The fact of the matter is that she doesn't want to see you."

"I don't believe you."

In my calmest voice, I reply, "Frankly, I don't give a fuck what you think. She asked me to intermediate. Not in an official way, of course. I'm not a divorce lawyer. But I am her attorney, as you know, as well as her friend."

"Divorce? Is she thinking about divorce?"

"I really don't know. But I wouldn't rule it out."

"Meaning what exactly?"

"Meaning that you screwed up. Big time."

"I know I did, Walt. That's why I'm here. What can I do? I need to see her, to speak to her."

"We're going round in circles at this point. You've admitted to me that you had an affair, ergo you lied to Maddy. Ergo you broke your wedding vows, and, most important, you broke her trust and her heart. *Allegans suam turpitudinem non est audiendus,*" I add rather pompously.

"What?"

"The translation is 'One who is alleging his own infamy is not to be heard.'" I know it is a bit much, but I can't help myself.

He looks at me, half startled, half with contempt. "So you're saying that I have no right to speak to my wife?" I can see his muscles bunching under his coat, his hands clenching into fists. I know what he is thinking.

"I didn't say that."

He stands up violently. "This is insane."

I do not move. He would like nothing better than to strike me. Instead I diffuse the situation. "Sanity is not the question here. Look, there's no one who's unhappier about this turn of events than I am," I say, somewhat disingenuously. "The last thing I ever wanted was for the two of you to find yourselves in this sort of position. But you are. And, not to put too fine a point on it, it's your own goddamn fault. So if there's a question of sanity, let me maintain to you, in a purely nonclinical way, that what you did was crazy."

He sits down again, defeated. The fight out of him. "I know." After a time, he raises his head and asks, "So what do you suggest I do?"

I am torn at this moment. I could offer advice, solace even. Or not. "I'm sorry. I don't know. All I can say is that, if Maddy changes her mind, she will let you know."

He absorbs the blow. "And Johnny? Don't I have a right to see him?"

"Again, that's not for me to decide."

He doesn't move; his great hands dangle between his knees. "Oh my god," he whispers.

"Look, Harry, I'm sorry I can't be of more help, but I have another appointment," I lie.

He looks up at me, befuddled. "Oh, right. Of course." He stands and puts out his hand. Unthinkingly I take it. "Thanks for seeing me. I really appreciate it. I can only imagine how difficult this all must be for you."

"Not at all," I reply, smiling. "I only wish I could be of more help."

"You'll tell Maddy that I came in, though, won't you? Tell her I want to see her?"

"Of course."

He turns to leave.

"One thing, Harry. If she, or I, need to contact you, where can we find you?"

He gives me a half smile. "I don't know, Walt. I hadn't really thought that far ahead. I suppose I had hoped that I'd be with Maddy and Johnny, but now I don't know. I'll be in touch, okay?"

I watch his broad back exit. I had always been so jealous of him. But not anymore.

6

THAT NIGHT ONCE AGAIN I WAIT UNTIL AFTER DINNER, AFTER THE second bottle has been opened and the dishes cleaned and put away. I ask her if she wants to hear about my meeting with Harry. This must be how a doctor feels when he has to deliver bad news to a patient. The spot on the X-ray is what had been feared. These are your options, none of them especially good. The patient, too, doesn't want to know the truth. These words will change their lives forever, cause irreparable harm, tear apart families. This is nothing they wanted. It is something being done to them. They have been betrayed by what they had always relied upon. There had even been moments of hope that, despite what they feared in their hearts, it was all a big mistake. Human error. The initial tests had been wrong and they would be spared. It takes a tremendous act of courage to listen, not to block up one's ears, not to lash out, but to accept and to act.

"I am sorry," I say after I confirm the worst.

Her elbows are resting on her knees. She is looking away, as though the news of Harry's guilt had happened to someone else, and we were talking about two other people whose lives are in tatters. "Thank you, Walter," she says finally. "I suppose it does remove any doubt." She lights another cigarette. "I'd like you to do me a favor."

"Anything."

"Can you tell Harry I appreciate his being honest with you? I am sure it wasn't easy for him."

"Of course."

"But also that I still don't want to talk to him."

I nod my head. "You can't keep on avoiding him forever, you know. What about Johnny? He keeps asking about his father."

She sighs. "I know. A few more days. That's all I ask."

DESPITE MY EFFORTS TO GET HER TO STAY IN MY APARTMENT, she and Johnny move back to theirs at the beginning of the month. It is a cold day, wet with rain. I suppose it is the right thing for them to do, but it seems awfully lonely without them. The night after they return, I insist on inviting myself over. I know she needs me.

It's odd being back here. The apartment is the bottom two floors of an old town house. They have the garden, which in many ways always struck me as a wonderful luxury, but I remember that Harry would complain about it. They had moved in shortly after Johnny was born, and the yard had been in pretty rough shape. Maddy had it landscaped, putting in cast-iron chairs and a dining table, as well as a jungle gym and sandbox for Johnny. "Worst idea we ever had," Harry would grumble. "It's like an invitation to every cat in the neighborhood. I should put out a sign saying "Welcome to Winslow's Fabulous Feline Facilities and charge the cats' owners a quarter each time they use it." Eventually, the sandbox was boarded up.

Aside from that, I remember many pleasant evenings having drinks while Maddy cooked steaks on the grill. They even had a heat lamp that allowed us to sit out on all but the coldest nights. Sometimes it would be just us; other times friends of Harry's, literary people mainly, would descend. Harry always loved parties.

The house is simple. A classic New York brownstone. The entrance under the stoop past a little courtyard. To the right of the front door a little breakfast area, where Johnny usually ate dinner. There is a long open-ended kitchen that gives onto the dining room, in which sit a magnificent matching set of Queen Anne chairs and a heavy ball-and-claw table Maddy inherited from her grandmother. Then down a few steps a sunken, open living room. Along its left-hand wall an enormous and very beautiful Edo-period screen depicting a scene from *The Tale of Genji*. Maddy bought it when Harry was stationed in Japan. The living room looks out onto the garden through an enormous picture window. The effect is surprisingly, and pleasantly, airy and modern.

One night at a particularly uproarious party, a drunken actor friend of theirs walked right into that window, breaking his nose and, so he claimed, costing himself the starring role in a film. I wouldn't have believed it if I hadn't seen it for myself. The actor maintained that he hadn't realized it was a window.

Harry joked that he was so vain he simply couldn't take his eyes off his reflection.

Upstairs is their bedroom, which faces out onto the street, and two rooms in the back overlooking the garden. One is Johnny's, the other Harry's office. The unfinished basement has an old Ping-Pong table, a washer and dryer, shelves of books, a boiler. I wonder what it is like for Maddy to be here now. His clothes in the closet. Photographs. Books. A favorite coffee mug. It would have been one thing for her to return to the Long Island house. Like my house, it had been built by her family. No one else had ever lived there. Any ghosts there were her ghosts. But not this place. It was hers and Harry's. Remove one from the equation and the math doesn't add up.

Harry, Harry, Harry. Even now I can't stop referencing him. He filled up everything.

Now Maddy lets me in. I hang my wet raincoat on a hook. She looks tired. "Hey, Walter," she says. "Come in." The house is strangely quiet, like a church on Monday morning. There is something different, not Harry's absence. No, something else. It doesn't dawn on me until Maddy says, "I hope you don't mind if I didn't cook. I just don't feel up to it."

"Not at all. I'm happy to order in." That's when it strikes me. There is no smell of food, no activity in the kitchen. A visit to Maddy's house always tantalized the senses, the aromas wafting from the various pots seducing the lucky guest. She was always hovering over a stove, happily chatting away while she diced carrots or reduced sauces. But since learning about Harry, she hadn't so much as warmed up a cup of coffee. I glance at the kitchen. It looks like a sad dog waiting for its master to return.

"Hey, Uncle Walt," says Johnny, tearing down the stairs freshly washed and in his pajamas, followed by their old babysitter.

"You remember Gloria, don't you, Walter?"

"Of course," I say, shaking hands with the Guatemalan woman who has helped look after Johnny since he was very young.

"Señor Walter," she says, blushing. Her English is not very good. Maddy speaks near fluent Spanish. My only other language is French, the benefit of having had a mademoiselle for several years as a child. As a result my relationship with Gloria consists of little more than smiling and bobbing at each other.

"I have a big surprise for you," I say to Johnny.

"What?"

I hold up two tickets to a Rangers game for next week. "You and me, pal. A week from Friday. Center ice. The Rangers against the Penguins," I say.

He takes the tickets from my hand and looks at them. His face a mask of disappointment. "Awesome, Uncle Walt." Children are terrible liars.

"What do you say?" prods his mother.

"Thank you, Uncle Walt." He gives me a lukewarm hug. To his mother, "Can I go to bed now?"

"Of course, darling," says Maddy. "I'll be right up."

Gloria follows Johnny up the stairs.

"That was pretty boneheaded of me," I say.

"No. You meant well."

"I just remember that Harry used to take Johnny to Rangers games. I thought it would be fun for him."

"You aren't Harry, Walter." She doesn't mean it the way it sounds, but it is still a slap.

I walk over to the bar and pour myself a large whisky. "I know. I'm not trying to be. I'm just trying to make him smile. He is my godson, after all."

"I know. I just wish you had cleared it with me first."

"He misses his father."

She nods her head. "Of course he does. Have you spoken to him?"

"He calls me every day," I say. Then, "What if I let him take Johnny to the game next week? God knows, I have no interest in hockey. That might be a nice thing for them both."

"Let me think about it."

I had again spoken to Harry that day. He was desperate to know Maddy's state of mind and wanted to find out when he could see her and Johnny. As usual, I put him off, deflecting his most urgent questions and doing my best to keep him both as informed and as off-balance as possible.

"When can I see her?"

"Soon, I hope. I think she realizes she needs to speak with you."

"Thank God."

"I am not sure if that's necessarily a good thing. For you, I mean."

"I don't care. I'm going out of mind. Please, you have to let her know how sorry I am and how terrible I feel."

"I have. I don't think it does much good."

Silence. Then, "I know."

"Have you found a place to stay, by the way?"

"Ned and Cissy's. But you can reach me on my cell anytime."

"Very good. Hopefully the next time we speak, I'll have better news for you."

228

"Thanks, Walt. You've been a real friend." It's true, I have been. The irony is that he thinks I've been a friend to him. Like an aging matinee idol, whenever he hears applause, he always assumes it is for him.

A WEEK LATER, OVER TAKE-OUT SUSHI AND BEER AT THE dining room table, Maddy announces to me, "I think I'm ready."

"What exactly are you ready for?"

"To see Harry."

"I realize that. I mean, just what are you ready to do?"

"I'm not sure yet. It would be so easy to push the whole thing over a cliff at this point, you know? Part of me wants to, just the way a child can't help but kick over a sand castle that she's spent hours building."

"And the other part?"

"The other part of me realizes this isn't a sand castle."

"Okay. How do you want to do it? Can I help?"

"Yes, you can. I've thought about this a lot now. I can't see him here, and I don't want to meet in a restaurant."

"So where do you want to meet then?"

"I need somewhere neutral but also private. That's why I was hoping you could let me use a conference room at your office."

"Of course. When do you want to meet him?"

"There's no point in putting this off any longer. I'd like you to call him tonight and tell him to come tomorrow."

"Time?"

"Let's do it in the morning. Can you get a conference room for ten?"

I nod. "Do you want me there?"

"No. I need to do this myself."

"All right. I'll be nearby in case you change your mind."

The next morning I go in early and arrange everything for the meeting. When I had called Harry after dinner, he was relieved to hear that Maddy was finally willing to see him.

"How does she seem?" he asked. "Do I have a prayer?"

"I honestly don't know," I answered.

"I'll take my chances."

He arrives a few minutes early, and this time I don't keep him waiting. He looks better than when I saw him last. His hair has been cut. His suit pressed, shoes shined. He looks like he's here for a job interview. I can tell he's nervous despite his broad smile and firm handshake.

"Where is she?" he asks.

"Follow me." Silently, I lead him to the conference room. We have many conference rooms. Some larger, others more intimate. I have chosen one of the latter. It is a formal room. The furniture and the paintings on the walls, mainly of horses, English. There is an Oriental carpet on the floor. It is where we often read wills. The blinds have been lowered to keep out the morning sunlight.

We enter. "Wait here," I say.

At ten on the nose, I return with Maddy. She is dressed in a red woolen skirt suit. It is the old Chanel she wears every year when she lunches with her trustee. She wears no makeup and her hair is tied back. She looks beautiful but severe.

Harry stands when she walks in. "Maddy," he exclaims, habitually moving toward her, but then halts when he realizes she doesn't want his embrace. It is the first time I have ever been in a room with them when they were not drawn to each other like magnets. She doesn't even look at him and instead takes a seat on the opposite side of the table.

"Thank you, Walter," she says. "If we need anything, I'll call."

"Take as long as you want," I say, closing the door behind me.

A little more than a half hour later, my line rings. "We're ready," she says. I hurry over with as much dignity as I can, nearly running down two junior associates. I knock and enter. Harry looks ashen. "Thank you, Walter," Maddy repeats. She remains seated while Harry struggles to his feet. I put my hand on his back to guide him along.

When we reach the reception area, Harry says, "I really put my foot in it, didn't I, Walt?"

I say nothing, but nod. What else is there to do? Even knowing his guilt, I still feel bad for him.

"She asked for a separation."

I raise my eyebrows. "I'm sorry," I say. "Are you surprised?"

He shakes his head. "No, I suppose not. Did you know?"

"No. She wouldn't tell me anything."

"No, she wouldn't," he says wistfully. "I've been with her for twenty years, and she's still a mystery to me."

"Well, you've been pretty mysterious yourself."

He takes the hint and smiles abashedly. "Fair enough."

"What are your plans?"

"Honestly? I don't know. I can't even go back to Rome—even if I wanted to, which I don't. New York is where Maddy and Johnny are, and I need to be near them even if Maddy doesn't want to see me. I suppose I'll mooch off Ned and Cissy a little longer, and then I guess I'll find somewhere to live. I've still got a book to finish."

"Well, good luck with it."

"Thanks. I'll be in touch. Maddy said something about a hockey game this Friday. I understand I have you to thank for it. It's damn nice of you. You know how much Johnny and I like our Rangers games."

"Don't mention it."

"She said it would be best for me to make arrangements through you, if that's all right."

"Of course." We shake hands. I can afford to be magnanimous now.

I watch him open the heavy glass doors, head to the elevator bank, and depart with a final wave, his leonine head standing out among the dark-suited attorneys and clients milling around him. Then I hurry back to the conference room where Maddy is waiting.

"Harry told me."

She nods. "It was the only answer that made sense to me."

"But you didn't ask for a divorce?"

"No, not yet. A separation will give us both time to wrap our heads around everything."

"How did he take it?"

"Pretty well." She sighs. "He cried and told me he was sorry and that he loved me and asked me to give him another chance. I told him I didn't think I could. I explained why, and he listened. I told him he could see Johnny, but I wanted him to go through you, at least for the time being. I hope that's all right."

"Harry mentioned. Of course it is."

"It just felt so damn odd seeing him, you know? It was like I was seeing a stranger. Someone I didn't even know instead of a man I've spent half my life with."

"I can't imagine."

"No, nor could I have. All I could see was just one big lie. I didn't see hands or eyes or hair. I just saw the lie. He actually repulsed me. I could barely even look at him."

I sit down next to her. "Maddy, how much do you know about divorce law in New York State?"

"I've been reading up on it online. I know we each need an attorney to prepare the documents and file them with the court. At the end of a year either of us can sue for a no-fault divorce if we still want to."

"That's more or less correct. That's only if you file a legal separation though. Is that what you want to do?"

"Yes. Will you represent me?"

"You know I will, even though it's not my area of expertise. It all depends on how messy things get. If there are issues surrounding support, child visitation rights, property distribution, things like that, it can get pretty complicated."

She nods. "I understand. I don't want to deny Harry the right to see Johnny. It would kill them both. As far as property and support, I discussed it briefly with Harry. I don't want anything from him. I have my own money."

"What about property?"

"We can work that out later. Harry said he'd agree to anything I asked."

"I'm sure he did. From what I've seen, though, that's fairly common. People can be very compliant at the beginning, in the hopes that the other will change their mind. Over time their attitudes can change. They can get angry and create all kinds of trouble. That's why it helps to have lawyers spell everything out in advance. Things can get nasty."

She closes her eyes for a moment. "Okay, Walter. Do what you have to do."

I nod. "Now what?"

"Now? Now I go home and try to figure out what to do with the rest of my life. I was sitting up last night after you left, thinking that, aside from you, I have almost no friends of my own anymore. Practically everyone I know is someone I met through Harry. It made me feel so damn lonely and depressed."

"You'll make new friends."

"Oh, it's not that. It's just that so much of my life has been wrapped up in his that I have actually had very little life of my own."

"That seems a bit harsh."

"Does it? I don't know. It certainly seems that way to me."

She stands up. "Thanks again for everything, Walter. I know I don't have to tell you how grateful I am to you for this and, for, well, just about everything you've done. I couldn't have done it without you."

Before I can say anything, she embraces me. I feel her familiar cheek against mine. The honeyed smell of her hair.

"Would you like me to come over tonight?" I ask.

She smiles and puts her hand on my arm. "No, better not. I need to start thinking about living on my own. I can't keep leaning on you all the time."

"I understand. There's a lecture at the club on Byzantine art I was planning on taking in anyway," I lie.

"Okay. Well, I need to get out of here. I'm dying for a cigarette."

Again I act as escort to the elevators, and we embrace.

"I'll check on you tomorrow," I say as the doors close, and she is gone, taking with her, as always, a piece of my heart.

7

"YOU'RE A FUCKING ASSHOLE."

"Come on, Cissy. Go easy on him. He's had a rough day."

"He's had a rough day? What about the kind of a day Maddy's had? What kind of month? Did you ever think about that?"

"She's right, Ned," says Harry. "I deserve everything Cissy says."

"Oh shut up, Harry," she hisses.

Her anger toward him has been simmering ever since he arrived. Whenever they were in the same room together, she gave him dirty looks and curt answers, but hearing that Maddy wants a separation causes her to boil over. And it infuriates her even more that he just sits there and takes her abuse.

"I wish the both of you would just shut the hell up," says Ned, his tie loose around his thick neck. They are sitting at the kitchen table. "Cissy, honey, Harry knows he's been stupid. You don't have to keep tearing into him. It doesn't do anybody any good."

"I don't care. I'm just so mad at you, Harry."

"I'm mad at myself, Cissy."

"Do you need a lawyer?" asks Ned before his wife can respond.

"Yes. Normally, I'd ask Walt for advice, but he's obviously taking Maddy's side."

"Can you blame him?" interjects Cissy.

"No, of course not. I'd have been astonished if he'd done anything else."

"Well, it serves you right," she says, walking out of the room.

"I might be able to find someone for you. One of the guys at work went through this sort of shit last year. Said his lawyer wasn't a total jerk."

"Thanks."

From the other room, Cissy angrily calls Ned's name and then slams the bedroom door.

Ned looks at Harry, rolling his eyes. "She's pretty pissed off at you." He stands up. "I better go see her."

"No worries. One troubled marriage at a time, right?" Harry says with a weak smile.

"I'll be right back."

Harry remains at the kitchen table, fiddling with the salt and pepper shakers. Ned returns a little while later. "Cissy's too mad at you to cook. She said if we want to eat, we're on our own. I told her she was just being spiteful, and now she's sulking and saying she's going to bed. What do you say we go grab a bite?"

❧

IN THE RESTAURANT THEY ORDER A DRINK. "YOU KNOW," says Ned. "Women can forgive just about everything but what you did. And it makes them almost as crazy when it happens to someone else because they're so afraid of it happening to them. Ever since you showed up, all Cissy can do is spit about you and keep asking me if I'm happy with our marriage and how much she loves me. I got to tell you, hoss, I'm having the best sex I've had in years." He laughs, and Harry smiles. "So who was it?" asks Ned casually, sipping his Scotch on the rocks.

Harry knows what he means. He shifts uncomfortably in his seat. "I'd rather not say."

Ned raises his eyebrows and then waves his big hand as though clearing the air. "Ah, forget it. It's not important. But, look, there is something I need to talk to you about."

"What's that?"

"Well, obviously Cissy's pretty mad at you. You're my best friend, and if it was up to me, you could stay with us as long as you needed. But she's my wife, and she told me she doesn't want you in the house. That's what we were talking about before we left. You can stay tonight, but tomorrow she wants you out. I'm sorry, man."

"No, it's all right. I understand. You've both already been kind enough to let me stay so long. It was a big help."

"So what are you going to do?"

"I don't know. I suppose I'll check into some cheap hotel and look for somewhere to rent."

"You need any money?"

"No, thanks. I should be all right. I'm still getting checks.

238

And my agent says a studio is looking to option my book, which would be some money."

"When will you find out about that?"

"I can't say for sure. These things take forever, apparently. They still have to work out all kinds of things, percentages, residuals, points, whatever. You know a lot of studios will option a book for a bunch of money and then never even make the movie? It's nuts, but with any luck, it should be sometime this spring."

"That mean you'd be going out to Hollywood?"

"I don't know. Maybe. Yeah. For a meeting or two. I haven't been out there for years. When I was stationed at Twentynine Palms, Maddy and I used to drive into L.A. from time to time. It's only a couple of hours. She had some distant cousin who lived in Brentwood. A crazy old lady whose father had been a famous director back in the day. Worked with guys like Errol Flynn and Bogart. She was an old drunk but very entertaining. She was living in this big, falling-down house with a blond golf pro who was even younger than we were. There were cats and dogs everywhere, even an ancient turtle. We used to go stay with her, and she'd take us to wild parties in places like Venice and Santa Monica."

"She still alive?"

"No, she died years ago. She was a lot of fun though."

"Yeah, well, good luck. You'd better invite me to the opening."

"You'll have front-row tickets."

But Harry was being optimistic, as usual, about his financial situation. The truth of the matter, as I later learned, was that he had spent a lot of his earnings. He had been with Maddy for so long and had always relied on her income to carry them through that he had no more financial sense than a teenager living on an allowance. What money he had been able to set aside had been placed with Maddy's people. Like many investors, they had lost money in the recent market crash, but sales of his book had helped offset most of his other losses.

His spontaneous spending had always put the biggest dents in his net worth. The Cessna had been bought on a whim. I remember Ned, who was a banker, had told him he'd be better off investing the money, but Harry had just waved him off.

"Gotta have the plane, Ned. It was a promise I made to myself. And besides, she's a beauty."

The next morning Ned is already gone when Harry comes into the kitchen with his bag packed. Cissy is standing at the sink, wearing a long bathrobe and staring out the window, drinking a cup of coffee.

"Sorry to disturb you, Cissy. I'm just leaving."

She says nothing but lifts her chin a little higher.

"Thank you for letting me stay. When I arrived I really hoped that things would turn out differently. I guess I've been wrong about a lot of things. I just wanted to say to you that, for what it's worth, I still love Maddy and will do everything I can to get her back."

Without looking at him she says, "Why do men do it? Why do they have to shit all over other people's lives just because they want to get laid?" Then, turning toward him, "Huh? Can you answer that? You've done it. Why did you?"

"I, I don't know," Harry stammers.

"What do you mean, you don't know? Did your marriage mean so little to you that you just hopped into bed with some slut for no reason at all?"

240

"No. It's more complicated than that."

"Complicated? How complicated was it? It seems pretty goddamn black and white to me. You were married. To Maddy, of all people, for chrissakes. Wasn't she beautiful enough? Wasn't she kind enough? Wasn't she a good enough mother? Wasn't she rich enough? Tell me, what didn't she give you that you had to go somewhere else? Tell me, I'd be really interested to know."

"No, Maddy gave me everything."

"So what was it? You wanted more? It wasn't enough to be a successful writer and father with friends who loved you? With a wife who adored you? Did you think that you were too special to live by the same rules as everyone else? Or maybe you just didn't really think about what impact your actions would have? That your selfishness would destroy everything? That's how a child thinks, Harry. That's not how a grown man thinks."

He can say nothing.

"You make me sick. God, why don't you just go already?" There are tears in her eyes.

That afternoon Harry calls me. "I just wanted to let you know that I've moved out of Ned and Cissy's apartment." He tells me he's found a room in a cheap hotel in the East Twenties. I have never heard of it. "It's full of German families," he says. "I'm the only guest not wearing Birkenstocks and carrying a backpack."

"In case I need to reach you, how long do you plan to stay?" I ask.

"I don't know. It's about two hundred dollars a night, so it's not too bad. I plan to start looking for an apartment today."

"Remember, it needs to have a room for Johnny," I tell him. "Otherwise a judge may not let him stay with you."

A few days later, he calls again, this time telling me he's found a one-bedroom in Murray Hill, near the tunnel. The next night is the hockey game. He asks me what he should do. Would it be all right if he picked Johnny up from home? I tell him I'll check with Maddy and get back to him.

I call her number and wait for the message to play out. I know Maddy. She hates the phone and never bothers to answer it. "Maddy," I say. "Maddy, it's me. If you're there please pick up."

"Hello, Walter." As I assumed, she had been waiting by the phone deciding if she would answer or not.

"Tomorrow night's the hockey game. Harry wants to know if he can pick Johnny up at home. If you're uncomfortable with that, I can take Johnny to the Garden."

She sighs. "No, that's all right. No need for you to be my errand boy. Tell him he can come here."

"All right. Why don't I take you out for dinner while they're gone?"

"Thanks. I'd like that."

The next night I arrive at Maddy's apartment at a quarter to seven. Harry is due at seven. "Come on in," says Maddy, offering me her cheek. Johnny gives me that familiar disappointed look when he sees that, once again, I am not his father. He is wearing his Rangers jersey. I ruffle his hair. "Have fun tonight, okay?"

"Go make yourself a drink, Walter," says Maddy.

"Good idea. Can I fix you anything?"

"No thanks."

I wander off to the bar and mix up a martini.

The doorbell rings. "Daddy!"

Johnny tears to the door and jumps into his father's arms. "Daddy, Daddy!"

Harry hugs his son tightly, lifting him off the ground, burying his face in his neck. "Johnny," he whispers. "I missed you so much."

"I missed you too, Daddy. You're staying, right?"

Harry looks at Maddy and places Johnny on his feet. Bending over so his eyes are level with his son's, he takes his hand and says, "Um, I can't, pal. I've still got to finish things up in Rome. I flew in just to see you, and, ah, I've got to fly back right after the game."

"Oh."

"Johnny, go get your coat," says Maddy, placing a hand on her son's shoulder. "You don't want to be late for the game."

The boy runs upstairs, calling, "I'll be right back, Daddy."

"You haven't told him."

Her face is like ice. "No. I thought it would be best coming from you."

"From me?" He looks away and then down at his feet, holding back his emotions, knowing he has no right to protest. "If that's what you want."

"I do. He'll blame me if I tell him that you won't be living here anymore. I'm not the bad guy here, and I don't intend to be. And frankly I'm not much in the mood to be one of those parents who fake a united front. It always seems so dishonest."

"I see. Hello, by the way. You look lovely."

"Thank you."

"Hey, Walt."

"Harry."

"So, do you have any idea what you want me to say?" he whispered.

"You're the writer. I am sure you'll be able to think up something."

He juts out his lower lip and nods his head. "Okay."

Johnny comes racing downstairs, jumping the last two steps and landing hard. Few things seem to give little boys greater happiness than the act of making loud noises. "Ready!"

"Okay, champ. Let's go."

"Bye, Mommy. Bye, Uncle Walt."

"Bye, darling. Have fun at the game."

The door closes behind them. Maddy turns to me and says, "You can make me that drink now, Walter."

We are sitting in the living room with our backs to the garden. Maddy is smoking. When Johnny is in the house, she normally goes outside. "I didn't know it would be this hard," she says. "I didn't know anything could be this hard."

There are tears in her eyes. "Damn," she says, wiping them away with the palm of her hand. "I don't want to cry."

"Haven't you cried once?"

She shakes her head. "Not really. Not like what I know I need."

"Maybe you should."

"I've been so angry I haven't felt like crying. But when I saw Johnny with Harry, I just felt so goddamn sad. We had this family, you know? We were happy. And now it's all gone. It's just not fair. How could he do it?"

I stand up and hand her my handkerchief. She blows her nose. "I don't know, Maddy. I truly don't. Of course, this sort of thing happens all the time. I just never thought it would ever happen to you and Harry."

She leans her head back over the chair. "Oh, crap. I was trying to be so tough. Tough for Johnny, tough for me, and, in a way, tough for Harry."

"Were you being too tough?"

"I don't know. Maybe. I mean, what does one do in this sort of situation? My father was divorced three times, but none of those had been much of a marriage. I was too young to remember my mother. His second wife, you remember her, Nancy? God, she was an evil bitch. I couldn't have been happier when she left. And his last wife, Ingrid, came and went while we were in college. I barely ever spoke to her."

I remembered the last two wives. Both were beautiful but just as dissolute as the father. Their lives seemed to be an endless round of drinking and pill popping. The second wife was notorious for sleeping around. Maddy even had a nickname for her: "the Bike," because everyone had a ride on her.

"There's no road map. You've got to do what you feel is right for you—and for Johnny. You're angry at Harry. What's more, you don't feel you can trust him anymore and don't feel you can stay married to him."

"I guess."

"You do mind that he had an affair, don't you?"

"Of course."

"And that he lied about it?"

"Of course."

"So don't be too hard on yourself. You didn't make this happen."

"Well, that's what I keep asking myself. What if it was something I did? I mean, I know we didn't sleep together as much as we once did, but Harry never complained about it."

"What if it was just sex he wanted? Men have been known to go through a midlife crisis. This could be his."

"You know, I don't think I'd mind if it was just sex. But he lied to me, Walter. And he seemed so distant at times. You remember when you visited us in Rome over Christmas? You sensed something was wrong, but I wasn't ready to admit to it. I kept thinking it had to do with his book and being in Rome."

"I remember."

"What really upsets me is that he may have fallen in love with someone else."

I say nothing. The thought to me is inconceivable.

"That's the only excuse, isn't it?" she goes on. "I mean, this wasn't a one-time thing. He was going away all the time—and lying about it. I wouldn't mind so much if it was just a one-night stand, but this was going on for months."

"How do you know there wasn't someone in Rome? No one knows yet who the woman was. I haven't pried because you didn't seem to show much interest. I can find out if you want me to."

"No, that's okay, Walter. I'll do it myself when I'm ready."

"How?"

"I'll just ask Harry. He's feeling so rotten I think he'd tell me anything I wanted."

"How do we know he's not still seeing this woman? If he had feelings for her, do you think he'd throw her over so easily?"

"The Harry I know is a romantic—and a bit of a sucker. So, yes, it's possible he's still seeing her. He'd even do it out of a sense of obligation. And what's to keep him? After all, I've asked him for a separation. He doesn't need to skulk around anymore."

"I spoke to Ned the other day. He was staying there, you know."

"Yes. Cissy and I have been in touch."

"Then you know she kicked him out."

"Not at my suggestion. I even asked her to let him stay on, but she couldn't do it. I think she's madder at him than I am."

"Yes, well, Ned told me that Harry had been genuinely distraught. He never went out at night and barely during the day."

"Meaning what?"

"Meaning that he wasn't exactly behaving like a sailor on leave. If he was in love with someone else, he'd be seeing her, wherever she is, not moping around Ned and Cissy's."

She put out her cigarette. "I don't know. Maybe. Look, I'm tired of talking about it. I thought you said you were going to buy me dinner."

I've had a number of romantic experiences with women over the years, but they have for the most part passed out of my life, distant as stars. This happened more when I was younger and when the girls of my age and background were on the hunt for suitable mates. Doubtless their mothers persuaded some of them that I was a desirable catch. I was almost engaged once to Agatha, Aggie, as she was known. She had lovely legs and a ready smile, and I think she liked the idea of being Mrs. Walter Gervais, at least the part that came with a large house in the Hamptons, a prominent name, the right clubs, and plenty of money.

She wasn't greedy. She was too well-bred for that, but by that time I already had enough experience in corporate law to recognize a potentially hostile merger when I saw one. Instead of getting down on one knee as she had hoped I would,

I took a trip—to visit Maddy and Harry, in fact—and when I returned, I told her that maybe we had better start seeing other people. She took it moderately well. I could tell she was disappointed, all those lovely aspirations coming to nothing, but she was hardly brokenhearted. I saw her several years afterward. She lived in Darien and had three children and was married to someone on Wall Street. Her hair was blonder, and she looked like she played a lot of golf. Clearly she had gotten what she wanted and bore me no ill will. "And you, Walt?" she asked. "How are you? Do you still have that lovely house?"

I informed her that I did. "And children?"

"No, sadly not. Still looking for the right girl, I suppose."

She gave me a patronizing little smile. It was a mixture of victory and compassion. "Poor you. Well, I can't say I'm surprised to hear it. You certainly didn't seem very interested in getting married."

It was true, of course. I suppose that's one of the reasons I wasn't too upset when I found myself on the wrong side of forty and still single. There was only one woman for me, and she was already taken. The notion of marriage to anyone else was unthinkable. What bothered me the most about dating was that I could always envision the end of the relationship. After a while, it seemed to me pointless, and maybe even a little cruel, to let someone form an attachment that would only be broken off.

Not all the women I dated took it as well as Aggie. Often there were tears and recriminations. The protestations. The anger. A few girls even broke up with me first, but rarely with any objection on my part beyond simple good manners. The reason, of course, was that none of the girls were Maddy. It was too much to expect that any of them would be, so eventually I just stopped trying.

As a result, I really had no idea what it meant to break up with someone you loved. Maddy and I had never been a couple, so there was nothing to break up. Based on my limited understanding, I could only imagine the agonies she and Harry were going through. But Maddy and I were still friends, which was what mattered the most to me, second only to her own happiness. Nor did I know what was going through Harry's mind when he thought of Claire, even though at this point I still didn't know of her involvement.

What was Harry going to do? How would he extricate himself? Did he even want to? As I thought about it after, he was caught between two women. One whom he had cheated on and who now despised him but whom, I believed, he still loved. The other was his lover. Both were beautiful and both were important to him. Would he fight a possibly hopeless battle to win back his wife, or would he accept that life changes and embrace the other? The risks were great. By choosing Maddy he could lose them both. By choosing Claire, he would lose Maddy forever. Would that make him happy? I know which choice I would have made.

8

HARRY ROAMS THE STREETS. STOPPING AT WINDOWS, DUCK-
ing in for coffee, occasionally a drink, browsing through book-
stores. He is a man unmoored. For the first time in his life, he
doesn't know where to go. His aimlessness, his loss. I pieced
this all together after.

He walks by Claire's building. Not for the first time. It is
during the day. He knows she is not there. There is no chance
she will walk out. She is at work. That is why he is there. He
repeats words in his head. What he will say to her. The different scenarios. *I am sorry. I can't do this anymore. You were right.
Let's run away. Somewhere in Mexico where they can't find us. Panama.
I have to stay with my son. I love my wife. I love you. I don't know what
to do. I have never been so confused in my life. Forgive me. One of you.
Both of you.*

He has been here every day, relieved that he is undiscovered. The only person who recognizes him is the man in the deli. Aztec eyes, a gold tooth. Two sugars, no milk. Then he walks around the block and then again, each time staring up at her window. Remembering what happened in that room, in that bed. Enshrining it in his mind. Wondering where his life went. It is still cold. The trees are bare, the buildings gray. Hardened, blackened mounds of snow cling stubbornly to the sidewalk. Every day he makes his pilgrimage. There is no one for him now. No one loves him. He has no one who will hold him to her. *I need you. I need someone. Not just anybody.* That is not the way he thinks. He needs warmth, love, acceptance, forgiveness.

One time when he's there, he thinks he sees her and panics, not knowing what to say or do. But it isn't her. He knows that if he wants to see her, all he needs to do is come here earlier. But that is not why he is here. It is in some ways enough to see the building. It is like playing a game of chance. I turn over a card, but what are the odds. He is being a coward. I am growing to hate him.

When he does call her, it is unexpected.

"Hi, it's me."

She is at work. "Harry?"

"Yes."

"Thank God. I've been so worried. Are you all right? How are you? Where are you?"

He had been prepared for anger. Its absence surprises him, encourages him. "I'm fine," he says. "I'm in New York. How are you?"

"Can I see you?"

"I'd like that."

"Tonight?"

"I can't tonight. It's my night with Johnny."

"Tomorrow?"

"Tomorrow."

"Come to my apartment at eight."

The next night he is back on the familiar street. He had stayed away that day. It is a few minutes past eight. This time, instead of passing by on the opposite side of the street, he walks up the short stoop and presses the buzzer. A moment later there is the answering buzz, and he pushes the door open. He climbs the familiar steps.

She is at the door. How does he greet her? Does he make a joke? Does he give her a polite kiss? Does he take her in his arms? Moments like these are crucial. They reveal everything. If it were me, I'd choose the polite kiss. But it is not me. It could never be.

It is a moment of confusion. Neither of them knows what the other is thinking. Standing in the doorway, halfway in, halfway out. Memories of her body. Shared breath. His hands. A powerful, undeniable attraction.

He embraces her, saying nothing. Remembering her scent, the feel of her hair. The beat of her heart. She grips him tightly, immersing herself in him. It is impossible to tell if it is a welcome or a farewell.

Her mouth finds his. Their lips meet. Again he is powerless.

"Oh god, I've missed you so much," she says.

"Me too."

Clothes are shed, resolutions shattered. It is too much for him, he succumbs. She, too, had been unsure how she would react. She had been angry at him, hurt by his absence. Feeling a fool, worse, a bitch. All of this I find out much later, when she tells me.

After, they are in her bed. He is talking. He describes what has happened to his life, to all our lives. Maddy's anger, her flight from Rome, her decision.

"What are you going to do?" she asks.

"I don't know. I'm not sure there is anything she wants me to do. I don't think she wants me to fight for her. I think she wants me out of her life."

"What about you? Do you want to be out of her life?"

"No. There is too much there. Too many years. Johnny. She will never be out of my life. It would be impossible."

"Do you still love her?"

"Of course. I never stopped loving her. I never will."

She closes her eyes. "Do you love me?"

"Yes. I love you both. Is that wrong?"

"Maddy seems to think so."

"And what about you?"

"I never asked for you to love only me. I never wanted to compete with Maddy. I loved you so much I wanted you to love me too, if only a little."

He pulls her gently toward him and kisses her forehead. "I love you more than that," he says.

In the morning, he is awake first. It is Saturday. Outside it is snowing lightly. The flakes melting on impact. Claire sleeps naked beside him, snoring gently, her hands under her head. He does not want to disturb her, so he lies there. Later they will go out for breakfast. Normally he would get up and go to the kitchen, make coffee and then go to his office to work. But there is no normal anymore. In the span of a few short weeks, everything has been upended. The office in Rome is gone, the office in New York is gone. His former life is a dream. He is an exile. In his rental apartment up five flights of stairs sits his laptop computer, barely touched, atop the small kitchen table. Inside is a novel he is at times reluctant to return to—so much has it changed, so much of his own circumstance has changed.

Is he surprised to find himself there? The woman next to him is not his wife, not the mother of his child. And yet. And yet there is something about this girl that is so important that he is willing to throw away everything. Is it her? Or is it something he wants to see in her? Yes, she is lovely, but not as lovely as Maddy. Yes, she is smart, but Maddy has wisdom. Is she as generous? As kind? As indomitable? I know she is younger. Less inured to the familiarity that two decades of marriage brings. She has not heard all of his jokes, does not know all of his moods or stories. To her he is still an undiscovered country where even the most mundane routines and rituals appear thrilling.

And why does she choose him? She may be young, but she is not a child. She is ambitious, that is plain. There are numerous other men who would have gladly taken his place in her bed. Much of it was opportunity. How many other prize-winning authors had she met? For her this was the first circle, the top table. It was not enough for her to be with a rich man. Clive taught her that. No, she had sampled those wares and found them wanting. She did not want to simply be an appendage. She had dreams of her own.

And then she met Harry. Handsome still. Lively. Successful, highly regarded. How could she not fall in love with him? He was everything she wanted. There would be a brief scandal if he left his wife for her, but in literary circles such exchanges are unremarkable and any antipathy would soon subside. Being with him would burnish her own career. The dinner parties, the open doors. Maybe even a novel of her own? They would be happy together, she could see that. She even began wondering what people would write about her one day in his biography. What view would history take of her? Home wrecker, partner, mistress, savior, or maybe just a footnote before he passed on to another woman.

But it is still only a fantasy. She needs him to sever the cord. That had not been her original intention, but now it seems the only way. Only that way can both Harry and she be happy.

Sitting in a booth at the local diner, she asks, "Does Maddy know about me?"

"No. She hasn't asked, and I haven't told her."

"Would you?"

"Do you want me to?"

She thinks for a moment. Would this be her life? Sitting across from him every morning watching him drinking his coffee, eating his eggs? He uses Tabasco sauce, she remembers that.

"I don't know," she answers. "I don't want you to lie if she asks."

"No, there have been too many lies."

"Let me tell her."

He stares at her. "You can't be serious."

"I am. I don't want her to hate you any more than she already does. I deserve some of the hate too."

"No, it's got to come from me."

"Listen to me. It makes sense. It might even make things

better. If I go in there and be honest with her, she might resent me, but she'll respect the truth."

He takes her hands. "Thank you. But it's impossible. I would never ask you to do it. Or even want you to do it. It would be cowardly. It's my responsibility. When the time comes, I'll tell her, but not before. Please understand."

She nods. "I understand."

A week later she is ringing Maddy's doorbell. It is raining hard. The sort of rain that makes an umbrella useless. She knows he will be angry when he finds out. But it is too late. She had not mentioned it again during the weekend. Waiting to see what he would do. If he would do it himself. When it seemed clear he wouldn't, she decided it was up to her to act.

She is nervous. Her steps had faltered as she approached. For a moment, she almost turned and fled. It would have been easy to find an excuse. Something came up at work. Let's try another time, shall we?

The door opens. "Claire," says Maddy, kissing her on the cheek. "Come in. You poor thing, you're soaked."

Claire enters. "Here," says Maddy. "Let me take that." She helps Claire off with her coat and hangs it on a hook. "I can't believe it's been so long. You look beautiful. I love your hair-cut."

Claire blushes and smiles. "Thank you. I forgot you hadn't seen it."

"I was so happy you called."

"Thanks for letting me stop by."

"Oh, don't be silly. It's just what I needed. It's wonderful to see you."

Maddy disappears into the kitchen. "Can I bring you coffee? Or would you prefer tea?"

"Tea would be lovely."

"I won't be a moment. Make yourself comfortable."

Claire remains standing. "I love your home."

"Thanks. It's too bad it's so miserable outside. When the weather's fine, it's nicest to sit in the garden."

"How's Johnny?"

"He's doing very well. He seems happy to be back in New York. His old room, his old friends. You know how kids are. Here we go."

Maddy emerges with a small silver tray, on which sit a porcelain teapot, two matching cups, creamer, and sugar bowl. Maddy has lots of lovely china she inherited from her grandmother. Did she use the Spode? I think so. "Hope Lapsang is all right. It seems like that sort of afternoon." She pours, and the smoky aroma fills the room. Claire is glad for the distraction. Her hand shakes when she lifts up the delicate cup.

They are in the sunken living room. Outside the rain patters against the glass, drums on the flagstones. Claire is again struck by Maddy's beauty, her poise. Her decency. It makes her feel insignificant. Doubly so now.

"So tell me about yourself," says Maddy. "How have you been?"

"Fine. Work's been good. I got a promotion. Better money. It allowed me to rent my own place."

"That's right. Walter mentioned something about that. He said he had a drink with you last fall."

"We were meant to get together again in spring, but something came up. How is Walter?"

"Same as ever, bless his heart. And romance? Any progress on that front?"

"It's been complicated."

"Oh, I believe it. Isn't it always?" Maddy laughs. "Speaking of which, I don't know if you heard this already, but Harry and I have separated."

Claire nods. "Yes, I know. I can't tell you how sorry I am."

"Thank you. It's not been easy."

Claire takes a breath. "Maddy, there's something I need to tell you. It's why I wanted to see you today."

"What is it?"

"I don't know how to say it so I'm just going to spit it out."

Maddy's eyes narrow. "Spit out what?"

"Oh god." Claire sighs. "I'm so, so sorry."

The hairs on the back of Maddy's neck rise. She knows what Claire is going to say almost before she says it and shuts her eyes. She doesn't want to hear it. It's too much.

"Maddy, Maddy. It's me," continues Claire. "I'm the one who ruined it all. I'm the one who's been having an affair with Harry. I'm so sorry."

Hearing the words makes it even worse than imagining them. Maddy's face turns white. The muscles in her jaw tighten, and she sits there in stunned silence, not moving a muscle. Claire leans forward, fearful, anxious. Making herself smaller.

"What did you say?" Maddy asks finally.

"It's me," she answers, almost inaudible.

"You're the one he bought the dress for in Paris?"

Claire nods her head and sniffs. "Yes."

"And all those other trips?"

"Yes."

Maddy takes a deep breath, staring at a fixed point on the wall. How do you react to something like this? The brazenness of the betrayal, the immensity of it. It offends all natural laws.

This is the sort of admission that leads to anger, no, worse, to murder. It's a stain that permeates everything. But Maddy does not reach across and strike Claire. She does not scream, she does not raise her voice. She is a woman who knows how to sit through a beating, who knows how to not give the afflictor the satisfaction of their blows, no matter how hard the belt falls.

In a measured voice she asks, "Do you love him?"

"Yes." Again, Claire nods, not daring to meet Maddy's gaze.

"I see. Does he love you?"

"I don't know. I think so." Love is, of course, even worse than sex. Sex is simply a betrayal of the body. Love is a betrayal of the heart.

Maddy stands up, walks over to a small table across the room, and removes a pack of cigarettes from a drawer. Her hand trembles slightly as she lights one. She takes a few drags, her back to Claire, staring out at the garden, watching the rain drip from the branches. Arms crossed, she turns again to face Claire and asks, "When did it happen?"

Claire blows her nose into her napkin, still avoiding Maddy's eyes. "Last fall. When Harry came to New York. We ran into each other at a party. I invited him back to my place for a drink. And . . ."

Maddy holds up her hand. "Thank you. That's enough. I really don't think I want to hear any more. I just want to ask you one more question. Why are you telling me all this?"

"Because I wanted you to know how sorry I am, and that Harry still loves you even if you are getting divorced. He doesn't know I'm here. He'd be furious if he did."

"You've seen him?" gasps Maddy. If it is possible for her to be even more shocked, she is.

"Yes."

"When?"

"This weekend."

"Did you sleep with him?"

Claire hesitates and then nods her head. "Yes."

Maddy closes her eyes. "I see."

Claire sits there expectantly. Waiting. Her cheeks moist with tears.

"Claire, thank you for coming. I can't say that I am glad to hear what you've told me, but I admire your courage. I don't know what you expected from me. And I am sorry to disappoint you if you thought I'd become hysterical or begin hurling insults or worse at you."

"No, I . . ."

"Please. Let me finish. What I do want to say is how saddened I am that you would betray our friendship as you did. When you first entered our lives last summer, I thought you were a very different person than you turned out to be. I, we, took you in, and this is how you repay us. I don't know how you can live with yourself. I really don't."

"Maddy . . ."

"I think you'd better leave now. I fell for your tears once. Please don't insult me even more by thinking I'd do it again."

Maddy walks toward the front door. Claire follows.

"Maddy, I, I wasn't sure what to expect from coming here today, but I had hoped that maybe you would at least try to forgive Harry and not hate me."

"I don't think I can promise you either of those things. Now will you please just go."

I ARRIVE THAT NIGHT. MADDY HAD CALLED ME IN A FURY. "That little bitch!" she had screamed into the phone. "That little bitch!"

She is already drunk when I arrive. A bottle of vodka is on the kitchen counter. Puddles of melted ice. It is hard to tell when she started. Probably not long after Claire left.

She is weeping now. Telling me about the conversation. The tea set is still on the glass Mies van der Rohe table in the living room. I notice that one cup has been hurled across the room, its obliterated remains lying in an expensive pile on the floor. Her nose is running, mouth bubbling, face slick with tears. I have never seen her like this in all the years I have known her. I offer her my handkerchief, which she takes and keeps.

"I should go see that Johnny is in bed," I say.

She waves her hand, incapable of speech.

I go upstairs. Gloria is with Johnny, reading him a bedtime story. "Hey, pal," I say. "Your mommy wanted me to tell you good night from her and that she loves you."

"What's wrong with Mommy?"

"Nothing. She's just feeling a little tired tonight."

"Is it Daddy?"

"No," I say with a little laugh. "Like I said, she's just tired." I lean over and kiss him on the forehead. It is clear he doesn't believe me. This is how children learn to mistrust adults. "She'll see you in the morning. Sleep well."

"Good night, Uncle Walt."

I nod good night to Gloria and pull the door to.

Downstairs, Maddy is smoking. I make us each a refill.

"Hope you aren't planning on eating," she says. "Food only gets in the way of the alcohol. Fuck food. I am never cooking fucking food again. I live in New York. I can order in anything I like any time I want. You want me to order you in something? Thai maybe? Mexican? Anything you fucking like. All it takes is a telephone and a credit card and some poor bastard on a bicycle brings it right to your door. Cooking is for chumps. Took me years, but I finally figured it out. See all those fucking pans? I'm going to sell them. The cookbooks I'll give away. What do you say, Walter? Want a fucking cookbook? Take your pick. I got a shitload of them. French, Italian, Greek, American, nouvelle, haute cuisine. You name it, I got it. I only ever started doing it for Harry. He seemed to like it so fucking much."

"No, I'm fine," I answer.

"Good night, Miss Maddy, Mister Walter," says Gloria, a quarter of an hour or so later. She is wearing her coat. It is almost nine o'clock.

"Good night, Gloria," Maddy responds cheerily. "See you tomorrow. Thank you for everything."

After Gloria closes the door and turns the lock, Maddy says, "What I don't get is why her?" I know who she means. This has been a steady topic of conversation all evening as she attacks the subject from different angles. "I mean, we were living in Rome. There were all those gorgeous Italian women he could have been fucking, but instead he chooses her. Where's the sense in it?"

I say nothing. She needs to talk it out. It is the double betrayal that stings the most.

"Look at me, Walter. I mean, I'm not bad looking for my age, right? Boobs still don't droop too much. My butt's pretty good, and I don't have bat wings yet, thank God."

"You're beautiful, Maddy. You shouldn't have any worries on that score."

"So what score should I have to worry on? Huh?"

"None from where I sit."

She smiles and puts her hand on mine. "Thanks, Walter. Sweet Walter. You've always been there for me."

"And I always will be."

She pats my hand again. "You know, I think I'm just a weensy bit drunk."

"Just a bit."

"I think I'm going to go to bed."

"Good idea."

She starts to stand up but stumbles. "Oopsy daisy," she says with a big grin. "You know, I might need a little help up the stairs."

I stand, and she puts her arm around my neck. I am just a little taller than she. Five-eleven in a good pair of shoes.

"You okay?"

"I'm fine—just don't go anywhere, or I might fall flat on my face."

I help her up the stairs and into the bedroom. She's laughing all the way. "I need to pee," she says, giggling. "Wait right here." I help her into the bathroom, and she emerges several moments later to the sound of a flushing toilet. "All better," she says. "Ready for night-nights."

I pull back the covers, and she throws herself on the bed. "Help me off with my shoes, will you, Walter?"

I take off the shoes. She unbuttons her pants. "Now the pants."

"I really don't think . . ."

"Oh, don't be such a poop. Put me to bed nicely. I deserve to be a little spoiled, don't I?"

The intimacy of the moment engulfs me. I look away when I slide off her pants, conscious of my desires. Still, I cannot help but glimpse a strip of lingerie before she places her legs under the sheets. "Would you like some water?" I ask.

"Yes please."

I go to the bathroom and return a few moments later with a glass of water. She is not yet asleep.

"I've got the spins," she says. "Shit. I haven't had the spins since college."

"Lie on your back and put one foot on the floor," I tell her.

She does. "That's better. Fuck, no it's not. I think I'm going to puke." She stands up, pushing past me, and weaves to the bathroom, careening off the closet and slamming the bathroom door. I wait a few minutes and knock. "Are you all right?"

I hear a flush and a groan. Worried, I open the door. She is curled around the bottom of the toilet. "I think I'm going to sleep here tonight."

The idea appalls me. "No, you aren't," I say. "Come on."

"No. Staying here."

"Honestly, you aren't. I refuse to leave you in this position. Come on." I grab her shoulders and attempt to hoist her to her feet, but she is too heavy. Or I am not strong enough. In any event, she remains on the floor. "Maddy, I will not leave you on the floor."

"What are you going to do about it?"

I remember her dares from childhood. She standing on the tallest branch threatening to jump off and I pleading with her not to. Once she did and broke her leg. I had to run home and get help. Robert had to carry her back to the house while Genevieve telephoned for the ambulance.

"You're being silly," I say. "You don't want to sleep on the bathroom floor."

"Yes, I do. It's very comfortable."

"You can't."

"Yes, I can. Watch me."

"I won't let you. What would Johnny think?"

"Oh, boo. You're being boring now. Stop being so boring all the time, Walter. Walter, Walter, always so boring."

That stung. There she was. Laying immobile, drunk on the floor. It was a challenge. Or at least I thought it was. It was impossible for me to allow her to remain in that position. After all, wasn't she my responsibility?

So once again, I try to lift her. "Oh, Walter," she taunts. "You're being so manly."

"Shut up," I say, "and cooperate."

To my surprise, she allows me to lift her. She is not fat, but she is a big girl, an ex-athlete, and weighs more than I thought. With effort, I haul her to her feet. She is laughing as I guide her back to bed.

"Just try to go to sleep," I say and turn off the light. "All right?"

"Not really," she murmurs.

"Can I do anything else?"

"Yes. Don't leave." She reaches out for my hand. I clasp hers.

"All right," I say, sitting in the armchair by the bed. "I'll wait until you fall asleep."

"No, not there. Come here," she says, patting the bed, her arm waving drunkenly.

"Well, I . . ." I stutter.

"Please. I think I need to be held."

"Oh, all right." I sit on the bed, on Harry's side no doubt, and remove my shoes and then recline, still fully clothed. She snuggles next to me, slipping her head under my arm and resting on my chest.

"That's much better," she says. "No more spins."

To my great shock, she starts to kiss me. Not sweetly, or even gently. Roughly, forcing my mouth open with her tongue. Her breath smelling of sick. Her hands slithering along my body. Surprised, I return the kiss at first. After all, it's not every day that the thing one has dreamt of for nearly one's whole life actually begins happening. How many nights had I envisioned this very moment? Her lips against mine, fused together in mutual ecstasy?

But it is not like that. This is not what I had dreamt about. There is nothing sweet about it. Not only is her breath bad but the whole thing feels wrong. I try to stand up. She is drunk. This is not romance. It is something coarse. I had wanted to give her choirs and rose petals.

"I should go," I say feebly, trying to unclasp her arms.

"No. Don't go," she whispers, her cheek against mine. Already I feel her hand on my belt. "I want you to make love to me, Walter. Please. If you don't, I'll feel like no one loves me. Please. For me."

I am torn. I feel like a classical hero, riven between what I want and what is right. She is on top of me. I sense myself becoming excited and she does too. I cannot help myself. "I know you want to stay," she says as she kisses me. And I do.

SPRING

1

WEEKS PASS. THE MORNINGS ARE GROWING WARMER. THE
more clearly one sees the world, the more it exists. Soon it will
be light in the evening. The earth will renew itself.

In the city it is raining. Heavy drops, harbingers of more
to come. Already puddles have formed in the street, garbage
swirling in the gutter. People run by on the sidewalk, clutching
umbrellas, holding newspapers over their heads.

Claire is in the gourmet market near her apartment. The
aisles are crowded with people, their jackets dripping from
the rain. Sausages dangle from the ceiling. The smell of fresh-
ground coffee. On the shelves, bottles of truffle oil, fresh pasta,
heirloom tomatoes, chocolates from Belgium. Garnet slabs
of tuna, breaded veal, marbled sirloin. Men and women in
white coats stand behind the counter talking knowledgeably
about cheese. Offering tastes, extolling the virtues of the Bleu
d'Auvergne over the Roquefort.

She does not come here often because it is so expensive, but she wishes she could. She would like to be one of those women, chicly dressed, like the ones in the checkout line with the Prada handbags, diamonds on their fingers. They seem to think nothing of stopping in quickly for a latte or lobster salad and paying for it all confidently with a platinum credit card. One day she knows that will be her. She is prudent. Never buying what she can't afford, making do with small economies, dutifully putting part of her paycheck away every two weeks into a retirement account. It is something she learned from her mother. She has a Frenchwoman's parsimony.

Tonight is different. Tonight she will splurge. I know she does not cook often. She has told me. At her office all day, she trolled different websites looking for recipes. She decided on French because it seemed the more ambitious and also the most familiar. Her mother had known how to cook, had introduced her to snails, sweetbreads, and ortolans, and had taught her how to eat oysters and artichoke hearts. She remembers the simmering burnt-orange Le Creuset pots that once lined the walls of their old kitchen. The bouquets of dried herbs. But that was a long time ago. Her father had never really enjoyed French cooking, preferring instead the homelier fare of his native New England. So their meals became simpler until they stopped altogether. For Claire, cooking felt like retracing steps taken in childhood, of half-remembered rooms and smells.

She had wanted to do something special, had even thought of showing off, but now she is not so sure she can do it. Her oven is so small, her cutlery inadequate. She has no roasting pans and barely any counter space. None of her plates match. For a moment she even thinks of ordering in, but quickly puts that thought out of her head. She clutches the list of ingredients and tentatively fills her cart. I think she made chicken, but it doesn't really matter. It could have been anything. I'll write chicken because it is easiest. A large chicken, shallots, organic baby carrots, French butter, new potatoes, two kinds of cheese, green beans, fruit. She wants it to be a real feast for Harry. This is the first time she has cooked for him. Another in a series of firsts. On her way home, she stops at a liquor store to buy wine. She tells the salesman what she is making, and he recommends a Médoc.

Outside, it is still raining. It is hard to carry her bags and hold the umbrella. A quarter of an hour later, she is home, her groceries unpacked, tying on an apron she has almost never worn. She looks at the clock; two hours.

Harry arrives a few minutes after eight. He is carrying a bouquet of flowers. "Hello," he says animatedly, kissing her at the door. His face is wet and rough with day-old stubble. "I brought you these." He takes off his damp coat and hangs it on the closet door.

She smiles and takes the flowers. "Thank you. Let me put them in water." She has an old vase, runs water into it, places the flowers inside, and puts it on the table. "They're lovely," she says.

"I also brought this," he says, pulling a bottle of whisky from a plastic shopping bag. "I figured you could use some more."

"Can I make you one?" she asks, taking the bottle.

"What an excellent idea," he says with a grin. "I was hoping you might suggest that. Will you join me?"

"Try and stop me."

She finds two glasses and fills them with ice. "I'm sorry," she says, handing him a glass. "Dinner won't be ready for a while."

"Anything I can do to help?"

"No, thank you. Just waiting for everything to cook at this point."

"I am sure it will be delicious. I'm starved. Cheers."

"Cheers."

She takes a sip, looking at him over the glass, feeling the sweet, peaty taste of the whisky against the back of her throat, savoring the moment. They are crossing another boundary. One day maybe it will seem like nothing. As simple as sharing a newspaper.

He sits in the chair nearest the tiny kitchen so he can see her. She is happy he is comfortable here. He knows the books on the shelves, the family pictures without looking at them. There is not much else. He fills the room.

"How was your day?" she asks. What she really means is, how is work coming on your book?

"Fine."

"Still having trouble?"

He shifts uncomfortably. "I'd rather not talk about it if you don't mind. I am just trying to work a few things out."

She has been waiting for him to take her more into his trust. At times it seemed almost as though he was about to.

"Sorry," he says. "I'm just not comfortable talking about it now. It's bad luck."

"I understand."

"So how was your day?"

"All right. I left a little early to go shopping. It's been a long time since I cooked properly. I don't mind telling you I'm nervous as a cat."

"Well, it smells good."

She opens the oven door and bastes the chicken. "Does it? God, I hope so."

He looks over at the small table, which is normally piled high with books and mail and her computer. Now there is a single candle and two glasses. An old tablecloth of her mother's. Paper napkins. Knives and forks. The bottle of wine sitting unopened. His flowers. "It looks lovely."

"Thank you. I wanted to do something nice for you."

He is behind her now, nuzzling her neck, smelling her hair. She closes her eyes. His touch still electrifies her. "You do plenty of nice things for me," he says.

She giggles and twists away from him. "Stop it. Don't distract me. The kitchen's too small. Go over there like a good boy and finish your drink. My oven's acting up, and I need to finish the beans. Damn."

"What's the matter?"

"I don't know if the thermometer's working. It's already been in for an hour and a half, but I can't tell if the chicken's ready or not."

"Try wiggling one of the legs. If it wiggles easily, it's ready."

"It's wiggling."

"Good. Take it out. It'll continue to cook. Just cover it with foil."

"Oh god, the potatoes aren't ready yet."

"How much more time do they need?"

"I don't know. Another fifteen minutes at least."

"Well, in that case, mind if I open the wine? Give it a chance to breathe?"

"What? Oh, sorry. I had meant to do that earlier."

"No worries. I'll take care of it. And I'll make us each another."

Fifteen minutes later, they are sitting at the table. Harry has carved.

"It's delicious," he says.

"No, it's not. You're sweet, but the chicken's overcooked, and the potatoes are undercooked."

"Not at all," he says, chewing the dry chicken. "It's perfect."

"Thank you for lying so nicely about it. I'm sorry it's not better."

"And the wine is excellent."

She smiles. "Okay, you can stop now." She puts her fork down. "How's Johnny?"

"He's all right. We had fun last night. We went rollerblading in Central Park."

She can tell this is something else he doesn't want to talk about. There is no question that she would join them. Maybe one day. But not now. It is too soon, he has told her.

This evening is part of her apology. He had been furious when she told him she went to Maddy. "I told you not to do that," he had yelled before storming out, slamming the door behind him. But she had run after him into the cold night in only her shirtsleeves and caught him on the street.

"I'm sorry," she cried. "I did what I did because I love you."

"You had no right."

"Love gives me the right."

"Dammit, it's more complicated than that. There's Johnny . . ."

"I know. But it's too late now. It's done."

He could only imagine what had happened. It made him physically sick. He turned to leave.

"No, don't go," she said, clasping him, preventing him from moving. "I'm sorry. It will be all right. I promise. Come back upstairs. Please."

He had followed her. She was conscious of her victory but also knew she had to be careful. She had taken a chance, almost too much of one. She had to win back part of his trust, part of his pride. This was about more than the two of them. This was about his family. She understood that better now. Would she have done it any differently? No, I don't think so.

In the weeks since, they had spent every night together except for the two nights each week he had Johnny. In that time, he had not spoken to Maddy once. When he called the house, Gloria answered and took down messages that went unreturned. When it became apparent that Maddy did not want to talk to him, he stopped leaving messages altogether.

After dinner he and Claire are getting ready for bed. The dishes have been cleaned and washed by hand. He now keeps a toothbrush by her sink.

"I'm tired," he says.

"Too tired?"

"No, not too tired. Just tired, you know."

"We don't have to do anything."

She doesn't mean it. Under the covers she is naked. She wants him inside her and then the peace that comes after.

"No, I want to."

"Good," she says. She trails her hands over his body, blowing in his ear, arousing him, as she knew she could.

"See, I told you I wasn't too tired," he says.

But when they are finished, he rolls over on his side, his back to her. She is used to sleeping on his chest. She reaches out her hand, lightly placing it on his back. He stirs in his sleep but doesn't move.

She gets up and quietly leaves the bedroom, fumbling in the dark for her robe. In her living room, she sits staring out the window with the light off. She can hear the sound of his breathing from the other room. This is how it starts, she thinks. One night they will not make love. There will be an excuse. One of them is too tired or too drunk. And then it will end— or it will evolve. Already they are brushing their teeth together before going to bed. Soon they will be sitting in restaurants, studying the menus with nothing new to say to each other. Is this what she wanted? Things are already very different from what they had been at first. Then it had all been new and exciting. There had been the house, the people, Maddy, myself, and, of course, Harry.

It's hard not to be caught up in the beauty of life from a summer lawn in the Hamptons. That had been followed by even more excitement. The first weeks of their affair. The sense of unreality, the mutual discoveries. The traveling, the mystery, the hotels, the restaurants. The danger. She had never felt so alive. Then the other night he repeated a story she had already heard him tell. It was a funny story, and she had laughed very much when he first told it to her. Hearing it a second time annoyed her. Didn't he remember he'd already told her this?

Was he already running out of stories? Had he already come to the point in his life where that was all he had left? Surely, it was only a matter of time before he told it a third time, or a fourth. She was in the phase of life when she was still making her own stories. Was that what Maddy did? Was that all wives did? Sit there and listen to the same stories over and over again? Was that what marriage was about? She remembered how she had felt during those endless afternoons in her grandparents' apartment. The sense that this was all there was, the old clock ticking in the hallway, the oppression of repetition.

She sighs and stands and stretches. On the street outside a young couple is walking. It is impossible to know how well they know each other. They are holding hands. They could have just met, or they could have been together for years. At the corner, they turn and kiss. Claire envies them.

2

IT HAS BEEN SEVERAL WEEKS SINCE THAT NIGHT WITH MADDY. I had woken early in her bedroom and quietly gathered my clothes. She slept heavily, snoring slightly. I left her there in the dark, sneaking out like a thief, hoping I wouldn't wake Johnny while I changed in the hallway.

Neither of us called the other that day or the next. I didn't because I didn't know what to say. I had no idea what was going on inside her head. She had been very drunk. Drunker than I had ever seen her. Did she even remember what had happened? I did remember, though, and the memory was uncomfortable. It had been painful, not in the physical sense but emotionally. Yet she was the one in true pain. I could tell she wasn't thinking of me, if she had been thinking of anyone. I was merely a device, a beating heart and racing blood. She had not said a word the whole time. Nor, for that matter, had I.

When we finished, she just pulled the covers over her and passed out. I didn't know whether to go or stay, so I lay there sleepless, not daring to move, staring at the ceiling, listening to her snore, pondering this unexpected turn of events, naked, stunned, and shamed, until I couldn't take it anymore and left.

A few days later, I called and left a message. I tried to sound as innocuous as possible. How was she? How was Johnny? Maybe dinner this weekend? I was convinced she was standing there the whole time listening to me leave the message, despising me. She never called back.

I tried again a few nights later. This time she picked up.

"Oh, hi," she said. "Sorry, I can't speak now. I'm already late."

"Call you tomorrow?"

"Great." She had already hung up before I could respond.

I was surprised to hear that she was late for something. She rarely went out, and when she did, it was with either Harry or me. Where was she going? Who was she seeing? For almost forty years, I had known her life almost as well as my own. Now I felt cut off. Or not. Maybe I was overthinking things. I wouldn't know until I could speak to her.

But when I called her the next day, she still didn't pick up. Nor the next day. Finally, I got tired of leaving messages. I shuttled back and forth between my apartment and office, looking for distraction in work but invariably finding my eyes drifting over to the photograph of Maddy and me on my desk. It had been taken years ago, by Harry I think. We were on the beach. I had more hair then and a slimmer waist. She looked just the same. Sometimes clients, making small talk, ask if she is my wife. I know it would look odd, having the photograph of another man's wife on my desk, so I usually lie and say she is my sister. It's almost the truth, after all, even though I am often tempted to lie and say that, yes, she is my wife.

The next several weeks were among the loneliest in my life. My one true friend seemed to have abandoned me. I had lived such a tightly circumscribed life, the fixed stars of my personal cosmos had always been centered around Maddy. As long as she was there, across the table or at the other end of the phone, what else did I need? But now I was completely aware of the emptiness. I felt like a pianist who had lost a hand.

I was at my club one night, having finished my fitful exercise routine and a steam, and about to enjoy a well-deserved martini, when another of the members came up to my table. "Say, Walt," he said. "Mind if I join you?"

"Not at all," I replied. I liked Dewey. He had been a few years behind me at school, but we knew each other socially from both the city and Long Island. Unlike most of the members, who came here to get away from their wives, I came here for companionship. He was agreeable, and we usually saw eye to eye on the decline of everything from the overall quality of new members at the various clubs of which we were both members to the general ineptitude of our elected representatives in Albany and Washington.

Dewey sat, looking uncomfortable. "Look here, I hope I'm not being out of line with what I'm about to ask."

"What's on your mind?"

"Well, I know you're friends with Madeleine Winslow."

"That's right."

"Maybe it's none of my business, but I saw her the other night."

"Nothing unusual about that."

"No, of course not. But what I mean to say is that I saw her with a man. Vicki and I had a sitter, and we thought it would be fun to go downtown to this little Italian place we've read about. I didn't recognize the fellow, but it most certainly wasn't her husband. I know Winslow slightly, and this man looked nothing like him. Darker. I just thought I should mention it, if you take my meaning."

"Ah," I said. I wasn't quite sure how to respond to this news. Another man? Who was he? Which little Italian place? I wanted to press, but tact prevented me. "Well, er, the Winslows have separated."

"Have they? Sorry to hear it. They always seemed like such a nice couple. She's a real beauty, and I remember him when he played hockey."

"Yes, it's very sad."

"Well, I guess that explains it. Sorry for busting in."

"Don't mention it. Glad I could clear things up."

He stood up to leave.

"Don't be in such a hurry, Dewey," I said. "Let me buy you a drink."

"All right," he replied, sitting down. "I'll have what you're having."

I wound up convincing him to join me for dinner too. Our conversation veered to the usual subjects, and, by the time we left the table, we had pretty much exhausted them. We parted on the street with vague but well-meant promises to get together for tennis once the weather warmed up.

As I walked home in the rain, my mind was turning over Dewey's news. Another man? What the hell was going on? Normally I would have called Maddy to tell her the gossip, but this time not only was she not talking to me but the gossip was about her. I was half-tempted to go by her house and get to the bottom of things. Despite the rain, I suppose I thought that seemed like a good idea because that's what I did. My reasoning was doubtless affected by the fact that I had drunk several martinis and half a bottle of the club's claret.

The lights were on in the house when I rang the doorbell. It was around nine-thirty. When there was no answer, I rang again. Eventually Gloria came to the door, opening it a crack, looking terrified, but she relaxed when she saw it was me. Still, she didn't invite me in, keeping the door chained.

"Mister Walter, *buenas noches*."

"Good evening, Gloria. Sorry to stop by so late. Is Mrs. Winslow in?"

"No, Mrs. Maddy is not here."

"Any idea when she'll be back?"

"No, Mister Walter. She out late every night. And last week too."

"Who is she out with?"

She shook her head. "I not know. Different men. Please. I go to bed now."

"I see. Sorry to disturb you. Can you please let Mrs. Winslow know I came by?"

"Yes, Mister Walter."

"Well, *buenas noches*."

"*Buenas noches*." She smiled and hurriedly closed the door. For a moment I thought about staying and waiting for Maddy to come home. But I had no idea when she might return or with whom. And I was getting soaked.

I had nowhere to go but home. Who else could I turn to? Harry? Not likely. Ned and Cissy? I supposed, but I didn't know if they'd be of any help. Claire? The idea was absurd. As I was lying in my bed, I realized I had to do this myself. I knew I had to find Maddy and speak to her. It was the only way. But how?

I also knew it would be almost impossible to know what Maddy was doing without her telling me herself. The only other way was for me to follow her. I imagined myself in a trench coat, hovering in the bushes and playing the fool, acutely aware it was something I could never do. But that didn't mean someone else couldn't do it. I knew our firm occasionally retained private investigators, and so the next day I had Marybeth get me the number of an agency we often used.

That afternoon a man named Bernie came to my office. He was stocky, had a mustache, and wore a florid tie and thick-soled shoes. I had never had a reason to use him in the past, but I knew that he was a former police officer and that a number of my colleagues vouched for him.

"How can I help you, Mister Gervais?" he asked.

"This is a personal matter," I explained. "I want to make that clear up front. So please be sure to bill me personally, not the firm."

"Doesn't make any difference to me, sir. What's the job?"

"I would like you to keep an eye on someone."

"Who might that be, sir?"

I handed him the photograph of Maddy and me from my desk.

"Your wife?"

"No, she's a friend."

He looked at the picture. "Nice-looking woman. You got any more recent photos?"

"I'll get some. But she looks just the same."

"Okay. So what's the situation?" He sat with an open note-book on his knee, pen at the ready.

"Her name is Madeleine Winslow. I have known her since we were children, and she is my oldest friend. She recently separated from her husband of almost twenty years, and it has been a real shock to her. Several weeks ago, she stopped re-turning my phone calls. That is unusual because we rarely go three or four days without speaking or e-mailing. A friend of mine told me he saw her out with a man the other night at a restaurant downtown. I spoke with her son's babysitter, and she told me that Mrs. Winslow has been out every night, usu-ally with different men. Frankly, I am concerned because she is acting very much out of character, and I need to make sure she is all right. I am also concerned about the welfare of her son, who happens to be my godson. What I'd like you to do is to keep an eye on her, find out where she is going, what she is doing, and who she is doing it with."

"Sure. No problem." He put his pen down.

Personally, I loathe it when people say "no problem." It is one of my pet peeves. When they are working for me, it's not their problem. It's their job. "And, of course," I added, after taking a deep breath, "I am sure I don't need to ask you to be discreet. She must not know she is being followed."

"Of course."

We then discussed his fee and a few other details. I prom-ised to e-mail him more recent photos of Maddy and then wrote out a check for his retainer. He said he'd be in touch in a few days if there was anything to report. I was impressed by his professionalism. We shook hands, and he left. I know some people might think I was going too far, sticking my nose into

Maddy's business, but I didn't care about that. The only thing that mattered to me was being sure she was all right. For the next few days, I waited. There was no word from Bernie or Maddy.

Following a weekend of worrying, I heard from Bernie on Monday morning. "I followed the subject over the course of three nights," he told me on the phone. "The first night, she left her house around eight o'clock. She took a taxi down to a restaurant in Tribeca. There she met a man. He's Greek, a Yannis Papadakis. Age thirty-eight, profession shipping. Marital status, divorced. Physical description, approximately six-foot, athletic build, brown hair, brown eyes, clean shaven, no distinguishing characteristics. I'll e-mail you his photograph."

I had never heard of him. "Go on," I said.

"The subject left the restaurant with Papadakis at just after eleven P.M. Both had a lot to drink. You'll find a copy of the receipt in the file I will send you. Papadakis paid the check with a Centurion card. There was a car waiting for them. A late-model Cadillac Escalade. It then drove them a short distance to Papadakis's apartment nearby on Beach Street. The subject entered his apartment. At three A.M. subject left the apartment and the Escalade drove her home. Shall I go on?"

"Please."

Bernie cleared his throat. "The next night, Friday, the subject again left her house around eight o'clock. This time she took a taxi downtown to an Italian restaurant in Soho, where she met a man named Steven Ambrosio. Age forty-two, profession investment banking. Marital status, single. Physical description, approximately five-eleven, slim build, shaved head, brown eyes, clean shaven, no distinguishing characteristics.

The subject left the restaurant with Ambrosio around midnight, and they took a taxi uptown to Ambrosio's apartment on East Sixty-Eighth Street. Again, around three A.M. subject exited the apartment and took a taxi home. Again, I will send an e-mail with photographs of Ambrosio and receipts. Any questions so far?"

Again, the man was unknown to me. "Not yet. Please proceed."

"On Saturday, the subject was picked up around three P.M. by Papadakis, this time driving himself in a Porsche 911. I followed them to Southampton, where Papadakis has a weekend house on Ox Pasture Road. It was difficult for me to park so I had to make do with circling the block. The neighborhood is home to many wealthy people, and the police patrol it regularly. I was, however, able to ascertain that the subject and Papadakis went to a party at a house in Sagaponack on Daniels Lane. It is likely that illegal substances were consumed. At approximately one A.M. subject and Papadakis returned to Ox Pasture. The next day they went for lunch at Nello in Southampton around one P.M., and then they returned to Manhattan. Again, Papadakis paid, and I can provide a copy of receipt. Subject arrived home around five P.M. She did not go out last night."

"Thank you, Bernie," I said. "Very thorough."

"Will you require my services further?"

"Yes." I was thinking. "Yes, I'll need you to keep following Mrs. Winslow. The only difference is the next time she goes out I want you to call me and tell me where she is."

There was silence on the other end of the line. Then he said, "I understand, Mister Gervais. I need to inform you that if you are contemplating assaulting the subject or violating her rights in any way, I would be considered an accomplice. I won't be a party to that, sir."

I laughed lightly. "Oh god, what? No, no. Please, Bernie. Don't worry about anything like that. I have no intention of assaulting Mrs. Winslow or breaking the law. I just need to speak to her. And since the mountain won't go to Mohammed, Mohammed must go to the mountain."

"Okay, Mister Gervais. I've got your cell phone number. I'll follow her again tonight, and if she goes out, I'll call you."

There was no call from Bernie that night. The next night, however, my cell phone rings shortly after eight. "Good evening, sir," he says. "The subject is on the move. I'll call you again when she has reached her destination."

"Excellent. Thanks." For the next quarter of an hour or so, I pace my apartment, clutching my cell phone, checking my watch, patting and repatting my pockets to make sure I have my wallet, a handkerchief, comb, nail clippers, pen. When the second call comes, I head to the elevator clutching the phone to my ear. Bernie gives me the name and address of a restaurant in the West Village. I am secretly relieved it's not out in Brooklyn somewhere. I can remember when traveling below Forty-second Street at night was as unusual as visiting the dark side of the moon. These days the most fashionable neighborhoods in New York are the ones that had once been the poorest. I step outside, where I have a car waiting, and give the driver the address.

"Subject is seated in a booth in the back," reports Bernie. "She is not with either Papadakis or Ambrosio. I haven't been able to ascertain the name of the man yet. Roughly fifty, graying hair, expensive suit."

"Thanks, Bernie. I won't require any more than that. If all goes well tonight, you can send me your bill in the morning. Wish me luck."

"Good luck."

Around nine o'clock, I arrive in front of a brightly lit bistro. I glance around for Bernie but don't see him. The streets here are still cobblestone. But the former slaughterhouses and commercial buildings have been renovated, and are now boutiques, hotels, restaurants, and nightclubs.

I tell the driver to wait, and walk inside. It's crowded with a cross section of hip, young Manhattan. Scruffy artistic types in black T-shirts commingle with young bankers, and pretty girls are everywhere. I can see why there aren't many older people. It's very hard to hear. I head to the bar and fight my way in. In my J.Press suit, I look out of place, like someone who wandered in from the wrong movie. Eventually the bartender acknowledges me, and I order a martini.

I look around the restaurant, searching for Maddy and praying she doesn't see me first. It's not easy because the seating area is not all visible from the bar. Finally, I spot her. Sitting in a corner with a gray-haired man, just as Bernie said. She is talking animatedly, the way she does when she's had a few drinks. I see there is an open bottle in a wine bucket near the table.

Immediately I duck my head to avoid being seen. I turn my back and try, with difficulty, to look comfortable. But pretty soon I am elbowed aside by a young man who hasn't shaved in several days. He's wearing a porkpie hat and orders drinks for a group of friends, and I retreat ignominiously to a corner. It is clear I can't just linger here. I need to act or leave.

Finishing my martini, I place the glass with resolve on the bar, leave a twenty-dollar bill, and start walking toward the back. I don't head straight for Maddy's table but instead pretend I am trying to locate someone at one of the tables, chin raised, sniffing the air like a lost bear. I am not much of an actor, but I didn't really need to be. There is only one person I have to convince.

"Maddy!" I say.

She looks up at me, surprised, beautiful. Her blue eyes wide. "Walter," she says. "What are you doing here?"

Grayhair looks confused and clearly doesn't relish the intrusion. I can't say I blame him.

I lean over and kiss her on both cheeks. "Meeting a client for dinner," I say. "Thought it would be fun to see why everyone makes such a fuss about this place. But I just got an e-mail that they're running late."

"Oh. Walter, let me introduce you to Richard," she says, indicating Grayhair as though my running into her in a downtown restaurant with a strange man was the most normal thing in the world. He looks like the Hollywood idea of a CEO. Jawline of granite, great teeth, full hair, gold watch. As I get closer I can tell he is more likely in his sixties.

"How do you do?" I say and, grabbing an empty chair behind me, ask, "May I?" I am already sitting, so they can't respond in any way other than to say yes without being rude. They are still holding their menus, meaning they haven't ordered yet.

"Not at all," says Grayhair, giving me a magnanimous boardroom smile. "Any friend of Maddy's is welcome."

"And not just any friend," I put in. "Her oldest friend.

Known each other since we were tots, haven't we, darling? So," I say playfully, turning and looking at her for the first time since I sat down. "Where have you been? I've been trying to catch you, but you've been so busy lately."

She gives me a dirty look. "That's right, Walter. I have been. Sorry I've been so hard to track down."

"Oh well, clearly I've been going to all the wrong places."

"Say, Walter, can I offer you a drink?" asks Grayhair. Obviously he comes from the school that believes the best way to control a situation is to pay for it.

"Why, thanks, Rich. That's awfully good of you." I hold up my hand and immediately flag down a waiter, asking him to bring me a Beefeater martini straight up with a twist. "So sorry to barge in on you like this. How do you two know each other anyway?"

Maddy says nothing but glares at me. Grayhair jumps in with "Oh, we met at a party in Southampton the other week."

"Southampton. Is that right? Nice part of the world. Lived out there long?"

"About ten years. I bought an old farmhouse and replaced it with something more modern. You know there was only one bathroom in the whole house? Realtor told me a family of seven used to live there. Imagine the line in the morning," he says with a practiced laugh.

I hate him, of course, but I also see his charm. I have sat across the table from many like him, grinding them down, taking my pound of flesh. I could do this all day—or night. It's like shagging flies.

I smile blandly at Grayhair and turn to Maddy, leaving him hanging. "How's Johnny? I haven't seen him in weeks."

"No, you haven't," she replies with the same kind of smile. Oh, I know her so well. "He's fine."

"Maybe I could pop over one night and see him, assuming you're ever around anymore?" I say to her. Then, back to Grayhair, "He's my godson. He's nine. Lovely boy." Before he can jump in with some trite observation about the virtues of nine-year-old boys, I turn back to Maddy. "So, I've discovered we have some mutual friends."

"We always have had, darling," she ripostes.

"Yes, well, these are new friends."

"Are they now? I am so happy to see you making new friends. You really do need to broaden your circle of acquaintances."

"Well, clearly I don't need to tell you that. You've been making lots of new friends too."

"I like people."

"Naturally, and from what I hear you've been enormously popular. That must make you feel so good. Being so popular with so many people. From what I hear you make a new friend almost every night."

"Fuck you, Walter," she says. Apparently playtime is over.

"Hey now, what's going on?" asks Grayhair, looking confused.

"Nothing, Rich," I reply. "Just a little light banter."

"It was so nice of you stop by, Walter," says Maddy. "What an amazing coincidence to run into you."

"I know? Wasn't it?" I say brightly, glancing at my phone. "Oops. Looks like my friend needs me to meet him at a different restaurant. Guess I must be going." I stand. "Thanks for the drink, Rich."

I lean over Maddy and whisper, "Are you crazy?" in her ear while kissing her good night. Then in a louder voice, "Let's talk soon."

Sitting stiffly in her seat, she says nothing. She is furious at me. Good. That's the reaction I'd hoped to elicit. One of them at any rate. "Well, so long. Hope you kids have a fun night," I say.

I walk casually through the restaurant to the exit. At the door I turn and wave. Grayhair, who has been staring at me the whole way, waves back, glad to be rid of me. Maddy just sits there. Outside, in the anonymity of the street, I breathe a sigh of relief. I realize I am sweating and feel the perspiration chill against my body in the cool of the night air. I look around for my car and walk over to it.

"Thanks for waiting," I say as I climb in. The driver, a Sikh, looks up from his cell phone. "No problem, sir. Where to?"

No problem. That awful phrase. I groan inwardly and say, "Nowhere just yet. Let's sit here for a while."

From the backseat, I have a good view of the restaurant's entrance. To my delight, not ten minutes later, I see Maddy and Grayhair emerge. I can't hear what they are saying, but Grayhair's body language suggests surprise, disappointment, and obsequiousness. He is trying to figure out what the hell is going on and how he can still salvage the evening. Maddy, tall and erect, her arm outstretched for a taxi, strides purposefully, disdainfully, like the prow of a ship. Getting a taxi in this neighborhood appears easy. There seem to be a dozen or so cruising around looking for fares. One pulls up in front of Maddy. She gives Grayhair a perfunctory kiss and jumps in, leaving him standing on the sidewalk bewildered and horny.

I watch Maddy's face in the back of the cab as she drives by. "Okay, we can go now," I tell the driver. "Please take me home."

I REMEMBER WHEN JOHNNY WAS BORN. MADDY HAD BEEN IN labor for forty hours. Then she dilated around six in the evening and pushed for the next three hours, Harry on one side, a nurse on the other, urging her to breathe, to push and push again. Johnny had been crowning almost the whole time. She pushed so hard she burst the capillaries under her eyes. Finally the doctor had to rush her in for an emergency episiotomy. A large male nurse had to keep a frantic Harry from following. Finally, Johnny was delivered, covered in his mother's blood, and she was able to hold him only for a moment because both of them required medical attention. Johnny was taken immediately to the neonatal intensive care unit.

The doctor, a little man with a German accent, told them about their son's heart. There was a congenital defect, something that had not been picked up in the prenatal examinations. They were keeping him under observation, and a pediatric cardiologist had been called in. There was the possibility of surgery. Harry was furious the doctor had let the baby crown for so long, making unnecessary physical demands on both mother and child, but Maddy calmed him with a touch of her hand. It's all right, she told him. And looking down at her, knowing what she had just gone through, he couldn't say anything more but just took her hand and kissed it and looked at her with love, amazed by her courage and strength.

The whole time I had been waiting anxiously in the lounge, chewing my head off, sick of CNN and as nervous as any expectant father. I have always hated hospitals, the stench, the sickness, the posturing of the doctors. It was torture, but for Maddy I was willing to endure it. When I first saw Harry's grim face afterward, I was relieved to learn that my worst fears had not been realized, even if the news wasn't what any of us wanted to hear.

"There's something wrong with his heart," he told me. "They have to keep him in the NICU. Maddy's in rough shape, but she'll be okay. They've given her a sedative to help her sleep."

We kept a vigil all night, alternating between Maddy's room and the NICU. I even suggested suing the doctor and offered to bring the suit myself. But Harry waved me down, concerned only about his newborn son, who was not yet named, who was lying there in his bubble-like bed, a little mask over his tiny face, electrodes attached to his chest, monitors beeping, a striped cloth cap covering his head, his eyes swollen with abrupt new life. I wasn't clear which of them appeared the more helpless, the father or the son. Harry looked exhausted too, having slept the previous night on a chair in Maddy's room while she had contractions. He would sleep at the hospital again tonight, if he was able to sleep at all.

The next day they wheeled Johnny into Maddy's room and let her hold him. It was a different room now, higher up and larger. Already there were several bouquets of flowers. The largest from me, plus a giant teddy bear. With her baby in her arms, Maddy looked beatific but half-dead. I had never seen her so drained. Her skin pale, her eyes blackened.

"He's so beautiful." She sighed.

"He'll be all right," I said. "The doctors here are the best. Plus I have a friend who's on the board. Don't worry. They're doing everything they can."

"Thank you, Walter."

The nurse returned and told us she had to take Johnny back. The look on Maddy's face was heartbreaking.

I also made a move to leave. "Before you go, Walt," said Harry. "There's something Maddy and I would like to ask you."

They looked at each other, holding hands, and then back to me. "Walter," said Harry, "I hope this won't come as too much of a shock, but we'd like you to be the godfather."

"I'd be honored." I looked at Maddy. I hoped my glance expressed the extent of my gratitude.

"If anyone can help get Satan behind him, it's you," said Harry with a smile, shaking my hand. Maddy held out her arms, and I leaned over to kiss her. "Thank you," she whispered.

"Do you have a name for him yet?"

"Yes," said Harry. "We've been talking about it for some time, but we only just decided it this morning."

"We're naming him John Walter Winslow."

I blushed. It's not every day your best friend names her child after you or asks you, in a small but real way, to become a de facto member of the family. I was very touched. From then on, Johnny became almost as important to me as his mother. I even set up a trust fund for him and named him my sole heir. One day he would be quite rich.

That night to celebrate I ordered in dinner from one of the city's best restaurants. It was July, and they sent over lobster and cold Pouilly-Fumé in ice buckets. They provided a table, linen, silverware, and even a waiter to serve us. It was very civilized. Maddy was hungry but exhausted. She ate a few forkfuls and had a sip of the wine but soon excused herself and said she had to sleep. I had tried to lure Harry away for a drink, but he declined, saying he wanted to stay with Maddy and Johnny.

The next several years were very hard. Johnny was in and out of the hospital, requiring a number of operations. The scariest time was once when he was three; he collapsed in the backyard of their house in New York, and Harry had to run him the whole way to the emergency room.

There was a further complication, but with Maddy, not Johnny. The doctor had taken Harry aside the day after the birth. The labor had been traumatic for Maddy. She had pushed for too long, and having another baby might be dangerous. I am sorry, he said. Harry did not tell me this. Maddy did, years later. I have often wondered what would have happened if there had been another child.

But I knew having a sick child had taken a toll on Maddy. Being a mother changed her. It made her more protective, less adventurous. Johnny became the center of her universe, and she refused to move herself out of orbit around him. But it also made her more determined and selfless than ever. And Harry was there every step of the way. He was working on his book then, the one that would make his name, and they shut themselves away for weeks at a time, living happily with only each other. I was always welcome, like the captain of the mail boat to a lighthouse keeper and his family, a source of diversion and news from the outside world, but I could tell they were never sad to see me chug away back to shore.

As Johnny's health stabilized, they became less reclusive. Then the success of Harry's book came, and, once again, he allowed himself to give in to his more social nature. He was always good in crowds, confident, amusing, attentive when he had to be. He liked parties, going to them or giving them. Maddy liked them less and rarely wanted to leave Johnny, so, more often than not, they invited people to their home. It was something she did for Harry and for herself too. And, of course, it didn't hurt that she was a good cook and beautiful and smart, and people always came.

But keeping Harry close, as she did Johnny, made her happiest. Maybe somewhere in her heart she feared that, if she didn't, she might lose them both. And that would have destroyed her.

That's why I was so disturbed to see her abandon Johnny the way she had. That was not the Maddy I knew. None of this was. Johnny needed her back, and so did I.

I call her the day after the scene in the restaurant. This time she picks up.

"That was a rotten trick," she says.

"I don't know what you mean."

"Oh, come off it. You know exactly what I mean."

"I'm sorry if I broke up your little date. He seemed like such a nice fellow too."

"You're an asshole."

"Am I?"

"Yes, you are. I don't know how you found me, but I don't believe that story about you meeting a client for one minute. You'd no more meet a client at a place like that than you'd vote for a Democrat."

It's true. I wouldn't. But I am not about to confess.

"Well, I guess we're all capable of doing new things. It's not exactly your sort of place either."

There is silence on the other end. Then, "My life is very different now than it used to be."

"If yours is, then so is mine."

"I didn't want it to be," she says quietly.

"I didn't either."

"What's wrong with my dating?" She is angry now. "I'm separated. And Harry's fucking Claire. Why do I have to stay cooped up? Shouldn't I be allowed to have some fun too?"

"Of course you should have fun. I just know you've been going out a lot. Isn't that rather hard on Johnny? He's going through a lot too. He needs you more than ever."

So far there has been no mention of our night together. I'm not about to bring it up, and neither, it seems, is she. I just want things to go back to the way they had been.

She sighs. "I'm thinking of going away for a little while."

"With Johnny?"

"No. He has school. He can stay with Harry. It'll be good for both of them."

"Are you sure that's the best idea?"

"No, I'm not sure about anything. I just know if I stay in New York right now I'll go out of my mind."

"Would you be going away by yourself?"

"Very funny. Yes. I don't want to be around anyone, see anyone. I just want to be alone. Go somewhere, sit on a beach, and think about what the hell I'm supposed to do next. Mexico, somewhere like that. I want green salt water. Green salt water so pure and clear it's the only thing between sand and sky."

I'm relieved. "That sounds like a good plan."

"I'm not asking for your approval, dammit."

"Can I help?"

"As a matter of fact, you can. Please check on Johnny from time to time. I know Harry will take good care of him. I just want Johnny to know that the other people in his life love him too."

"Of course. It'd be a pleasure. How long will you be gone for?"

"I don't know. A few weeks. I'd like to disappear for a year, but I know I can't do that."

"When are you thinking of leaving?"

"If I can, I was thinking next week. The sooner the better. When I come back, we can open up the house. I know how much Johnny loves being there. I can't believe it's almost the summer again. God, what a year," she says with a laugh.

ON THE NIGHT BEFORE MADDY'S FLIGHT, HARRY COMES TO the brownstone to pick up Johnny. Naturally I had asked if she wanted me to be there. To my surprise, she said it wasn't necessary, but she tells me about it the next morning when she calls from the airport to say good-bye. I had already asked her to give me her contact information. I don't like the idea of not knowing where she is.

"It was nice to see him. I was surprised," she says.

I am equally surprised to hear her say so. It's the first time she has talked civilly about Harry since the whole episode came to light. Until now, she hasn't expressed anything other than contempt.

"What do you mean?"

"He was being so sweet. And he gave me his old Saint Christopher medal. The one he always wears when he flies. He told me he wanted me to have it."

"Did you take it?"

"Of course. He knows how much I hate flying."

"What else did you talk about?"

"Johnny. I told him I didn't want Johnny to be around Claire."

"How did he react?"

"He agreed. Said he understood. Then he tried to apologize again."

"What did you say?"

"I said I didn't want to talk about it."

"Did you talk about anything else?"

"Not much. You know, chitchat. Mexico. You know, it's one of the few places we've never been together. Maybe that's why I wanted to go there. Anyway, we had a drink. Sat in the living room. It was strangely cozy, you know? He said his book was coming along. The funny thing is that he even made me laugh. You know how he is when he gets going. No one can tell a joke like Harry, and, even though I had promised myself I'd be immune to his charms, he had me roaring. I had been so angry with him that I couldn't believe he could still do that, but he could. For a moment I almost forgot about what he did and how angry I am with him, and it was almost like none of this had ever happened. And Johnny looked so happy too. I could tell what he was thinking."

I let this sink in. "Are you having second thoughts?"

"What?"

"Second thoughts. About the divorce."

"Oh, I don't know. Isn't that normal? I was reading that happens a lot. Halfway through you get cold feet and wonder if it's really the right thing to do. We're so quick to chuck our whole lives overboard. I mean, my father tried to fuck anything in a skirt whether he was married or not. But that wasn't why his wives left him. Life can be so lonely, you know?"

I knew that better than most. "Do you still love him?"

"I don't know. I spent the last twenty years of my life with him. It's odd not having him around. I miss him sometimes. I really do. And of course Johnny does. He's been so excited about spending time with Harry that I almost resent it. I asked him if he was going to miss me, and he said sure, but I could tell he almost couldn't wait to leave with his father." She laughs.

"So what are you going to do?"

"Nothing for the time being. Go to Mexico. I can think about things while I'm down there, and hopefully I'll be able to get some perspective. I'll be back in a couple of weeks. Then, if I change my mind, I can deal with it. Or not."

"Okay, well, good luck and *vaya con Dios.*"

"Thanks, Walter. Thanks for everything. You've put up with so much from me. I really don't think I could have made it without you. You know I love you. You're the one man who's never let me down."

"I love you too," I answer, but I don't mean it the same way she does.

I CAN IMAGINE CLAIRE'S FACE AS SHE ABSORBS THE NEWS. HE has taken her out to dinner to the little bistro near her apartment. They must have had a few martinis, and then the frisée salad sprinkled with lardons followed by a steak frites dripping butter. A bottle of red wine. She would be happy, enjoying an increasingly rare night out. She had even made him meet her at the restaurant so she could go home and change out of her work clothes.

"There's something I have to tell you, and I hope you won't mind," he says. "Johnny needs to stay with me for the next three weeks. Maddy is going on a trip. She called me yesterday and told me. She's not taking Johnny."

"There's nothing bad about that," Claire says, not quite understanding. "I'd love to help take care of Johnny. He's wonderful."

"I'm sorry. I'm not so sure it's a good idea for you to see Johnny right now. Maddy and I discussed it."

"Oh, you did, did you? What did you say? Did you stick up for me at all?"

He is surprised by the suddenness of her anger, but maybe he shouldn't be. "It wasn't like that," he says with a shrug, cutting into his steak.

"Oh really? So I'm meant just to disappear for three weeks until Maddy comes back?"

"It's not such a long time."

"That's not the point."

"Okay, so what is the point? Are you suggesting that I should place you ahead of my son? You know me well enough to know I could never do that. Anyway, what choice did I have? I need to do everything I can to ensure that a judge gives me equal time with Johnny if the divorce goes through."

"If? Don't you want it to go through?"

The question startles him. "Of course I don't want it to go through."

She stares at him. "What?"

He looks at her quizzically. "You heard me. I don't want to get divorced. I don't want to lose my family. I'm sorry if that's not what you want to hear, but it's the truth."

"So does that make everything else a lie?"

"No, not at all. There's no need to twist my words like that. I care for you very much. I hope you know that. But I also thought you understood how I felt."

She looks down, biting her lip. Finally she asks, "And what about me? I'm tired of it, Harry. I love you, but I need to know you love me too."

"We've been over this. You know I love Maddy and Johnny. They're my life. I screwed up, and Maddy hates me, but I'd do anything I could to get them back. I thought you knew that. I'm sorry if I made you think anything else."

She looks away. "I'm such a fool," she says. "God."

"Why do you say that?"

"To have ever thought you would choose me over Maddy. When she asked for the divorce, I thought I might have a chance, but now, even when she doesn't want you, you still want her more than me."

He lets her words drop. "I do."

Hatred flashes in her eyes. "You're a taker, Harry. You never think about anything other than what you want. You

never think about what other people want or how your actions affect other people. I know you didn't think of me for one
minute when you were talking with Maddy. And you know
how that makes me feel? It makes me feel like shit."

"I'm sorry."

" 'Sorry'? Is that all you can say?"

"This is my family we are talking about. We were happy
together until . . ." He pauses.

"Until what? Were you going to say until I came along and
ruined everything?"

He opens his mouth to speak but knows it would be pointless.

"Forget it," she says, standing up. "Since you want to spend
the next three weeks with Johnny so much, why don't you just
start now?"

"Maybe that's not a bad idea."

"What?"

He sighs. "Maybe we shouldn't see each other anymore.
I've been thinking about this a lot lately. You're wonderful, but
I still love my wife. I need to do everything I can to save my
marriage and my family. And, besides, you're so young. Did
you really think this would become anything?"

She looks at him, stunned. Finally she says in a barely audible voice, "Bastard."

"Claire . . ."

She puts one arm hurriedly through the sleeve of her jacket,
and then the other, and gathers up her purse.

"I'm sorry," he says again but does nothing to prevent her
from leaving. They look at each other like strangers.

He watches her walk out the door, the remnants of their
dinner before him. There is still wine in her glass. Her meal sits

half-eaten, the knife and fork where she left them. The napkin thrown on the seat. He almost gets up and follows her but instead signals to the waiter for the check. Diners at tables nearby who had stopped talking once again resume their meals.

He finishes the wine, leaves his money. He is a generous tipper, counting out the precious bills.

Leaving the restaurant, he starts walking toward Claire's apartment, partly from habit. She has not yet given him a key. He could, he supposes, ring her buzzer. Tell her over the intercom that he has changed his mind and hope for the click that releases the door, a sign that all is forgiven and that he may once more go to her. But when he reaches the front of her building, he is still unsure what to do. His legs feel leaden. His finger presses the button by her name, once, then again. He is relieved when there is no answer. He steps back out on the sidewalk and looks up to her window. No lights are on. She is not home.

He walks down the street to a bar on the corner. Narrow, dimly lit. He enters and orders a whisky from the bartender. He stares at himself in the mirror. Anger overcomes him. Anger at himself. What the hell has he done? What the hell had he been thinking? Why is he here at all? He had once had so much love and had squandered it. Maybe Claire was right. He had taken too much, and he would never be able to get it back. But he had to try.

He finishes his drink and leaves, turning once again toward Claire's building. Looking up, he sees the light is still off. His apartment is blocks away, and the air is still cold, but he isn't ready for bed yet. He turns and walks in the opposite direction, wondering if he will ever be here again.

4

When my father died it was, to reverse the old line, sudden and then gradual. It was the day before Thanksgiving when my mother called me at the office. "Your father's unwell," she told me in her precise, elegant tones. "The ambulance just left. They are taking him to Southampton Hospital. I think you had better come out."

I knew it must be serious. No one in those days went to the hospital in Southampton.

"What's the matter? What's wrong?"

"He had a seizure. He had been feeling off recently. I found him on the kitchen floor and called 911."

"I'll be right out."

I had been planning on driving out the next morning anyway to have Thanksgiving dinner with them. It was a family tradition. A few friends of my parents would come for drinks around two in the afternoon, and then we would sit down to a bird prepared by Genevieve and served by Robert. Between the turkey and the dessert, which was usually an array of pies also prepared by Genevieve, we would wrap ourselves up and stroll down to the ocean and back to work up an appetite. Then, the next day, my parents would depart for Florida and shut down the house until April.

In the old days, Maddy; her brother, Johnny; her father; and whichever one of his wives happened to be in the picture sometimes joined us, but that was usually more at my insistence. My mother didn't care much for Mister Wakefield, and I suppose she knew he drank, but she was too well-bred to say anything, in front of me at any rate. When they came, Mother always put out the smaller wineglasses and had only one bottle of wine brought up from the cellar. I am sure Maddy's father knew what was going on. He was too smart not to. As for my father, he could find the good in anyone, and since the two men had been neighbors since childhood, even though my father was the elder by the better part of a decade, they had more than enough to talk about. And Mister Wakefield could be very entertaining as long as he hadn't had too much to drink; then he would become mean as a snake. They stopped coming the year they sold the big house, which was the year after Maddy's grandmother died, but by that time, Maddy and I were already at Yale.

After my mother's call, I hung up the phone and went to find my boss, a prematurely aging striver who had recently been made partner and commuted every day from Manhasset. I was a young associate then and not my own master. We were working on an important contract and had been in the office well past midnight every day for the past several weeks. I explained what had happened, and he sighed and told me reluctantly I had better go. Death is still one of the only things that the legal profession respects more than the needs of the client.

I had an old green Audi then and drove it as quickly as I could out to the hospital. The holiday exodus had already begun, and it took me longer to make the trip than I would have liked, even though I knew all the back roads. This was before many people had cell phones too—I certainly didn't, although I did have a beeper from work—and I didn't know what the situation was when I pulled into the parking lot.

My mother was in the waiting room, looking remarkably composed. Not a hair out of place. After she called me, I'm sure she had carefully selected the right skirt suit for the occasion, chose the appropriate earrings, handbag, and shoes, and sat down at her desk to write in her distinctive cursive instructions for Genevieve in her absence. Only then would she have had Robert drive her to the hospital in the big old Cadillac.

"How is he?" I asked, after giving her soft, old cheek a perfunctory kiss. As always, she exuded a subtle hint of Chanel No. 5.

"He is under observation," she replied in a firm voice. "The chief of medicine is attending to him."

He should have been. My parents were generous supporters of the hospital.

My mother stopped a passing nurse and asked her to have the doctor come out to explain to me what was happening. That was a harder thing to do than it sounds, but she had always had the knack. Nurses, waiters, stewardesses, taxi drivers, government officials. There was something about the way she spoke and carried herself that commanded attention, even of those who in most cases would be least inclined to stop. It may have helped that her father was a general, but I think it was something she was born with.

My father was a gentler soul. Tall, serious, kindhearted. On my mantel at home, I have a photograph of him as an undergraduate in the late 1940s. No one would have called him handsome, but he had a solid, reassuring face and the broad shoulders of an oarsman.

When my parents married and had me, they were older than most of their contemporaries. It was, I think, a happy marriage. She played bridge and ran their lives. He worked at one of Wall Street's great banks, where he was apparently greatly respected for both his fiduciary acumen and his integrity. He traveled a good deal on business, usually accompanied by my mother. For a while, he even served as an undersecretary of the Treasury in the Nixon administration. One of the senior partners of my firm, who had known him for years, remarked to me shortly after joining, "I have always admired your father. He was an indispensable man to many dispensable people."

It was difficult to see him lying on the hospital bed unconscious, an oxygen mask over his face, intravenous tubes in his now skinny, pale arms, a catheter, a battery of blinking machines in the background. Ever conscious of his dignity, he was a man who wore a necktie even on Saturdays, always kept the tail of his tennis shirt tucked in, and I don't think ever swore, even when another driver swerved in front of him. He would have hated the thought of being poked and prodded by a group of strangers, and I was secretly grateful he had been sedated.

"We are not sure what exactly caused the seizure," the chief of medicine informed me. "We have run a series of tests, X-rays, CT scans. So far nothing is conclusive. Your mother has filled us in about his diet, sleep patterns, and exercise. We had his personal physician in Manhattan fax out his records, and nothing's presenting itself yet."

"But surely you must be able to tell something?"

"We will continue to run tests. For the moment, it is better to keep him sedated. We will keep you posted."

My mother and I dined at home that evening, attended by a worried Genevieve and Robert. Mother had already been on the phone after returning home, calling up the handful of guests who were expected for dinner the next day.

"Oh, I am so sorry," I heard her say from her office near the drawing room. "But I am afraid I have to cancel Thanksgiving dinner tomorrow. I know it's terribly last minute, but poor Hugh's not well, and we had to take him to Southampton Hospital this morning. Yes. Thank you for being so understanding. No, no, please, no need to send anything. I am sure he'll be home in a few days, right as rain." Click.

"How are you, dear?" my mother asked me from across the table, putting an emphasis on the pronoun. "Any news?"

I was startled by her questions. Her husband of three decades was lying in the hospital, quite possibly dying, and she was keeping up the façade. I wanted to tell her what I really thought but instead only answered, "No news, Mother. I've been working hard, but that's to be expected."

"Any girls?"

"Alas."

She sighed, so I said, "You mentioned on the phone this

morning that Father hadn't been well for a few days. Do you have any idea what was wrong with him or whether it's connected to his seizure?"

"Dr. Marshall told me the tests were inconclusive, as I believe he told you. I am not sure what good it does to speculate. Neither of us is a trained medical professional."

"Yes, that's true, but I was wondering if there was anything you told the doctors that could shine a light on why Father's in the hospital."

She shrugged and took another bite of her dinner. "I told the doctors what I know. I am sure you do not appreciate it when a layman tries to tell you how to do your job any more than a doctor does."

My father lingered for days. Thanksgiving was a joyless affair. Just my mother and me. After dinner I went for our traditional walk to the beach but did so alone. It was cold, and I wore a scarf around my neck, my tweed jacket protecting me from the wind. I stood there overlooking the waves for a long time, praying silently for my father's recovery. I had already offered up more vocal prayers that morning with my mother when we went to Thanksgiving services at St. Luke's. By then news had spread around the congregation, many of whom were my parents' friends from the club. The rector stood by the door in his long white surplice and held both my mother's and my hands warmly, tendering his most sincere thoughts and prayers.

Mother's friends were no less attentive. "Oh, Elizabeth," they said, swarming around us, the older ladies dressed like my mother, skinny, artificial hair; the men in blazers, tweeds, and club ties, most of them walking with sticks and with hearing aids in their ears. The men tended to hold back while the wives pressed forward. I couldn't blame them. It must have been damn depressing for them to see one of their own go down, leaving each of them to wonder who would be next.

On Friday a battery of specialists came out from Manhattan. Nephrologists, neurologists, cardiologists, even tropical disease specialists. "Had your father been to Brazil in the past six months?" one of the last asked me brightly.

The next day my father woke up, groggy and confused. I was there when he did, having spent each night with him, as I knew he would have done for me, sleeping on a chair. "Walt," he said, a look of panic in his eyes, "what the hell is going on?"

"You're in Southampton Hospital, Dad. You had a seizure at home. They've been keeping you sedated."

I could tell he still didn't quite comprehend what I meant, so I repeated myself. "You've been here since Wednesday."

"Since Wednesday? What day is it today?"

"Saturday."

He looked away from me. "My god," he said, the reality of the situation beginning to press in on him. "And your mother? How is she?"

"She's fine, Dad."

He patted my hand. He looked so small and etiolated. Not my father but a pale shadow of him. "Walt, could you ask the nurse to bring me some water? I'm awfully dry." He ran his hand over his face. "I also need a shave. I must look like a bum."

For the next several days, he had moments of lucidity, but the doctors usually tried to keep him pretty dopey. I would go home every morning to shower and have breakfast, and then, unless my mother needed me to run an errand for her, I returned to the hospital. Of course, I grew to hate the place, the beginning of my apostasy toward the medical profession in general. It was so depressing, the smells of shit, disinfectant, and death. The lonely people moored in those impersonal rooms, televisions blaring, the coughing and moaning from behind pulled curtains, doctors and nurses walking in clusters up and down the fluorescent hallways. The lack of information, the air of superiority, and yet, for all their training and experience, they still hadn't been able to find out what was wrong with my father.

It often seemed to me as though the tests were making him worse. They kept trying out different medications, many of which made his heart rate increase, or they pumped him full of solutions so the scanners could do their job. The worst thing, for me at any rate, was that there were always new doctors popping in, many of them absurdly young, scanning charts and asking me the same questions over and over. How much did he drink? (Not much.) Was he a smoker? (Quit years ago.) Did he exercise? (Several times a week.) Was there any family history of heart disease? (Not that we knew of.) Had he been to Brazil in the past six months?

It went on and on like this. It was exasperating. I kept wondering what the scrawls and hieroglyphics on those charts actually meant. Why didn't the doctors confer with each other? If lawyers handled our profession the same way, without any communication between the different attorneys working on the deal and going back to ask the clients the same questions repeatedly, it would lead to utter chaos. It was a joke. But now, faced with a crisis, these doctors seemed less competent than the man at the office who fixes the copy machine.

314

My father was a stoic man. He had been born and raised during the Depression with a sense of the deprivation that most of his countrymen endured, although his family's wealth had shielded him from the brunt of the impact. He had joined the Navy after Yale in the postwar years, and his knowledge of languages, the legacy of a French governess and a German fräulein, as well as several years spent traveling abroad with his parents and siblings in the 1930s, had earned him a position as an aide to Admiral Sherman, who was at the time chief of naval operations. After resigning his commission, he joined the bank. In all the years I knew him, I cannot recall my father raising his voice or complaining about anything other than politics and the New York Yankees.

And so it came as an even greater shock when, one afternoon, I was sitting there, trying to work—my office having sent the papers I was to review—and my father called out to me. "Walt," he said. "Come here."

I leaned over him, and he gave me a wild look, a look I had never seen before. "You've got to get me out of here," he pleaded. "You've got to get me out of here. I'm going to die here if you don't."

I looked at him, trying to tell if this was the real man speaking or just someone who was still loopy from the cocktail of medications they had dosed him with. Had he woken up from a bad dream? Or was he genuinely terrified? The look in his eyes told me he was serious. I felt helpless. I looked at the tubes being fed into his body and could only imagine what it would entail to remove any of them. And how was I supposed to get him out of there? Carry him? I imagined the two of us limping down the hallway, shrugging off security guards, clinging to an IV stand. Would they let me use a wheelchair, or should I just wheel him out on a gurney? And then what? Take him home? How? In the Cadillac? In my Audi? Would they let us use an ambulance? I knew it was irrational to even contemplate such rash action, but I did anyway. I would have done anything for my father, but I couldn't do this. Lord knows, I didn't want him to be there any more than he did, but to remove him now seemed the height of irresponsibility.

"Dad. I'm sorry. I can't get you out of here. You've got to stay. The doctors are doing everything they can."

"I don't believe you. They're going to kill me. You've got to get me out of here."

"Dad, they aren't trying to kill you."

He gripped my arm. "Please."

"I'm sorry."

"The hell with you," he said and started to sit up. He was old and frail but not without strength. I had to put my hands on his shoulders to keep him from getting out of bed.

"Dad, you've got to stay in bed."

"You're no son of mine. Let me go."

I ignored him and instead called for the nurse. She came and injected a sedative into his arm while he struggled against us both. Within seconds he was asleep.

The next day he seemed back to normal. He was sitting up in bed clear-eyed and was getting a shave when I returned. The remnants of a breakfast tray sat on the table, his first solid food since he had been admitted.

"Morning, Walt," he said, evidently pleased with himself. "Can you do me a favor? I have a board meeting next week, and I need you to have the papers sent out. Can you please arrange that?"

I was heartened by this turn of events. The doctors still hadn't determined what was wrong with him or what had caused the seizure, but they were as relieved as I. They informed me that, if he continued to make such progress, they would be able to move him out of the ICU to a regular room. I spent the day with him watching football on TV. He napped occasionally, but mainly he was interested in catching up on what had been going on in the world. I had saved the past week's worth of *Wall Street Journal*s and brought them to him. This made him very happy, and he told me that I didn't need to spend the night with him. Grateful to sleep in my own bed, any bed, I stayed until eight P.M. For the first time since I was a child, I kissed him good night.

At his insistence, I returned to the office the next day. He and I talked on the phone that afternoon. He told me that, if everything went well, he would be out in a few days. He said my mother had already booked their flight to Florida and called the housekeeper to give her a shopping list. It was the last time we ever spoke.

At four that morning, the phone rang in my apartment. I had again worked late but sprang out of bed at the first ring. It was my mother's voice on the other end. "Your father died," I heard her say. I stood in my bedroom not comprehending. "He had a heart attack."

I fought back the urge to shout or cry but instead said, "I'm so sorry, Mother."

"The nurse said it would have been painless," she replied. "I'm afraid you'll need to come back out again."

The funeral was that Saturday, attended by the usual retinue of guests. Maddy couldn't make it because Harry was stationed in California at the time, but she called me that night. I told her about how my father had asked me to get him out of the hospital, and that I couldn't help feeling guilty that I had somehow let him down, that if I had succeeded in spiriting him away he might still be alive. Maddy told me I shouldn't think like that, that the person who'd asked me that wasn't my father. It was someone else. Her father had already been in and out of several sanatoriums by this point, and she had experience being around someone who was on psychotropic drugs.

That made me feel better, but it didn't entirely deaden the sting. I loved my father very much and was furious at his doctors for, in my opinion, not ever finding out what was wrong and for killing him. It wasn't that the doctors hadn't tried their best. They had. It was just that their best wasn't much damn good.

My mother died two years later. Also of a heart attack, but under circumstances less dramatic than my father's. One morning in Florida, Genevieve was bringing in her breakfast, and she just simply didn't wake up. I always thought it was the perfect way for her to go.

I was thirty then, and I inherited the house and much else besides. I told Genevieve and Robert they would be welcome to stay on at full salary if they chose, but that I wouldn't be requiring their services as my parents had. They remained for another few months, mainly to help me clean out my parents' apartment and put the Long Island house in order. But they were getting on in years themselves and, thanks to a sizable bequest from my parents, decided to return to their village outside of Lausanne and retire in comfort. They had been a big part of my life, and I was sorry to see them go. I visited them once a few years back, and we still exchange cards and gifts at Christmas.

My father's death, instead of making me more aware of my own mortality, made me avoid doctors. Until then, I had always been responsible about going to the doctor every year. Even then my cholesterol was a bit high, and I could have lost some weight, but otherwise I enjoyed rude good health. But doctors are a little like priests—they claim to possess a secret knowledge that imbues them with an air of unwarranted superiority and most of us turn to them only when everything else has failed.

5

I RECEIVED THIS LETTER FROM MADDY:

Dear Walter,

I can't believe I have never been here before, but I feel as though I have known this place all my life. It is so beautiful. The Gulf of Mexico stretches green and lazy to the horizon. The sand is clean and white. Little fishing boats depart at dawn and return in the afternoon. Wisps of clouds occasionally break up the brilliant blue sky, and at night there are millions of stars. I am staying at a small hotel in the Yucatán. On the first day I arrived, I went to the five-star resort where I had reserved a room and took one look at the people and the perfect lawn and the unnecessary fountains, the faux-Mayan architecture and the silent, well-groomed staff, and I knew I had to get the hell out of there. So I asked the driver if there was a place less formal, and he drove me down a dirt road to a little hacienda on the beach where there was a dog tied to a stake in the courtyard that barked the minute we stopped and chickens and goats and it looked perfect. The woman who runs the place gave me a nice room with a balcony that looks out over the water and a bathroom down the hall. There is no air-conditioning and no room service, but there is a little bar and a small restaurant that makes the most delicious shrimp I have ever had in my life. These shrimp were literally just plucked from the sea and then boiled with garlic, cilantro, lime, and jalapeño. Delicious. Washed down with a cold Tecate, I could eat them all day.

It's not all perfect, though. The cockroaches are the size of cats, there are some very unpleasant odors, my room is not terribly clean, and it's incredibly hot during the day. I am convinced I will come down with diarrhea any minute, every man leers at me like a potential rapist, there is no safe, and it's a good bet my wallet and passport are going to be stolen at any moment. The owner of the hotel, a lively woman named Sonia who is also the cook, tells me not to worry, but when I go for a walk on the beach, I tend to attract a number of admirers.

But walk on the beach I do. There's not much else to do, which is fine. I thought about renting a fishing boat, but Sonia told me the skipper she uses is away. When will he be back? She wasn't sure. Maybe the end of the week. Maybe not. I realize I should have rented a car, but it seemed an unnecessary expense when I booked the trip. One day I did hire a driver to take me out to Chichén Itzá, the large Mayan ruins near here. What an astonishing place. I've never been in the "ruin" of a long-dead civilization. In Europe they just keep building over everything and in the U.S. nothing's that old. But Chichén Itzá is old, and it is dead, its culture and people no more existent than the Sumerians or Hittites. It's amazing to think that this civilization flourished for thousands of years and built this beautiful city and then one day a small group of Spanish guys with guns and armor appear out of nowhere and, poof, the whole thing's over in less than a hundred years. It's heartbreaking to think of the people who once lived here, the children, the families, the warriors and the priests—yes, even the ones who performed human sacrifices—and lost everything. Their lives, their homes, their culture, their language. Gone. Obliterated. All that remain are ruins like this and a few descendants whose ancestors escaped into the jungle centuries ago and hid for their lives until everything was forgotten but their fear.

I was smart to come here. I knew I had to get out of New York. You were right. I was going a little crazy. I am not a self-destructive person and have never been. I grew up around self-destruction, my father raised it to an art form, but I have always fought against it. Still I knew it always existed within me, that urge to lose control, to give in to rage and despair. To throw away everything important to me simply because I could, and because one day I woke up and realized that everything was a lie.

I feel a little like the Maya. I was content in the center of my little world, believing I was protected and powerful—but then something more ruthless came along and tore down my defenses. Who wouldn't become self-destructive at that point? What was left to fight for? Isn't that what happens when civilizations implode? The looting starts. My culture lay in ruins too, and it all looked so hopeless. In the grand scheme of things what did it matter what happened to me? Did I think I was above it all? That I could somehow skate through life

*believing I would remain untouched? History is full of such
self-deception. Look at the Maya, look at the French during
World War Two. They thought they could hide behind the
Maginot Line, but the Germans just went around it.*

*But did that kill the French? No. France persevered. Its
language, its culture, its people, its traditions fought back
despite the Nazis, collaborators, and the very human belief
that sometimes it can be better to give in rather than resist.
Of course, many French did give in, but the greater number
did not. Which would you rather be? I'd like to think I
would have been among the fighters, and that's why I am so
disappointed in my life and myself that so far I have given in
to what has happened to me. Rather than fight, I ran away.
I thought I was being brave, but maybe I was just being a
coward. If I really loved what I loved, if I really believed in
it, then I should have stayed and faced my problems. I might
not have been successful, but at least I would have known I
had done my best.*

I am tired of running away. It's time to fight.

*I hope you are well. I am sorry if I have not been myself
recently. I hope you know how much you mean to me and
how important your love and friendship are to me. Thank
you for everything. I'll see you soon.*

XXXX
Maddy

*P.S. The French didn't do it alone. They had help. I am
counting on you for that help. I know I can.*

P.P.S. I had a nice letter from Harry.

6

HARRY IS JOGGING ALONG THE RIVER. EVERY MORNING HE takes Johnny to school and then jogs back home. The mornings are still cool. He is wearing his old gray sweats and has a wool cap over his head. The distance is more than fifty blocks, which is more than two miles. He cuts down to the East River and crosses over, passing other joggers, dog walkers, mothers pushing strollers. He is out of condition. His lungs burn, and his muscles creak. Perspiration streaks his face. The body is evil and must be punished. When he returns to his apartment, he does sit-ups and push-ups until he is exhausted. Then he takes a shower and sits down to write until he has to leave to pick up Johnny. Work on his book is finally going well. The logjam has broken. Words flow.

Maddy sent them a postcard. She sent them both love. The weeks have gone by quickly. Too quickly, he feels. Seeing his son only two nights a week isn't enough. It never could be. The intensity of his love sometimes threatens to overwhelm him. He is amazed by his son. Wants to know what he thinks. Wishes he could see the world through his eyes and experience his joys and sorrows. He wants to run his fingers through Johnny's hair, to make him laugh, to feel the warm smoothness of his cheek against his own. Their hands are the same. There is no one in the world he could be closer to. Not Claire. Not even Maddy.

They go for long walks. Sometimes in the park, sometimes just meandering. Johnny is a great walker too. They talk about Johnny's school, the other children, how Jeremy thinks he's so cool and Sean gets on his nerves and Jack made Willa cry on the roof. They talk about the Rangers' dwindling chances in the Stanley Cup playoff. They play a running game of *Jeopardy!* where Harry asks him the names of presidents and state capitals and Johnny gets each one right. They are starting on English kings. "Which king had his head chopped off?" Harry played this same game with his own father. One night they even talk about Darwin's theory of evolution.

"I don't see what the big deal is, Daddy," says Johnny. "I think it's cool to be descended from monkeys."

At night, they order in pizza or Harry cooks, usually steak or spaghetti. He helps Johnny with his homework. At bedtime Harry tells him a story or reads to him. The Penguin King is still a favorite, and the ending always has to be happy now. Then Harry sits back down at his table, pours himself his first drink of the night, and starts to write again, happier than he has been in months.

I know this because Harry tells me. A few days after Maddy

leaves, he calls me unprompted at the office. "Hey, Walt," he says cheerily, sounding better than I have heard him in months. "Thought I'd just check in with you and give you a status report on Johnny in case Maddy called."

"Is everything all right?"

He laughs. "Everything's fine, Walt," he says. "Johnny and I were wondering if you'd like to come over to the Palazzo Winslow one night for a bad meal. You haven't been here, and we thought you'd be curious to see how the other half lives."

Johnny's voice comes through the receiver: "Please, Uncle Walt."

I can hardly say no. And besides, hadn't Maddy expressly asked me to check in on him? "I'll see if I can," I answer. "What night were you thinking of?"

"How about tomorrow? You bring the wine. Something old and expensive, and I'll make something young and cheap."

The next night I arrive at his apartment and climb the flights to the top floor. It is clear that money is tight for Harry.

The apartment is small, sparse, in an old tenement near the Midtown Tunnel. The street below is an endless procession of cars and trucks entering and exiting the city, horns honking, engines spewing out carbon monoxide. Through grimy windows, the view is only of more tenements and fire escapes. Harry says the old Hispanic woman down the hall blasts her television. Occasionally he hears fights, shouting. He imagines it is her boyfriend or son coming to borrow money. The smell of cooking oil lingers in the hallway. Sirens heading to Bellevue punctuate the night.

Harry has set up a single bed in the bedroom for Johnny, and he has a couch in the living room for himself. A large poster of a hockey player hangs on the wall. There's a table where he works and eats. Books are stacked on the floor. There's a small television with one of Johnny's video devices hooked up to it. Unlike many bachelor apartments, it is neat, thanks to Harry's military training. Clothes are folded away, there are no dishes in the sink. He kills cockroaches with his shoe. It is a place to change clothes, to work, as impersonal as a hotel room.

In spite of it all, both seem well. Harry and I shake hands as though the past several months had never happened, and Johnny gives me a big hug, which is extremely gratifying. A steak sits marinating on the counter. The tiny kitchen is part of the living room. Harry pours me a whisky and sits at the table. I sit on the couch next to Johnny.

"Thanks for coming, Walt. Not your usual stomping grounds."

"I've seen worse."

"Well, hopefully it won't be for too long. I only signed a six-month lease. With any luck, if Hollywood makes me a good offer, I'll be able to afford somewhere better."

"Or maybe we could live in Los Angeles," says Johnny.

I keep my opinions to myself.

"Whoa, pal." Harry laughs. "Let's not get carried away."

We talk about Johnny's school. What he's studying. Once a week there is chess after school, another day piano. Johnny's school is near their old apartment, but it is several stops away for Harry.

He then tells me he is nearly two-thirds of the way finished with his book, and thinks that it's the best thing he's ever written. The words have been flying out. But he won't tell me what it's about. "It's a surprise," he says with a wink. "But you could say it's a love letter to my wife." He tells me he gets up every morning at five and writes until seven, when it's time to wake Johnny. Then he comes home and works until it's time for pickup.

Dinner is pleasant, like old times. Even though Maddy is not here and the locale is different, I am drawn into Harry's orbit, like the gravitational pull of a planet on a smaller moon. For a night I find it impossible not to like him. Just as Maddy did, I had meant to be distant, aloof, but it was inevitable that he would have me roaring with laughter. Johnny fights to stay awake, and when Harry says, "Come on, pal. Time for bed," I stand up and try to make my excuses, but Harry waves me down. "Don't leave yet. Let me get Johnny ready for bed and then we can have a more serious talk."

And, again like old times, I stand in the doorway listening to Johnny be put to bed. Teeth brushed, he says his prayers, and then Harry tells him one of his stories.

"Thanks for staying, Walt," says Harry, carefully closing the bedroom door behind him. "Can I get you anything else?" The wine has been drunk, and he makes us both whisky sodas. We resume our places at the table.

"Look," he says, "I want to say something, and if you can pass it along to Maddy, I'd appreciate it."

"What is it?"

"That I still love her. Maybe more than ever now. And I don't want us to get divorced. That I screwed up, and that I will spend the rest of my life trying to make it up to her, but we—her, me, Johnny—won't ever really be happy unless we are all together as a family. Please, can you tell her?"

"Have you told her?"

"I wrote to her last week."

That must have been the letter she referred to. "Well, good luck. I guess it all depends on her frame of mind when she returns. I'll mention it if it seems appropriate."

"Thanks, Walt. I know how much she thinks of you."

I get my coat and head to the door. It's not that late, but it's time to get going.

On my way out he asks, "One more thing, Walt. You wouldn't know anyone who'd be in the market for a plane, by any chance?"

"What do you mean?"

"I've decided to sell my plane. It's costing too much, I don't use it enough to justify the expense, and frankly I could use the money. Maybe one of your rich clients might be interested."

"I'll ask around," I reply. That damn plane.

ON SATURDAY, HARRY AND JOHNNY DRIVE OUT EAST FOR the day. Maddy is returning the next evening. It is their last day together. They leave early. It is still dark. Johnny sleeps in the backseat while Harry drives, drinking coffee. As the sun rises, the morning becomes beautiful, as he had hoped. He had been checking the National Weather Service for the past few days, and the forecasts are for fine weather.

There are already leaves on the trees as they get farther from the city. He has not been out here since the fall, when he came with Claire. That seems like a lifetime ago. He notices the new stores and restaurants, their façades freshly painted, waiting for the bounty of summer. The farm stands are still closed, the fields flat and untilled.

They pull into the airport shortly before nine. There are only a few people in the small terminal. While Johnny sits groggily on one of the chairs, Harry gets more coffee and checks the weather report.

"Hey, Marty," he says to the man behind the counter. "How's it going?"

"Harry! Long time, man. Where you been hiding?"

"Spent the fall and winter in Rome."

"Nice."

Harry shrugs. "Jimmy around?"

"Out back."

"Thanks. I asked him to prep and gas up the plane. Been a long winter."

"I'll say."

"See you around."

"Take it easy."

Harry and Johnny walk out onto the tarmac, Harry's hand on his son's shoulder. The wind sock hangs limply, and the sun is already bright. He spots the little Cessna. Jimmy has taken off the tarp that covered it all winter. The battery has been charged, and the pitot and static vents cleared of bugs. He looks under the cowling, and checks to see that the flaps and wheel bearings are properly lubricated.

"Everything okay?"

Harry turns and sees Jimmy, and the two men shake hands.

"You remember my son, Johnny, don't you? Shake hands with Mister Bennett, pal."

"How do you do, Mister Bennett."

"Good to see you again, Johnny. You're getting real tall, aren't you?"

"I'm the tallest in my grade."

"Good for you." Then to Harry, Jimmy says, "I found a family of mice in the engine but cleaned 'em out and replaced some wires they'd chewed through. Let me show you."

The two men walk over, and Jimmy lifts up the cowling. "See? Good as new."

"Looks good, Jimmy. Thanks."

"She's a pretty little thing."

"That she is. Thinking of putting her up for sale."

"Oh yeah?"

"Yeah. Know anyone who might be interested?"

"Sure. I know a bunch of guys who'd like a 182."

"Cool. I'll talk to you about it later. Going to take her up for one last spin."

"Good day for it."

"Couldn't ask for better."

"Well, Harry, good seeing you. Let me know about the plane."

"You bet. Thanks again. Send me your bill."

Harry walks around the plane, completing the preflight procedures, reminding Johnny again how to check the empennage, elevator, and rudder. He runs his hands over the flaps and ailerons, and inspects the nose wheel and fairings, removing the tie-downs and chocks as he moves clockwise around the plane. He then walks back to the terminal to file his flight plan with the tower. He and Johnny have been talking about doing this for days. They'll be heading up to the Cape and then maybe stop for lunch on Nantucket. There isn't a cloud in the sky.

Warmed by the sun, the cockpit is stuffy. Removing his coat,

Harry opens the windows and checks that Johnny is buckled in correctly. He switches on the engine, and it coughs to life, the blade of the propeller suddenly a blur. With a practiced eye, he looks over the controls to make sure they all appear to be functioning normally. He radios the tower and asks for permission to depart. "East Hampton Tower, this is Tango Gulf Niner Niner requesting takeoff."

The radio crackles. "Tango Gulf Niner Niner, you are cleared for takeoff."

There is no one in front of them. He taxis the little Cessna from the run-up area and points it down the runway. He smiles at Johnny.

"Ready?" he calls out over the thrum of the motor.

The boy smiles back and gives him a thumbs-up. Harry slowly advances the throttle all the way to full. The oil pressure and oil temperature are in the green. At around thirty-five knots, the airspeed indicator comes alive. He pulls back slowly on the yoke when the plane hits sixty-four knots, and then they are in the air. The plane climbing high, banking left over the airfield.

"Look, Daddy, our house."

Harry looks down. He sees the large pond, then the big house, and then the cottage behind, always marveling at how small it all seems. He has been looking at it for years from this height, the first thing he always checks, his heart leaping at the thought of possibly spotting a tiny Maddy, maybe watering in the garden or playing on the grass with Johnny, her golden hair sparkling in the sun.

Now, he realizes that, if things cannot be resolved with Maddy, he may never see it any closer again. It makes him feel like a ghost looking down on the loved ones he's left behind.

He remembers the first time he ever saw Maddy. She had been crossing the quad. It was early in their freshman year, and he had already been adopted by members of DKE, many of whom had been upperclassmen in his boarding school and knew what a good hockey player he was. They introduced him to New Haven—where to drink, where to eat, which classes to take. They took him to the parties freshmen were rarely invited to attend. He had been walking in the opposite direction when one of his friends, a junior on the hockey team, snickered and said, "Check out the fresh meat."

The first thing he noticed was her hair. He had never seen hair like it. Golden with hints of red, rippling halfway down her back. Then he saw her face. It was a proud face, chin jutting out, the nose sharp. She walked like a man, he thought. Strong, purposeful. He could tell she wasn't afraid of anything. She also dressed like a man, with the tails of a man's shirt hanging out over her jeans. At the time the shirt intimidated him. He thought it was a boyfriend's. An older man's. It suggested undreamt-of levels of sophistication. It communicated that she had seen more of the world than he had. Her beauty, her self-possession, her insouciant manner, all combined to create an aura around her that made her stand out from all the other girls he had seen so far at Yale.

Unlike them, she wasn't easy to categorize. She wasn't preppy, she wasn't Goth, she wasn't a hippie or a dyke or a jockette or a geek. She just seemed so uniquely herself. He had never seen anyone like her, or anyone so beautiful. None of the other boys said anything as she passed by. They, too, were awed. And she ignored them, her brilliance making everything around her dull. After she was out of sight, one of them finally said, "I'd like to nail that."

Harry said nothing but just kept his eyes transfixed on the door through which she had walked. His chest felt tight. He felt like punching the boy who had spoken but knew he would have been out of line. "Shut up," he said. But his words were lost as, at the same time, one of the other boys playfully punched the boy who had spoken in the arm. "Yeah, right. Never going to happen, man." The rest of the boys laughed, reasserting their manhood, but Harry frowned, thinking only of the girl.

Freshman year was a triumph for Harry. He easily made the varsity hockey team, the first freshman to do so in two decades. With its mix of prep school heroes and working-class prodigies, the squad was one of the best Yale had put on the ice in years, winning the Ivy League title and getting as far as the NCAA semifinals. He even dated a pretty, pneumatic creature from Greenwich, a field hockey player if I remember correctly. Or it could have been lacrosse. It's not important. But the whole time he was thinking about Maddy. They shared no classes, nor were they in the same college. Occasionally he would catch a glimpse of her, sometimes crossing the street, entering a building, driving by in her car. She was like an angel of good intention, hovering always just out of reach. And yet each time he saw her, his heart would race, and for a few seconds a rush of joy would surge through him. She was still here, he hadn't imagined her, and, yes, she was as beautiful as he remembered.

Inevitably, this momentary elation would be followed by a crushing despondency that would carry him through the rest of the day. He wished he could simply call out to her, "Hey! Stop!" But even if he did, what would he say? Once he had seen her walking right toward him, and he'd panicked and ducked quickly away. Normally, he was easy around women, but her beauty was so extreme that it made him feel foolish. He knew nothing about her, where she was from, what kind of person she was, what she was studying. He didn't even know her name. All he knew was that she was beautiful, and for some reason she terrified him.

Then one night in the spring, at a party thrown by the daughter of a wealthy German industrialist, who had converted an entire town house in New Haven for one night to celebrate her twenty-first birthday, they met. Hundreds of guests had been invited, including Maddy, Harry, and me. The engraved invitations told us the dress would be formal, shorthand for not dressing like slobs. So Maddy actually had made an effort that night, unlike most evenings.

The weekend before, she and I had visited several boutiques in Manhattan, and she had picked out a skintight, low-cut, sparkly green dress that fell just above the knee. Needless to say, she looked stunning in it, and I was enormously proud to be her escort for the evening. The dazed, admiring looks of the other men confirmed what I already knew, that not only was Maddy the most beautiful woman at the party but she was the most beautiful woman any of them had ever seen. There was much whispering going on behind our backs, and doubtless a few of the women made catty comments, but none of that mattered.

At one point, I recognized an old prep school classmate I had not seen much during the year and walked over with Maddy to introduce them. I have to confess this was pretty selfish of me; I wanted as many people as possible in the room to know I was with Maddy. It was my finest hour.

My former classmate was talking to a big fellow with his back to us, wearing a too-tight dinner jacket, obviously borrowed, but I barged in anyway. "Hey, Frank," I said. "Where have you been hiding?" Frank turned and shook my hand and then stopped when he noticed Maddy. "Frank, allow me to introduce Madeleine Wakefield."

Frank recovered his composure and smiled. "How do you do? And may I introduce Harry Winslow?"

I recognized the name from the *Yale Daily News*. He had been a frequent subject of front-page admiration.

"You're 'Winner' Winslow?" I asked. It was a sobriquet that had been given to him for his hockey prowess.

"Just Harry," he said with a shy grin.

"Well, then, Harry, I'm Walter Gervais, and this is Madeleine Wakefield."

He didn't look at her. He couldn't look at her. "How do you do?" he mumbled.

"Walt, guess who's here? Rocky came over from Princeton for the party. He's at the bar. Want to see him?"

"Maddy, I'll be right back. We need a refill anyway. Harry, can I ask you to look after Maddy? I won't be a minute. That okay?"

Maddy nodded.

And then the moment Harry had dreamt about all year, and yet dreaded, was upon him. His mouth was dry. His brain shut down. It was agony. He stared at Maddy, struggling to come up with something to say so he wouldn't just be standing there staring at her like an idiot.

"Nice party," he ventured. "Are you having fun?"

Maddy turned and looked at him. He had never been so

close to her. Her eyes were a sparkling ice blue. "I don't sleep with hockey players," she said and turned and walked after me, leaving Harry gaping like a trout.

This became a story they told quite often afterward, and it always got a good laugh at dinner parties. But Harry didn't talk to Maddy again for the rest of the term. When we did catch sight of him, she would either look the other way or make a disparaging remark. At the end of the year, we all dispersed, some to jobs or internships, others to country clubs and beaches. Maddy worked that summer in Washington for a congressman and had a brief affair with one of his aides. She wrote to me about it in excruciating detail, letters which I read in the evening while I was living in my parents' empty apartment, interning at one of the city's oldest law firms. It was our first summer apart. She came up only twice. We had one week together at the very end, however, by which time, thankfully, she had broken off the affair, and we went to the beach every day and just hacked around at night, going to parties or a movie or just staying in. Harry, meanwhile, went out to Oklahoma, where he worked building oil rigs.

It was fated they would meet again. It happened in the fall term of our sophomore year. The irony is that I was the agent of bringing them together. They had not spoken since the spring party. I had been invited to join one of the university's elite literary societies, which I considered a great honor. At the initiation dinner, in the Leverett-Griswold House, I was surprised to see Harry at my table. Previously I had thought of him as nothing more than a star athlete. I would never have guessed he was also interested in literature. In my past experience, the two were usually mutually exclusive. But there he was.

I did not know yet that his father was an English teacher, and he had practically cut his milk teeth on Shakespeare and Milton. I had always prided myself on my knowledge of Shakespeare, but his surpassed mine. Not just his ability to recite many obscure passages with relative ease but also his sensitive appreciation of the human emotions that made the plays great. With his looks and memory, if he hadn't been such a fine hockey player, I am sure he would have been a terrific actor. In any event, we soon became friendly.

One night I arranged a dinner in New Haven, to which I invited a number of guests. Maddy came, of course, and so did my new friend, Harry. It was at a Thai restaurant, and there were eight of us at a large, round table. The staff brought out many courses: coconut soup, prawn curry, roast duck, diaphanous rice noodles, fish in dry red curry sauce. We were drinking Thai beer and doing shots of ginger vodka. Maddy sat on my right, and Harry, as it turned out, sat on her right. At one point I noticed the two of them hadn't spoken all night. It was like there was a glass wall between them. With me and the rest of the party, Maddy was more animated than usual, laughing, shouting questions to the people on the opposite side of the table, cracking jokes. Harry, on the other hand, looked as though he was at a funeral. He spoke occasionally to the woman on his right, but spent most of the evening sitting quietly, barely touching his food.

After dinner we all walked back to Maddy's off-campus house on Elm Street, and she invited everyone up for a glass of wine. Most of us accepted, but not Harry.

"Thank you," he said. "I have practice early tomorrow."

Several days later, I got a call from Maddy. "You'll never believe it."

"What?"

"Harry Winslow asked me out."

"He did? What did you say?"

"I said yes, of course. Any reason why I shouldn't?"

I could think of many, but all I said was "None that I know of."

What was so momentous about this was not that someone asked Maddy out—although it happened less often than people thought—but that she actually accepted. I had been with her on many occasions—on Long Island, in Manhattan and New Haven—when men approached her. They were usually older, more confident. She was never rude. She never told anyone to buzz off or flipped them the bird, or anything so vulgar. She just politely said "No, thank you." Sometimes the more persistent ones, if we were in a bar or restaurant, sent her a drink; others even sent flowers if they knew where she lived. If they were too pushy, we just left. But in almost every case, she demurred.

With Harry, not only did she say yes but clearly she had thought about it and, having done so, liked the idea. It is possible she even expected it, from that first moment at the spring party. She was not a spontaneous sort of person. We shared so much, but we had not shared this. This was hers. It was a part of her life that was shut off to me. I resented this concealment, of course, and was jealous of it, but I also knew there was little that could be done about it. If she wanted it, I wanted it too. She was the shark, and I merely the pilot fish.

Their first date was at an Italian restaurant, an old-fashioned red-sauce place near Wooster Square that closed years ago. Harry didn't have a car, so Maddy drove with him squeezed into the passenger seat of her red MG. After dinner, they went to a bar and then back to Maddy's room. There, as she told me later, they stayed up all night talking and looking at her photo albums. Old Kodaks, the edges serrated, their colors muted. Pictures of her childhood, when she was raised by her grandmother, as an infant, later skinny in a one-piece on the beach. Birthday parties, swim meets. Photos of her father, young and muscular with his shirt off, his hair still full and blond, at a friend's wedding, playing golf, at Christmas. Her brother, Johnny. A succession of stepmothers. A yellow Mercedes convertible that later wound up wrapped around a tree. Men in turtlenecks with sideburns, women in Lilly Pulitzer and bouffant hair. Everyone smoked. I know these images well. They were my life too.

It was a month before they slept together, she said. During that month, I barely saw her. Suddenly, the two of them had become inseparable. They met after class, dined together at Mory's or in her apartment, where funnily enough Harry did most of the cooking because Maddy, being a child of privilege, had never learned how to navigate a kitchen. Instead of driving down to New York with me, she went with Harry now. The city was still new to him, and she delighted in showing it to him. She took him to all our favorite places, Bemelmans, the White Horse, Vazac's, the Oak Bar. They spent hours at the Frick and the Met, drove out to Luger's in Brooklyn, danced at Xenon. She took him to "21" for the first time and charged the meal to her father's account.

After that first month, there was another and then another, until it blurred into a year. It was clear to me, and to them, that they were in love. I had never seen Maddy so happy. She glowed. And I knew the only course of action available to me was complete and utter acceptance. I could not have her to myself anymore, and, if I fought it, I would risk losing her entirely. Instead I became an acolyte, lighting the candles, carrying the cross, swinging the thurible. Initially, I hesitated, wondering if it would last, waiting for the relationship to break off under its own weight. But it never did.

In the summer after sophomore year, they traveled to Europe together, staying with friends in England, hiking in the rain through the Lake District, traveling down to the Côte d'Azur, stopping at vineyards along the way, visiting old friends of her grandmother's. Then they went to Santorini, where they slept on the beach and got brown as nuts, swinging back through Marrakech and then Barcelona before coming home.

I did not join them but every few days got enthusiastic postcards from Maddy. I was wildly jealous, but what could I do? I had another internship, my sights already fixed on law school. When in our senior year Maddy told me they were going to be married after graduation, I was genuinely happy. I could see that Harry loved her. Not for her beauty but for herself. He had penetrated beneath the armor to see the soul inside and knew that what he found was gold. I had been aware of it all along, of course, and it gave me a certain satisfaction to know I had been there first, that, in this one thing, he would always follow me.

HARRY'S PLANE TOUCHES DOWN AT NANTUCKET MEMORIAL Airport. It's still low season, and the airport is relatively empty. It's a little after eleven. Johnny has to use the bathroom, and they have a late breakfast at the little restaurant in the terminal. Johnny has pancakes and bacon. Harry, coffee and scrambled eggs. The restaurant is full of pilots, a few in uniform, but most of them recreational fliers like Harry. They fly over for the day, have lunch, and fly back. They are doctors, small business owners, retirees. It is a small confederation. They like nothing better than sitting around talking about flying. Normally Harry would join them, but not today. Today he has Johnny. He wants the day to be about his son.

"How did your mother seem before she left, pal?" he asks.

"Okay, I guess," Johnny says, swinging his legs distractedly. "She was a little sad sometimes."

Harry nods his head. He can barely bring himself to look into his son's eyes. They are Maddy's eyes. Her sadness is his fault. It is all his fault.

"How are you, Daddy?"

Harry is surprised by the question. It might be the first time Johnny has ever asked anything like that, revealing a maturity, a growing awareness of others that is so often among the last traits to develop in children, if it does at all.

"Well, I guess I'm a little sad too."

"Why?"

"Because I miss your mommy, and I miss you."

"Maybe if you came back home, then both you and Mommy would be happy again."

Harry looks away and pats his son's hand. "I'd like that very much. Come on, pal. It's wheels-up time."

7

THEY ARE BACK TOGETHER AND ONCE AGAIN IN THE HOUSE
on Long Island, the sound of laughter and music and voices
emanating from the house. It is summer. Outside the sun is
shining, the sky is blue. There they are on the lawn, planning a
beach excursion or a dinner party or just sitting in chairs reading. Sailing on the pond, where on Sunday afternoons there
are regattas. Maddy cooking or in the garden. Johnny playing
with a friend. He is older now. Taller, slender like his mother.
He has her beauty.

His heart condition has gone away. It's as though it never
happened. He plays tennis now. I let him use my court. There
are even a few girls around, an inkling of what it will be like in
a few years. He will be devastating. Women will fall at his feet.
Harry comes out of the house, looking well. He completed his
novel. It was another bestseller. His last book is being turned

into a movie. Who else is there? Well, I am, of course—happy to have my proxy family united again, warm in their shared love, contented as a favorite uncle. Ned and Cissy are there too. She is carrying her first baby in her arms.

How did it all happen? How does anything happen? They realized they loved each other too much. And, like all truly happy couples, they were complete only when they were together. Pain is transient but love eternal. Harry and Johnny landed, and Maddy returned from Mexico. When Harry brought Johnny back home, Maddy invited him in. Inspired by her trip, she had just been to the store and was roasting a pork shank. Making chile ancho relleno. Would he like to stay for dinner? There was cold beer in the refrigerator. They sat around the table as they had so many times before, wearing the comfort of being together like an old coat. There was laughter. Maddy told them about Mexico. About the color the sea turned at sunset, about the parrots in the jungle. She brought back Indian blankets, a sombrero for Johnny. They told her about their flight. Johnny showed off his knowledge of English kings. It was King George the First, he said. He came after Queen Anne. He was German. They clapped, and he smiled, appreciative of the applause but happier still that his mother and father were together again.

After dinner, they put Johnny to bed the way they always had, with stories and a kiss on the forehead. Then they talked deep into the night, soaking up each other's thoughts, laughing from sheer joy in each other's presence. There were tears but no recriminations, no anger, no fear. There was no need. It was as though their lives had never been altered. When it was time for bed, there was no question whether Harry would stay.

He simply followed her upstairs, and she expected nothing less. They then made love, slowly, securely, happily, the way they once had, the only way two people who are truly in love can.

And Harry never left. Love endured. They grew older. They got dogs. Johnny went to Harry's old school, then Yale. He never played hockey, but that mattered to no one, least of all Harry. Instead he had a flair for languages and spent a term abroad in Paris, staying with friends of the family. We all came over and visited once and took a cycling trip through the Loire Valley. Johnny knew Italian, Spanish, and French, and was learning Mandarin. He was interested in foreign relations. Maybe even law.

He and I had lunch a few times a year. I drove up to New Haven, and we ate at Mory's, or, when he was down in the city, we met at one of my clubs for lunch. Every year during the Christmas holidays, we went to a Broadway play or musical, just like when he was a boy. I loved hearing about his life, about his interests. In addition to his mother's looks, he has her passions and sensitive nature, and his father's sense of humor and knack for making everything look easy. He is such a perfect combination of the two. I couldn't be more proud of him.

In the spring we would all go skiing in Breckenridge for a week. Summers were spent on Long Island, and Johnny came out as often as he could, usually bringing with him one in a succession of beautiful, tan girls with white teeth and honey-colored hair. They would join us in trips to the beach, their firm breasts barcly concealed by their bikinis. Johnny, lithe and tightly muscled, the scar on his chest just visible when he had his shirt off, paddling one of the canoes. There were still swimming races. Maddy still won most of the time, but one time I saw Johnny hold back and knew he was letting her win. He was now much taller than both of them. Maddy still had her figure, but Harry had put on weight. Both of them had gray hair.

After graduation, Johnny didn't join the Marines, as his father had, but he did spend a year in Cambodia teaching in a remote village. He wrote me e-mails from there, describing the people, their customs, their gentleness. He also sent photographs of him helping build a well, leading a water buffalo, astride a motorcycle. Then he returned and entered law school. He joined my firm, at my encouragement, of course. He was well-liked and was soon on the fast track for partner. But I knew he was too spirited to remain for long. Guided by nobler instincts, he moved to Washington, where he went to work for the Department of Justice. It was there that he met Caroline, who would become his wife. She was English and worked at the British embassy.

Her parents flew over to meet Maddy and Harry, and spent a weekend on Long Island. Everyone got along famously. Her father, Gerald, was in the City. Caro's mother, Jilly, was a homemaker and somehow related to E. M. Forster and had literary interests. She had read Harry's books—there were four now—and was very excited to meet him. Caro had two brothers, one an officer in the Blues and Royals, the other still at Cambridge. Their flat was near Eaton Square. They had a weekend place in Gloucestershire. It was a typical Cotswolds house, the golden limestone, with views sweeping down a green valley. Every August they went to Tuscany for their summer holiday. In the winter, they rode to hounds.

Johnny and Caro were married in the Cotswolds. Several

hundred guests came. Many of Johnny's friends flew over. So did some of Maddy and Harry's friends. Ned and Cissy. Me. There was a big marquee on the lawn. Champagne flowed. The men wore morning coats, the women wore hats. Maddy looked beautiful in a soft green dress that brought out the blue in her eyes. It was a charming village. The reception was only a short walk from the church, which predated the Norman Conquest. There were swans in the river. Harry was best man.

We saw less of Johnny, but that was to be expected. In their second year of marriage, Caro announced at Thanksgiving that she was pregnant. Harry, grinning enormously, patted his son on the back. Maddy kissed Caro. The baby was born in May. He was christened Walter Wakefield Winslow. There followed two more soon after, Madeleine and Gerry. I gave them all gold spoons with their names on them. They were all beautiful and healthy children.

One year Johnny and Caro lived in Shanghai, another year in London. He had left Justice and rejoined the firm (where, by now, I was of counsel) as a partner. They returned to New York. I bought them a town house. I know, it was absurdly lavish, but what else am I going to do with my money? Besides, as I pointed out to Johnny, it was all going to him one day anyway. The children entered school. I dutifully attended school plays, concerts, and games, just as I had done with him.

Maddy and Harry were always there as well. They still moved like lovers, hardly ever standing out of reach of each other. Harry's hair, still thick, was white, and he still carried himself with the slight, shifting gait of an aging athlete. He had an operation to repair one of his knees. Maddy's hair was white too. She had cut it shorter, so it no longer ran down her back, but her eyes were just as bright. She had that delicate, parchment-like beauty that only a few older women possess. She and Harry traveled from time to time. Harry was asked to teach a seminar at Yale, to be a fellow in Rotterdam. He gave graduation speeches. They never spent a night apart.

For the first few years, Johnny and Caro would come out on the weekends and would stay in Maddy and Harry's house, but as they had more children and the children got bigger, it was plain that they had outgrown the house. I should have thought of this sooner, but, after talking it over with Harry and Maddy, I told Johnny and Caro I was giving them my house too, along with a small trust to be used for its upkeep. Once again, they protested, but I pointed out the fruitlessness of any argument and that it made no sense for one man to ramble around in a big old house by himself when what it really needed was a family with children to live in it.

So I went to live with Maddy and Harry, using Johnny's old room as my own. I was very comfortable and, frankly, felt safer. If I had fallen down the stairs in my house, it might have been a day or so before anyone found me.

I am old now. Nearly bald. I need to keep wiping my shoulders to brush away dandruff. I don't hear as well as I once did, nor do many other things work as well as they once did. I have become one of those elderly men who fill their days with trips to the doctor. I stop in at my office every morning, but there is less and less for me to do. I mainly act in an advisory capacity. I still sit on a few boards. I am on the library committee at one of my clubs. I still have one martini every night, even though I have been told it is bad for me. Maddy and I go for long walks. Not as long as we once did, but it is enough. She uses a cane now, an elegant gold-handled one that belonged to her great-grandfather, the land baron. Whether in the country or the city, at night I go to sleep in my bed with a light heart. I have no regrets. I have known love, it has blessed me nearly every day of my life. I couldn't be happier.

Except none of this is true.

8

THEY FIND THE PLANE'S WRECKAGE LATE THAT AFTERNOON.
Only the mangled landing gear is visible above the waterline.
It is a clear day, wind blowing from the southwest. Almost no
turbulence. The tower had received a distress call from Harry
around two o'clock, reporting that he was losing altitude and
asking for clearance. That was followed by some static that the
air traffic controller couldn't make out, and then silence.

An eyewitness who had been surf casting on the beach says
he saw a single-engine plane come in low and attempt a water
landing. On contact with the surface, it flipped over several
times and broke apart. Divers locate the body of a young boy
first. He had been decapitated. The water is cold, the current
strong, and visibility is limited. The divers can only stay down
for fifteen minutes at a time. They don't find Harry's body until
the next morning.

I learn of the crash the way most people do. I read about it online. It is a Saturday, and I am spending a quiet afternoon at home in New York. AUTHOR AND SON FEARED DEAD IN CRASH runs one of the headlines. I did not know that Harry and Johnny had flown that day. I click on the headline absentmindedly, and, with mounting horror, I read the story, stunned and disbelieving until the phone calls start. Friends, acquaintances want to know if it is true. I don't know, but I fear the worst.

Then I receive an official call from the local chief of police, a man I have known for many years. His father had been our butcher. I remember the son working in the shop when he was a teenager, a few years younger than I, his apron smeared with dried blood. His thick hands, short blond hair. I had been listed as an emergency contact.

"Mister Gervais, I'm sorry to tell you this . . ."

It is all I need to hear. Maddy is still away, her flight due in the next day. I have to notify her. I try information to get the number for her hotel and finally find it online. There is no answer. I call the Mexican consulate in Manhattan but am told by the answering service to call back Monday morning. I don't even know what flight she will be on. I then place a call to the home of the man who heads up our firm's Mexico City office and tell him what happened. I tell him Maddy is staying in a hotel in the Yucatán, and, after much grumbling, he eventually arranges to have the police locate and inform her.

It is the only way. I can't risk her arriving at the airport and finding out what happened by glancing through the newsstand. That would be too cruel.

Late that night Maddy calls from Mexico. I have been expecting it, dreading it. I pick up the phone before the end of the first ring. She is hysterical.

"What the hell is going on, Walter? Is this some kind of crazy joke? I just had two Mexican policemen wake me up and tell me to call you."

I tell her what happened. The cry that emanates from the other end of the phone is otherworldly. It is a mixture of anger and pain I have never heard before. "I'm so sorry," I repeat. "I'm so sorry." There is nothing else for me to say, so I stand listening to her sob, wishing I could be there to comfort her. After a quarter of an hour, I ask her what time her flight gets in. I have to ask several times because each time she tries to answer, she begins to cry again. Eventually she manages to stutter out the time.

"Don't . . . hang . . . up," she pleads, drawing in breaths, fighting now for control.

"I won't."

We stay on the phone for another hour. Occasionally we speak, but mostly we are silent or Maddy is crying.

In the morning she has to fly early to Mexico City and then to JFK. She won't arrive until the evening. When she does, I am waiting. She is in a wheelchair. Despite a tan, she looks waxen, her cheeks hollow. I walk up to her but can't even tell if she recognizes me. Her eyelids flutter. She is being escorted by an airline representative and a porter, who carries her luggage.

I nod as the pretty, dark-haired girl asks, "Are you here to meet Mrs. Winslow? She has been given a sedative. She slept the whole way from Mexico. Do you have a car waiting?"

This time there is no stretch limousine. I take Maddy to my apartment and put her in my bed and let her sleep.

For a few days, it is in all the papers. They all use the same photograph of Harry, the one from the dust jacket of his book. One of the tabloids even found a class portrait of Johnny standing with a bunch of other boys in jackets and ties; they run it with a circle around him. Another has a diagram that shows what happens to a plane when it hits the water. I can't look at it.

There is speculation over the cause of the crash. Was it pilot error? A technical malfunction? Did Harry have a stroke? Was Johnny flying, attempting a landing under his father's supervision? Had a depressed Harry driven his plane into the water on purpose? The National Transportation Safety Board moves the pieces of the plane to the Air National Guard base in Westhampton Beach to determine what happened. Autopsies are performed on both bodies.

Maddy wants them cremated. She is a little better now but still walking around my apartment like a somnambulist. It is up to me to make the arrangements. I speak with the funeral home on Pantigo Road. I fill out the necessary forms. The *New York Times* calls about the obituary, so do the *East Hampton Star* and *Southampton Press*. I have a lot to do and hate leaving Maddy alone. I am seriously concerned she might just walk to the window and throw herself out. I come home and find her still at the breakfast table, staring at a cold cup of coffee, smoking, fingering Harry's Saint Christopher medal. The heap of stubbed-out cigarette butts is the only indication that time has passed.

I drive us out to my house. That is where the reception will be. She told me she can't return to her own house. I put her in the Victorian Room, and, instead of using my own room, I sleep next door, in my great-grandfather's monk-like chamber. In all the years I have known her, she has never spent the night in my house. I make dinner, but she doesn't have an appetite. She has barely eaten a thing in days. All she seems to consume is vodka and nicotine. I urge her to eat something, tell her that there's no point in starving herself. I carve her meat as though for a child. I even put it on the fork. She just stares at me.

In the morning, the caterers arrive. I am not sure how many guests are coming back to my house afterward. I can count on Cissy and Ned, Harry's agent, his publisher, other friends. Maddy's brother, Johnny, is coming from Oregon, where he works as some kind of addiction counselor and teaches yoga. These were the ones I knew to invite. I knew she wouldn't want too many. Only the closest family and friends. Some of them I hadn't seen in years, but I suppose they had kept in touch with Harry and Maddy.

Shortly before eleven, I drive us to the church, St. Luke's, the same one where we had my father's memorial. I still regularly attend services, whether out here or at St. James's in the city, but I know that Harry and Maddy were mainly Christmas and Easter only. The new rector is a woman who has been there for the past few years. She greets me warmly and with great sensitivity, then lets me slip past as I have my arm around a sedated Maddy. I had to help her get dressed.

A few guests have already arrived, but I ignore them, escorting Maddy to the front of the church. There are many flowers surrounding the altar, and two large photographs of Harry and Johnny. I feel myself tearing up, and I can only imagine how Maddy must be feeling, if she is aware of anything, and I hold her tightly. A few people come up to Maddy, but I politely try to shoo most of them away.

I look around and see Harry's father sitting by himself in a pew opposite. A widower now, he has come down from New

Hampshire, where he lives in retirement. I am once again struck by their physical resemblance. It is like looking at Harry in thirty years' time. His father is staring at the photographs of his son and grandson. His whole legacy wiped out in a single instant. I would have gone over and greeted him, but didn't want to leave Maddy.

Ned and Cissy appear. Cissy slides in next to Maddy, not saying a word, chin up, clutching Maddy's hand. Ned looks shrunken. A few more people file in, but I keep my attention focused on Maddy. The service begins, the familiar words: "I am the resurrection and the life." There are no speeches, no remembrances. Maddy would not have been able to bear it. It is over quickly.

I move Maddy back outside to my car, which is parked in front of the church. I barely notice the guests as I walk out but catch glimpses of a few familiar faces. There are more people than I had expected. Funerals always attract the curious, especially if the deceased is a celebrity of sorts. Only about ten cars follow us back though.

I had brought boots for Maddy and myself, and help put hers on. We walk slowly through the mud toward the pond, followed by the others. Ned takes one of the canoes and carries it down the dock. I follow behind with Maddy. Ned and I help her into the bow, where she sits facing aft. Then I get in, sitting in the stern, as ever. Cissy hands me the tin. No one says a word.

The other guests have gathered on the dock, all of them still in their dark suits and dresses. They are silent. The only sounds come from my paddle, my breathing, and my heart roaring in my chest. The sky is overcast, a milky translucence. The water is dark, calm and opaque. A few seagulls circle overhead. Most of the estates on the pond are still shut for winter. Trees are wrapped in burlap. Lawn furniture stowed away. Swimming pools covered by tarpaulins littered with brown leaves.

I paddle us out to the middle of the pond and open the tin. There is only one. She wanted them mixed together. Gingerly, she takes it from me. Dipping her fingers in, she removes a handful of ash and then throws it out over the water. She begins to sob. Or, rather, continues sobbing, because she really hasn't stopped for days. Again and again, she reaches into the tin and scatters the ashes until they are all gone. She looks at me, and I understand it is time to return. Her eyes are red and swollen, mirroring the tears running down my own cheeks.

We return to the dock, and Ned and Cissy help us out. Again, I shepherd Maddy back to the house. "I can't," she whispers. I tell her I understand. I take her to her room, where she collapses on the bed. I pull the comforter over her and turn off the light. "Please tell them I'm sorry I can't come down. I just can't see anyone."

Downstairs the mood is somber. Everyone has gathered in the Green Room. It has been years since so many people have stood here. A white-jacketed bartender is mixing drinks. A waiter passes hors d'oeuvres. I greet a few of the guests. Harry's agent, Reuben, comes up to me, confidentially placing his hand on my arm.

"How is she doing?"

"It's been a terrible shock," I reply.

"It's been a terrible shock for all of us. I can't believe Harry's dead. Or Johnny. What a tragedy."

I circulate among the other guests, my mind still on the grieving woman upstairs. I try to be a good host, tell them what I know, commiserate with them, shake my head. I look for Harry's father and find him on the patio, staring at the water.

"Can I get you anything, Mister Winslow?"

Startled, the old man looks over at me, focuses, and shakes his head. "No, thank you, Walter," he says. Then he asks, "What do you think happened? I mean, up there." He gestures with his chin up at the sky.

"I really don't know. The autopsies haven't come back. Nor the results from the NTSB."

"The hell with all that. They won't tell you anything."

"What do you mean?"

"It was hamartia."

The term is familiar to me, but its meaning is lost. "Hamartia?"

"From Aristotle's *Poetics*. The fatal flaw. I know what my son had done. I know he had sinned. He told me about Maddy and that other girl. It's always that way. When the hero does something stupid or wrong, the fates won't let him forget it. And yes, my son was very much a hero. He always had been. But being a hero doesn't prevent one from making terrible mistakes. Or from suffering the consequences."

I listen in silence. He is an old English teacher. It is how he thinks. If he had been an engineer, he would have a different explanation. He has doubtless constructed this theory, based on a lifetime of lecturing, during his long, solitary drive down from New Hampshire. There was no such thing as a technical malfunction in *Hamlet*, nor did Oedipus have any pilot errors. Harry's father's world is governed by certain inviolable rules. Cause and effect. The tragic error could result only in more tragedy. It is the only thing that makes any sense to him.

"He was a Marine pilot," he adds. "He could fly anything in any condition. Planes just don't fall out of the sky."

I look at him. Clearly, he is in pain, desperately trying to rationalize the irrational.

"I wish I knew," I respond eventually. "If you'll excuse me, I need to go check on people." I leave him there, still staring out at the water. He may not have even realized I had left.

We all need to make sense of our loss in a way we understand best. I didn't mean to be rude, but I didn't see him again before he left. For all I know, he may have gone straight to his car after our conversation. People are gone by two o'clock, and the caterers are packing up. I had ordered too much. There are plastic containers holding several dozen deviled eggs crammed in my refrigerator. An entire lasagna in a foil baking tray. Half a ham. Gallons of whisky, vodka, white wine. Bread. Lemons. Seltzer. I could live off it for weeks. Ned and Cissy are the last to leave.

"Call me if you need any help with Maddy, okay?" says Cissy. I tell her that I hope they can come out soon.

"Thanks, Walter," says Ned. "I've been meaning to tell you. We recently bought our own place in Bridgehampton, near the ocean."

The news comes as a surprise. "Congratulations."

"It happened about a month ago. Harry knew, but I never had a chance to mention it to you. I told him it was time we stopped being such freeloaders," he adds with a weak grin. I can tell he is about to cry.

"Don't be silly. I'll miss you guys, but I am very happy for you," I tell him. But I'm not really happy. It is one more loss. Our old life has come unglued, and it can never be put back together.

9

I walk Ned and Cissy out to their car, sorry to see them go, feeling emptier than I ever have. I pay the caterers and then go up to check on Maddy. We are alone again in the house. The sounds of her breathing in the darkened room tell me she is sleeping. I will look in on her again later. I wander downstairs. The kitchen is clean. It's too early to get drunk, but I figure there is nothing else to do. I pour myself a large whisky and flip on the television in the library, but there is nothing I want to watch.

Instead I wander over to the bookshelves. More than one hundred years ago my great-grandfather had begun collecting and binding copies of *Punch,* the once-great British humor magazine. My grandfather and father kept up the tradition. We have every single issue, going back to the 1840s. I pull out a volume from the early twentieth century and absentmindedly flip through the yellowed pages of cartoons of Punch himself, the Kaiser, village curates, noble British military heroes with mustaches, slender, long-necked beauties personifying all that was good and noble in the world. It was probably here in these pages that I first developed my sense of ideal womanhood. Small wonder that the women in the drawings bore such a strong resemblance to Maddy. I had loved leafing through these volumes ever since I was a child, but I have no appetite for it today.

Restless, I decide to go for a walk. I pull on a coat and exit quietly, making sure not to slam the door. I hate to think of Maddy waking up alone in the house, in that strange bed, quite probably disoriented, calling out but with no one there to answer her.

Despite the melancholy of the day, or more likely because of it, it feels good to be outside in the April air. The ground is soft, and there are signs of life in the daffodil beds. Already jack-in-the-pulpits are pushing up. It's still cool, but spring is here. Soon all the trees and flowers will be in bloom, the lawn will smell of fresh-cut grass, and on the pond the cygnets will swim after their parents. I first walk around the house, inspecting gutters, drains. I had the power lines buried years ago. Raccoons and squirrels used to leap from tree branches onto the roof and burrow into the attic, too often winding up trapped in the heating ducts. For this same reason, the trees need to be pruned back regularly. I make a mental note to have the groundskeeper trim the box hedge, repair the deer fencing, and put up the tennis nets.

Then I walk down to the water. To my surprise, someone is standing at the edge of the dock facing out over the pond. It's a woman, dressed in a beige raincoat and rubber boots. All the funeral guests are long gone. It's not Maddy.

I recognize her shape as soon as I see it.

Claire.

"Hello, Walter," she says, turning to look at me. I had forgotten how lovely she is. She had been in the church. I remember her coat, but her face and head had been concealed by sunglasses and a scarf.

I hesitate. "Claire," I say. "This is a surprise."

"Is it?" She gives me a rueful little smile.

"Yes."

"I had to say good-bye. I knew I wouldn't be welcome, but I had to come."

I say nothing but walk up behind her. The dock is too narrow for us to stand side by side.

"Maddy's in the house, you know."

"I assumed she would be here. How is she?"

"Inconsolable."

She sighs. "I understand," she replies in a soft voice. "How are you?"

I take a moment to respond. I haven't been thinking about myself. "Incredibly sad," I answer finally.

"I am so sorry. About this. About everything."

"We all are. It's a terrible waste."

"I know. I can't stop thinking about Johnny."

"None of us can. There's nothing sadder than the death of a child."

"Maddy's lucky she has you."

I nod my head. It is surreal standing here talking with her. "Thank you. You know, Claire, I can appreciate why you wanted to come, but I am afraid I have to ask you to leave. I can't risk having Maddy wake up and see you here. It would be too much for her in her present state."

She sniffs and smiles at me. "Of course. I understand. I had hoped I could just slip in quietly, unobserved and say good-bye. I did love him, you know. Very much. I've been crying for days."

"We will all miss him."

"You know, he didn't really love me. I know that now. But there was never any question in his heart. He loved Maddy the most—and Johnny, of course. For what it's worth, I hadn't seen him for weeks. Not since Johnny came to stay with him. We had a fight."

"Why are you telling me this?"

"So you can tell Maddy. I don't know if she knows that. He never talked about her, about their family. He kept that to himself. I think that's important. I know it would be if it were me."

"Thank you. I'll tell her."

"And don't think I haven't suffered or won't suffer. I will always carry part of Harry with me."

I look at her, not knowing what to say. I remember the first time we met. How fresh and new she had seemed then.

"Good-bye, Walter." She puts out her hand. "I hope we won't be enemies."

"Of course not. But it might be hard to be friends."

"I understand."

I watch her walk away and then hear the faint sound of her boots as they crunch down the drive. She must have parked on the road. I feel sorry for her. She isn't a bad person. I believe that in my heart. And I can't blame her for falling in love with

Harry. He was hard not to love. And she, like so many of the young, was looking for a shortcut, an edge over the competition, always in a hurry, not yet realizing there is no benefit in speeding up the journey, that the destination is not the point but merely part of the process. They also don't fully appreciate that their actions have repercussions. That lives can be ruined. Of course, the young don't have a monopoly on selfishness. We want what we want. The bitter truth is that it rarely makes us happy once we get it.

I turn and walk back to the house. I don't want to leave Maddy alone for too long.

EPILOGUE

MADDY NEVER REALLY RECOVERED FROM HARRY'S AND Johnny's deaths. Eventually she returned to a semblance of life. It was impossible for her to go back to either of her homes, so she continued to stay with me. I know she often thought of killing herself, so I watched her like a hawk. "I just want to die," she'd say. "Will you help me?" And I, I who would have done anything for her but that, always told her no. At times I wondered if I was doing the right thing, that maybe it would have been better to let her go. Her pain was unbearable. She would break down in the middle of a meal. We never went out, seldom saw anyone.

When Harry was alive and they were together, we had all been so content with the world built around their marriage that we had few contacts beyond it. We didn't need any. People found us. But no longer. She remained heavily medicated. I even stopped going to my clubs, afraid of leaving her, if only to make sure she ate a little dinner or didn't accidentally leave a cigarette burning near a curtain. During the day, I hired a nurse to look after her so I could go to the office, but at night it was just us.

She was tormented by nightmares. I could hear her screaming in bed and would rush to her door and wait and listen. Sometimes I would knock, but mostly I just let her sleep. But she always knew I was there.

"Walter," she would cry. "Are you there?"

"Yes," I would answer. "Do you want me to come in?"

"No, it was just another bad dream."

Usually, after one of her episodes, I lingered there until she had calmed down. Other times I wasn't able to go back to sleep and instead read or puttered around until dawn. One day I had to rush home early after receiving a panicked phone call from the nurse telling me that Maddy had locked herself in the bathroom and wouldn't come out or even respond. When I arrived, I knocked on the bathroom door and desperately asked Maddy if she was all right. To my relief there were signs of life and no sounds of running water. I was seconds away from calling the police when I heard the tumblers turn in the lock, and Maddy walked out past us both. She had cut off her hair, that glorious hair that now lay scattered in the sink and on the bathroom floor. I had the locks removed on every door in the apartment the next day but said nothing about it to Maddy and gave the nurse a raise after begging her to stay.

Gradually, we moved Maddy's belongings to either my house out east or the apartment in the city, but we left much more behind. We packed for her the way one packs for a journey.

Take only the essentials, leave everything else. She wanted little. A warm coat, underwear, rain boots, a ratty sweater of her father's, a stuffed bear from her childhood. A few old family photo albums, medals from her swimming days. Some jewelry of her grandmother's that wasn't in the safe-deposit box. She left behind her cookbooks, her pots, her knives. It was as though she was leaving behind the last two decades of her life. She took nothing of Johnny's, nothing of Harry's. I had their things boxed up and put into storage.

When it became clear she would never return to either of her two homes, I broached the subject of selling them, or at least renting them out. "I don't care what you do," she told me. "I can't go back." I had no qualms about selling the Manhattan apartment. It held no real memories for me. The cottage was a different matter. Not only did it hold a special place in my heart but also I was concerned that some boorish hedge fund manager would buy it, tear it down, and throw up some horrid modern mansion I would be forced to look at every day. So instead of selling, I bought it and, at her instigation, had it razed. Today it is an empty field, where wildflowers bloom in summertime.

We did, however, place a large rock, more like a boulder really, at the edge of the pond, near where she had scattered the ashes. It weighed several tons and needed to be put in place by a crane. A stonemason had carved in Harry's and Johnny's full names, the dates of their births and deaths, and an epitaph Maddy composed that read I WILL LOVE YOU ALWAYS. We also placed a little stone bench beside it, and she planted flowers around the base. Every day she went down there and sat for hours.

We were married the next year. It may come as a surprise, but it shouldn't. She was healing, and, to me at least, it seemed the right thing to do. The only thing, really. I had proposed several times, and she always told me she wasn't ready. She thanked me for helping her and wondered why it mattered anyway. We were already together and could we please just not talk about it? Still, I kept asking. I had my reasons, of course. Partly I believed that, if she married me, she would be better able to heal her wounds. But also I wanted it so very much.

There were practical reasons too. As her husband, I could visit her in the hospital. I could do things for her legally that I could not do as just a friend. Also, call me old-fashioned, but I believe in the proprieties, and if we were going to live together under the same roof, we should do so as man and wife. Eventually she relented.

We told only a few people. Ned and Cissy, but only afterward. There was no reception. The ceremony was held in the town hall, my groundskeeper and the golf pro from the club were the only witnesses. We exchanged rings. I handed over the check. Afterward, the two of us went to the movies. Maddy loves the movies.

We still slept in separate rooms. Sex was never an option. It would have been impossible for both of us after all that had happened. Nor were children—even though Maddy was too old, we could have adopted. But that was beside the point. It was enough for me that Maddy was now my wife. I know she agreed to this only out of a combination of apathy, gratitude, and fear. While she was recovering, she became unnaturally afraid of being alone. The thought of having to spend the night by herself was terrifying. We always kept a light on.

Fortunately, I was senior enough in my firm that I could arrange my schedule to accommodate her, as Maddy, in addition to being incapable of being alone at night, also refused to fly. As a result there were more than a few overseas deals I was forced to delegate to other members of the firm. I don't blame her, but it was just one more constraint we were forced to live with.

It wasn't all bad, though. There were good days. Maddy resumed playing golf, a game she hadn't played since she was a child, when she and her father, who was a scratch player, won the father-daughter tournament at the club so often that they eventually just gave them the cup. Harry had never been interested in the game, finding it too slow, so she simply stopped. Her form was perfect, and she could hit the ball as far as any man. She could have been very happy playing thirty-six holes every day, starting early in the morning and going hard until evening, regardless of the weather. I am an indifferent golfer at best, despite taking lessons since childhood, but I was happy to play for Maddy's sake.

She didn't care that she was better than I. It was enough for her to be concentrating on the ball, the wind, the green. She even enjoyed the comradeship of fellow golfers, and we often made up fours with other members, or she would go by herself if I was unavailable. Her beauty, athleticism, and the air of mystery around her made her quite a compelling figure at the club, of course, and at first we were deluged with invitations to cocktail parties, dances, dinners. We politely declined every single one. Small talk on the golf course was one thing, in someone's home it was another entirely.

One of the worst times of year for her began when the club

closed the course for the season. To help her feel better, I eventually bought a place in Florida in the same club north of Palm Beach where my parents had once had a house. There were still a few elderly women there who remembered them. The house, a pink stucco one-story Spanish Colonial with a swimming pool, a bedroom for each of us, and a little apartment over the garage, was right on the golf course.

We began spending more time in Florida, taking the twenty-five-hour train ride down to West Palm right after Thanksgiving and staying there through April. That's where Maddy began to socialize again and became more animated. By now, her hair had grown back, but it was not as long, or as golden, as it once was. She still never cooked, but we began to accept a few invitations, and she began to enjoy going to the golf club or the main club at night for dinner. These were new friends, people not associated with her past life. Many of them were happily illiterate. The books on their shelves, if they had any, were spy novels for reading on the beach, manuals on how to improve one's golf game, a few hefty biographies that may never have been opened. They also had the usual assortment of coffee table books with lush photographs of architecture and gardens. It would have meant little to these retired bankers, lawyers, and CEOs that Maddy had once been married to Harry Winslow, the author. This allowed her not only a welcome anonymity but also a chance to start over. In this world, she was only Maddy Gervais, not Wakefield, not Winslow. I won't say she was happy, but she was in less pain, and for that I was extremely grateful.

Gradually, she began to come back to life. It had started with golf and continued with that other great Sunday activity, going to church. After Maddy came to live with me, I had fewer and fewer opportunities to attend Sunday services. I gently asked her if she had any desire to go, but she declined, saying bitterly, "I don't think God would care to hear what I have to say to Him."

Then one Christmas she agreed to join me. We hadn't attended a Christmas Eve Mass together in years. We were in Florida, and Christ Memorial Chapel was wearing its holiday best, festooned with garlands and wreaths, a manger in the corner, the choir in their surplices, red candles burning in every sconce. It was the "midnight" service, which meant eleven P.M., and the church was full of people in their Christmas finery, lots of red and green neckties, their seasonal cheer buoyed no doubt by a good dinner. Sleepy children dozed on their parents' shoulders, old ladies sat together.

The rector greeted us warmly at the door. He read the traditional Christmas Eve service in a warm Scottish burr, while children playing the parts of Joseph, Mary, the shepherds, and the three kings acted out the story. We sang hymns, and I was very pleased that one was a favorite of mine, "The Holly and the Ivy."

Afterward, as we were driving home, Maddy said, "I forgot how much I liked going to church. Can we go again on Sunday?" So we returned the next week and then every week following. When we were on Long Island, we also went. And while I remained purely a Sunday goer, Maddy started taking Bible classes, and before long, she had graduated to community outreach programs. She worked on clothing drives, served in soup kitchens, visited people in the hospital, and delivered food to the elderly. Eventually she became a member of the vestry.

By now, I had more or less retired from the firm, a decision that had been one of the easiest of my life. I kept an office there still and went in from time to time, but mainly for distraction because there was little for me to do except sign the odd paper and peruse the *Wall Street Journal*. Maddy and I didn't need the income, of course. In addition to my money, Maddy still had her own trust, which I now looked after. She also had the money from the sale of her homes and from Harry's books, and, for the first time in her life, she was really quite rich.

Sales of Harry's books surged after his death, and, after much dithering, a movie came out based on his second. Thanks to the inclusion of one of Hollywood's more bankable stars, the film performed relatively well at the box office. We were, of course, invited to the premiere but inevitably declined. Maddy had no desire to see the movie. I snuck out to see it one afternoon and found it mildly diverting, but it was nothing like the book. Still, I couldn't help but think how much Harry would have enjoyed seeing his book made into a movie even if he might have been disappointed with the final product. I know he certainly would have appreciated the money. His agent, Reuben, had been after Maddy for years to share the draft of his last book in case there was anything salvageable. But she made sure that no one ever saw it.

Well, that's not entirely accurate. I did read it without her knowledge. One of my responsibilities in the aftermath of the accident was to settle Harry's estate, which also meant removing his belongings from the rental apartment. There hadn't been much, but there was his laptop. Everything else I had boxed up and sent into storage, but I kept the laptop. It was not too difficult to figure out his password—it was, incidentally, "Maddy"—and this allowed me to find and download his novel. He had several hundred pages in the most recent file. I gave Maddy the computer, but secretly I kept a copy of the novel for myself. I did so out of curiosity. She was still so fragile I didn't want to do or say anything that might upset her.

It was a good book—better in many ways than his last. It was all about us, although it wasn't really about us. I suppose that's how writers do it. There was a happily married family, a handsome husband, a beautiful wife, a sweet boy. They were loved and admired. There was even a family friend. Into this idyll comes a young woman, beautiful, sensual. But she is not a snake in the garden. She is smart, full of life, eager for love. There is an affair, followed by heartbreak and remorse. The descriptions of their first night, Paris, all the trips they took, the time they spent together—things that only the two of them would know were there. That is why I know so much. Harry wrote it all down. What was different was that the story ended well. The husband and wife were reunited. It was a story of forgiveness. Some readers may have found such a conclusion unrealistic, treacly even, but it made sense to me. It was, as he told me the last time I saw him, a "love letter" to Maddy.

I never told Maddy I had read Harry's last novel for fear it would cause barely healed wounds to burst open again. I could not bear for that to happen. But it did make me curious. There was much I hadn't known, that none of us, except for Harry and Claire, knew about their affair. But every year, again without Maddy's knowledge, I reread the manuscript, hoping to glean something new about Harry's feelings for Maddy, his feelings for Claire. There was a certain masochistic pleasure in doing so, of course. While I was only a minor character, it was strange to read about myself, even if it was supposed to be fiction. Is that really me? one asks. Is that the way I talk? Is that how Harry—or any author—really sees it? One doesn't know whether one should be insulted or flattered, or both simultaneously. What seems important to one person is peripheral to another. Still, I went back to the book every year, immersing myself once again in those prelapsarian days and then the inevitable fall.

Much of the writing was quite beautiful too, at least it struck me that way, because he caught their life, our lives, making them so recognizable and yet so much more. There were certain words, passages that gave me chills whenever I read them. But, like all secrets, after a while it became too much to bear alone. I had to share it with someone. Obviously, I could never discuss the book with Maddy. Our golfing friends would be incapable, and even old friends like Ned and Cissy, whom we did not see that much of any longer and who were minor characters in the book, would have merely been sounding boards. I needed to share, but, more important, I needed to know more.

There was only one thing to do. I contacted Claire. Nearly a decade had passed, and she wasn't easy to find, but eventually I tracked her down. She was surprised to hear from me, of course, but was good enough to agree to meet me for lunch. She was living in Old Greenwich now, and asked if we could meet somewhere near Grand Central because she would take the train right back out. The only place I knew in the vicinity was the Yale Club, so I suggested that.

❧

WHEN THE DAY COMES—I MAKE SURE TO COVER MY TRACKS with Maddy by telling her I have a big client lunch, of which I have fewer and fewer nowadays—I enter the club for the first time in months and am greeted by Louis at the front door. "Welcome back, Mister Gervais," he says. "I hope you had a good winter."

I am early and wait for her downstairs in the lobby. Her train was scheduled to arrive shortly after twelve-thirty. A few minutes before one, she walks through the door. Her hair is longer, her face not as fresh as it had once been but still beautiful, the almond eyes, the pillowy, slighted parted lips. It is late April, and she wears an elegant gray coat over a subdued but well-cut fawn-colored, knee-length dress. She is a little heavier, but her legs are still good. I spot on her left hand a wedding band and a good-size diamond.

I stand up to greet her. "Hello, Walter," she says, putting out her hand. "It's been a long time."

"Yes, thank you for coming in all this way."

"Don't mention it. I'll take any opportunity I can to get down to New York."

"How long have you lived in Old Greenwich?"

"Four years."

We go up to the rooftop dining room. It is quieter, more intimate than the boisterous Tap Room. I recognize several of the members sitting around the room and nod to them. The maître d', Manuel, is also pleasantly surprised to see me. I shake his hand warmly, and he shows us to our table. Would we like anything to drink? he asks.

"Martini?" I ask Claire.

"No." She smiles. "No more martinis for me. Just a sparkling water, please."

"Well, I will have one, if you don't mind, even if my doctor would disapprove. Beefeater up with a twist, well-shaken, please."

Manuel leaves with the drink order, and I turn to Claire, taking her in fully this time. "It's nice to see you again," I say. "You look very well. The country air agrees with you." I wish I could say the same for myself. Even though I have only recently returned from several months in Florida and have a nice tan, my doctor is after me about my cholesterol, and he tells me I need to lose about twenty pounds.

She laughs. That same laugh. Silver bells. "Oh, I don't know about that. I suppose I can't complain, but sometimes I do miss New York."

"Why did you move up there?"

"Well, David, that's my husband, is from there, and we thought it would be the best place to raise a family. He commutes in every day, and I stay at home and look after the children."

"How many children do you have?"

"Two boys so far, but I'm five months pregnant with my third."

"Congratulations. How old are your boys?"

"Nine and three."

"It sounds like a lovely life."

"It is. A little boring at times, but we have good friends up there, and David and I always make sure to spend at least one weekend a month by ourselves in New York. We stay in a hotel, go to a play, see friends, try new restaurants. That way I get the best of both worlds."

"And where does David work?"

She tells me. He is in finance. One of the big banks, but maybe he'll go out on his own in a few years. He has an MBA from Harvard. They met at a party. They went on their honeymoon in the Galápagos.

We chat some more about her life.

"How are you, Walter? And Maddy?"

I tell her. About Maddy, about what has happened in the years since the accident. How our lives have changed. Our marriage. Florida. But not about the book.

Lunch comes. I have the Baker soup followed by a rare steak. I indulge myself when I can. Claire has only the salmon, most of which she leaves on her plate.

"So why did you want to see me?" she asks. "I can't believe you simply called me up out of the blue after all this time and all that happened back then just to chitchat."

Now I tell her about the manuscript—and that I am the only person who has ever read it. About how good it is and that I read it every year. I also let her know it left me with more questions than answers. Was that what it was really like? Was that how it really happened? There are too many gaps. Can she help me fill them in?

"It was a long time ago, Walter," she says. "I was so young."

But I press, and in the end she relents. We talk about their love affair, about Paris, about the thrill of the beginning, about the anguish at the end. There are tears welling in her eyes as I pry deeper. I want details that are often painful.

"I haven't thought about any of this in such a long time," she says. "I've tried not to."

She gets up and excuses herself to go to the ladies' room. When she returns, she looks more composed. Her makeup is retouched. "Sorry," she says. We order coffee. "Did they ever find out what happened, about the crash, I mean?" she asks.

"The reports were inconclusive."

She nods her head. "What do you think happened?"

This is a question I have asked myself many times. I even hired private investigators to review the medical records and the NTSB reports. "I don't know," I reply finally. "I will tell you what I do know. Contrary to what some of the newspapers reported at the time, I don't believe Harry did it on purpose. The book was going well. He adored Johnny and would never have done anything to hurt him. And he still loved Maddy, and he told me he was going to try to win her back. And, what's more, I think she would have taken him back. From what I can tell, there was no reason why he would want to kill himself or Johnny."

"So where does that leave us?"

"Well, it's possible there was pilot error, but that's unlikely. Harry was too good a flier. It could have been a blocked vent. Or they could have hit a bird. The NTSB did not find any indication of technical malfunction, but the plane had been so badly damaged it was impossible to tell. Of course, the manufacturer sent their lawyers to argue that it couldn't have been the plane's fault and waved a sheaf of reports testifying to the safety of the plane and its design. No, it's a mystery."

"I've often thought about it too," Claire says. "I've never been able to think of a good reason either. At first, I thought it was God's way of punishing me for sleeping with a married man, but then I realized it wasn't me who was being punished." She laughs mirthlessly. "Isn't that just typical? When we are young, we think it is all about us."

We cross Vanderbilt Avenue, and I say good-bye to her at the entrance to the station.

"You know, it happened ten years ago this week. I thought maybe that's why you called me."

"Yes, I suppose it is. Ten years is a long time."

"But it's funny how things work out, isn't it? I mean, you've gotten what you've always wanted, haven't you?"

"I can't say I look at it like that."

"Oh no?"

"No, I would much rather that Harry and Johnny were still alive."

"But then you wouldn't be married to Maddy. You wouldn't have had her all to yourself."

"I never wanted her all to myself. I love her. I always have. All I have ever wanted is her happiness. But she doesn't love me, not the way she loved Harry."

"Well, she is very lucky to have you."

I find her attitude maddening and slightly offensive. "And you don't feel in the least bit culpable?"

"Culpable? Me? For what?"

"For what happened, for the pain you brought about."

"That I brought about? No, I don't think you understand."

"What don't I understand?"

"I am blameless. I was young, and I was in love."

"So it was Harry's fault?"

"Yes. It was something he chose to do. I didn't know what I was doing. I look back at myself then, how naïve I was, and it seems so long ago. The irony is that I won in the end. At least in a way I did. But there were times when I didn't think so."

"What do you mean?"

She smiles and puts her hand on my arm. "I loved him, you see. I will never know if he really loved me or not, but I know that he loved his family more. Now that I'm a mother, I understand why he chose the way he did, but I couldn't back then. And, of course, we never had a chance to find out what might have happened. But I have tried to make up for it. And I've been very lucky to find someone who loves me for who I am in spite of everything."

She then looks at her watch and says, "I'm sorry, but I have to go. My train is about to leave." She places a quick kiss lightly on my cheek. "Thank you for lunch. It was lovely seeing you again." She turns and stops, taking an envelope out of her purse. "I wasn't sure if I was going to give this to you. It's been so long, you see. I had no idea what it would be like. But I think it's all right. I hope you'll understand. You can tell Maddy if you think it's a good idea."

She hands me the envelope. It is normal letter size, ecru. My name is written in ink on the front.

"Good-bye, Walter," she says. She squeezes my hand. I stare into the deep brown of her eyes, and for a moment I am reminded of the girl she had been and why we had all been so dazzled by her.

I watch her descend the grand marble staircase and then walk briskly through the milling crowds to her track.

I walk back to the club and up to the reading room on the second floor. In the after-lunch pall, the space is nearly empty. A few older members like me are dozing in their armchairs.

The younger members, squash-fit and keen, have already returned to their jobs. I take a seat by the window. A waiter appears and asks if I want anything. I think about a Scotch and
soda but instead ask for a coffee. I still have to drive back out
to the country to see Maddy.

I take the envelope from the inner breast pocket of my
jacket and slide my thumb under the flap. It opens easily; the
gum had been only lightly licked. The paper is heavy, expensive. The lining marbled. An address in Old Greenwich is embossed on the back flap. Inside are three photographs. They
are of different ages and sizes. I shuffle quickly through them.
I have not seen any of them before. The first is of the seven of
us—Claire, me, Maddy, Harry, Johnny, Ned, Cissy. Taken on
the beach. Harry stands in the middle, his arm around Maddy.
They are both laughing. Their hair windblown. Johnny is on
his other side. I am next to Maddy. Claire, in a bikini, is next
to me. I can't believe how young we all look. Even I, who never
truly felt young, am struck by the comparative firmness of my
muscles and smoothness of my face.

I remember that day. We asked someone passing by to take
the photograph. It is a jolt. I haven't seen a photograph of us
all together in years. I had put away whatever we had for fear
of upsetting Maddy. I stare at it for several minutes, dumb with
memory. Wishing I was back there again.

The waiter returns with my coffee, disturbing my reverie. I
sign the chit and then look at the back of the envelope. There is
a date and the words *Georgica Beach* written in black felt marker,
but nothing more.

I pick up the second photograph. It is of Harry and Claire.
They appear to be in Paris, and I silently congratulate myself

when I turn it over and see the words *Basilica Sacré-Coeur* written on the back. They stand side by side like honeymooners. The lawyer in me rises. This is the proof, the smoking gun, if you will. Not that I ever doubted it, but here at last is the physical evidence that it all really happened.

The last photograph is actually a Christmas card. On it is a portrait of a happy family. Claire and her husband are sitting on a green lawn with two boys and a golden retriever. The husband is dark, like Claire, handsome, slender, white teeth. He looks sinless, like the kind of person who does triathlons. His hand is on the shoulder of the smaller of the two boys, a copy of the father in miniature. The other boy, considerably older, is on the other side of his mother. Unlike his brother, he is fair, his eyes blue. There is something familiar about him.

How old did Claire say her oldest son was? I do a quick mental calculation. It adds up. Had she even known she might be pregnant that day of the funeral? And yet, through all the years, she had said nothing, asked for nothing. I put the photographs back in the envelope and replace it in my pocket.

I drive out to the country that evening, arriving before dinner. Maddy is in the library staring at the television when I walk in. A half-empty vodka and soda is in front of her, the condensation from the ice forming a little puddle beneath the glass. There are old ring marks now all over the table. I switch on the lights and place a coaster beneath her glass. It's still cool in the evenings, and I light a fire. She says nothing.

This is a bad time of year for her. We rarely talk about it, but I know the anniversary of the crash always weighs heavily on her. Aside from making sure we have plenty of vodka, cigarettes, Prozac, and Ambien in the house, there is not much

I can do for her. Despite the pain she feels, she refuses to go anywhere else. Year after year I suggest we stay in Florida, but she won't. It is important for her to be here, to be as close as possible to the place where they were last alive.

As usual when we don't go out or order in, I cook, something I've never been any good at. But Maddy doesn't care. I could serve her anything—filet from Lobel's or cat food—and she would eat it with the same degree of disinterest.

"How was your lunch?" she asks, cutting an overcooked lamb chop.

I appreciate her asking. It is an effort on her part. Her doctor has been encouraging her. I know she couldn't honestly care less how I spend my days. Of course, in this one particular instance, if I had told her where I really had been and with whom, she would have cared a lot.

"Fine. It was an old case. Tying up some loose ends."

"Hm. Oh, good." She has already lost interest. We eat in silence at the old kitchen table with the waxed yellow cloth, where Genevieve and Robert used to sit lifetimes ago, having decided that the formal dining room, the one with the Zuber wallpaper, was too formal.

I look over at her. She is older now, more careworn, but she still takes my breath away. As always, I want to tell her I love her, but I cannot. It would only upset her. It is painful for her to think about love. And so I simply breathe the words to myself, offering them up like a silent grace.

After dinner, Maddy goes to bed as usual, and I wash the dishes. Then I pour myself a brandy, open the windows, and put on Verdi. Wearing a coat against the cool April night, I go out to the back lawn, carrying my snifter, to take a seat in one of the Adirondack chairs that face the pearlescent water of the pond. It is a beautiful evening. There are millions of stars overhead.

The strains of *La Traviata* caress the air. This is one of my favorite times. My mind is free to explore, to commune with my memories. My eyes play over the familiar view. The other-worldly, nocturnal brightness of the pond. The shadowy shapes of the trees rise up like old friends, rustling gently in the breeze. I love this somber fugue of colors, all the purples and silvers and blacks. The tree nearest me, maybe fifteen feet away, is well lit by the lights from the house. It towers above me, inclining slightly as though it, too, is listening to the music. I look at how the branches mount into the canopy of new leaves. I am struck by how tangled the boughs are yet at the same time how beautiful, the filigree impossible to follow, as complex, and yet as simple, as a shower of diamonds. How tall, how graceful, how noble are these trees, how long they took to grow so high and yet how easily they can fall.

A strong wind, an ax. Man or nature. It doesn't matter. I could call my gardener tomorrow and have them all chopped down and turned into mulch. We are all of us vulnerable. For a long time I think about the photographs, about what Claire wanted me to know. It is more than I can do.

I carry my glass back inside and remove the envelope from my suit jacket draped over one of the kitchen chairs and walk into the library. The fire is still going, and I stoke it with a poker. Verdi fills the room. The flames leap higher. I take the photographs and the envelope and toss them all into the fire. I stand there waiting until every trace of them is gone, making my silent apologies.

❧

THAT WAS YEARS AGO. I STILL THINK ABOUT CLAIRE. ABOUT Maddy. About Harry and Johnny. They are never far from my thoughts. In my mind, they are still there, laughing, young, untainted. Maddy and I are old now. She is slowly dying in the next room, breathing on a respirator, a shrunken figure curled up on the bed, attended by round-the-clock nurses, the curtains drawn. She never could quit smoking. There was no point in arguing. She asked to come up here from Florida to die, and I consented. It was the last thing I could do for her. So I hired an ambulance to drive her the whole way while I followed behind in a car.

"Thank you for everything," she wheezes. I sit holding her tiny hand in the darkened room, trying to be strong for both of us but knowing that she is secretly relieved to be finally released. I have done nothing for her, while she has been everything to me. "It's all right, my love," I whisper. "You rest. It will all be over soon. You will be with them again soon, I promise."

And I know in many ways she already is, on her mouth the faintest trace of a smile, welcoming the peace that has been denied her for so long. These last decades of her life had been a sort of hell for her, and not for the first time had I wondered how God could create someone as fine and pure and beautiful as Maddy, only to torture her. It was cruel. It made no sense. It was like the artists who were gassed in the Nazi concentration camps. All those poets, musicians, dancers, people who after years of study, years of sacrifice so they could spread hope and enrich life, were killed, cut down, their voices lost forever.

Why? What is the point of having special gifts unless you are allowed to use them?

Maddy had done nothing wrong, yet she was the one made to suffer. I know deep in her heart, she partly blamed herself. "If only I hadn't gone to Mexico," she had screamed countless times. I told her it was not her fault, that it had nothing to do with her, but she could not bring herself to believe me. Her doctors had attempted to do the same but with similar results. The human heart needs to burden itself, to take responsibility for its losses, otherwise it will explode.

I scatter Maddy's ashes over the pond too. There are only a few people in attendance. Ned and Cissy join me, but Ned is no longer able to carry the canoe by himself. I hire some young men to help with that, grandsons of friends. They paddle me out to the middle of the pond, and I weep silently while I gently throw the powdery remains over the water. I am surprised by how light and insubstantial they feel. These had once been the person I had loved most, her skin, her eyes, her hair. All reduced to powder. To nothing. Dissolving in the water. Gone. And yet I know this is where she wanted to be more than any other, and I am happy that I could bring them together in death at last.

The next day I have her name and dates added to the cenotaph alongside those of her husband and son. I comfort myself to think that, if there is a heaven, they are reunited now. It is what I pray for, at any rate.

I have lived with ghosts for years. The ghosts of Harry and Johnny, the ghost of my father, and, even while she was alive, the ghost of Maddy. They haunt me, unable to truly die because they are still alive in memory. They are my heroes, my North Star, and I have been trying to follow them my whole life. At the end, I am left with the pain of what might have been. We make so many right decisions in life, but it is the wrong ones that can never be forgiven.

ACKNOWLEDGMENTS

I WOULD LIKE TO THANK MANY PEOPLE FOR THEIR HELP IN THE creation, both directly and indirectly, of this book. First of all, I want to thank Sharyn Rosenblum, who was a good sport and agreed to read the unfinished manuscript more from common decency than common sense, and who then opened so many doors. I would also like to thank, in no particular order, Chris Herrmann, Joseph Lorino, Charlie Miller, Brendan Dillon, David Churbuck, Chris Buckley, and Bill Duryca for their friendship as well as their helpful feedback. I would also like to thank Margaret Douglas-Hamilton, who threw open her beautiful home in Lakeville, where I wrote much of this book. I have also been lucky in the people I have had working with me to make this book a reality, especially my agents, Britton Schey and Eric Simonoff at William Morris Endeavor, and, of course, my prescient, diligent, patient, good-humored, and wise editor, Henry Ferris at William Morrow.

Last, I want to thank my mother, Isabella Breckinridge; my sister, Alexandra; my stepmother, Barbara; my late father, Arthur; my son, William; my daughter, Lally; and my beautiful wife, Melinda, for all their love and support.